The
Invisible
Valley

The Invisible Valley

A NOVEL BY
SU WEI

TRANSLATED BY
AUSTIN WOERNER

Small Beer Press
Easthampton, MA

Small Beer Press
150 Pleasant Street #306
Easthampton, MA 01027
smallbeerpress.com
weightlessbooks.com
info@smallbeerpress.com

Distributed to the trade by Consortium.

Library of Congress Cataloging-in-Publication Data

Names: Su, Wei, 1953- author. | Woerner, Austin, translator.
Title: The invisible valley : a novel / by Su Wei ; translated by Austin
  Woerner.
Other titles: Mi gu. English
Description: First American edition. | Easthampton, MA : Small Beer Press,
  2018.
Identifiers: LCCN 2017047744 (print) | LCCN 2017049832 (ebook) | ISBN
  9781618731463 | ISBN 9781618731456 (alk. paper)
Subjects: LCSH: Teenage boys--China--Fiction. | China--History--Cultural
  Revolution, 1966-1976. | Psychological fiction.
Classification: LCC PL2904.W43 (ebook) | LCC PL2904.W43 M6313 2018 (print) |
  DDC 895.13/52--dc23
LC record available at https://lccn.loc.gov/2017047744

First edition 1 2 3 4 5 6 7 8 9

Text set in Centaur 12pt.

Printed on 50# 30% recycled Natures Natural B19 Cream paper by the Maple Press in York, PA.
Cover illustration © 2018 by Liu Guoyu.

Contents

In the late 1960s, at the call of Chairman Mao, twenty million Chinese students of middle- and high-school age streamed from the cities to the countryside as part of the "Down to the Countryside" movement. For years they lived among the peasants, separated from their homes and families, forced to give up formal schooling to be "re-educated" through hard agricultural labor. It was a time of great idealism and incalculable hardship.

In the southern province of Canton one million students were downcountried, many of them to state-run rubber plantations in the tropical highlands of Hainan Island.

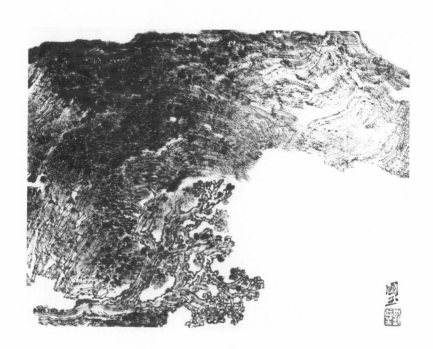

Chapter 1
Ghost Bride

Blood-red snakeclouds gathered in the western sky, and the rubber trees glowed as if on fire. Lu Beiping counted the pits he'd dug that day on the recently denuded hillside, picked up the squad leader's notebook, recorded his number, and stood scanning the list of names for Fong's mark.

Nothing. She'd vanished. And their squad leader, Sergeant Fook, was nowhere to be seen either. With a sigh, Lu Beiping swatted away the head that hovered inquisitively over his shoulder.

—Okay, Chu, I don't need the National Joint Newscast to tell me that they're off Seeking Peer Support again. Am I right?

Seeking Peer Support: It was a fashionable term in those days. Sometimes they called it a "Revolutionary Heart-to-Heart."

—Well, said Chu, smirking: I can't speak to her whereabouts. But she did mention she was hoping you'd pick up her share of pork scraps at the ration supp tonight. And some of that frozen fish they just brought in from Whitehorse Harbor.

Maybe I should stop by the supply co-op and pick up her monthly allotment of TP and sanitary napkins while I'm at it, Lu Beiping thought sullenly, since it appears I've become the errand boy. Then the whole goddam world would see how steadfast her affections are.

And yet, as he gathered his satchel and books, he felt a quiet thrill at the thought of his special ration-collecting status.

—Oh, Chu added: One more thing. Fook wants you to write another propaganda piece for Operation Red May.

—How about this: Pork Production Continues to Soar on the Ass Cheeks of Our Fearless Squad Leader . . .

I

Fook was what passed for fat in those days. He might be a model re-ed, but he was no match for Lu Beiping in terms of looks—Lu Beiping liked to think.

He said he didn't give a damn, but the truth was, Lu Beiping cared far too much.

Long shadows slid past them as they hiked down the twilit trail. Lu Beiping fell back to the end of the column, where he could listen to the raunchy banter of the plantation hands and occasionally add his own two cents. This was a nightly ritual. Most of the city kids would blush to hear the workers, women included, riffing in elaborate and colorful detail on the subject of one another's intimate habits, but Lu Beiping was one of the few re-eds who'd cultivated a tongue sharp enough to join in the game. Pointing at the shadow cast by the satchel swinging from his hoe, Lu Beiping remarked upon its resemblance to the shape of a fat mother cat being humped by a scrawny old dog. This won him a few guffaws, and several hands crowded round for a closer look. Too late! Lu Beiping cried, jiggling the hoe so that the two forms quivered languidly: You missed it, the big moment's over. A storm of laughter erupted, then a shrill woman's voice called out over the others: Your turn, Lu! Take her, she's yours! Surveying the crowd for the offender— probably the company gossipmonger, Choi—Lu Beiping said: Sure! But only if you show that old dog a good time tonight.

—Listen to the mouth on that boy! the workers hooted. Shame these ears!

Just then, as the wail of a pig being slaughtered echoed up from the direction of camp, Sergeant Fook's shadow loomed from behind.

—Low-minded Sentiments! You people should do yourselves a favor and quit indulging in these Low-minded Sentiments!

Not seeing Fong there among them, the squad leader hastened away, and as his silhouette rolled off down the trail Chu said something snide that Lu Beiping didn't catch. Stiff-faced, Lu Beiping meandered away from the crowd, putting some distance between himself and the hands, then pointed at the shadow of his satchel and said to Chu with a grim smile:

—Will you look at that. That dog and cat are at it again.

Right at that moment, their eyes fell simultaneously upon a flash of red not far from the dog's hindquarters.

(It was right over there, Lu Beiping told Tsung years later as they walked up toward the trailhead near the old base-camp entrance: It was lying at the edge of that stand of rubber trees we just passed. In those days, Lu Beiping explained to Tsung, the country's entire agricultural administration had been restructured as a military hierarchy: A work unit was a company, a plantation a battalion, and the system of state-run farms on Hainan Island was known collectively as the Agricultural Reclamation Corps—Agrecorps for short.)

A scrap of red paper lay in the dirt, stabbing into Lu Beiping's vision.

He stooped, picked it up. The edges were sticky with mud. He unfolded it, squinted at a few lines of scrawled inkbrush characters rendered nearly illegible by the damp, thought it odd, and was about to throw it away when out of the bushes, cackling and clapping, ran Mrs. Kau, the foreman's wife.

—Bounty and bliss! Bounty and bliss! Congratulations, friend Lu, bless your soul and bless the soul of my poor little girl! Your brother-in-law could come into his next life a horse or a cow or a mule and not have paid back half the good turn you've just done him, oh, bless your soul, bounty and bliss! Come along, right this way, quit making such a fuss, step right on in, make yourself at home, and don't you run off now, Chu, have a cup of yammings while the pork's still stewing. You city boys are all manners, don't be shy, oh, bless my poor girl's soul down in the dark place! Now where'd Lu get to? There he is! Here, son, you have a cup too, mercy me, don't just *stand* there, have a seat, move over, brother, this young man's the reason we're having this party. Come on, Lu, don't be a stranger, you're part of the family now . . .

(Chance, Lu Beiping would say to Tsung years later. You can make a joke out of a lot of things, but Chance—no. Chance is no laughing matter.)

❧

It was at the end of a long and tedious journey that Tsung decided to make Lu Beiping the main character of his novel. Of course, this choice was itself pure chance. The journey was a routine field survey for a boring research project run by Tsung's tedious American grad-school advisor, and Lu Beiping, their escort from the Hainan Foreign Visitors Office, had done little to relieve the prevailing ennui. Lu Beiping, Tsung gathered, had spent most of his adolescence in these hills, working on this very plantation, in fact; yet he seemed to have nothing at all to say about it, and instead spent the trip leafing through Tsung's professor's Taiwanese magazines and crowing at the alien wonders therein. At last Tsung said: God, I'm bored out of my skull, I think I'll write a novel. About what? Lu Beiping piped up. Anything, Tsung said. Like . . . He glanced over at Lu Beiping, who by this point looked even more washed-out than Tsung, though still trimly dressed in jacket and tie, speaking always in clipped, proper Mandarin, the perfect image of an anonymous bureaucrat: You, for example, Tsung said, without really meaning it.

At that offhand remark, Lu Beiping began to tell his story.

Really, he said, you can't make light of Chance.

He couldn't remember how she managed to drag him, flapping like a captive chicken, her bony fingers digging painfully into his arm, all the way down to the Kau family's cookhouse; nor could he remember who was sitting in the shadows of the smoke-filled room as he was manhandled onto the only unoccupied stool and, sweating profusely, was forced to down round after round of yam beer on an empty stomach. He remembered watching in a drunken daze as the foreman's son Wing, his mother egging him on, bowed to him and toasted him with a cup of beer, then Mrs. Kau tried to get him to kneel, and he refused to kneel till finally the foreman strode into the room and the boy sank grudgingly to one knee. He had a memory of Wing struggling in his mother's grip as she tried to get him to perform some kind of ritual gesture, and then of Foreman Kau's arm shooting out to stop her, quick and reflexive, like a military salute. Then for a moment the foreman's booming shout jolted Lu Beiping out of his stupor, and he heard voices chorusing in the surrounding smoke: Bless this feast! (Or was it *Rest in peace*? Lu Beiping couldn't remember.)

Ghost-married. I've been ghost-married.

These were the words echoing in Lu Beiping's skull as he lay crumpled in bed later that evening after heaving out a great torrent of half-digested pork onto the floor, his mouth still burning with the rank aftertaste of yam beer.

—Congrats, pal! So you're the lucky one. The whole unit owes you for ration supp tonight—

—Fuck you to hell!

Chu's head disappeared quicker than it had appeared around the door, leaving Lu Beiping alone to ponder a gleaming morass of meat, beer, and bile.

When Lu Beiping regained consciousness later that night, he shook Chu awake on the neighboring cot and, with his help, managed to piece together the story in which he'd come to play such a pivotal role.

The time had arrived for the foreman to find a wife for his son Wing, but there was the problem of his eldest daughter, Han, who died from malaria the winter the re-eds came, when the fever was raging and many had perished in the lands surrounding Mudkettle Mountain. Han fell into shadow the year after she graduated from elementary school, so she'd be almost twenty now, had she lived. Nobody knew the origins of the rite—was it Hakka? Or native Hainanese? Foreman Kau was a retired army veteran of Hakka blood, but his wife was born and raised on the island, near Lam-ko. Everyone knew how it worked, though: Only if a mate were found for the soul of the unmarried older sibling could the younger child marry without calamity. Otherwise the dead one's shade would stir against the living, and that meant sons dying without heirs, daughters giving birth to horned abominations; in short, it meant no end of trouble for the entire family.

(In those days, the head of a work unit should theoretically have been called the Captain, Lu Beiping explained to Tsung. But for whatever reason, nobody called him that in our unit; they just called him foreman.)

For the Kaus, the question of a ghost marriage was fraught with complications. The foreman, who was also the local Party branch secretary, naturally worried for his reputation—in that era of Rectifying Ideological Outlook and Eradicating Antiquated Thinking, the slightest suspicion of harboring superstitious beliefs might cause one to be tarred as a reactionary. Mrs. Kau, however, was adamant. Which comes first? she asked—the Party or your son? According to whispered reports circulating in the village, this family matter had caused a livid Mrs. Kau to storm into the next branch committee meeting, causing such a stir that the division clerk and the funds officer both had to come out and intervene. So the Kaus quietly sent a man over the mountains to Lam-ko to consult a well-known spirit elder, who checked the almanacs, chose an auspicious day, and set off the chain of events that ended with Lu Beiping picking up that scrap of red paper at the edge of that particular rubber grove on that particular evening. One hour before sundown, on a west-facing slope; every detail was set according to the elder's prescriptions. Inside the folded paper were written the dead Han's birth figures, and all that remained was for some unwitting male to pick up the note and bind the worlds of light and shadow.

That morning Mrs. Kau had taken a stool and a bundle of cane strips for basket-weaving out into the rubber grove and sat there all day, weathering sun and rain-shower, weaving and waiting. Officially the night's ration supplement was meant to celebrate the launch of Operation Red May, but everyone knew that the Kau family's ghost wedding was the real reason for the party, and nobody thought too hard about politics when there was meat and beer to be had. But the cookhouse was already jammed with guests and still nobody coming down the path had taken any interest in that little piece of red paper lying at the edge of the grove—even a wet-diapered infant would've done the trick, though females didn't count, and Mrs. Kau, crouching in the trees, had a few extra notes ready in case a girl picked it up. Darkness fell; the air grew cold; all throughout camp rose the cup-clacking clamor of workers toasting the end of a month's meatfast; and the foreman's wife sat anxiously in the forest, hoping her future "son-in-law" would soon appear.

(Married to a ghost, Lu Beiping exclaimed to Tsung: It was just my kind of luck!)

—Help! Come quick! Lu's in trouble!

Chu told Lu Beiping that after Mrs. Kau had hauled him down to the crowded cookhouse, he'd run off immediately to tell Cigar, an older boy who'd come with them from Canton and who'd since become something of a bigwig among the re-eds, in hopes that he'd step in and rescue Lu Beiping. But Cigar just smiled and said: Lu's head is way too big for his shoulders. This could be a valuable part of his re-education.

—Hmph! Chu grumbled, he's just jealous that you stole away the prettiest girl in the unit. He wants to watch you suffer.

In the course of an evening, Lu Beiping had become "ghost son-in-law" to the foreman. Limp as a rag doll, the taste of bile still lingering in his mouth, he lay awake for the rest of the night listening to the creaking song of an oxcart somewhere deep in the hills beneath Mudkettle Mountain.

When the first bar of May morning light lay across his blanket, Lu Beiping woke to see Fong standing in the door.

—They tell me you got married last night? Fong said with a giggle. To a ghost? Gosh, Lu, sounds like a real adventure.

The expression of naïve wonder that she so often wore, which in the past had struck Lu Beiping as faintly seductive, now had a chilly edge to it. Her syllables fell like pins on a frozen lake.

Camp after morning bell was indeed a frozen lake, empty and silent. Even the distant, echoing creak of the well rope sounded cold.

—You know the whole company's talking about it, right?

Lu Beiping closed his eyes.

—Say something! If you're the foreman's ghost son-in-law, what does that make me?

—Where did you go last night after work? I couldn't find you.

—Is that your business? Why should it matter to you where I go after work?

She's toying with me, Lu Beiping thought. She knows that she's at her most alluring when she's just on the verge of anger.

—Oh, and what about my fish? I did ask you to pick up some frozen . . .

—Your *fish*? Lu Beiping burst out. I almost got hounded to death last night, and you're asking me about your stinking fish?

As soon as the sentence was out of his mouth, Lu Beiping noticed that Fong had had her hand over her nose the whole time they'd been talking, her eyes twinkling with amusement as if she were watching a frog drowning in a dye vat. Then he noticed the smell in the room, the reek of yam beer mixed with the fetid odor of half-turned pork, and all at once the embarrassments of the night before—vomiting all over the floor, the whole sequence of mortifying events that led up to it—flooded back to him in a vivid rush.

—Alright, I'm leaving now, Fong said, then she turned and walked out the door.

As she left, Lu Beiping watched the swaying curves of her limbs, so round and perfect they made one ache.

Months later it would dawn on Lu Beiping that Fong had been waiting for the first convenient moment to break off the thing between them, and that the ghost wedding had provided her with just the excuse she needed. She'd even taken care to sever the last remaining vestige of their bond—that frozen fish. At the thought, Lu Beiping laughed out loud.

The sun was in his eyes now. He decided to go down to the well to wash his face. When he stepped out the door he felt like he was treading on loose soil, his feet sinking into cushions of dust, and as he carried his twanging bucket alongside the re-ed dorm building he imagined faces watching him from every window. Stop imagining things, he told himself. But he thought for sure he'd heard laughter. As he picked his way down to the well in the bowl-shaped hollow below the mess hall, the slope above him seemed like an amphitheater, its seats crowded with silent spectators waiting for him to speak. Standing at the well's edge, he swore at the top of his lungs.

—GOD! DAMN! MOTHER! FUCKING—he went on to evoke the female reproductive tract with the most eloquent profanities in the Cantonese language, words that he'd never have said ordinarily even if a thug in the alleys of Sam-kok Market had been twisting his ear—BITCH!

No response, not even an echo. His maledictions were swallowed by the silence of the morning, as if they'd fallen into a pile of cotton balls.

As he climbed back up the hill, he passed the division clerk, whom he recognized as one of the people who'd poured him beer last night in the smoky clamor of the foreman's cookhouse. The man nodded at him and smiled pleasantly. No work today? he asked. With a small blackboard tucked under his arm, probably from the evening literacy school, he hurried on his way.

Lu Beiping stood frozen for a moment, struck by a sudden thought. At first he'd imagined that the whole company would take delight in his suffering, slapping their thighs at the ridiculous charade of Lu Beiping being crowned "ghost son-in-law." What he hadn't realized was that this role had a flip side—he was the foreman's son-in-law now, ghostly status notwithstanding. Nobody dared laugh at the foreman's own kin. The camp, with its dirt paths and long brick-and-plaster barracks, was exactly the same as before the raion-supplement party; nothing had changed. But now its everyday appearance seemed faintly uncanny, and this unnerved Lu Beiping, like a subtle insult to which he had no retort.

As he pushed open the door to his room, he glimpsed, at the edge of a nearby stand of rubber trees, a woman clad in black, sitting on a small cane stool. It was Mrs. Kau—his "mother-in-law" (ha!) who'd shanghaied him into marrying her dead daughter (good god!) and who now, for some strange reason, was sitting near his dorm room and studying him (monitoring him? protecting him?) with an unfathomable gaze. He supposed he ought to pitch a fit, make some kind of a scene; but then a great lassitude overcame him (what was the point of making a show of force to your mother-in-law?) and, pretending he hadn't seen her, he let the door slap shut behind him.

His world had changed overnight, changed utterly and irrevocably. He had become a stranger to himself, and the world had become alien to him.

(Crazy, right? Lu Beiping said to Tsung. It's hard to imagine a more surreal transformation than that. But what made it so odd was that it didn't feel in the least bit unreal.)

All day the image stuck in his mind: Mrs. Kau, dressed in black, sitting by the rubber trees, watching him.

And as he pondered that image, he couldn't help imagining—no, it was silly—a face, the face of a girl he'd never known: Han, his ghost bride.

He lay in bed, writing in his diary. He knew that Chu had begged leave for him that morning.

—It's been a big night for you, Chu had crooned ghoulishly in his ear, just as the first rays of dawn were filtering through the window and Lu Beiping was drifting back to sleep: I think the foreman'll understand!

Then Lu Beiping had rolled over and vomited again.

❧

Three days later Lu Beiping, driving a herd of cattle, set off deep into the hills.

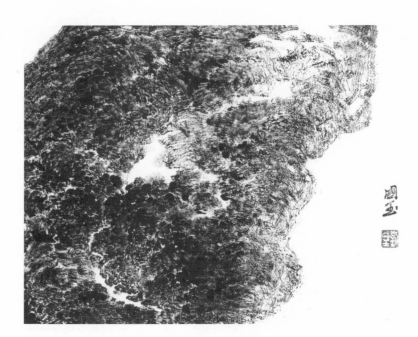

Chapter 2
Smoke on the Mountains

Fiery sunsets aren't an unusual sight in the tropics of Asia, but it's only on Mudkettle Mountain that you'll see snakeclouds. On clear evenings these bright red cloud formations come teeming over the horizon like bloody apparitions, thick and bulbous and coiling, filling the sky with eccentric shapes. Perhaps it's some vagary of the climate in this hundred-mile reach of the Hainan highlands, where deep jungles breathe out miasmic vapors, that produces these fantastic displays: pendulous scarlet coils, each coil haloed with black, the scarlet made more bloodcurdlingly scarlet and the black more chillingly black by the contrast. Looking up, you could easily believe—as many here do—that a thick, cold mass of "snake air" is writhing in the sky above you, flicking out invisible forked tongues. The Cantonese frequently use the word "snake" to describe objects of a particularly striking hue, so the big red imported apples in Canton markets are colloquially known as "snakefruit," and the brilliant-green, thick-leaved, aromatic grass that grows in the hills is often called "snakegrass." Some say that this explains the clouds' curious name. But the locals would tell you, as they told the re-eds fresh off the ships from Canton, that the snakeclouds owe their name to the mountain's pent-up snake air. Deep in the mountains there dwells a giant thousand-year-old python: the Snakeweird, font of the land's bounty and of its ruin. Never, never, wake the Snakeweird. As Lu Beiping drove his cattle into the foothills, the thought of the Snakeweird was never far from his mind. Never mind if what they said was true; here he was, having recently donned the eerie mantle of "ghost husband," pressing ever deeper toward the monster's legendary haunting place. He felt as if he were departing from the land of the living and crossing into the country of shadow—thinking this, he felt a pang of dread, and a faint tingle of excitement.

They call this place the Mudkettle. Mudkettle Mountain is actually the westernmost arm of a range called the Mo-Sius, and the Mudkettle is the large, thickly forested valley encircled by the mountain's several peaks. Out through this valley flows Mudclaw Creek, its looping course tracing out the five fingers of a hand or claw, separating the plantation's rubber groves and windbreaks from the wild forestland above. For the first few days, Lu Beiping grazed the cattle mostly between the thumb and forefinger of Mudclaw Creek, where the slopes were gentle and the forest open, so it was easier to control the herd. The work was new to him and the animals were unruly, so he played it safe, fearing that he might commit some beginner's blunder that would rob him of this fantastic new job. Every day at morning bell he'd herd the animals out of the corral near the trailhead, up through a dozen sectors of rubber forest and over five or six hills, till he reached this semi-wild place where grassy meadows opened between rank vegetation, and the cattle could eat their fill. When he could, he'd drive them farther, quickening his pace and calling sharply, leaving behind the clangs of the work bell and the shouts of the grove hands. Before long he found himself in the midst of a tropical rainforest, tall curtains of vines and epiphytes rising on all sides, a daunting labyrinth that was a challenge for the cattle to navigate. But once they got through, new vistas greeted him: narrow creek-cut gullies filled with emerald profusions of grass, in any one of which the animals could happily feast away the day. Then Lu Beiping would find himself a sunny slope, recline into the shade of a broad-leafed tree, open his satchel, fish out a book, and, with his right leg swinging over his left, sink into the bright dreamworld between its pages, while the air around him prickled with the contented munching of the cattle.

This was a typical Lu Beiping pose. Or rather, it was a pose typical of a certain sort of character rare but conspicuous among kids who'd been downcountried for re-education: the loner, the introvert, the solitary outsider. Among the more radical re-eds—the mainstream ones, that is—you'd never see that dangling right leg. It marked a person out as an eccentric, wayward type who'd have been common in less extraordinary times: the ravenous but homework-hating bookworm, the non-stamp-collecting oddball obsessed with basketball stars, the meticulous bather whose room was never neat, the deadpan joker who spoke only to mock. Lu Beiping was just such a character, typical among late-adolescent males. But in that drab, gray era whose knee-jerk conformity erased all usual expressions of age and sex, it was this ordinariness that made him unique.

I like your independent spirit, Fong had always told him. She said it in a vague, lofty tone that he knew was meant to convey Seriousness, a quality by which, in those days, a person's worth as a human being was frequently judged. It was now clear to him that, just as her habit of praising Sergeant Fook for his Competence—You're *so* competent, sir—reflected her own slippery kind of competence, so her desire to appear Serious reflected her own triviality. *The most beautiful women have trivial minds.* What novel was that from? He wouldn't call her one of the *most* beautiful women—but if there was one thing he was sure of, she was damn trivial.

He laughed. Well, he had to admit that ever since that fateful evening last week, he'd been a little jealous of Mr. Competent. Even his vacation in the mountains couldn't cure him of that.

Speaking of which, this new job, which had all the appearances of a special arrangement that Lu Beiping had purposefully contrived, had in actuality just fallen into his lap, foreman's orders. The morning after the ghost wedding, as Lu Beiping lay truant in bed after heaving out his insides for the second time, Fook had dropped by his dorm room to inquire about the new propaganda piece for the wall gazette. Lu Beiping curtly refused. He wanted a new assignment. He couldn't bear the thought of watching his former girlfriend and his own squad leader dallying around right under his nose. Fook said quietly: Listen, Lu, there's an inspection team coming to camp this week, why don't you just write the prop piece and then I'm sure the foreman'll see to your redeployment. There was a beseeching note in his voice, as if he were begging on the foreman's behalf. But as it turned out, Lu Beiping didn't have to write the piece after all—later that day a call came from battalion HQ saying that the inspection team would be arriving ahead of schedule. When the foreman hung up the phone he went straight to the trailhead, cornered the cowherd, Gaffer Kam, and demanded the keys to the corral that the old man kept tucked in his waistband, which shortly afterward Fook dropped with a clink into Lu Beiping's palm.

What a boondoggle. The job was usually reserved for those members of the unit who were officially registered as elderly, handicapped, or otherwise unfit, and with good reason: Though the hours were long and it put you outdoors in all sorts of weather, once you got the animals to a nice grassy slope you could just kick back and relax. They were meat cattle, seventy-eight head in total, loaned from battalion HQ for the sole purpose of fertilizing the rubber groves, and as long as they ate plenty, shat plenty, and the "corral count" stayed high, you could lie around reading novels and nobody would mind your business. Only later would Lu Beiping realize how much the Gaffer resented him for taking this job away from him. Needless to say, he was grateful to leave behind the sweat-dripping, hoe-swinging life of the grove hand—he was his own squad leader now, commander of bovine battalions. Better this, even, than substitute-teaching in the base-camp schoolhouse, the assignment Fong had always coveted.

—Hell, I wish I'd picked up that piece of paper, Chu lamented theatrically when he learned of Lu Beiping's good fortune. Ghost husband? Sure! I'd love to be the foreman's special boy. Get drunk, lie around for a few days, drag yourself out of bed and land the best slacker job in the world. Now there's a position with benefits!

—Well, Chu, when I get down to the Land of Shadow I'll file for a divorce, then Han will be fair game for you. How's that sound?

—Whoa, not so fast . . .

Marrying a ghost: The thought made Lu Beiping chuckle. When he was little, after his father spanked him, he'd ask his mother: When can I get married?—leaving her to wonder at the strange non-sequitur. Of course, every little kid fantasizes about marriage. For a child, marriage symbolizes adulthood, freedom, independence; it means coming into your own, having a job and a family; it means being in charge and getting anything you want; it means Love, and Romance, whatever that means. But what did it mean to marry a ghost? What does ghost marriage symbolize? In those days, among re-eds, one's Political Issues were a topic often discussed loudly and publicly, and when one "resolved" them—by getting recommended for Party membership—it was an achievement to be trumpeted to all. But Personal Issues—love, marriage, sex—were freighted with a host of ominous-sounding abstract nouns. One night, he and Fong had been standing by the well, talking quietly, feeling a tacit understanding growing between them, and Lu had reached out to touch her arm . . . only to be repulsed as if by an electric shock. My god! she gasped. What are you . . . what are you doing? I didn't think . . . I hadn't imagined you'd harbor such, such . . . Low-minded Sentiments!

Lu Beiping was dumbfounded. Speechless, his vision swimming from embarrassment, he watched her sashay briskly away with her still-empty water bucket ka-wonging on her hip, rubbing ruefully at the hand that had just touched and been slapped away by a woman's. He felt like she'd spoken to him in a foreign tongue. Low-minded Sentiments? What was that supposed to mean? That and Interpersonal Entanglements, Inappropriate Intimacy, Male-Female Liaisons, Deviance Issues, Lifestyle Issues: clanking polysyllabic jargon probably invented by some hairy-cheeked occidental like Heidegger or Hippocrates. That searing glance, that trembling touch, those heart-quickening curves, all reduced to Entanglements and Liaisons and Issues . . . god! It made the whole thing seem like a terrible chore.

Well, he thought, now things are different. I'm "married." And that means—(yes, it's true!)—my Personal Issues (ugh . . .) are resolved! Ghost-married . . . to Han. Who is Han? Who is this mysterious woman—my "wife"? Ghost wife, ghost husband. Shadow bride, shadow groom. Ha! In those tasteless, insipid, white-rice-and-pot-likker days, could one imagine a more tantalizing, titillating, fantasy-kindling spice for the imagination than—being married to a ghost?

So, Lu Beiping imagined with relish: What if right now Han came gliding out of the mist-clouded forest, searching for her shadow mate? What would I do? Lying between the gnarled roots of a tall fruit tree, leaf-filtered sunlight shimmering in his eyes, he tried to picture her face. A gentle oval, maybe, slightly pointed at the chin, like one of the leaves of that epiphytic plant dangling from that branch on the far side of the creek. Her hair: a ponytail tied high up on her head. No, not a ponytail, that was too much like Fong; how about pigtails then, a pair of thin pigtails hanging behind her ears. She'd be shy and quiet, with a delicate voice, not loud-laughing and shrill-giggling like Fong. Her footsteps: quiet and delicate too. Not quiet—soundless, coming from There. A wrinkled baby-blue blouse, a bit too small for her frame. I've seen you before, friend Lu.

A voice quiet as a mosquito's buzz.

The day you city kids arrived from Canton. Remember? I was standing at the edge of the road with a group of students from the village junior high. They were banging drums and gongs, and I was standing in front, waving a red flag with tassels. I was class prefect. Your truck braked and spattered me with mud, and I heard you all clamoring in the back as it lurched to a stop. Then a boy jumped out, shouting frantically: Where's the bathroom? Where's the bathroom? That was you, right? You charged over to us, yelling: I gotta go! Where's the bathroom? We all burst out laughing. None of us had ever heard of a bathroom. Finally we figured out what it was you meant, and little Leung pointed toward the woods and said, The squat's over there, the privy. Bathroom, right? We girls watched your face turning colors and giggled till we got stitches in our sides.

Wow, sounds like I made quite an impression. How cruel of you, laughing at a guy in such desperate straits.

We couldn't help it! You sure did put on a show. I'll never forget the look on your face as you stood staring off into the woods, before you went staggering off down the path, all hunched over on one side, hee hee hee . . .

So, Han, since you mentioned it, do you want to know where I actually took my first piss in Tam-chow County?

Shame my ears.

There was such a big crowd at the base-camp entrance—the foreman and all the farmers, everyone cheering and banging drums and shooting off firecrackers—that I couldn't just walk over to the forest and drop my pants in broad daylight. So I hobbled to the crossroads like a wounded soldier, my bladder ready to burst, and made a dash for a little thatched hut I saw not far from the path. An outhouse, I thought: a privy. It was dark as a cave inside. I tore open my pants and let it rip. Whoooosh! It was heavenly. Then my eyes adjusted to the dark, and guess what I saw? A stove. I'd pissed straight into a peasant's frypan. What are you laughing at, Han? You think this is funny? Only later, after I started work, did I finally figure out whose kitchen equipment I'd anointed. Can you guess? Yes! It was Choi, the lady who goes around beating her breast and crowing, Mercy me, mercy me! I took my first piss in Choi's cookhouse! Hahahahahaha—

Heeheeheeheehee-kreek-KREE-kreek-KREE-kreek-KREEEEEEEEE!

A jungle partridge, spooked by his laughter, exploded out of a thicket at the edge of the creek and flapped right past him, its wings almost grazing his head. Jolted back to reality, he threw a glance around the forest. Goose bumps rose on his skin. The air smelled rank and moldy, with a hint of a burnt odor, like the smell of angelica root. All around him shimmered blue-white ripples of mist, like cirrus clouds or sheens of diffracted light, gliding slowly through the air. Through the humid curtains of summer heat he made out a faint buzzing sound, growing louder and then fading, tensing and then relaxing, as if someone were plucking at the mountain's nerves. His vivid fantasy flashed once more before his eyes, and the soles of his feet went cold. The cattle—where were the cattle? They had all disappeared. Had they . . . had they sensed her presence, and been scared away?

—No, he muttered to himself, sitting up hastily among the roots: No, no, no. It's nothing.

Then he sprang up, walked a few paces, opened his fly, and proceeded to take a leak. Damn it, he thought—might as well. They say ghosts are afraid of dirty things, right? Hey, Han, look at this! Do you think this is funny, now? Take a nice long look!

That jungle fire was a strange affair. Only months later would Lu Beiping realize just how fishy it was.

He'd been cowherd for a little over a week, and his cattle calls were still no more effective than a bullwhip fashioned from bamboo shoots. Often, after he'd gotten lost on the forking paths around Mudclaw Creek and the cattle had stomped the bamboo thickets flat trying to find their way back home, Lu Beiping would have to rely on the sixth sense of one highly intelligent white-nosed bull—the herd's lead bull, whom he'd later name Alyosha—to guide the battalion, lowing up ahead, out of the green labyrinth.

It was near evening, the sky piling thick with snakeclouds, and Lu Beiping and his troops were once again lost somewhere inside the third bend of Mudclaw Creek. They were hunting for the haggard old bull who always wandered far from the herd, searching greedily for fresh grass—Lu Beiping would later name him Judas—when they emerged into a strange valley. It was a shallow ravine roofed with a low ceiling of branches, which shut out most of the sunlight, leaving the valley in deep shade. Every tree trunk, branch, and bush in sight was crusted with fist-sized fungal tumors, and all over the ground bloomed clusters of mottled gray mushrooms that looked for all the world like human brains. Glistening pustules pimpled every visible surface; it was enough to set anybody's teeth on edge. Through cracks in the canopy above Lu Beiping glimpsed glowering ropes of red-black snakeclouds, and an alcoholic odor with a fishy undertone cloyed the air, so pungently tangible that Lu Beiping could almost feel it condensing and diffusing across his skin, like the languid licks of a huge, invisible tongue. From all sides the tiny heads of the fungi craned, snickering conspiratorially to one another, weeping pus-laden tears. Lu Beiping had never seen anything like this. *Skinnyface!* he hollered into the trees. *Where are you?* When he got no response, he started to panic, threw back his head and howled:

—*Heeeeelp! Is anybody there? Anyone?*

His voice died away instantly, as if muffled by a wet blanket. No echoes sounded in the dim, vacant valley.

Weeks later, when he told the story back at camp, one of the hands would leer at him knowingly and say: Friend, that was it—you found the baleglen. It was rumored that the jungles of Tam-chow County contained a wandering valley, which was the source of the malarial vapors that sickened the villages surrounding Mudkettle Mountain. Yet the mushrooms that grew in this valley—blue gnarly-knots, gray monkeyheads—could be sold in the markets for a staggering price. Few people could claim to have set foot in the baleglen, because, it was said, the valley moved constantly throughout the foothills, materializing in a different place every fortnight, on the first and fifteenth of each lunar month. One couldn't set out to find it, only hope to stumble into it by accident. Many had burned incense, prayed, and cast hexes in hopes of divining the next appearance of the baleglen—so called because of the bale it inflicted on the land, or the many bales' worth of rice that had been scattered in such spell-casting attempts. And it was true, in the following months Lu Beiping would never manage to find the strange valley again, though he and his bovine comrades came to know every nook and cranny of these hills. In fact this seemed to be true of many of the wondrous sights Lu Beiping discovered in the jungle: enchanted, hidden places that seemed to wink out of existence the moment he left them. (Years later, when he went back to school, Lu Beiping would try to construct a scientific explanation for the baleglen—maybe, he reasoned, there wasn't really any such place; maybe those rare fungi grew only under very specific topographical and climatic conditions, so that when all factors aligned they'd suddenly effloresce, then wither and vanish in the blink of an eye. Such an explanation might account for the illusion of a wandering valley, flickering like a specter throughout the foothills of Mudkettle Mountain. And if that were true, those mushrooms would be all the more precious . . .)

But that's a sidenote. At the time, Lu Beiping was too flustered to ponder the ecological origins of these strange fungal growths, and as he grew increasingly uneasy, the sky grew darker. His hoarse shouts drew no reply from the mist-covered hills; instead, they seemed to tug the scarlet coils of the snakeclouds closer to his head. The mist was getting thicker. The red sky yawned over him like the bloody maw of a giant serpent, ready to swallow him and his cattle alive. Soon the haze grew so thick around him that it was hard to see, hard even to breathe. The cattle began lowing in distress. Then, just as Lu Beiping felt himself nearing the peak of loneliness and desperation, he saw, with a bolt of terror, a bright tongue of flame leap upward out of the canopy directly ahead of him. No—this wasn't mist. It was smoke!

God, no. Not a jungle fire. Lu Beiping tensed; his hearing sharpened; first he made out the pip-popping crackle of burning rattans, then, in the distance, he heard a vague, low roar. In summer, when thunderstorms were frequent, everybody lived in fear of lightning-lit wildfires. But it had been drizzling on and off for days; the air was heavy with moisture, and he hadn't once heard thunder. Maybe it was a manmade fire? The Tam-chow hill folk and Loi tribesmen often set fires when they hunted wild hogs. No sooner had this thought occurred to Lu Beiping than a tumultuous clamor rose around him, like a herd of swine pummeling through the underbrush—or . . . no! He shouted in vain at the stampeding cattle. Stooping, he bounded ahead through the trees, then smacked into what felt like a solid wall of heat and reeled back, choking and gasping for breath.

Wait, Lu Beiping thought—is that a person?

To his amazement, a dim figure rushed out of the smoke, bent over and clutching a bulging mass to its stomach. Upon seeing Lu Beiping the man let out a yell, then dropped to the ground crying, *Fire! Fire!*

Before Lu Beiping could get a good look at him the man had scrambled to his feet and vanished again into the haze. There immediately followed a loud splash, and when Lu Beiping turned to look he was surprised to see water glinting through the trees. What on earth . . . ? Somehow, he couldn't imagine how, he and the cattle had managed to loop all the way back around to the creek's second bend, where the water widened into a shallow pool.

Seconds later the man rose from the water, now naked from the waist up, and charged back toward the flames, swinging his sopping undershirt and shouting, *Fire! Fire! Fire!* Lu Beiping still couldn't see the man's face, but without wasting any time, he yanked the machete out of his belt loop, sawed at a shrub till with a *crack* the whole thing came free in his hand, dunked the branches in the creek, then ran, water droplets dancing off of the leaves of his makeshift firefighting tool, back to where the flames raged.

Far down in the valley the bell began to ring, wracking the air with metallic spasms.

This wasn't Lu Beiping's first encounter with a jungle fire. In the hills such fires came often and unexpectedly, roaring to life without the slightest warning and driving people in terror before their sky-blotting fury. Only by quickly deploying waterfronts and firefronts could such fires be brought under control. A firefront was backburn set to thwart the fire's advance; a waterfront was a chain of workers heaving buckets, the conventional line of defense.

Luckily this fire hadn't spread far yet. The head was small and mostly smoke, probably because the forest floor was still damp from several days of rain. Wielding the wet branches, Lu Beiping beat at the flames, while through the choking wall of heat he heard the rhythmic *whap-whap-whap* of the other man flogging at the burning foliage with his wet undershirt, overlaid with his shouts of *Fire! Fire!* He still couldn't make out more than the man's dim silhouette. Minutes later a confusion of scuffling footfalls filled the haze around them as the grove hands, alerted by the sound of the bell, swarmed in from nearby sectors to put out the blaze. After a moment's thumping, thrashing commotion, the fire began to recede. With its retreat cut off, the head guttered out, leaving scattered embers flickering fitfully beneath a jumble of charred branches.

A few workers walked to and fro with rubbermilk pails full of creekwater, splashing out the last hissing pockets of flame. As the smoke thinned, Lu Beiping glanced around the glade, looking for the man who'd fought the fire alongside him. But all he saw were the ghostly forms of the tappers floating through the haze. Suddenly, from the far end of the grove where smoke still swirled, the foreman's voice rang out like a gong:

—Damn hill folk and their damn hog fires! Who found it this time? Which one of you spotted the fire?

Lu Beiping listened, expecting his mysterious fellow firefighter to reveal himself. In those days, being the first person to report a wildfire was a ripe opportunity for advancement, and few would pass up the chance to snag an official accolade.

No one answered.

—Speak up! boomed the foreman, his tall silhouette looming out of the haze. Nobody here wants a citation?

—A citation? Lu Beiping heard somebody snicker. I'd be afraid I'd get denounced as a Class-Enemy Arsonist!

That was Chu, never able to keep his mouth shut. The foreman chuckled.

—Well, son, maybe you're the arsonist I'm looking for!

—Hell, no. I mean, no, sir. I mean, I'd never . . .

The workers crowded round Chu, jostling him and offering congratulations.

—It's Chu! Chu spotted the fire!

—Never thought you had it in you, pup.

—Hey! one of the hands said suddenly, What about Lu Beiping? He runs his cattle this side of the creek. It must've been him that spotted it first!

All eyes fell upon the cowherd. Indeed, the soot was blackest on Lu Beiping's skin.

—No! It wasn't me, Lu Beiping said hotly, advancing toward the foreman. I was hunting for a lost bull when I saw a guy come running out of the smoke, hugging something. It wasn't till I saw him that I realized there was a fire.

—Hugging something? the foreman said, his expression growing serious. Did you see who it was, son?

—No, sir. But I saw him run off and jump in the creek, then rush back and beat the flames with his shirt. It was he who started getting the fire under control.

—That was me! Chu yelled from off to one side. I'm the class-enemy-vanquishing, firefighting hero!

—Cut the bullshit! the foreman snapped. His expression was harsh now; all jocularity was gone from his voice. His eyes swept the gang, paused somewhere in their midst, and his brow furrowed. Then he said in a firm voice: Lu, the prize is yours. If you hadn't cut that bush to beat the flames, we'd never have gotten the fire under control. I'm going to recommend you for a certificate of merit.

—Huzzah! It was Lu! the gang started shouting again. Well done, boy!

—It *wasn't* me, Lu Beiping insisted, turning red with embarrassment. I'm serious! I don't want a certificate of merit! This stuff is none of my god-damn . . .

He swatted away the arms that began raining congratulatory slaps on his back, then lost his temper, and thrusting a finger at the crowd he bellowed:

—Son of a *bitch*! It's not like this is some sort of crime! Who *was* that guy? Who ran and jumped in the creek? Who the hell puts out a forest fire and then doesn't have the balls to admit it?

The crowd fell silent, taken aback by this sudden show of anger. Hands and re-eds traded glances. Wow, Lu Beiping thought, people actually listen to you when you're the foreman's son-in-law. Chu was still sniggering and whispering wisecracks when Lu Beiping's palm swung out of nowhere and smacked him squarely in the temple.

—Fuck you, Chu. Why don't *you* take that prize?

25

Chu staggered back, dazed. Then his face went white and he snatched a hoe out of the hand of a nearby worker.

—Shit, Lu, have you gone crazy? Motherfucking . . .

The gang fell upon the two and pulled them apart. Now that their post-firefighting high had been thoroughly dampened, the foreman had no choice but to step in, chuckling conciliatorily, and try to dispel the bad air.

—Cool your heels, boys. Chu, give over that hoe. Lu, your modesty is commendable, but what a temper you've got! Alright, folks, back to work.

The workers and re-eds shepherded Chu, still cursing under his breath, off into the trees and dispersed toward their respective sectors. Lu Beiping, dour-faced, broke free of the crowd and hurried away to hunt for his cattle. As he passed a pair of workers walking side by side he overheard them talking in hushed voices:

—Sure is strange, scrapping like that over a citation . . .

—Foreman's got a terror of fires . . . must be something on his mind . . .

It was getting dark. Off in the trees the cattle were lowing impatiently, eager for their master to take them home for the night. Lu Beiping began hollering to them, then out of the corner of his eye he glimpsed a familiar, sopping-wet figure walking among the scattering grove hands. He veered toward the figure, then broke into a run, but the young man, hearing his footsteps, slipped into the crowd and was gone.

This time, though, in the smoky twilight, Lu Beiping made out the anxious face beneath that green army cap. Well, who would've thought—it was Wing, whose older sister's spirit Lu Beiping had just married, who was now Lu Beiping's brother-in-law by ghost marriage: the foreman's much-adored son, who, as everyone knew, could do no wrong.

The snakeclouds were fading in the darkening sky. Really? It was Wing? As he called to the cattle, Lu Beiping's heart quickened. And as he herded the animals out of the thick stands of jungle grass and into the open aisles of the rubber grove, he made another surprising discovery. Not far from the pool, scattered beneath charred branches, were hundreds of grains of white rice.

Rice? Who had been scattering rice here?

Only then, thinking back on his earlier misadventures and remembering the shadowy, fungus-covered glade, did Lu Beiping recall a conversation he'd once overheard among the hands: talk of a hidden valley, and something about rice. Had those grains of rice somehow issued from the glade? he wondered. Or had someone scattered rice near the pool as some kind of religious observance, or in an attempt at witchcraft? What, come to think of it, had Wing been carrying when he rushed out of the smoke? What did the rice have to do with the fire, with Wing, with that thing he'd been holding? As he mulled over these questions, Lu Beiping smelled an odor like burnt porridge wafting in a cloud of mist that had drifted off the pool, and through the mist he heard the quiet sob of lapping water. He turned around, gazed out of over the rolling backs of the cattle in hopes of catching a last glimpse of that strange valley. But he saw nothing but somber ranks of rubber trees with crimson clouds scudding over. The sinister valley, with its cadaverous fungal blooms, had vanished; and after a minute, so had the cloud of odd-smelling fog. It was as if, with a flick of the wrist, someone had yanked away the whole scene—the hills, the sky, the bend of the creek—then yanked it back again, slightly altered.

As Lu Beiping walked toward the fading sunset, the cattle lowed contentedly.

Two weeks had gone by since Lu Beiping had received his new assignment, and the cattle commander was starting to get the hang of things.

He now dressed in a long-sleeved work suit, like the sewage workers who came and went by night through the streets of Canton. The ends of his sleeves and his pant legs he tied tight with twine. This kept out the bugs, and most importantly the flying leeches—those bloodthirsty, deformed-looking, wormlike creatures common in Hainan jungles at elevations higher than a thousand feet above sea level. The hands told terrifying stories about the "flitleeches," said they'd penetrate any chink in a person's clothes, burrow their way into navels, vaginas, and assholes, suck a body to a leathery corpse. He wore knee-high rubber boots too, despite the heat. The undergrowth was always wet from dew or rain, and when he drove the herd out in the morning he'd be soaked before reaching the second hill, so the boots were an indispensable shield for his shins. Plus, there were the "hourlaters," tropical rain showers that blew in like clockwork every afternoon, each day an hour later than the last, sheeting down furiously and then gone the next minute; in the hills, these often broke into full-fledged thunderstorms. When the sky shuddered gold and bolts of lightning blasted the trees above him to charcoal, Lu Beiping was doubly grateful for his rubber boots.

The heat wasn't a big deal, surprisingly—he now understood the true breadth of human endurance. Toiling shirtless in the groves, Lu Beiping had found the heat unbearable, but now, sheathed in cloth, he somehow managed to nap under the blazing sun. The real problem was the smell. Not of cowshit—of his feet. Even he couldn't stand the stink of his own feet. And no wonder, since he spent the whole day stumping through the sweltering jungle with his legs encased in rubber. It was like wearing a pair of pickling jugs. After work he'd yank off his boots, tip out a good pint's worth of sweat, and watch as the soil sizzled and ants fled in panic. Even his stout bovine regiment broke ranks before the billowing waves of stink. The first few evenings he'd tried to bring his boots back into the re-ed dorm, which resulted in a memorable uproar. Dammit! Chu cursed. Give us a break! Next time, leave those things in the Underworld! *Us*, Lu Beiping thought: if this was "us" against him, he'd happily play the villain. From then on he peeled off his sweaty work clothes right next to the corral, immediately in front of the camp's main gate, flaunting his malodorous footwear for all to see and smell while a band of camp brats swarmed around him, giggling. Sometimes he'd hang his boots from the end of his machete—like an outlaw fleeing to the marshes with spear and wine flagon, he joked to Chu—and prance barefoot down to the well, eliciting shrieks from the re-ed girls who gathered there after work to wash their hair. Gaffer Kam, hearing the commotion, would rush to the scene and then stand on the sidelines jeering at Lu Beiping in hopes of currying favor with the city girls. Hey, smelly boy! he yelled. Keep away from the ladies! Wait till I get my pick!

Bliss. Pure bliss. It had been a long time since Lu Beiping had had so much fun. He gave his cattle exotic foreign nicknames—Jesus, Abraham, Julien, Vronsky, Rudin, Natasha—harvested at random from the Russian and European novels he loved to read, plus his *Bible Stories* anthology. In those days this was a provocative thing to do, and he felt a secret thrill whenever he belted those awkward syllables. *Move it, Raskolnikov, rattle your hocks!* he'd shout as he brandished his switch at the moseying black bull. *Quit mucking around in that ditch, Emma!* he'd bark, gripping a shrub while he tugged the spotted heifer up the slope by her single curly horn. Of course Alyosha was his favorite, with a lean, colt-like body, a noble red-brown face, and a white stripe running down his nose; Lu Beiping imagined him as the Lord of the Cattle, his clairvoyant animal familiar. And the gaunt-faced, sinister old bull who always wandered off to graze in secret he knew as Judas, the Horned Betrayer, and regarded warily.

Adam and Eve didn't join the roster till much later, after some alert bystander had reported Lu Beiping's suspicious naming habits to the goose-stepping Sergeant Fook. One evening, Fong, feigning casual interest, strolled over to the corral, pinching her nose against the smell. He'd had no contact with her for almost a month, but the company beauty queen was coquettish as ever. In her usual tone of fakey, theatrical awe, she asked him why his herd of Bible characters was missing Adam and Eve. Did this omission have some special significance?

—JUDAS! he bellowed to the Betrayer, who was lingering stubbornly outside the gate, causing Fong to hop back with a shriek. He

laughed darkly. Special significance? he said. Well, you know, over *there*
Adam and Eve came first, before Jesus and Judas. But on this side of
the world, Jesus and Judas will be long dead before we have an Adam
and Eve.

—What . . . what . . . Fong stammered. What do you mean? Stop
being subversive!

—So report me. Go rat me out to your friend Fook, maybe he'll
put a big gold star on your Party rec.

He hadn't even taken off his boots and already she was hightail-
ing it away.

Screw it, he thought. Who cares?

The truth was, Lu Beiping cared far too much.

Several weeks ago he'd gotten intel from Chu that at a meeting at
battalion HQ not long after Lu Beiping had started on as cowherd,
Fong had solemnly announced that Sergeant Fook would be her Party
Entrance Recommender.

See no evil, hear no evil. It was time to put himself farther out
to pasture.

At the third bend of Mudclaw Creek he built himself a crude
hut and cattle corral. It took an extra half hour each way to get the
animals out to decent grazing, and on this pretext he'd suggested to
the foreman that he corral them in the hills, so they wouldn't defatten
on the trail. He'd even live there himself, he offered, so he could keep
a better eye on the cattle, monitor the corral count. Good man! the
foreman said with a grin and extra emphasis on the "good," sounding
like a general in a model opera. Good man! Is this your personal contribution to Operation Red May? Wish they'd sent us more fine pups
like you! Lu Beiping listened expressionlessly as the foreman lauded
his initiative, feeling like he'd just fulfilled some secret wish on the
foreman's part. In the past, during the winter months, when the grass
near camp became too thin to sustain the herd, the company herds-
man often corralled the animals in the hills, so there was precedent
for Lu Beiping's request. But now—the foreman eagerly concurred—
what with all the hubbub clearing bush for Red May, the animals were

skittish and grazing poorly, so it made perfect sense for Lu Beiping to move into the hills early this year. He told Lu Beiping to get rice and cooking oil from the quartermaster, pick up a barn lantern, slicker, flashlight, and extra work clothes at the storehouse. Don't think you'll need a flintlock, he said. We used to give one to the Gaffer but there's nothing to shoot at on the mountain now but hogs and rabbit deer. Don't you believe that nonsense about the Snakeweird.

There they stood, the foreman and his ghost son-in-law, shooting the breeze in broad daylight in front of the camp gate, as if there were nothing at all shady about this arrangement.

Two days later, the foreman sent a team of workers with an oxcart full of thatch to make some much-needed improvements to Lu Beiping's hut.

—Damn it, same pot gets a different handle, groused the Gaffer, toiling in the rubber groves, to anyone who would listen.

Dreamless Vale, Lu Beiping wrote in his journal. This was on his third day living alone in the hills. He'd christened the gully with this florid name mostly as a counterweight to fear—to the awful, nameless fear that these wilds had woken in him.

On the first night, the jungle revealed its terrifying true face. First, there was the silence, a huge, all-encompassing silence that slid shut over him like an iron lid. Actually, the jungle at night was filled with noises: the moaning of the wind, the shrieking of birds, the howling of wild animals, the buzzing of insects; but together these added up to a single, oppressive silence. Every sound threw the silence into sharp relief, added another kilogram to its steadily accumulating weight. As the silence grew heavier, deeper, thicker, acquired mass, volume, and density, an irrational fear seeped out of Lu Beiping's bones and hardened around him like a shell. (When you're so afraid that you no longer know why you're afraid, that's true fear, Lu Beiping said to Tsung, years later.) By day, flanked by his brawny bulls, he could fancy himself intrepid; but at night, the fear that lay coiled inside him would slither out ready to swallow him whole. Every rustle in the forest was a raiding party sent in advance of silence. Light the lamp and it became a malevolent ghost's eye, staring at you; snuff it, and darkness fell over you again like a vast, wet, moldy-smelling curtain, suffocating you—sometimes Lu Beiping actually felt short of breath. He sat bolt upright in his hut, which was open on four sides, with just a low wall separating him from the elements, unable to sustain a supine position for ten minutes, much less sleep. Whistling, singing, going for night strolls were all futile distractions. Every rustle, every cheep was a knife blade on his nerves. He tried to avoid brushing anything with his frigid toes and fingertips; his extremities had become conduits through which fear could flow, and the slightest movement might swell its influx. For several nights he could do nothing but sit against the corner post next to his bed, clutching his sheet, clenching his teeth, his eyes squeezed shut, waiting for morning to come. The only thought that warmed his cold, muddled brain was a keen sense of nostalgia for·his bare board bed back in the re-ed dorm. If it hadn't been for the gentle murmur of the cattle chewing their cud in the corral next door, soothing his nerves and bringing him back to reason, he'd have screamed, leapt up, and beat a hasty retreat back to camp.

Driving cattle by day, driven by fear at night—it strained him to the point of exhaustion. Then, when he had finally mastered fear, boredom became the greater enemy. When you were around other people, boredom was an accent, a quarter rest in the march of daily life; but when you were alone with a herd of cattle, a mountain, and a vast, dark forest, it became an all-enveloping medium, like air. A mind needs an Other in order to exist, an object to reflect back its own consciousness and feeling; otherwise, herding cattle is boring. Cooking is boring. Making faces at the creek is ridiculously boring. Masturbation is boredom pushed to its final, empty extreme. After each of these desperate episodes he'd hit himself, curse himself, sink into a deeper funk. Isolation and boredom were a slow burn, withering him, wasting him, emaciating him. He needed activity; he needed talk; he needed a sense of mission. He needed to rescue himself. With mock formality he laid out a Cattleherd Five-Year Reading Plan, forcing himself to read his books according to complex schedules broken down by page, line, hour, and minute, all the while taking notes. His dwindling journal entries took on a new form: catalogues of elaborate sobriquets for every single plant, animal, or object in sight, chosen with far more painstaking thought than he'd given to his cattle's foreign nicknames.

For example. There was that huge gorgontree at the head of the trail, the most frequent source of nighttime creaks and rustles. Probably because it stood on an exposed rise, the slightest breeze would send it into a disheveled frenzy. This was the Tree That Dances in the Wind. On sunny days, down by the creek where he cooked and bathed, he noticed four or five blue dragonflies always flitting around him, and he would whistle to them, start conversations with them, imagining them to be emissaries of the shadow kingdom sent to keep a lonely ghost husband company. These, he decided, were the Blue Dragonflies of Fate. In the thick, clammy evening air he'd sometimes catch whiffs of a keen aroma given off by some jungle plant, making his hair bristle; this was Nerve Perfume. And that strange sound that he heard from time to time, both during the day and at night, whose source he could never ascertain—it wasn't a bird, nor was it the call of any mammal he'd ever heard; more than anything it sounded like a baby's wail, but hoarse and alto, calling up memories of sad, wizened infants he'd once seen on a school field trip to an orphanage—this, he concluded with a shiver, was the Child Crying from Beyond the Grave.

In the end, it was with music—with his little Dunhuang harmonica, its tin surface etched with two flying nymphs—that Lu Beiping vanquished boredom and fear. After the first few sleepless nights he began to achieve a kind of mental discipline that allowed him to face the darkness without quailing. First, after bathing in the creek and spreading fresh straw for the cattle, he'd turn on his transistor radio and listen to shortwave broadcasts from one of the foreign stations that did Chinese-language programming. Then, by the light of the hurricane lantern, he'd read his books, jot notes, write in his diary.

Finally, when his eyes began to smart, it was time for Harmonica Hour, unshakable as the daily trumpet practice that his musician dad had imposed on him when he was a kid. He'd pick up the instrument, draw a deep breath, and pause, waiting for a lull in the jungle's racket; then he'd blow a long G major chord, sustaining it till his lungs gave out. Like a boomerang the merry tone sailed out, rebounding off the bowl of the Mudkettle and arcing back into the gully, glancing off the water's surface, ricocheting between the cliffs. A one-note phrase became a symphony of lapping echoes, the sound filtered by the night air to an aching, crystalline purity. Warbling glissandos, ululating arpeggios—Mudkettle Mountain was his own experimental speaker box. The ethereal sounds he'd once conjured from homemade subwoofers welded from spare parts, to the oohs and aahs of friends, couldn't compare in the least with the Mudkettle's enormous natural amplification system. While in the mood, he'd play through all the Soviet songs that kids back then knew by heart; then, from the depths of his memory, he'd dredge up tunes to nursery rhymes his parents had sung—*Mama hen, mama hen, lay me an egg; the rain, the rain, it falls and falls, old ladies carry parasols*—and perform them all, from beginning to end, in varying concert order.

Thus, with the help of his harmonica, Lu Beiping learned to converse with the mountain. His dejection at losing his girlfriend and having to marry a ghost, the gloom of his dreary new jungle exile, his feverish adolescent wants and nameless night fears, his unmoored feeling of isolation and helplessness; all these were held at bay by the harmonica's piping voice, a sound blissful as skating by moonlight, cool as ice cream; they were gathered up in each inhale, expelled in each exhale, and one by one quelled, extinguished.

It was by chance that he discovered the tobacco patch.

Before long his Cattleherd Reading Plan had sprouted a complication. Ever since he'd moved into the hills he'd been curious about the distribution of trees throughout the jungles of the Mudkettle. That shadowy stand across the creek from his hut—was it first-growth forest, or second-growth? If it was first-growth, why were there no tall trees? If it was second-growth, why was there no trace of human labor, just dense thickets of cane and fern and jungle grass and impenetrable walls of wild banana trees? The epiphyte clinging to the tree above his head—was it a vine, or a tree itself? The bottom half looked like a vine, but the upper half was woody, like a tree. Was it an epiphytic tree growing on an epiphytic vine? Or a tree-vine hybrid? And why was this slope covered with conifer trees that looked like they belonged in a temperate northern forest? As he drove the cattle through these incongruous pines, he concluded that he needed a book on botany so that he could better appreciate the strange wilderness into which he'd been flung.

This meant a trip back to camp to rummage through the books he'd packed when he'd been downcountried. Surely he'd brought a plant-identification handbook—one on tropical plants would be best. But no. Sadly, he'd neglected this area of his library. The best he could find was a thin pamphlet at the bottom of the crate printed by the Revolutionary Committee of the South China Institute of Agricultural Sciences, part of the pre-departure PR packet they'd been issued: *Industrial Crops of the Tropics at a Glance.* Yes, here was a half-page insert titled "forest resources," listing tree species along with distribution, use, identifying characteristics, and medicinal properties (this was probably intended for barefoot doctors). He stuck the pamphlet in his bag along with a couple more novels, remembered the night's chill and grabbed a sheet and a change of clothes, then hurried out the gate and up to the trailhead, where he was immediately buttonholed by Choi, the notorious gossip from squad 7.

—Mercy me, mercy me, Choi tittered, her quick eyes taking him in: It's a crying shame to see a nice city boy like you get caught up in such a shadowy affair. Crossed!

She curled her lip in the direction of camp. He wasn't sure if she meant this exclamation as a curse or an expression of pity. He was numb to the topic of the ghost marriage by now, did his best to deflect Choi's platitudes (You look so thin, friend, you must be wasting away up there!) and was about to bid her good-day when she grabbed his wrist, pulled him into the trees, yanked his head down so his ear was level with her lips, and murmured:

—Poor thing, she really was crossed.

He stared at her, and wanted to ask her what she meant, but she thrust him away and dismissed him with a flick of the fingers.

—Go on. Get yourself as far away from here as you can.

After he'd gone a pretty good distance he glanced back through a gap in the hills and saw that Choi was still standing at the edge of the rubber grove, warding him off with an outstretched hand. He dug out his pitiful brochure and started filling the holes in his knowledge of tropical botany. Parrot camphor, deer plum, lyre tree, flowering pear . . . it was hard to imagine this somber sylvan congregation going by such fanciful names. Ah, it said these were rare tropical hardwoods, traditionally offered as tribute to emperors. Nut palm, hogbark, gray-wood, gooseberry . . . these were the commoners, whom he stood a better chance of getting to know; it said they often grew in large stands. Maybe that was a difference between tropical rainforests and temperate woodlands; here, you never saw large stands of anything, it was all mixed and motley, trees of every stripe crowding cheek by jowl. The rarer the tree, the less likely you'd find it among its own kind. That was one lesson from his remedial botany class, perhaps. He meandered through the forest, glancing back and forth between the trees and the list in his hand, but all the while a small voice whispered in the branches brushing past his ears: *Poor thing, she really was crossed . . .*

Damn it, he thought. All this nonsense about ghosts and spirits is really starting to go to my head.

A moment later he heard a swishing sound far off in the trees. He stiffened. No, it was nothing. The jungle was a sea of strange noises, he'd drive himself nuts if he gave too much thought to any of them. He tried to scatter his attention, focus on anything but that soft swishing noise intruding stubbornly at the edge of his hearing.

But amid the soughing, creaking, rustling, plopping, gurgling, whirring hubbub of the jungle, the *swish-swish-swish* of human footsteps persisted, intermittent but unmistakable to an ear sensitized by long weeks of isolation and silence. And they were growing louder, getting more distinct; in fact, they were hurrying now. Yes—they were coming directly toward him! The hair stood up on the back of his neck, and his heart started to race.

When you're the only person for miles around, the silence can be terrifying. But when you *think* you're the only person for miles around, then the silence is broken by the sound of another human being— that's doubly terrifying. For weeks he hadn't encountered another living soul in this dark expanse of woodland, besides his cattle—who could this be, then? (Or rather, *what* could it be? A wild animal? A ghost?)

Doing his best to stay calm, he slipped into the trees and padded stealthily toward the source of the sound. But when he ought to have been just feet away, the sound ceased, then whatever it was turned tail and scampered away like a spooked deer.

A flurry of pitter-pats dwindled into the forest, like an animal fleeing on tiny hooves.

Lu Beiping swept back a curtain of creepers and tore after the sound, his fear forgotten. In the middle of a weedy, sun-dappled clearing he stopped—for a moment he'd glimpsed, disappearing into the trees at the far edge of the clearing, the unbelievable figure of a naked boy. The boy's bare back had a strange metallic sheen, like armor, but there was no mistaking it: that was a human being, a child, buck naked, skin tanned to the shade of copper.

In the trees up ahead he could hear his startled cattle moaning in alarm.

That was when he found the tobacco patch.

He was on the far side of the creek's third loop, on a wild, gently sloping hillside where one could still make out faint paths worn through the underbrush by travelers or hill folk long ago. It was at the fork up ahead that he'd parted ways with the animals earlier that afternoon, leaving them to wander to their favorite grazing grounds. When he passed through this area yesterday he'd noticed this sunny clearing, probably an old swidden. In the hills one was always coming across such places, where hunters or travelers of years past had left their marks upon the landscape. The swidden had long gone to waste, overgrown by a profusion of shrubs that covered any trace of cultivation, but he couldn't help noticing these clumps of broad-leafed plants growing among the weeds—they were low, full, and leafy, but the cattle hadn't eaten them, which made him curious. He'd also caught whiffs of a familiar scent rising into the morning air, but he'd paid it no mind; just as his ears tuned out the jungle's constant clamor, his nostrils were inured to the tides of strange and familiar scents washing over him from dawn till dusk. In the evening the grassy smells were strongest: herb-like medicinal aromas and, once in a while, the cool, cutting clarity of Nerve Perfume. Mornings, when the woods were milky with mist, he'd catch puffs of a light, sheepy odor not unlike the smell of semen. He'd imagined it was probably a mixture of dew, night air, and rotting leaves, but the similarity was uncanny, and though the thought made him queasy at first, before long he was pulling Chu aside and gleefully sharing his lewd discovery. So it hadn't occurred to him that these aromatic plants might be anything out of the ordinary—hadn't he seen, in every ditch, draw, and riverbed around here, scads of these shrubs with their broad, slightly furry leaves?

No. He recognized that smell. It tugged at him, it was rich with memories.

As soon as he caught his breath, he pegged it: This was a tobacco field. He'd smelled that aroma as a child; these were the leaves with which his father had filled his pipe. Because now, through tangles of weeds, he saw them, lying on mounds of turned soil: crisp, tan leaves tied in bundles and left to bake in the sun.

It was then that he looked up and studied the curl of smoke hanging against the far mountainside. He'd noticed it a few days back and suspected it might be smoke from a cooking fire. But the mountain was always wreathed in vapor, and he spent the whole day wading with the cattle through seas of mist. There was little reason to single out that one white wisp clinging like a smear of salve to the mountain's flank.

For some reason this discovery saddened him. There had to be some connection between the tobacco field and that naked boy, and the boy couldn't be living by himself in the hills. Lu Beiping now realized that he'd been deluding himself: Mudkettle Mountain wasn't his alone to enjoy. In the end, there was no escape from the human race, which he found increasingly detestable.

The munching of the cattle, which had calmed him in the past, now just put him even more on edge. The bugs racketed away, and the air was insufferably hot. He unscrewed his aluminum canteen and took a swig of musty, lukewarm water he'd boiled hastily that morning, as the creekwater couldn't be drunk straight. He hollered to the animals and led them from the clearing, stripped off his sweaty work shirt and draped it on a clump of wild myrtle so that the beasts, smelling his scent, wouldn't stray; then he padded furtively back into the clearing, carrying his canteen and books. Tilting his frayed straw hat to shield his eyes from the sun, he reclined into the knotty roots of a cassod tree. A vein in his temple throbbed, beating a tattoo against his taut eardrum. That bare-assed kid would be back, he'd put in a second appearance at his tobacco patch, Lu Beiping was sure of it. Some part of him wouldn't rest till he'd gotten to the bottom of this business. If he and his cattle shared this mountain some other soul—or souls— he couldn't ignore the fact.

He'd guessed right. The boy hadn't gone far. The vein in his forehead had barely quit thumping when another flight of pitter-pats set off sirens in his brain.

Silent, Lu Beiping lay in wait at the edge of the tobacco patch, half-obscured by brush, his glasses glinting beneath the rim of his straw hat.

Once more the child's nude silhouette appeared among the trees, his skin gleaming like a suit of copper armor. With swaggery grace he leapt into the clearing and danced through and around the bushes, flattening weeds with his small brown feet. Now and then he stooped to pick up a bundle of tobacco leaves, his eyes flitting reflexively around the clearing.

Before long those eyes caught sight of Lu Beiping's trail through the brush and, following it, alighted on straw hat, canteen—

The boy sucked in a sharp breath, leapt back, fled a few paces; halted, turned round, fixed Lu Beiping, who'd just removed his hat, with a defiant glare, and warbled shrilly:

—Oy! You're not Kambugger! Who are you?

Lu Beiping knitted his brow, puzzling out the boy's meaning through his thick accent. There was a stilted, archaic sound to his speech, like a nobleman in a singshow, and hearing it from the mouth of this swarthy wild-child, he couldn't help chuckling.

The boy grinned.

At that, all the hostility in the air evaporated.

(That kid, Lu Beiping said to Tsung years later—it was as if our meeting was arranged by Fate. We were friends from practically the first moment we laid eyes on each other. It felt like we were acting out a script.)

He stood up, patted himself off, walked over to the boy. The boy narrowed his eyes, and Lu Beiping realized that he was squinting against the glare off of his white undershirt. The boy repeated, as if passing a verdict:

—You're not Kambugger. Who are you? I'm not feared of you.

He pronounced his vowels like a northerner, or a Hakka. But his features were like those of the Hainan hill folk: deep, dark eye sockets; broad face; broad, flat nose.

Lu Beiping laughed.

—You might not be scared, but you sure gave *me* a fright.

The boy stood like a drawn bow, black eyes glinting, as if he were about to pounce on Lu Beiping or turn and bound off into the trees.

Lu Beiping saw that the boy's face was covered with sweat. He smiled and offered him the canteen.

—Care for some water? How old are you? What's your name?

The boy, still eyeing him warily, gathered up the bundles of tobacco leaves and swaggered boldly after him into the shade of the cassod tree. Lu Beiping threw a calculatedly casual glance over the boy, taking in the features of his dark colt-like body. Every protruding feature—nose, collarbones, nipples, the little bat dangling from his crotch—shone as if it had been lacquered.

The two sat beneath the tree and fell to talking, the boy fanning himself with Lu Beiping's hat, as if they had known each other for years.

His name was Smudge. He wasn't sure how old he was, stuck out a pair of grubby hands to count—seven, maybe. He was talkative, spoke shrilly in an odd, unplaceable brogue that sounded at times like Cantonese, at times like Hakka, and at other times like Jiangxi or country Hunan speech. Kambugger, Lu Beiping deduced, was their name for his predecessor, Gaffer Kam. The Gaffer, it turned out, had planted this patch of tobacco plants in secret while he'd been herds-man, and sold its produce to Smudge's people. They hadn't known the job had switched hands, and when the patch went wild and they finally ran out of leaf, they'd sent Smudge down in search of the Gaffer, only to find this four-eyed stranger in his place. It was Smudge whom Lu Beiping had heard scampering through the trees—when Smudge realized "Kambugger" had been replaced, he'd dashed back up the mountain to alert his folks, then steeled himself to return and harvest the unclaimed leaf.

—I wasn't thieving, he explained, shaking the bundle. My pa says, we can take what's Kambugger's then give him back money later. We're not thieves, Pa says.

—Where does your pa live?

Smudged gestured in the direction of the smoke.

—Where do your folks come from, Smudge? Are you from around here?

—Pa and us, we're driftfolk. Do you wit what's meant by that, driftfolk?

Ah, of course. How could he not know about the driftfolk? In those days the two most backbreaking jobs on the island were construction—baking bricks, framing buildings, mortaring and plastering—and woodsman's work, harvesting timber in the mountains and hauling it out to the Agrecorps camps. The driftfolk, itinerant laborers from the mainland who roamed the hills, were inevitably called upon for such work, which was thankless but required certain skill. They were homeless, unpapered, "invisible," and often paid in grain. Usually they'd pitch camp in the mountains not far from a village or base camp, then drift off when their work was done, leaving empty shacks. When, though, had a band of driftfolk stolen onto Mudkettle Mountain, and why were they camped so deep in the jungle?

He knew a child couldn't give him clear answers to these questions, so he didn't ask. But Smudge had plenty of questions for him.

—I see you got double eyes, sir. You from Canton?

He nodded, fingering his glasses reflexively. He often forgot they existed.

—Thought so. Canton folk ever speak pretty.

He bobbed his head with grave authority, noodling with Lu Beiping's canteen strap.

—Why are you here with the kine? What happened to Kambugger?

Lu Beiping pursed his lips, studying Smudge, trying to think of a good way to answer this question. In Smudge's black pupils he saw reflected in duplicate the uneasy expression on his own face.

—Because of the smell of my feet.

Smudge nodded.

—I wit, yep, I wit . . .

His fingers paused.

—What's meant by that?

Lu Beiping laughed.

—Come on, you must "wit" smelly feet.

He tugged off a boot. Smudge skipped away, holding his nose and shrieking with laughter.

—I wit, I wit! Oy oy oy, I wit!

He chortled, doubling over, swaying back, his whole body wriggling like a small brown eel, pinching his nose all the while. Lu Beiping laughed too, kicking waves of the odor in Smudge's direction.

In the surrounding forest the cattle, disturbed by their laughter, began a call and response of concerned lows.

—Oy, that's smelly alright! Oy, oy, oy . . .

Smudge's laughter diminished to titters. When they were done Lu Beiping put on his boot again and asked:

—So who lives up there with you, besides your pa?

Smudge danced back another few paces.

—I won't tell!

He charged over, grabbed the bundles of tobacco leaves, and flew out of the clearing on diminutive hooves.

—Pa says tell nobody!

The boy's silhouette, then his voice, melted away into the trees. Above the forest arched the dark curve of the mountain. There was no sound except for the tinny ring of dying echoes. Lu Beiping felt like he'd woken from a dream.

The cattle munched grass, the sound soothing as water. The sight of the green hills was like a cool, refreshing breeze.

Lu Beiping sat in dumb silence. *Pa says tell nobody.* Smudge's odd cadences lingered in his ear.

The curl of smoke was thicker now, and tinted pink. It must be supper time up there, he thought. Supper time for me too. It was time to drive the cattle home, get a fire going, prepare for the night.

He dug out his harmonica and played his animals a slow, brooding serenade.

Chapter 3
"Pa"

That night, Lu Beiping couldn't sleep. Because of Smudge. Or rather, because of the eerie premonitions that Smudge's appearance had aroused in him. Was this another of those chance encounters that would change everything, like when he'd picked up that slip of paper lying at the edge of the forest on that fateful, crimson-skied evening less than a month ago? It made him uneasy to think that the quiet order into which he'd reined his life might soon be thrown to the winds—to the winds of this volatile wilderness, where anything could happen, and where whatever happened, he'd have to face it alone.

There was a cold breeze that night. He'd put too much wet wood on the fire, and smoke had filled the hut, making him hack and wheeze. He got up and prodded the embers with his machete, causing sparks to leap and light to shudder on the ceiling. He listened to the ruminating cattle, to the wind soughing in the thatch. He'd built the hut too close to the water. Where water goes, wind follows, the hands always said. Every year when the typhoons came, the wind would snake along the rivers, scything the bluffs on either side clean of trees. Autumn was typhoon season. When autumn came the wind would have its way with this hut, for sure. But at least it was sturdier now that the foreman's team had reinforced the frame. They'd swapped out Lu Beiping's randomly cut branches for real beams, dug a shallow drainage ditch around the hut and filled it with lime to keep out vermin. Out here, everything attracted bugs. Building houses in Hainan required special attention to wood quality; if a structure wasn't built from solid heartwood, the insects would chew it up in no time, honeycomb the beams like the intricately carved ivory tusks he'd seen once at a city museum. On the first few nights the bugs had kept up a constant drone in the rafters, and when he stuck his finger into the wood, dust had rained down. The sound had soothed him, lulled him to sleep. Now his new beams had banished the insects, traded their gnawing for the jungle's cacophonous silence.

He couldn't sleep. The creek gurgled below him, abrading his ears. He felt like he was sleeping in a hanging coffin, like he'd read about in books—those mysterious caskets clinging to cliffs over hundred-foot chasms.

Nope, it was no use. He just couldn't sleep.

For some reason he thought of the Gaffer—"Kambugger," Smudge called him. Lu Beiping chuckled. So, the tobacco patch was that geezer's little secret. After working the Gaffer's job for close to a month, he'd started to wonder why the old man bore him such a grudge. It turned out that being herdsman wasn't such a carefree existence after all, what with the rain, the cold, the constant battering of the elements. And the Gaffer had always vehemently refused to camp in the hills during winter—he said he'd seen spirits, heard wispwomen cackling in the trees after rain, had even, one night, glimpsed the great serpent itself, the Snakeweird. He'd demanded a gun from the unit, said the smell of sulfur scared off haunts. But even then he'd refused to spend nights in the jungle. Why, then, after Lu Beiping had willingly shouldered his thankless assignment, did the Gaffer start spreading nasty rumors about him behind his back? Lu Beiping smiled; it all made sense now. The truth was, the Gaffer had far overestimated his powers of inference. Private Crop Cultivation was a crime policed only erratically in those days—the Weeds of Capitalism were too many to be pulled, and whether such clandestine farming got punished depended on who noticed and took an interest. But Lu Beiping was notorious among the re-eds as a political "laggie." Didn't the Gaffer know that? An independent spirit, Fong had coyly called him. Yes, he'd always be a misfit, out of step with the rest of humanity. At this thought, Lu Beiping felt a strange pang of grief. *A loser like you*, Chu had said with a grin, *makes a perfect husband for a ghost.* (The little bastard.) Didn't the Gaffer know that he had nothing to fear from Lu Beiping?

He rolled over in bed, and his thoughts drifted to Han. His ghost spouse had become very concrete to him now. Even now, in the wavering firelight, he could picture her face: eyes twinkling with merriment, a lock of hair hanging over one eye, as she giggled over Lu Beiping's frantic quest for a "bathroom." *Poor thing, she really was crossed.* He mulled over Choi's cryptic words. If Han really had suffered some wrong, as Choi hinted, then his ghost wife's spirit was indeed an unquiet one. He wasn't afraid that she'd come looking for him, nursing some old grievance; if she came looking for anybody, it would be the person who wronged her. But what if, out of the jungle's cavernous darkness, a vengeful phantom—like the ghost in the *The Black Urn*, the opera that his percussionist father so adored, in which he said you could discern in the patterns of drumbeats the different footsteps of the living and the dead—came gliding toward him right now, crooning its desperate song, accosting him like the poor pot-seller in the story? *Ere I open my lips, my tears flow down; hark, hark, old man, hear my tale . . .* His father had loved to sing those lines, lingering melodramatically on the high notes, and boasted that he could do the pot-seller's voice in three different vocal styles. What if Han's ghost came to him singing like that—good god!—long sleeves rippling, hastening through the jungle in search of her lonely cowherd . . . Would he shout out a brave *Ho! Who goes there?* Or would he turn tail and run? (All this Lu Beiping wondered in half sleep, with a half smile, half-frightened and half-amused.) He thought of the Snakeweird, the serpent-demon the locals claimed could swallow a whole village, thought of the "wisp-women" the Gaffer said could be heard cackling and wailing in wild banana groves after rain. They said that the Snakeweird, like Confucius's leocore, appeared only once a millennium, but while the leocore brought bounty to the land, the Snakeweird brought ruin. What were wispwomen? Hadn't he read about them somewhere? Yes, in that old poem by Qu Yuan—they were shapeshifting spirits who lived in the mountains, whose songs lured travelers off their paths. Spirits were afraid of the smell of sulfur; snakes too. The Gaffer had said that. But on Midsummer's Day you used something else to ward off spirits. What was it? Orpiment. Bloodstone. He didn't have any sulfur or bloodstone, but he did have a pair of abominable-smelling boots. Ha! Were ghosts afraid of smelly feet?

So Lu Beiping mused, turning fitfully on his bamboo cot, unaware that it had begun to grow light outside and the mist from the creek had risen up the slope and was pouring into his hut. Through the fog of sleep he heard the cattle snorting and moaning in the corral, hollered, *Peter! Judas! Quiet down!* then drifted off again. In a dream, he saw a figure walk into his hut, fiddle with his clay jug and frypan, then sit down. Was it Han? he wondered half-consciously. Had she climbed out of his water jug, like the Snail Maiden, so that she could clean his hut and cook him breakfast before he woke? But the movement ceased. Apparently his supernatural helper had gotten lazy. He rolled over, murmuring; then he heard, seemingly just inches from his ear, a quiet, tittering laugh. He came awake with a start.

Through the mist he made out a small figure sitting in the middle of the hut, a plastic rain tarp draped over its head.

He sat up in bed. It was Smudge. The tarp slid to the floor, showering water droplets. The boy was naked like before, his unkempt hair sodden with dew. He was sitting bent over, engrossed in Lu Beiping's harmonica.

Hearing Lu Beiping stirring, Smudge looked up and grinned at him. Lu Beiping noticed that his teeth were almost black.

—You're a lazybones too. My pa says I'm a lazybones. Where've you been? I've been all over the mountain, looking for you.

—How long have you been here, Smudge?

—Can't read hours, Smudge said, pointing at the alarm clock on Lu Beiping's nightstand. I feared I'd rouse you, so I waited.

Something about the expression on Smudge's face struck Lu Beiping as extremely worldly for a seven-year-old.

—What do you want, Smudge?

Smudge opened his left fist. In his palm lay several wet, crumpled bills.

—Pa'd be pleased if you give these to Kambugger. For the leaf we took.

—I can't, said Lu Beiping, now fully awake. Tell your pa your folks need to give it back themselves.

He reached out and closed Smudge's fingers over the bills.

—Why?

—Money's complicated.

Smudge nodded.

—I wit.

He was silent for a moment, then said:

—Pa'd be pleased if you come visit, come jolly with us awhile.

Lu Beiping laughed at this quaint turn of phrase.

—I'm sorry, Smudge, I really don't have time to jolly. I've got to take care of the cattle.

—Liar. That's not so. Kambugger'd ever come jolly with us. Even when we didn't ask. And he nay ever slept nights on the mountain.

Passing the rain tarp to his left hand, Smudge reached over and tugged at Lu Beiping's arm.

—Come along, he said cajolingly. When I told them about you and your smelly feet they near about laughed their supper bowls off the table, said you should come jolly with us. Won't you come along? Please?

—No! Smudge, listen to me—Lu Beiping peeled the boy's fingers off of his arm—I can't go. I overslept. The animals are hungry. I want you to run home now and give that money back to your pa. I'm afraid you'll lose it, jollying around down here.

Smudge opened his fist again, considered the bills gravely, looked back at Lu Beiping, then edged reluctantly toward the door. Turning and meeting Lu Beiping's gaze, he said:

—Liar.

As he said this, the boy wore the same sensitive, sorrowful expression as before, a look that made him seem old beyond his years.

Lu Beiping threw on his work clothes and followed Smudge out the door, saying nothing in response to this accusation. The warm, pungent odor of sun-baked excrement filled the air. The cattle were frisking in the corral and lowing impatiently. He gave Smudge's rump a farewell slap and watched as the boy made his way across the creek, hopping from one round stone to another in the swirling mist. On the far side Smudge lingered for a moment, pouting. Lu Beiping waved at him, then turned his back to the boy as he unwound the thick wire that held shut the corral gate. The animals surged forward, accompanied by a gust of odorous air, a pleasant mixture of manure and the morning smell of jungle grass.

As he pulled on his legendary rubber boots he heard a high-pitched voice calling mischievously from across the creek:

—Cow got loose! Run, smellyfeet, catch her!

That little joker. I must have offended him, Lu Beiping thought.

Lu Beiping would never be able to say whether his first meeting with Smudge's "Pa" came about by chance, or whether he'd willed it subconsciously. He'd known that, sooner or later, he'd cross paths with the people who dwelt beneath that wisp of smoke—after meeting Smudge, the encounter was inevitable. And yet, for some reason, he kept putting it off. He felt an inexplicable dread at the thought of facing this band of strangers alone in the wilderness. What sort of people were they? And how many? Whenever a certain restlessness rose in him, a tantalizing mixture of curiosity and temptation, he had to force it down by deliberate effort before he could be at ease. He needed some time to adjust.

Three days went by, during which Smudge didn't show himself. The humid summer air, aside from being occasionally pulled taut by a scuffle between bulls, hung deathly still. The sky was an oppressive gray, and drizzled endlessly. Lu Beiping found that he couldn't stop thinking about Smudge. The cattle, too, seemed to be on edge; they grazed in an aimless, restless manner, riffling haphazardly through one patch of forest and then galumping off to another. The herdsman's bottom was afforded no comfortable perch, and his mind found no refuge in his books.

The area where Lu Beiping had set up his bivouac was a hilly patch of forestland enclosed by the third finger of Mudclaw Creek, where the stream flowed out toward the valley bottom. On the third day he decided to ford the creek and venture higher into the hills, toward the fourth finger, where he might discover fresh pastures. Even before the morning mist cleared his hunch was rewarded. This was a great spot; the cattle were grazing with gusto. He knew that the sun set earlier in these steep ravines, so when he woke from a nap after an afternoon spent reclining against a fallen tree reading Turgenev, his first thought was to drive the cattle back across the creek before darkness fell. Hollering their outlandish names, hurling rocks and dirt clods as he'd once flung discuses in track and field, he flushed the animals out of the leafy crannies into which they'd strayed. Southern yellows always kept in herds, never wandered far. As he rounded them up, he counted off by fives and tens. Seventy-five, seventy-six, seventy-seven . . . one missing, as usual. That would be Judas, the gaunt-faced straggler.

—*Judas!* he bellowed. *You lousy bastard! Quit playing hide and seek!*

He thrashed through a prickly wall of shad cane, tugged aside several thick curtains of bloodvine, shouted again:

—*Judas! You*—

He fell silent. On a solitary, moss-covered log in the middle of a clearing sat a woman, her face framed by two thick braids, a cigarette burning between her fingers, eyes fixed on Lu Beiping.

Beyond her he heard the bright whisper of the creek. He had emerged above the creek's fourth finger, where an open, sunny meadow rolled gently down to the water.

Silhouetted against the dark curve of the mountain, the woman's form radiated a deep, placid composure.

(Years later, telling his story to Tsung, Lu Beiping would return again and again to this scene.

He said: I felt like Fate was sending me a coded message.

Something about this woman struck me immediately, Lu Beiping told Tsung. Catching Fong's eye, or holding her hand when we were out of others' sight, I never felt this deep tremor of apprehension. In my books I'd read about solemn coming-of-age ceremonies performed by young men of Western religions: My own coming-of-age ceremony, odd as it might sound, was a gaze exchanged with a woman in the wilds of Mudkettle Mountain.)

She sat in a slash of shade cast by the afternoon sun, smoking a hand-rolled cigarette while arranging something in a wicker basket on her knees. Immediately he noted the way she wore her hair: two fat braids tied with purple yarn and looped once above the ears, a hairstyle seen on almost no woman in those days. Even stranger, she wore a pair of bracelets, one of silver and the other of a dark red wood he would later learn was called snakesbane—an aromatic, supposedly snake-repellant wood. From her ears dangled, shockingly, a pair of earrings, which he'd only seen on feudal-society women in movies; hers were short jingly bangles inlaid with mica or some other glittery substance. Her skin was ruddy but smooth, her features broad. He couldn't tell at first glance how old she was, but her gaze had a steady, mature woman's power.

Lu Beiping smiled and gave a slight bow from the waist, a wordless salutation. This was a gesture with which city kids of a certain class were accustomed to greeting guests or older relatives. Later, she would mock him for it.

He walked toward her. She put out her cigarette, slowly set aside her basket, and stood up.

Lu Beiping felt his own feet grow clumsy.

—You must be . . . she began, then she stopped. Finding no better words, she said: You must be the four-eyed cowherder with the smelly feet.

He grinned, and she smiled back. The uncomfortable moment was gone.

(If I were Napoleon, Lu Beiping said to Tsung, my feet might have changed the course of history. If every wild, unbelievable, ecstatic,

harrowing thing that followed could be traced back to that meeting—
should I thank my smelly feet?)

—Strong men stink, she said with a chuckle. It's the strength that
smells. Eh? Or is it just cowshit?

He flexed a black-booted ankle, not sure how to respond to this.
At last he said:

—I'm looking for a lost bull. An old spotted bull. Have you—

—Smudge is sick, the woman said, cutting him off. It's the fits.
I'm picking medicine.

—The fits? Smudge has malaria?

Lu Beiping was alarmed.

—What kind of medicine are you picking?

—Viperwort, she said, lifting a handful of leaves from the basket.
You ought to come see him. He's been lying in bed two days, shivering
and giggling about your smelly feet.

Lu Beiping noticed that her voice had no trace of Smudge's brogue.

Smudge sick, and with malaria no less. There was no getting out
of this one. Did she really think that a funny-named herb was going
to save Smudge from that terrifying disease?

The woman gazed at him unflinchingly. He noticed that her eyes
had a far-gazing quality, a look of serene, unbroken attention always
fixed on something in her immediate surroundings. Later on, this gaze
of hers would follow him frequently.

He tried to discipline his own eyes, which kept straying without
his permission. She wore a white flowered blouse with no sleeves or
collar, and above the round neckline the faint beginning of a valley
showed. Below her breasts were two dark half-moons of sweat, and
through the thin, damp fabric he could see the texture of her skin, the
flesh full and plump, the pores like fine, dark grains.

—I can't go, he said, feeling a little flustered. I've got to drive the
animals back down to the corral. I'll go see him tomorrow. I have
medicine.

—Bring the cattle then. Autumn can help you herd them back
tonight.

Who was Autumn? Strangers were popping out of thin air. Just how many people lived up there? Well, he'd soon find out. For some reason he felt liberated: If he was to go, let it be with a thundering herd of cattle, at the heels of this strange wild-woman; let him march up boldly into the riddle of that mountain valley. The cattle would give him courage.

On the far side of the creek rose a steep bluff ablaze with orange myrtle. The sun was low in the sky, and the forest teemed with shadows. Now he heard the faint sound of a dog barking. He couldn't tell where it came from. It didn't sound close by, but it wasn't far off either. Just then Judas, displaying unusual timeliness, appeared in his field of vision, nibbling his way with haughty steps out of a vine-tangled ditch. Lu Beiping swore and ran after him, heard the woman shout from behind:

—Round up your beasts and follow me!

Basket in hand, she waded into the water, her plastic sandals treading the stones on the shallow creek bottom. She pointed up the creek.

—This way.

The path didn't continue on the other side of the creek. Later Lu Beiping would learn that most hunters, woodcutters, and travelers who ventured into the forests of the Mudkettle stopped here at the creek's fourth loop, where this precipitous slope created the illusion of a dead end. Few noticed that the creek itself formed a narrow, burbling passageway. The water wasn't deep, and as Lu Beiping stepped into it the woman was already wading upstream, entering a shadowy tunnel formed by flanking bluffs and overarching branches. The cattle debarked tumultuously into the creek and sloshed with pleasure up the cool waterway. Sandwiched between their jostling bodies, Lu Beiping watched the woman's silhouette far ahead winking in and out of visibility in the light reflected off the water's surface. He now noticed her loose knee-length shorts, her dark calves scissoring in the sunlight, slender but firm looking, and the curves of her hips distinctly outlined against the bright water.

The thought that leapt into his brain then was absurd. But still, he could hear his own blood gurgling like the creek.

Rhrhrhrhrhrawf! Rhawfrrrrrawf-rhawf-RHAWF-rrrrrrrr-RHAWF!

When he emerged he was greeted simultaneously by Smudge bowling toward him, wrapped in a threadbare cotton blanket, and by the vicious snarling of a dog. (The cattle, rumbling up out of the tunnel of branches, must have frightened the scraggly mutt the drift-folk kept, provoking this gut-wrenching tantrum of howls.) Strange, Lu Beiping thought—why hadn't he heard the dog before? At night, in his hut on the far side of the mountain, he'd heard everything from the booming calls of baboons to the wails of hyenas to the weird bickering sounds made by mating snakes. The barking of a dog should have been obvious.

—Wildweed! Hush! Cut it out!

This was the woman, raising her voice over the dog's invective. Lu Beiping was thoroughly rattled by this unexpected aural assault, and Smudge capering around him and tugging at his arms disoriented him even more. Even after the whole herd had assembled on the bank, he still hadn't caught sight of the dog, whose endless, lunatic barking seemed an ominous welcome to this unfamiliar turf. Twice Smudge tried to shout something in his ear, but the animal drowned him out.

—Wildweed, enough!

A deep voice rang out like a thunderclap, and finally the dog fell silent. Echoes hummed in the ensuing quiet. The gurgling of the creek grew loud again.

That voice must be Smudge's pa, Lu Beiping thought. Shame on me for thinking those things.

The man, like the dog, remained invisible.

The woman took charge of the cattle and herded them onto a nearby slope. In the sudden silence, Lu Beiping came to his senses and took a moment to survey the hollow into which they'd emerged.

Here Mudclaw Creek came to an end, trailing off into a necklace of shallow, pebble-bottomed pools. Later Lu Beiping would learn that the actual source of the creek was higher up, behind the next shoulder of the mountain, a deep spring-fed pond that the driftfolk called the Sea's Eye and said bubbled up from the ocean itself. The hollow was a half bowl cut into the mountainside, hidden from sight and sheltered from wind, and the bluff that Lu Beiping had seen rising above the creek was one of its walls, seen from the back. Its inside slopes were crowded with trees whose gnarled figures looked like they'd been carved by the passage of centuries. The place was like a scene from a Ming novel: an exile's hiding place, a mountain sanctuary. (Later, he and Autumn would make a discovery in the mountains above the hollow that would suggest that this wasn't too far from the truth.) Two thatch-roof lodges, one large and one small, had been built at catty-corners near the water, and by the door of the larger one, clearly the sleeping quarters, leaned a jumble of saws, ropes, and bamboo shoulder poles. The smaller lodge was open at one end, and out of it poked a stone cooking hearth from which a tendril of smoke rose. The ground between the huts was littered with planks and boards, and piles of logs sat soaking in a pool clearly deepened for this purpose. As he walked along the pebbly bank a ragtag flock of chickens swarmed around him, and he noticed one tall, craggy-faced rooster who seemed to be their leader, with a sure strut and a calm, imperious gaze.

At first he saw no one else in the hollow. Smudge tugged him a few paces toward the lodges, then released him abruptly and dashed away. It was then that Lu Beiping saw beneath one of the bluffs, sitting at the foot of a lychee tree partially disfigured by lightning, a pair of children, slightly younger than Smudge; a big, scrawny dog tied up with a cane-twine rope; and two men, perched opposite one another on a wooden frame, trading pulls on a long two-handled saw.

The shadow of the bluff deepened the shade cast by the tree, and it took Lu Beiping a moment to make out the men's figures. When he did, he was quietly shocked. Both men, like the kids, were naked. The one seated lower on the frame, his back to Lu Beiping, wore a pair of briefs, but the swarthy, bald man facing him, higher up, astraddle the frame, wore not one thread of clothing, and as he hauled on the saw the bundle that hung between his thighs swung impudently. But the charcoal hue of his skin made his body's contours seem somehow gentle, and this lessened the awkwardness of the full-on view.

Kids and men alike gazed at Lu Beiping with varying mixtures of curiosity and distrust.

Lu Beiping smiled and gave a slight bow, as he'd done when he met the woman. He heard the dog breathing heavily.

Must have been the bald guy who shouted just now, Lu Beiping thought. I'll bet he let the dog bark for a while on purpose, just to intimidate me.

The woman, who'd disappeared a moment before, now reappeared at the door of the smaller lodge and yelled:

—Time to call it a day, boys! Show some respect, get down off that thing and say hello to our guest.

The men laid aside the saw and dismounted from the structure. Lu Beiping saw that the log they'd been sawing was nailed with big metal staples to the wood-cutting frame. Though they wore no clothes, they'd sweated so hard that the log and the frame both glistened with moisture.

The two kids ran over and clung to the woman's thighs, but Smudge hung back timidly. The woman barked at him:

—You happy now? I brought back the four-eyed smelly-footed cowherder you've been going on about.

Four eyes and smelly feet. Once again the magic phrase lightened the atmosphere. He heard the two men, who had yet to offer him any sort of greeting, chuckle quietly.

—Get back inside now, the woman ordered Smudge. Look at you shivering. You ought to be in bed.

Smudge, pulling the blanket tighter around him, gave Lu Beiping a conspiratorial look.

—I'll go with him, Lu Beiping said quickly.

Leading Lu Beiping by the arm, Smudge tugged him in the direction of the lodge from which the cooking smoke rose.

Lu Beiping wished he'd had the presence of mind to ask Smudge what it was he'd whispered in his ear while the dog was barking. But it was too late—dinner was ready.

—Suppertime! the woman yelled out the door. Wash up and come eat!

A minute later three men trooped into the lodge. *Another* man, Lu Beiping thought. He was the first to enter, a tall, heavyset fellow with a crew cut and skin as dark as the others'. Now, probably to show politeness toward their guest, the men had washed off their sweat and covered their nether regions. The heavyset man and the lean, bald man both wore red-and-white-checkered Teochew waistcloths, and the man he'd seen from behind, who had longish hair parted down the middle, had swapped his briefs for a pair of faded running shorts. As if they'd coordinated, each man carried a fat bamboo water pipe. The big man, stooping as he came through the door, was the first to greet Lu Beiping.

—Care for a smoke? he asked, offering the blackened tube.

The three kids probably slept jumbled together on the big bed in the middle of the room. Beneath a tattered and patched mosquito net lay a heap of rumpled, line-dried clothes, a baby sling, and a worn wooden comb tossed off to one side. Another water pipe with a piece of red yarn tied around it leaned against the bed—this one obviously belonged to the woman.

The two younger kids played at the woman's knees, following her back and forth between the hearth stove and the long, low dinner table, which was nailed together from scrap boards of various sizes.

The man with the crew cut grinned and chuckled.

—Soon's I heard Wildweed barking up in Crackbowl Hollow I wit it was our smelly-footed friend come to jolly with us. And sure enough. Pleased to know you. My feet've been stinking for years, but these folks nay ever took such an interest in them, as in yours.

He talks like Smudge, Lu Beiping thought.

The woman slapped the man's wrist reprovingly.

—Sit down and eat. You'll make us all sick, talking like that.

The other men laughed. The bald man took a gurgling drag on his pipe and acknowledged Lu Beiping with a perfunctory nod.

The fellow with the center part, who looked younger than the others, caught Lu Beiping's eyes in silent greeting. His skin was dark too, but his features were delicate, with a somber cast. The big bamboo pipe looked rather incongruous in his hand.

Lu Beiping studied this motley gang, trying to piece together the relationships between them. Smudge seemed to be a point of convergence, having both the woman's features and the heavyset man's accent. Was he their kid? But the bald man appeared to be the one who called the shots—Smudge was skittish around him, and the woman looked at him frequently. He must be the head of the household, if a household was what this was. As for the younger guy, the only time any animation came into his eyes was when he glanced at Smudge, suggesting some kind of allegiance between them—this was another mystery.

(A Shangri-La? Lu Beiping said, smiling at Tsung's question. I wouldn't call it that. More like a den of thieves, an outlaw hideout.)

Before he could come to any conclusions, the woman brought out the food. A crock of boiled taro and another of yam porridge, small dishes of pickled bamboo shoots, taro pickles, salt turnips, fish jerky. Lastly, after a wink at the bald man, she carried out a steaming black-and-yellow wood-ear scramble, then went back into the kitchen and returned with a massive, foul-smelling bowl of yam beer, whose cloudy depths swung and glinted when she plunked it down in the middle of the table, to the general excitement of those gathered.

Crap, Lu Beiping thought. Yam beer. He wrinkled his nose. The bald man gave a pleased grunt and elbowed him.

—Help yourself.

God, no. Lu Beiping could tell that once again he wasn't thinking straight. He had to say something, couldn't just sit there like a mute. But he didn't want to make a fool of himself like he'd done in the Kaus's cookhouse.

—No, no, he spluttered as he picked up his chopsticks: Elders first! Help yourself, Mr. . . .

But by this point he'd already started to reach for the food. He froze, glanced at the others, then looked back at the bald man.

—I'm sorry, sir, I don't even know your name.

Poor Lu Beiping. Just at that moment, the woman had gone to feed the dog.

—Well, Lu Beiping blurted, I guess you must be Smudge's pa.

Smudge gave him a vicious pinch under the table. His wits returned to him, and he realized that the atmosphere around the table had turned ice cold. The bald man's face had grown so dark it looked like it might burst into thunder and lightning, and his chopsticks hung motionless at the lip of his bowl. The other two men slurped porridge intently, pretending they hadn't heard.

(As soon as that yam beer came out, I completely lost my head, Lu Beiping told Tsung. I was overwhelmed by the reeking memory of that night in the foreman's cookhouse. Even as I opened my mouth to ask the question, I knew it was the wrong thing to say. That it actually escaped my lips was purely an accident.)

The woman, who'd heard too late what had happened, hurried through the door.

—Mercy me! she said, giving Smudge a sharp look. Then she lifted the beer bowl, sloshed some out into a cup, shoved it in front of the bald man, and said to Lu Beiping with a tense chuckle: You've got the wrong idea, friend. *I'm* Smudge's pa.

—You are not.

The bald man glared at her. Looking back at Lu Beiping, he said slowly, punctuating the air with his chopsticks:

—Son, you're welcome to eat at our table, but only if you don't sin against our laws.

Now it was the woman's turn to be offended. She reached out and flicked the man's chopsticks with her own.

—Damn it, give him a break! You want to talk laws, do it someplace other than at supper.

But right after she said this she drew the bald man's head to her breast and fondled it. Smiling at Lu Beiping, she said:

—Shame on me for not making things clearer. This mean-eyed bastard's my friend Kingfisher, the toothless baboon. All howl and no bite.

Lu Beiping felt himself blushing. The woman's peacemaking attempts were just making him feel more sheepish. He knew that Cantonese country people had some unusual naming customs, but he'd never heard of a mother being called "pa." And why did the man object so vehemently to this? Just what was the woman's relationship to Smudge? And to this Kingfisher fellow, and to these two other men?

—All howl and nay bite, eh? the big man cut in. As I've ever heard it, he bites and you do the howling.

He howled with laughter, and soon the others were laughing too. Now the woman went to the big man, circled him with her arms, and slapped him playfully across the lips.

—Listen to this man, flapping his jaws like a monkey wrench without a screw. Four Eyes, this is Stump. Thick as a hunk of wood—she rapped his head—in case you couldn't tell.

—Heh! Kingfisher chortled. A hunk of wood. You'd know, wouldn't you?

Now the woman went over and embraced the man with the center-parted hair, who hadn't said a word throughout all of this.

—And this is Autumn. He'll help drive your animals home tonight. He's like a brother to me, he's my bloodless kin.

—Bloodless kin? A bond boy! Kingfisher whooped, and Stump gave a hoot of assent.

—You've got some nerve, talking like that about an educated man. Autumn, I think you'll like our friend here, he's a scholar. Bows like this—she aped Lu Beiping's courteous bend at the waist—and hauls around a big bag of books when he's out herding, so Smudge says. Even calls his animals by queer foreign names, Thisky and Thatsky, Maggie-laggie and Rascally-cascally-kov and such. Like handmaidens for some European queen!

She laughed, gesticulating more and more energetically as she spoke. By now the three men had almost emptied the big bowl of beer. From beneath the woman's dancing arms Autumn gave Lu Beiping a knowing smile. Lu Beiping nodded back, feeling like they'd established a kind of rapport between peers. Autumn's eyes had an unmistakably melancholy look, Lu Beiping thought.

The woman seized the bowl and drained what was left of the beer, then grabbed the two roughhousing kids and dragged them to her side.

—And these brats are Tick and Roach. Tick's almost six, she's about old enough to start helping round the house. And Roach, he's in charge of wetting the bed. A right mess, just like his Uncle Stump.

She grinned wickedly at the big man.

—Smudge you already know. And I'm Jade. I'm the den mother. I cook and clean for these bandits.

—You're drunk, den mother, Kingfisher interjected, wrestling the bowl from her. Don't mind her, Four Eyes. Drink makes her run at the mouth. You look hungry, eat some more.

—I'm eating, I'm eating, Lu Beiping said automatically. Now that Kingfisher had relaxed a bit, Lu Beiping thought that there was something noble looking about his craggy, iron-dark face. This woman, though—Jade—had thrown him into total confusion. Den mother. She clearly wielded some kind of domestic authority. But what was her relationship to these men? She seemed to have a measure of intimacy with all of them. He had a hunch, which had been gathering momentum throughout this conversation, but his thoughts were now cut short by Jade shrieking in alarm:

—Smudge! Heavens above!

Lu Beiping turned and saw Smudge lying in bed, his face deathly pale, gripping the blanket and shivering violently. Smudge hadn't made a sound all throughout dinner, Lu Beiping realized. He put down his chopsticks and was about to rise, but Kingfisher stopped him short with a bark.

—Eat! Can't we have one goddam meal in peace around here?

He glared at Jade.

—Woman, you have a guest. That boy's been twitching for days now, you ought to be used to it.

Jade ignored him. She hurried from the kitchen with a bowl of medicine broth and sat down at the bedside.

Kingfisher sucked porridge loudly. Once again, the mood had gone to ice.

The cattle rested on the slope. They'd grazed their fill and now sat huddled together in the grass waiting for their master. As Lu Beiping approached, a few steps behind Autumn, the animals raised their voices in warm, baritone greeting.

Lu Beiping hollered to Alyosha, and as the herd assembled and began trooping down the hillside he heaved a huge sigh of relief.

Strange place. Strange people. Nothing he'd experienced in his life up to this point had prepared him to understand this kind of strangeness.

The chilly moonlight refreshed him. Splashes of silver shone on the dark bluffs to either side, and framed in the hollow's mouth lay the sprawling form of the mountain, like an octopus easing its tentacles in deep, moonlit waters. There was a cold breeze, and when Lu Beiping stepped into the creek he gasped despite his rubber boots. Autumn was barefoot. The cattle sloshed along happily, hastening homeward with an eagerness that Lu Beiping didn't share.

Once again the jungle's fermented odor filled his nostrils. Amid the familiar night noises he searched for something to say to Autumn, something to break the silence. He felt a sudden need for talk.

—The dog's not barking, he said finally. When I came up he was making quite a scene.

—It was me that tied him up then, Autumn said, opening his mouth to speak for the first time since Lu Beiping laid eyes on him that afternoon. You scared him good, marching up there with your thunderous army.

They both laughed quietly. After walking in silence for a while, Autumn spoke again.

—How old are you? When'd you come to the country?

—Guess.

—I can't tell. City people's features all look alike to me.

—City people's features? Lu Beiping repeated, chuckling.

—I'd say you're younger than me, Autumn said. I graduated from junior high in sixty-five. You?

—I would've graduated in sixty-nine. But I actually never went to junior high, at least not to class. They closed the schools right after I finished sixth grade. Three years later I got downcountried.

—But you know Jesus, Peter, Judas. Where I come from, even high schoolers don't know those names.

Lu Beiping glanced at Autumn. He knew them, obviously.

—Yeah, but there are a lot of things I never learned. Like, Rectify Ideological Outlook. Never Forget Class Struggle. Venerate, Emulate, Integrate, Participate, Evaluate, Interrogate, Repudiate, Annihilate. That stuff gave me a headache. I failed every current events test.

Lu Beiping laughed and slashed with his machete at the grass that grew alongside the creek. Autumn smiled tensely.

—Let's not talk about that stuff.

Lu Beiping wanted to ask Autumn where exactly he came from, and how long he'd been in Hainan. But he felt that he shouldn't press a "driftperson" for these details, so he bit his tongue, trying to think of something else to say. The two young men waded on down the creek. Up ahead Lu Beiping heard a quiet swishing noise in the water, probably some creeping night creature, and was about to fling his machete in order to scare it off when Autumn laid a hand gently on his arm.

—Don't. It's a snake, crossing the water. Don't rile the snakes, don't wake the spirits. That's one of Kingfisher's laws. I should've told you.

That was something to talk about.

—So, what law of Kingfisher's did I break back there?

Autumn was quiet for a moment. Then he said:

—Kingfisher has lots of laws . . . lots of sins. I'm one.

Lu Beiping turned and gazed at him. In the branch-filtered moonlight his expression looked even more somber and remote than usual.

—Smudge's dad died, Autumn said slowly. Was smudged. We don't say die, we say smudged. Smudge's dad was smudged flat by a falling tree. When Smudge was born, his dad named him that, said mean folks need mean names, give a man a low name and death'll pass over him. But death took him instead. Smudge crossed his own dad. So—Autumn lowered his voice—*they* don't like him.

They? Lu Beiping remembered the rude scene at the end of dinner and felt a chill.

—Is Jade Smudge's mother? he asked.

—Yep. He's her oldest. She mothered Tick and Roach too.

—By . . . Kingfisher? By Stump? Lu Beiping asked carefully.

—Yep, Autumn said. But it's Smudge she cherishes most. She has him call her Pa in secret. Never when Kingfisher's around.

—So, Lu Beiping said, now brimming with curiosity: What about snakes? Why can't you rile them?

Autumn gazed at him for a moment, then said slowly:

—On account of what your people call Antiquated Thinking. Some folks hold that everything has a spirit. I believe that. The way Kingfisher says it, spirits of warm-blooded animals are good spirits, divines. But spirits of cold-blooded animals, snakes and insects and the like, are haunts. Weirds.

—What about dead people? Lu Beiping asked with a catch in his voice, thinking of Han. Are their spirits good or bad?

—Dead people's spirits are cold-blooded. Warm blood turns cold, that makes shadow air, killing air. Kingfisher says Smudge has got the killing air about him.

—What about you? You said you're . . . a sin?

—They say I'm cold-blooded. They're right.

Lu Beiping shuddered. He thought of Han again, couldn't bring himself to think further, and walked on in silence.

After a while he asked:

—Who do you all report to? Are you part of a unit? How do you get by, felling trees up here in the mountains?

—We belong to Whitesands County. This bluff here is the border between Tam-chow and Whitesands. Whitesands is afraid you down in Tam-chow are about to burn the mountain clean of wood, so they let us up here to log and ship timber down to sell. Kingfisher has papers.

He spoke reflexively, as if recounting a well-worn story. Sighing, he said:

—Logging's hard work. Who to do it, but us driftfolk?

The cattle had stopped. They'd come to the clearing from which Lu Beiping and Jade had waded into the creek that evening. Lu Beiping hollered them onward, then turned to Autumn.

—You can go back now. I know the way.

—It's early yet, Autumn said. I'll walk with you a spell, take a look at your . . . abode.

Lu Beiping laughed inwardly to hear his hut described in such lofty terms.

—Sure. Actually, that's a great idea. I can give you medicine for Smudge. That's not . . . against your laws, is it?

Autumn smiled bitterly, and the two quickened their steps at the thought of Smudge's illness. After skirting a ravine they emerged at the third bend of the creek, and the cattle celebrated their arrival with cheerful lows. Familiar smells filled the night air, and the beasts trumpeted and fussed eagerly. Before long they were shouldering at the corral gate, and managed to kick it open. Lu Beiping hollered sharply to Alyosha, raked down some of the hay that he kept piled near the corral and tossed a few armfuls through the fence slats, then as the cattle crowded round to feed he leapt up onto one of the shafts of the oxcart and counted them.

—Seventy-six, seventy-seven . . . Perfect! Seventy-eight.

Autumn watched him with a look of wonder, as if surprised to see Lu Beiping make these nimble, practiced motions.

—Soon there'll be more than that, Lu Beiping said with a hint of pride. At least two of the cows are pregnant. The miracle of life, eh? Before long I'll be looking after a whole new generation of mooing youngsters.

Autumn said nothing, and for a moment his expression darkened.

The hut smelled of damp air and sweat, of new thatch and the longstanding reek of his boots. Lu Beiping lit the lamp, glanced back and saw Autumn still standing outside, the same look of melancholy on his face that he'd worn at dinner up in the hollow. He called to Autumn, but the man didn't move. Lu Beiping turned and fished hurriedly in his bag, found the pouch of pills he'd brought with him into the mountains. Crap, there was no quinine left—after moving to his jungle camp, he'd been so scared of catching that dreadful tropical disease that he'd swallowed a pill every night, not even knowing whether it could be taken prophylactically. Now he had nothing left but piddling things he'd loaded up on at the clinic, Silverwing Detoxifiers and Blue Licorice Extract and such. He grabbed the Silverwing bottle, handed it to Autumn.

—Here, this might help, till I can get some better stuff.

He turned and searched the hut for something fun to give Smudge, reached hesitantly for his harmonica. But when he looked back Autumn had slipped away without a sound.

He ran out, saw Autumn's shadow vanish into the trees on the far side of the creek, leaving nothing but moonlight and murmuring water. Another strange one, Lu Beiping thought.

Chapter 4
At the Water's Edge

In the mountains, nobody counts the passing days. So if it hadn't been for Kambugger's unexpected visit, Jade wouldn't have known it was an important day for her, and been reminded of her own sorrow.

He'd come for the leaf money. The first question out of his mouth after Wildweed quit barking was this:

—Does he know?

—He? Who's he?

Jade played stupid, cursing the man silently. Filthy cur. There's nothing he'd be ashamed to take a sniff at.

—That Canton pup they put in my place. Four-eyed city pup, got ghost-married and sent up here to mind the cattle. You seen him?

—Excuse me?

Jade raised her eyebrows, laid aside the shirt she'd been washing. Kambugger waved the bills she'd just handed him.

—You know damn well what I'm talking about, Jade.

—How would I know what he knows? Jade said, whipping a pair of patched waistcloths on the rocks. I don't know anything but what Smudge told me, which is that his feet stink, and that he's the new cowherd.

—Heh, his feet stink, that they do.

Kambugger nodded as he slipped the money into his pocket.

—Well, if he doesn't know anything, I don't know anything either. As long as he's got no dirt on me, all's well. So long, Jade.

Jade watched from a distance as he waded into the creek, his gaunt, stooped figure looking like a little brown shrimp. That man is just a pile of trifles and gossip, Jade thought. For him, everything's dirt. To think that there are some people who make their way in the world like that, collecting dirt on other folks.

—Hey, Kambugger! she called. Wash your mouth out before you come talk to me next time. Don't forget, I've got some dirt on *you!*

—Wash my mouth out? the old man said, tossing an arm dismissively and kicking at the water. Lucky thing it's Midsummer, I can wash it right here in the creek, rinse the evil spirits out of it, get it extra clean. Midsummer's Day, they do say the waters have that power.

He looked back and leered at her.

—Maybe you should tell Smudge to tell that stinky boy to take a Midsummer bath too.

He slipped into the lemongrass and was gone. Jade felt weak all of a sudden and sat down heavily on the bank.

That's right. Midsummer. Today's Midsummer. Smudge's pa's day. And Smudge still in bed with the fits, shivering and twitching.

On Midsummer, go down and bathe in the water, never go up into the mountains. Climb the mountain on Midsummer and you'll wake the snake air. That's what Kingfisher always said. Like in the singshow, *Tale of the White Serpent*—wasn't it on Midsummer that the young scholar woke the white lady's snake air, so a whole storm of spirits came out to make trouble? Smudge's pa didn't believe in powers, he went up the mountain to log on Midsummer, against their warnings. And then . . . No wonder the men had washed themselves in the creek first thing today, then sat all day under the lychee tree smoking and sawing instead of hauling in the timber they'd felled yesterday. If Smudge's pa were here, he'd be wrapping rice dumplings right now. Rice dumplings with salt water and rock sugar, with pork and sweetpaste, with dates and lotus butter, every flavor and color you could think of . . . No more. When Horn went, so did the rice dumplings. She'd heard that people here in the Hainan hills didn't mark Midsummer; Midsummer was a water holiday. But her people were water people, she was born and raised by the water, and it was down by the water that she met Horn.

Jade rose and stumped over to the tree, laid a slap on Kingfisher's bare back.

—You devils. Why didn't you tell me it was Midsummer?

Kingfisher glanced up at her, grinning mischievously.

—Keep that up, Jade, slap me again. It's been a long while since you've laid such a kind hand on me. Give me a thump down here, will you?

He squirmed his big naked body. Stump, up on the frame, also naked, laughed.

—Mercy, Sis! On good days we're glad to share your sweets, but on ill we'll leave you be. *Spittle in the eye dries swiftly, Princess, but true love'll nay ever deplete! Still thy weeping, tear not thine hair . . .*

Stump launched into the crooning recitative from *The Emperor's Daughter*. Jade turned to leave, not in the mood to banter with the men.

—Where's Autumn? she called back. Where's he off lazing at?

—Soon as we finished stacking boards he scampered up into the high valley to study that tombstone or whatever it is, Kingfisher said as he yanked on the saw. I think he's aiming to become an archae-ologist. I always said, your brother friend won't ever be content with what's served at the driftfolk table.

Jade went briskly toward the smaller of the two cabins. As she walked in, Tick and Roach, who'd just woken up, ran to her clamoring:

—Auntie, Auntie! What's wrong with Smudge? He's . . .

Jade rushed to the bedside and drew Smudge into her arms. For days he'd been burning up with fever, his face flushed, his mouth foam-ing, his limbs twitching. She brought over some herb broth, pried open his clenched teeth, and fed him a few spoonfuls, calling his name softly. Hot tears ran down her cheeks. She laid him down, reached under the mat for some incense sticks, lit them. With the smoldering sticks clasped in her hands she knelt before Horn's memorial tablet, closed her eyes, and murmured to his soul in the darkness:

—Horn, brother. I know it's your day. Please don't call Smudge to you now. I won't let you take him. Please, please, brother, show me a sign, show me you're listening . . .

Midsummer—it was no wonder the sun was so hot that day. They said that on Midsummer, with the sun highest in the sky, shadow was at low ebb, and light ruled all. He must have chosen this day to go, she thought. He was that kind of a man, big, strong, and fiery-tempered, a straight-hearted, honorable man. He couldn't bear the awful things they'd said about him, the awful things they'd accused him of, back when he'd been chief quarryman at Ho Chong and the head family had hounded him out in the name of Purification. The struggle meeting had turned into a flat-out clan feud; he'd hit people, hurt people, then fled with his brothers and took to the river. They'd drifted for years, living by hook and by crook, roaming all the way from the Hundred Hills in Guangxi to Five Finger Mountain in Hainan, to the Mo-siu Mountains, to Mudkettle Mountain. Some had turned back, unable to bear the hardship. Some had been caught and thrown in jail, others had risen and prospered, become foremen and Secretaries. Once I've stuck my head out, I'm not sticking it back, Horn said. I'll keep drifting till there's no place left to drift to. They were boarding the ferry at Kwun-chow Crossing when he saw her, come out walking by the water to escape the company of her village sisters, wearing trouble on her brow. He said: Come drifting with us. We need a woman. She studied him for a long moment, and he said again: Come, we need a woman. That bold, honest look and those bold, honest words—*we need a woman*—were what made her get on that ferryboat. Horn was the third man in her life, but it was he who turned her into a woman. Driftfolk need a woman like a tree needs its taproot, he'd always said. Horn had cleft her stony soil, seeded her with Smudge; she'd roamed with him across half the province, never staying in one place for long, watching the band grow and split. It had been no easy thing, holding this crew together, making their way across the sea and into these hills. On Mudkettle Mountain they'd found some peace at last. And then . . .

For driftfolk, what mattered most was staying on luck's fair side. Like most West Canton people they observed name laws: Children called parents Uncle and Auntie, spouses addressed one another as

Brother and Sister, so as to mislead baleful spirits that might bring them harm. But lately, in secret, knowing Kingfisher would disapprove, she'd had Smudge call her Pa. That way, whenever her son called her name, he seemed to be addressing two people, one in light, the other in shadow.

She heard Smudge stir on the bed behind her.

—Pa, he groaned. Pa, I'm dying . . .

—Hush! Jade said. She gathered him into her arms and, bringing her lips close to his ear, whispered: Smudge, today's the day your pa passed on, your other pa. I lit a stick for him, why don't you say something to him.

—I'm dying, Smudge whimpered. I'm dying, Pa, I—

—Peh! I spit on that!

She slapped the bed frame and rose. Then without warning she began bellowing furiously:

—Hell on you for saying such a thing! I spit on that! Like you haven't been enough afflicted. They say you crossed your own pa, and here you go crossing yourself! Heaven help us, Smudge. I spit on that! I spit on you, and I spit on that!

Like a madwoman she began spitting in every direction, thrusting a quivering finger at Smudge, at Tick, at Roach, at the spirits gathered in the surrounding darkness. The two little ones began to cry.

—I spit on that! she wailed in a crazed voice. I spit on you! I spit on all that! Gods in heaven . . .

Smudge, who had now awoken completely, sat up and stared at Jade with a blank look in his eyes.

—He's here! Smudge squeaked. Pa! He's here!

—What? Jade said, trembling. He's here? Smudge, did you call him here? Your pa's spirit? Quit scaring me, Smudge—

—Pa, he's here! Stinkyfoot's here!

Outside the dog gave a few loud yaps, then fell silent. Still half mad with desperation, Jade ran to the door, her thick braids falling out of their coils, and collided head-on with Lu Beiping.

—Smudge, it's your pa! He's come to save you!

She threw her arms around Lu Beiping and sank to her knees, tears streaming down her cheeks.

Lu Beiping, walking in on this bizarre scene, was caught completely off guard. Dazed, he glanced back and saw Kingfisher, Stump, and Autumn, who'd rushed over to see what was the matter, standing outside the door in varying degrees of nakedness, staring in dumb silence at him and Jade.

He freed himself gently from Jade's embrace. Autumn came over and helped her into bed.

Slowly Jade came to her wits, saw Lu Beiping standing before her, then looked at the others. She clutched Smudge tight and began to sob.

—Is she okay? Lu Beiping mouthed to Autumn, then without waiting for a reply he fished the box of pills from his pocket and said: This is for Smudge. It's Western medicine, special medicine for malaria.

All eyes in the room fell upon the paper box lying in his outheld palm.

—Four Eyes, Kingfisher said at last: You're a saving rain. I wouldn't wonder if Smudge's pa himself called you here today. We cooked up every kind of cure we could think of, but this morning Smudge's fever got so bad we just about busted our heads . . .

—Smudge, you're a right lucky pup, Stump said. When you called out for Stinkyfoot I'll bet you had no notion you were calling down your own savior. Better hie to it and make thanks.

Jade gave a teary laugh, tossed the hair out of her eyes, and pointed at Lu Beiping.

—Bullshit, it was *me* called him here. I got down on my knees and prayed the eights, and in he came. You think Horn's spirit could bring about a thing like that?

Kingfisher, mid-drag on his pipe, gave a loud snort of laughter, expelling a mouthful of smoke.

—Did you hear that, Four Eyes? She said she prayed the eights for you. How many times have you prayed the eights for Horn, eh, Jade? How about me and Stump? I don't believe you'd pray the ones and twos for us. Heh!

Laughter filled the room. Lu Beiping, his face serious, interrupted:

—You should give the medicine to Smudge now. It's called quinine. Give him one pill three times a day, morning, noon, and night. I should get going now. I left the animals grazing in the meadow down there, but I can't leave them for long.

He stood up, repeated his instructions about the dosage to Autumn, tousled Smudge's hair, then strode quickly out the door. Four pairs of amazed eyes watched him as he waded into the creek, hastening away without a backward glance.

—Well, bless me sideways! Stump said to Autumn. He looks a mite peeved. You've got an ounce or two of ink in you, did we say something unmeet?

—Why'd he run off so fast? Smudge piped up after swallowing his pill, grabbing Jade's neck and scrambling up into her lap.

Kingfisher sucked gravely on his pipe for a long moment, then whacked its butt on the ground and bellowed:

—Lie down, Smudge! Why? On account of you, that's why! Always for you! We've gone and riled up every spirit on this mountain once again, on account of you!

The cattle rumbled through the gap. (I felt like I'd just come back from a harrowing military campaign, Lu Beiping joked to Tsung.)

By this point he'd already vowed to himself never to visit the hollow again. Today had been an exception—for Smudge's sake, for the sake of that packet of quinine he'd made a special trip back to camp to pick up.

Just two visits to the hollow had been enough to confirm Lu Beiping's suspicion about the migrants' unusual arrangement. Jade, the "den mother," was a woman held in common. With the possible exception of Autumn, whom she regarded as her "little brother," she was wife to the entire band—to three men, when Smudge's father had been alive; now to two, or maybe two and a half. Autumn might not share her bed, but he probably kept no secrets from her. The three children—Smudge, Tick, and Roach—were all hers, by different fathers. Actually, this kind of family structure wasn't unheard of among frontier migrants, for whom women were a scarce commodity, and in those days rumors of such polyamorous unions abounded in the Hainan highlands. But for Lu Beiping, a well-bred city boy whose father had played percussion in a Western-style symphony orchestra, such an anomaly, confronted in the flesh, seemed freakish beyond belief. From the first moment he set foot in the hollow, when he was greeted by the bloodthirsty snarls of the dog, he'd sensed some lurking aberration, and had the distinct feeling that Fate, which had grown quite fond of toying with him lately, was preparing to toss him from one absurdity into an even greater one. As if marrying a ghost hadn't been enough, he'd now come face-to-face with a conjugal configuration that made his own seem conventional by comparison. Three naked men, a pipe-smoking woman, strange taboos and curious accents, a mother who made her son call her "Pa"—this was a real-life ghost marriage. He'd barely come to grips with the first absurdity and already this new one was bearing down on him, courting him with eager insistence, ready to draw him into its warm embrace.

No, absolutely not. He couldn't rid himself of the first absurdity, but he'd do his best not to get tangled up in this one.

So, beginning the very next morning, he started herding the cattle in the opposite direction, back toward camp. From the third finger of Mudclaw Creek he drove them down the valley to the slopes surrounding the second finger, sometimes even to the first, back toward the shouts of the workers and the clangs of the work bell. But every familiar face he saw, every how-do-you-do he exchanged, was a reminder that if he wanted to escape from the second absurdity, he'd have no choice but to return to the first. Out of every stand of rubber trees the foreman might stride; in every whiff of burnt grass from the constant bush-clearings he might detect Han's insidious presence; in every grassy draw where he might park his bottom he might find left-over scraps of red envelope paper, evidence that Mrs. Kau was busily preparing for her son's upcoming nuptials. The cattle, munching grass, debated the mysteries of ghost marriage; the rustling leaves of the rubber trees whispered news of Fong and Fook's budding Interpersonal Entanglement; with every breath, he thought of the Gaffer; with every step, he pictured Choi; at every turn, he glimpsed out of the corner of his eye a fluttering crimson banner announcing the launch of Operation Red Something or Other; and whenever he sneezed, he heard Chu's voice prattling on about the latest "intel" circulating among the re-eds . . .

God, no. He was fed up with all that stuff; it made him sick to his stomach.

No choice, then, but to remain on his own small patch of turf, hole up in his lonely mountain redoubt. His hut and cattle corral between the second and third bends of the creek were, he did his best to imagine, the sole safe haven offered him by Fate; they were a quarantine, a no-man's land, a demilitarized zone between two bristling absurdities.

For several days he drove the cattle back and forth like trapped houseflies between the narrow limits of his domain, avoiding like the plague any open hillside from which he might glimpse the white wisp of smoke hanging against the mountainside; avoiding also any south-facing slope where he might hear the tolling of the work bell down in the valley. The cattle were antsy; he was antsy; even his books offered no escape.

And then, one evening, Fate brought him to the water's edge.

No, not to some mythical riverbank where fairies and wisp-women cavorted—just to the narrow pebble beach down by the creek, a minute's walk from his hut through a stand of wild banana trees, where he cooked and bathed every evening after work. Here, where the water was deep and long grasses trailed in the eddies, where smooth stones cobbled the creek bottom and the fat fans of the banana trees formed a natural screen, he liked to beguile the early evening hours, eating and reading, humming along to the tunes on his shortwave radio while he scrubbed off the sweat of the day's labors, till darkness fell and his hut beckoned. Only on rainy days would he cook in the dim cave of his hut, and this was a much less pleasurable activity. Usually he'd build a fire on the bank and put on water to boil before taking his bath; but today he was so sweaty that he didn't bother filling the pot, just peeled off his work clothes straightaway and tossed them into the stream, followed by his illustrious rubber boots. Then he leaned down, dabbled his fingers in the shallows to test the temperature, took off his glasses and perched them on a rock, splashed some water on his ears and chest, took off his briefs, and waded into the creek till the water came up to his waist.

A daub of rosy light lingered between the hills. A light breeze blew, and the water felt less chilly than normal. He glanced down at his naked silhouette reflected among the dark shapes of the banana trees. Life in the countryside had changed his body, added some bulk to his etiolated bookworm physique. He had actual shoulder muscles now, and the lines of his buttocks and thighs formed two taut curves. It was in hopes of growing muscles like that these that he and his seventh grade pals had once flocked to the school gym to hoist barbells and swing sandbags, fired by early, whispered discussions of human biology. Now those muscles seemed to Lu Beiping to be the single, unasked-for reward of his lonely backwoods adolescence. He hadn't shaved in a month, and a bristly fisherman's beard now clung to his cheeks and chin. He'd always been hairy, probably thanks to the mixing of his father's northern genes with his mother's southern ones. Back at camp, when he washed by the well, he'd always been embarrassed to reveal his hirsute body to the public eye and suffer the inevitable jeers of "hairy occidental." But now, gazing at the luxuriant black tangles that sprouted on his lower belly and between his thighs, he felt a melancholy sense of wasted potential. The breeze blew, gentle and cool. Once again, on this still-young evening, he could hear his own blood gurgling like the creekwater.

The water was alkaline, and it left his skin feeling slippery. Still he didn't forget to wade back to the bank for his cake of Trolley Car soap—one piece every two months, doled out at the co-op—and attend to the sweatiest places on his body. In those days scented bathroom soap was unheard of, and even coarse lye soaps like Trolley Car were considered quite decadent. Reflected among the dark shapes of the banana trees, his body looked exceedingly pale, even after a month of daily beatings from the sun. Smelly feet notwithstanding, he was quite meticulous about personal hygiene. He had his dad to thank for his iconoclastic streak, but it was to his mother, a nurse, that he owed his strict sense of discipline and his healthy eating habits, which she'd drilled into him from an early age. It was these very habits that had allowed him to adapt so easily to life as a jungle-dwelling hermit; from day one, he'd run a tight personal ship. What was his mother doing now? he wondered. Silent, long-suffering, always the pillar of their household, now suffering through the absence of her son and two daughters . . . He pictured her sitting in the living room, watching dust motes fall through the slanting evening light while his father, bitter and bereft of music, tapped out a bored rhythm on a cardboard box.

The creek chimed and chattered. As he scrubbed himself, turning these things over in his mind, he felt a spot of warmth growing on his back and had the uneasy sensation that he was being watched. He turned, saw nothing but green walls of foliage and the fat trunks of the banana trees standing like a row of silent, buxom women. Damn it, stop overreacting, he thought, and waded deeper into the stream. Then he heard, very distinctly, a quiet giggle, the sound of laughter just barely contained.

Before he could figure out where the giggle had come from, an explosion of impish cackles ricocheted down the slope, followed by Smudge's barreling brown body.

—We found you! We found you! Where have you been, Stinkyfoot?

Lu Beiping turned and saw Jade walk out grinning from behind the banana trees. She caught his gaze and gave a loud chuckle.

—I've never seen a man wash with such care, Four Eyes. That's a nice, trim body you've got. We've been watching you for a while now, we didn't want to disturb you.

For a moment Lu Beiping said nothing, just stood frozen to the spot, mortified to have been caught out in the open with no clothes on. Meanwhile Smudge was thrashing toward him through the water, a small, bare-bottomed cyclone of glee.

—Water fight, water fight! Let's have a water fight, Four Eyes!

A volley of spray slapped him in the face. Lu Beiping remembered that he'd left his glasses on the bank.

—Smudge! he protested. Quit it, okay? But it was no use; Smudge kept shrieking and splashing water at him, caught up in raptures of silliness.

—Hoy, Pa! Come down here! Come water fight! Come on!

(That kid was my nemesis, or my guardian angel—I'm not sure which, Lu Beiping joked to Tsung. So, what was I supposed to do? Back at camp, when we boys went down to the well to bathe wearing nothing but our briefs, the girls would go scurrying away with squeals of embarrassment. Was I, a grown man, alone in the wilderness, going to take flight at the sight of a grinning woman? And with Smudge capering around me like some fey river spirit, insisting that I join in his horseplay, refusing to take no for an answer—could I reasonably, even in my state of undress, just turn tail and run?)

But of course, this was all an after-the-fact rationalization. In the moment there was nothing to it but this: In order to preserve his own masculine dignity, or perhaps guided by some mysterious intuition of whose workings his conscious mind was ignorant, Lu Beiping made one of the most important, and strangest, decisions of his life.

Okay, he thought. Just go with it.

Laughing, he plunged into the rosy glow of the sunset, infected by Smudge's merriment, and joined in the fun.

—Take that, Stinkyfoot! Smudge cried, beating water back at him. You've been hiding from us, haven't you? Take that!

Smudge pranced around him, lashing water, kicking up iridescent blooms of mist, seeming to unfold on all sides of him like a water lotus, his soprano cries echoing throughout the twilit valley. All at once the melancholy that had been weighing on Lu Beiping's heart lifted, and, as if heaving it all off his chest at once, he bellowed:

—Take THAT, Smudge! And THAT! And THAT!

Mustering his old schoolyard hell-raising abilities, he beat salvo upon salvo of water at Smudge, from the right, from the left, whipping hissing arcs of water at the boy, while Smudge, wriggling like a brown mud-eel, flopped in and out of the waves of spray. At last Smudge gasped through a mouthful of water:

—Pa! Help! Come down here, quick!

Before the words were out of his mouth Jade had hopped into the creek and was advancing on Lu Beiping, splashing water at him with both hands while shielding Smudge with her body. But even together they were no match for Lu Beiping; just a few one-handed salvos sent her reeling and spluttering. She beat water at him with all her might, but it seemed as if the spray were magnetically repelled by his body, pummeling back pitilessly into her eyes, nose, and mouth.

—Enough, Smudge! she cried, choking and gasping. Stop it, you'll make yourself sick again!

By now her flower-patterned blouse was soaked through. When Lu Beiping and Smudge, panting, let their arms fall slack by their sides and silence descended abruptly over the gully, Lu Beiping realized that the thin fabric of Jade's blouse had become nearly transparent, and he was now standing face-to-face with a naked woman. Their eyes met reflexively; her gaze faltered, and he looked away.

—Whew! You sure are strong, she said after a pause, her chest heaving from exertion.

—He's a demon! Smudge crowed. He's the Bull Devil!

Laughing, Lu Beiping waded back to the bank. As he climbed, dripping, out of the water, he saw that it was nearly dark, the last rays of twilight glowing on the undersides of the tree branches. A breeze blew, cold against his skin. He sucked in a sharp breath, drew Smudge, still protesting, up onto the bank, and held out a hand for Jade. She looked up at him for a moment, then put her hand in his.

He hoisted her up onto the bank. At the squeeze of her soft, big-boned fingers, a shiver ran through him.

—It's cold, she said. He felt her fingertips brush the hair on the back of his hand.

—Quick, let's get back to the hut.

He gathered up his clothes, glasses, and radio, took Smudge under his arm and, sheltering him from the wind, hurried up the slope. Jade picked up a basket she'd left on the bank and followed, trembling from the cold.

It was strange the way the air temperature fluctuated in the hills. A little while ago it had been swelteringly hot, but now that the sun had set, it was cold as snowmelt.

The fire crackled, warming them and loosening their tongues.

—Sorry it's such a mess in here, Lu Beiping said as he squatted to tend the fire after tugging on a pair of shorts and a sleeveless under-shirt. I never have any visitors, so I never clean.

Smudge, butt-naked as always, was clambering around on Lu Beiping's cot and fiddling with his numerous playthings: alarm clock, radio, flashlight, harmonica.

Jade stood in the doorway, her head tilted to one side, wringing out her hair and studying Lu Beiping with a faint look of amusement in her eyes. The two thick braids that she usually wore coiled above her ears now spilled down over her shoulders, gleaming purplish in the light, and drops of water rolled down her skin.

Lu Beiping felt her eyes following his busy movements. He poured water from the jug into the frypan, hung it over the fire to boil, then turned and tossed her a spare set of work clothes.

—Here, put these on. You'll catch cold.

—Dole clothes, Jade said, sniffing them mischievously: Do they smell too? Guess I'll wear the magistrates' cloth while my own dry.

Locals often referred to the government-supported mainlanders, both the military and the Agrecorps, as "dolers," people who "wore the magistrates' cloth." Lu Beiping chuckled.

—Okay, glad to hear you're okay with magistrates' cloth for now.

He watched her out of the corner of his eye as she went to the far end of the hut and, briskly and without any trace of self-consciousness, stripped off her wet blouse and shorts. This was the first time he'd ever seen a woman naked, and his head snapped away immediately at the sight. Yet he was conscious of how every detail had printed itself on the backs of his eyelids. Her skin had looked paler than usual in the firelight and appeared to be suffused with a faint glow. Her breasts were big and solid-looking, their twin curves etched starkly against the shadows. And that dark patch on her lower abdomen, the sight of which made his insides lurch: Really? he thought. Women have it too? Once, back in the city, when the Revolution was going full tilt, he and several of his male classmates had stolen into the boarded-up school library and raided the stacks in search of those albums of "pornographic Western artwork" that the students all had been warned against yet secretly longed to see. When the pages fell open to those startling naked figures—Eve, Venus, the Greek goddesses—the hypnotic triangles between their thighs had all been glossy and bare.

This careless discovery lent fuel to the perilous feeling that had been growing inside him. He steered his reluctant body over to the cot and forced himself to play with Smudge while a hot, prickling sensation crept up the insides of his thighs.

Jade, looking dry and refreshed, returned to the fireside, where Lu Beiping had tented three sticks for her to hang her wet clothes on. The first words out of her mouth as she reached to pick up the basket that she'd left by the door nearly made Lu Beiping faint from surprise.

—Four Eyes, she said, arranging her shorts and blouse carefully over the sticks: Why do you wear clothes? I'm like to die of heatstroke, watching you go about buttoned to the chin in this June heat. And you even tie up your wrists and ankles too. What makes you want to hide such a fine body beneath so much clothing?

—A fine body? Lu Beiping said with an uneasy laugh and a little, unconscious flex of his arms: Well, I should ask you the opposite question. Why *shouldn't* I wear clothes? I mean, with Kingfisher, Stump, and everybody up there walking around naked as the day they were born, isn't it a bit . . .

Awkward, he wanted to say, but didn't.

. . . unusual? And unhygienic too. Aren't you afraid that Smudge and the little guys are going to get bitten by mosquitos and get sick?

—Unhygienic? Jade said, pausing to consider this alien word, perhaps encountered once or twice before in a commune literacy class. Then she said disdainfully: Wearing clothes, that's what you call hygienic? You dolers get your cloth tickets every year, you eat out of a magistrate's hand. But we driftfolk, where are we going to go for our . . . hygienic? My pups grow like bush cane in July, give them a set of clothes and a month later they'll be busting the seams.

She reached over and flicked off some straw that clung to her blouse, then continued:

—That day after you ran off so quick, me and the men got to talking about your clothes. You see, Stump and Kingfisher and them are so tanned the flitleeches can't get their teeth into them. Kingfisher says, man's a child of the sun, if he hides from the sun he'll lose his brightness, his light air, and that means shadowy things like bugs and snakes'll glom on to him. Going around in high summer with every inch of your body covered will turn you into a big sack of shadow, they said, it'll draw haunts and tempt ruin. So I said, you just wait, before long I'll get him to take off his clothes and sup on some sun. They even bet me I couldn't! But what do you know, today me and Smudge saw you supping sun, just as easy as that!

She leaned back, chortling heartily, sticking out her crossed bare feet in the process. Two rows of plump ivory toes intruded at the lower edge of Lu Beiping's vision, catching like burrs in his eyes. Still chuckling, Jade pulled Smudge into her lap and said:

—Pity this rascal couldn't keep from laughing!

Supping sun. She spoke so frankly, so matter-of-factly, about what had been for him a moment of awkwardness more intense than any he'd ever experienced. Imagining his own naked body being drunk in so studiously by a pair of strange female eyes, and recalling that spot of heat growing on his back, Lu Beiping fell silent. Light air, she called it. Could it be that Kingfisher's superstitious mumbo-jumbo really had some truth to it?

Jade collected herself, then got right to the point, pulling the cloth off the basket to reveal a layer of snow-white rice cakes. Lu Beiping's eyes lit up. As a kid he'd loved to eat those soft, sweet cakes, which in Cantonese were called "virtue cakes" for some reason he'd never learned. Speaking quietly now, Jade said:

—Four Eyes, you know, bringing that medicine saved Smudge's life. I thought for sure I'd weep another Midsummer. Kingfisher insisted we give you a proper thanks, cook you a batch of virtue cakes to show you how grateful we are. But when I came down the mountain with the first batch I couldn't find hide nor hair of you. I cooked a second batch, same thing. This here's the third batch. Kingfish said, third time's the charm, we're going to thank that boy if means sitting by his hut till the sun falls out of the sky. Someone saves your child's life, shines some light on you, you'd better thank him or you're asking for trouble. Even if—

—I hid all day long in those trees, waiting for you! Smudge cut in. I saw the kine, and I savvied you wouldn't be far.

—Quick, Jade said, let's eat these while they're fresh. I made them just this afternoon. Smudge, Four Eyes saved your life, isn't there something you ought to do for him?

—No! Smudge yelped, wriggling in protest: He's a demon! He near about drowned me! I won't!

—Smudge, Jade said reproachfully, Don't butt heads with me, now. Show Four Eyes some respect, or this'll be the last time you get to jolly with him.

Before the words were out of her mouth Smudge had flopped to one knee in front of Four Eyes. Lu Beiping, to whom the traditional forms of etiquette were utterly foreign, tugged at Smudge's arm while spluttering anxiously:

—Wait, Smudge! Don't! I—

Jade watched him with a look of barely concealed hilarity, holding one hand over her mouth to keep from laughing.

—Four Eyes, she said, Why don't you bow back, like you did with me? She mimicked the slight bend at the waist with which Lu Beiping had first greeted her, then flew into a paroxysm of laughter.

Hahahahaha-HAH-hahahaha-HAH-hahahahahahaha . . . !

In the jungle, on summer nights, the brightest sound isn't the wind, the rustling of leaves, or the calls of wild animals. It's the insects. The moment darkness falls it's as if a floodgate has been pulled open, and a tide of strange noises inundates the forest: *googook . . . googook . . . chiggacheep, chiggacheep . . . GYAK! gyak GYAK! gyak GYAK! gyak . . .* There are noises like infants suckling, like the buzzing of thin silk strings, like moaning dogs trapped inside crock pots, like throbbing drumbeats, like rolling thunder . . . And yet there are no sad sounds. No; on summer nights, there isn't a single melancholy sound to be heard in the jungle. Even those sounds that ought to be terrifying are terrifying in a lurid, clownish sort of way, like the costumed devils in a southern Ghostmas parade, or a masquerade ball out of a European novel . . .

They sat by the fireside, eating rice cakes, talking. Wow, Lu Beiping said, these are great. And saved me a meal's worth of firewood too. Jade said, Come up and eat with us from now on, then. You can save yourself a meal's worth of firewood every day. No, Lu Beiping said, I can't do that. I eat out of a magistrate's hand, remember? Well, Jade said, I guess I can't compete with the magistrates. Lu Beiping laughed and said: You wouldn't say that if you'd tasted the magistrates' cooking!

They ate, laughed, shot the breeze. The evening wore on. Throughout all this Lu Beiping tried to maintain a measure of distance, a neutral attitude; but time and again he found his feelings slipping away from him, sidling off in the same direction without his permission.

Smudge finally figured out how to turn on the radio, and after a burr of static the dulcet voice of Radio Moscow's Mandarin-speaking female announcer filled the gully. If this had been heard down at camp there'd have been hell to pay. Yet, though tuning in to Enemy Broadcasts had in fact become one of Lu Beiping's favorite pastimes in the jungle, now, in the presence of Jade and Smudge, all these concerns seemed unspeakably remote, pointless, irrelevant, and he let Radio Moscow play on. A murky-sounding choral arrangement of "Su Wu the Lonely Shepherd" (*Thirteen years on the icebound plains, so far, so far a-waaay from boooome . . .*) played for a minute or two, then Smudge turned the dial again, cutting to the warbling gobbledygook of a European or American station.

Irrelevant. Yes, completely irrelevant. Jade gazed into the flames, deaf to the sounds of the radio. Smudge twiddled the knob, eliciting a fit of shrieks and squawks, then got bored and turned his attentions to the on-off switch of Lu Beiping's flashlight.

These people live in a completely different world from me, Lu Beiping thought. *He* was impossibly distant from *her*. This distance brought a simultaneous sense of novelty and security, and as they talked he became more and more convinced that the shame he felt when she saw him "supping sun," the initial sense of propriety he'd tried so hard to maintain in Jade's presence, was a silly thing, of no account. Did he try to maintain a sense of propriety while bantering with Choi and the other female workers down at camp? Just go with it—yes, just go with it. This was a good thing; there was no need to remain on his guard, to affect reserve just for the sake of reserve.

As she sat by the fire, talking with Four Eyes, Jade experienced a similar rearrangement of her emotions. Not once since Horn died had she passed an evening in such quiet, attentive conversation. When she looked up at him Lu Beiping recognized the same placid look she'd worn on their first meeting, that expression of deep, imperturbable serenity flashing from time to time from behind her eyes.

—Kambugger came up the mountain a few days ago, Jade said. When he collected his leaf money he asked after you. He was anxious to know whether you . . . *knew*—she grinned—whether you had "dirt" on him.

Lu Beiping laughed. He'd been expecting this.

—So, did you tell him? No? You didn't? Well, you know what, I don't care. What's it to me whether he earns a few bucks selling tobacco? Is that my business? Damn it, this country is getting stranger and stranger. People are so paranoid now that they'll practically burn down their own houses in order to destroy every scrap of evidence that could be used against them. Everybody takes it for granted that other people *care* enough about what they do to *want* to dig up dirt on them! It's terrifying!

Lu Beiping was rather surprised to hear this impassioned speech issue from his own mouth. He would never have expressed these sentiments in the company of the other re-eds, not even Chu. Yet even as he spoke these words he felt strangely distant from the reality they described. Jade, though, appeared quite intrigued by them, and gazed at him even more intently, as if expecting him to go on.

—So, Lu Beiping said, changing the subject: I've been meaning to ask you, why do you call him Kambugger?

—Kambugger is a mother-plugger! Smudge interjected shrilly. He does nasty things!

That kid's sharp as a tack, Lu Beiping thought. Even while he's absorbed in his own games he doesn't miss one word the grown-ups are saying.

—Really? he said, looking questioningly at Jade. So . . . he ventured, what kind of nasty things does the Gaffer do?

Jade guffawed.

—Smudge'll tell you.

—He diddles the kine! Smudge crowed. When he was kinekeeper, he diddled a mama cow! I saw him chasing her all over the mountain, and Uncle Stump saw him too!

Lu Beiping stared in disbelief. Really? a voice clamored in his brain. No way! Holy crap! Jade giggled through her fingers, then picked up the story:

—When he couldn't get inside he'd fly into a rage and beat the cows bloody. Stump caught him at it, and not just once. He said: Get a woman, Kam! What kind of man lets it out on a dumb cow? A man with grit enough to come alone into the hills ought to find himself a real woman to plow. Hell, I'll find you one! That sent Kam running. You should've seen the look on his face, Stump said!

She fell into another fit of laughter, then went on:

—That's a right nasty thing, don't you think? So on account of that, Kambugger's convinced we've got some kind of "dirt" on him, gives us free smoke-leaf, and comes up to the hollow all the time to make nice. He's got eyes for me, but he'd never dare. When I tease him he gets all wincey. Hmph! You call that a man?

—Kambugger's afeared of my Uncle Stump! Smudge boasted. He's afeared of me too!

The flames leapt and crackled. Lu Beiping said nothing, studying this strange mother-son pair in the firelight. These were a man's most personal secrets, the very darkest corners of his life, and here these two sat gabbing away cheerfully, tossing the horrible topic around as if it were a plaything. They really do live in a different country than I do, Lu Beiping thought, and for a moment he pitied the crabbed, cringing old man. The Gaffer's constant digging up and hoarding of dirt had twisted him into something not quite human. But he and the Gaffer had more in common with each other than with these two; they were countrymen, compatriots. In their world, human affection—love, lust, sex—was a liability. It was dirt.

For a short while nobody spoke. Outside the night sky was a rich, deep blue, and the moonlight thinned the forest shadows. Only on rare evenings, when the moon rose above the treetops and its pale light filtered down through the branches, did the sky turn this particular cobalt color, and the whole jungle seemed suffused with a dim luminescence. The insects fell quiet, and the water grew loud. It was getting late. They should probably get going, Lu Beiping thought.

Smudge, who had been busy fooling around with Lu Beiping's harmonica, accidentally summoned a note.

—It sings! he cried, squealing with amazement. Thrusting the harmonica into Lu Beiping's lap, he commanded him: Play it, Stinky-foot! Make it sing!

Called back from his reverie, Lu Beiping again became aware of Jade's ivory toes curled just two feet away from him in the firelight, and felt her big, far-gazing eyes weighing upon him.

—Make it sing! Please!

He glanced at Jade, picked up the harmonica and blew a few chords, then set it aside, not in the mood to play.

—Next time, Smudge.

—No! Play it! Play it now! Please!

With a weary smile Lu Beiping lifted the harmonica to his lips, played a warm-up arpeggio. But halfway through the first phrase of "Red River Valley" he stopped.

—Sorry, Smudge, I really can't play tonight. I'll play for you next time, I swear, or I'm a dirty son of a dog.

Jade, sensing the change in the atmosphere, stood up.

—Smudge, time to go.

She turned to Lu Beiping.

—My clothes ought to be dry now. Just a minute, got to go change out of my government garb.

While Lu Beiping tried to mollify the pouting Smudge, Jade turned and in the blink of an eye had swapped his "magistrate's cloth" for her shorts and flowered blouse. When she came back into the firelight her braids were once again neatly arranged at her ears. She looked clean and fresh, the way the cliffs did after rain, when the patterns and textures of the rock became suddenly vivid. Strange, he thought—this woman, for all her wild and, at times, uncouth ways, possessed a lofty, even noble kind of beauty.

—Oh, Jade said, glancing down. My slippers. I left them by the creek. She lifted one of the bare feet upon which Lu Beiping's eyes had by now lingered several times; said to Smudge, Wait here; and went quickly out the door. Lu Beiping took the flashlight and hurried after her.

It was pitch black outside. The moon had passed its zenith and been swallowed again by the mountains, and the forest was dark as a cave. Smudge seized the flashlight from Lu Beiping and, shrieking with laughter, whirled its beam around like a searchlight, momentarily illuminating pale wisps of mist gliding among the black trunks of the trees. Lu Beiping led the way down to the bank. But in the darkness they couldn't find the place where he'd bathed that evening, and Jade lost her footing on the stones, almost slipping into the water.

Lu Beiping reached out a hand and grabbed her.

For the second time that day, Jade took Lu Beiping's hand by the water's edge. When her unsuspecting hand was caught up in the boy's thick-knuckled grip, Jade's fingertips brushed the hair on the back of his hand again, and she shivered.

Lu Beiping also felt a twinge of electricity. The treetops swam. He snatched the flashlight back from Smudge and, pulling Jade behind him, combed the ground beneath the banana trees. Behind one of the trees, among the leaves of a calla-lily plant, the flashlight's probing glow at last alighted on a pair of cast-off plastic sandals—this, then, was the hiding place from which Jade and Smudge had watched him "supping sun."

The ring of light hovered briefly over her feet as she put on her sandals. As she leaned on his arm, still gripping his hand, Lu Beiping felt her fingers press twice against the inside of his palm.

His mind reeled. He'd never come so close to a female body, not even to Fong's, and never in darkness. From the first moment he laid eyes on Jade he had imagined her to be a kind of wild gypsy woman, fierce and forthright, undaunted by the wilderness and the dark. But something about this squeeze of her fingers betrayed a docile, even childlike dependence.

Even after she put on her sandals she still held his hand tightly. As he led her back up to the hut he heard the cattle, startled by their approach, lowing in the corral.

Finally she released his hand. Lu Beiping handed her the basket. She took it, started to walk away, then turned, looked at Lu Beiping, and said slowly and deliberately:

—Four Eyes, I want it to be good between us.

—Oy! Smudge yelped nearby. I want it to be good between *us* too!

Again the silhouettes of the trees blurred and swam. To hide his own alarm Lu Beiping threw the flashlight beam onto Smudge's face. Smudge tossed his head back and bellowed into the night:

—BULL DEVIL! I WANT IT TO BE GOOD BETWEEN *US!—TOOOOO!*

In the flashlight's glare Smudge made an impish face.

(Years later, Lu Beiping would tell Tsung: When he turned off the flashlight and Jade and Smudge vanished back into the dark forest, he remembered, with a wry grin, the Chairman's Immortal Words.)

Revolution is inevitable.

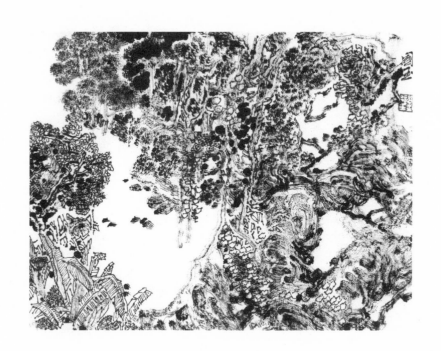

Chapter 5
The Haunted Grove

He bounded like a leopard through the jungle, driving the cattle before him in panicked disarray. A hot ferment seethed on the summer air, turning Mudkettle Mountain into a massive wine cellar. Every leaf, frond, fruit, and flower exhaled a heady, intoxicating scent; even the roar of the cicadas in the treetops seemed to ooze an alcoholic fragrance. Lu Beiping romped beneath the boiling sun, his face a mask of roasted flesh, like a pig's face grinning from a banquet table. Gone was the nameless dread of his first nights in the jungle, gone the emptiness and the angst—he'd banished them to Java, flung them to Timbuktu. Just as the light, the sounds, the quality of the air all seemed subtly changed as if in sympathy with a subtle change within him, the world outside the mountains seemed also to be undergoing a mysterious transformation. A scorched odor drifted on the humid air. Flocks of birds alighted hectically in the trees, then exploded like shrapnel back into the sky. At certain times of day the waters of Mudclaw Creek grew inexplicably turbid, and in the evening after work he saw white-bellied loaches lolling in the shallows below his hut. An occasional cross-breeze carried hints of a far-off noise, a buzzing, multilayered hubbub like overlapping radio waves, which seemed to radiate from the folds of the mountain itself. Sometimes it grew louder, sometimes faded into the distance, and always it ceased before he could make out what it was. Bleached clouds hung motionless in a crystal blue sky. At every turn the mountain slouched belligerently in his vision. The cattle, it seemed, were the first to sense the change; they were edgy and quick-tempered, with no appetite for grass, and spent the days frisking from slope to slope and getting into fights with one another so that Lu Beiping, their helpless master, spun after them like a leaf on an erratic wind. The sun beat down, seething over him, turning his body into a hunk of glowing charcoal, and soon his "magistrates' cloth" was a suit of salt-crusted armor, hardened by wave after wave of drying sweat.

And so he thought: Might as well try "supping sun."

He peeled off his thick denim work clothes, rolled them into tubes and tied them around his waist, then removed his wet undershirt and turbaned it on his head, tying it with a twist in front like an old Shaanxi farmer. He still brandished his long-handled machete, still set the valleys echoing with cries of ABRAHAM! and RASTIGNAC!, and yet, in the sweat sizzling on his skin, in the wind beating against his chest, he sensed the miraculous new relationship into which he and this mountain had entered. The nature of this bond was still a mystery to him. But when he bathed in the creek that evening, offering his bare body to the effulgent sunset, he heard—could actually, distinctly hear—the sound of the sweat droplets that sheeted off his shoulders clattering on the water's surface below. At the same time, wafting off his long-confined skin, he noticed a scent that he'd never smelled before—the odor of sunlight. Light air, just like Kingfisher said. It smelled petulant, and sort of blue-black, like gunmetal; wild and lonesome, like the songs of Yangtze river boatmen; brash and imperious, like the hoofbeats of ironshod horses carrying weapons to a war on a distant frontier. He splashed water on his chest, his soul soaring. The smell carried him back to his childhood, back to the smile on his mother's face as she hung sheets out to dry in the first rays of post-monsoon sun; back to the touch of his grandmother's wispy hair on his cheek as she told him bedtime stories about flying cats and talking flowers. He felt as if he'd knocked open the door of time. As he drove his cattle deeper into the hills, from the first finger of Mudclaw Creek to the second, the third, the fourth, he had the strange sensation that he was traveling into time itself, into the past, into his own interior, into a dreamlike, unknown dimension.

Listening to the babbling creek, he felt a swooning bliss, like the hiss of a white-hot ingot plunged into cold water. He thought: If I keep going, if I go all the way to the end, what will I find?

A surprise visit from Chu and his friends revealed to him how much he'd changed.

Just after sunset Chu arrived with a posse of re-eds, bringing, in addition to peals of impudent laughter, two pounds of raw pork from the day's ration supplement. Apparently, unbeknownst to Lu Beiping, the unit was mobilizing for a massive pan-battalion Agricultural Reclamation Operation. There'd been Orders From the Top, and Chu and his pals were preparing for deployment; the meat was a special morale-boosting measure, distributed at the pre-campaign Pledge Rally.

—Soon as I heard there'd be a ration supp, Chu explained, I thought to myself, we can't forget about our poor cowherd up in the mountains. But guess what? Turns out I wasn't the only one thinking of you. After I'd picked up your share I discovered that the foreman had already set aside a pound of top-notch jowl meat for you. Everybody's supposed to get one pound of meat, but you get two, thanks to my misunderstanding. And to your . . . ahem . . . special status!

Laughter filled the hut. Cigar drawled:

—Lu, you've missed out on a lot of scuttlebutt, squirreled away up in here in the mountains. Chu's too modest to tell you—he got promoted to platoon leader! Lieutenant first class! Hell, he could pull rank on any of us.

—Lieutenant! Lieutenant! Man the cannons! someone yelled, and everyone groaned at the predictable war-movie quote.

Watching their faces in the firelight, Lu Beiping felt strangely remote, as if he were gazing at his old friends from the far side of a primordial ice river. The guys yammered on, dishing out sundry pieces of camp gossip: how so-and-so had been busted for cheating during the Champion Tapper Competition; how this Canton re-ed had been given so-many demerits for picking a fight with that Swatow re-ed; how this year's Personnel Call for Trainees and Students allotted so-many slots to Battalion Three . . . Their voices slid back and forth across his eardrums, trying futilely to pry their way into his brain. Orders From the Top, Pledge Rally, Champion Tapper Competition . . . those words were like dim memories from an antique past, bearing whiffs of dust and mildew whenever they issued from Chu's mouth. All this talk of platoons, battalions, and campaigns seemed to Lu Beiping a kind of arcane cant, murky, mysterious, and utterly unrelated to his present life. He stood off to one side, arms crossed, eyes wandering around the hut, while his friends' voices babbled over his ears like a brook in the dry season. From time to time he gave a chuckle or a grunt, like an idle traveler loitering on the bank, tossing absentminded pebbles into indifferent eddies.

—Hey, Lu! Why are you wearing so little clothing? Chu said, calling him back to the present. Funny; only a week before, right here in this hut, he'd asked a similar question of Jade. And yet, though very little time had passed, that question now tasted like vinegar bottled in another century. Lu Beiping surveyed the gang, noting the post-work attire of his re-ed comrades: sleeveless white undershirts and blue-striped sailors' shirts, pants of army green or navy blue, "commando" sandals cut from used truck tires, straw hats sporting chipper slogans: "Wide Horizons, Bigger Dreams!" "Together, We Can Move the Mountains!" In the flickering firelight Lu Beiping's own sunburned, sinewy frame must have looked to them like the silhouette of a prehistoric animal.

Whap! Someone flattened a mosquito against his cheek, then exclaimed:

—God, look at the size of that thing! Lu, how do you keep from getting bitten to death out here with nothing but a pair of shorts on?

The others chimed in:

—Yeah! And it must be freezing at night! Aren't you afraid of getting sick?

—Take care of yourself, huh? Once the unit's gone on campaign there'll nobody here to look after you.

Finally, something to talk about, Lu Beiping thought. With a cavalier wave he said:

—I'm used to it. Once your skin's good and tanned and you've built up plenty of light energy, the bugs won't touch you.

He knew those were not his own words, but Jade's; yet they slipped so easily out of his mouth.

—Right on, tough man, a few murmured in assent, and Chu quipped: What are you, Lu, some kind of monk?

They were on completely different wavelengths, he and these young men. Listening to their laughter fade down the hillside, watching their flashlight beams play among the trees till the voluminous black silence of the jungle subsumed them, Lu Beiping felt suddenly regretful, worrying that he'd thrown a bucket of cold water on his friends' pre-campaign high. He hadn't meant to snub them. He bore them no ill will, these old mess-hall companions with whom he'd been friendly to varying degrees. But though he'd wracked his brains trying to find some shared topic of conversation, some angle by which to jump into the old-time banter, he'd come up short. Mudkettle Mountain, Lu Beiping was beginning to think, exerted a strange and powerful influence upon its inhabitants, stripping them of some part of themselves. What it took, though, and what it gave back—that he wasn't yet sure.

But the odd sense of remove that Lu Beiping felt as he stood by the fire dissipated briefly at the end of the evening, and for a moment reality jutted through the fog. As the other boys sloshed merrily across the creek, Chu grabbed Lu Beiping by the shoulder and pulled him aside, into the shadows.

—Listen, he whispered, there's something fishy about Han. Be careful, Lu. Just before we left camp, Choi cornered me and muttered a bunch of weird things about how terrible it was that you got ghost-married, how you should never have been sent up here into the hills. Whatever happened to that girl, it must have been shady.

Han. Who *was* this girl? Lu Beiping wondered. Who was this "wife" he'd been saddled with? Ever since Smudge had drawn him into the world of the driftfolk, he'd all but forgotten about his ghostly spouse. As he stood by the door of his hut, lantern in hand, watching the last glimmer of his friends' flashlights disappear into the dark valley, he realized that Han, a ghost, a phantom, was his last remaining bridge to the outside world. A specter from the netherworld had become a trail beckoning him back to the real one. Curiosity ate at him. He hung the lantern from the gate of the corral, tossed a few armfuls of hay through the fence slats, and stood gazing in the eerie, phosphorescent light at the dark forms of the cattle slumbering inside. A few lowed at him genially out of half sleep. Alyosha's face, with its jaunty white blaze, glowed with a warm, halo-like light, while Judas's gaunt countenance looked wintry and ominous. Lu Beiping felt as if he were standing at the gates of the shadow kingdom, peering in at its horned inhabitants. For a moment Han's face flashed through his mind, and he shuddered.

A yellow mist glided in, smelling faintly of mold. Lu Beiping ducked back into his hut; it was best to avoid such noxious vapors. Already he'd forgotten that the jungle could also harbor this kind of insidious influence.

The hourlaters are a special kind of rainshower unique to summers in the Hainan highlands. First, in the early afternoon, the heat builds to an almost unbearable point, so hot it could melt steel like butter, render the fat out of pig iron. In the morning, when the sun has just shown its face, the dew pitpatting down from the trees is still refreshingly cool, but once the sun has climbed a hand's breadth, the dry leaves and grass become banks of bristling blades. The slightest breeze sets the forest clashing, enveloping you in a murderous, saber-rattling gust of heat. If you're unfortunate enough to be in the forest at this hour, you'll feel as if you're being flash-fried in chili oil, a chicken at the mercy of a Sichuanese chef. Hot, spicy, numb—you'll escape none of these treatments. Even the shade is a deviously designed trap. When you're out in the sun, your sweat dries the moment it exits your flesh, like breath freezing in an arctic winter. But the instant you set foot in the shade your sweat comes gushing out in viscous torrents, plugging your pores like starchy water. Soon you're a potsticker in a bubbling vat, stifled in your own bodily fluids, unable even to spit. Then, as the sun mounts higher, the air hangs around you like a white-hot steel curtain, and you begin to fear that it will sear off the outer layer of your skin. Even the glittering, crystal-hard sky seems too flimsy to withstand the punishing force of the heat. Then, at a certain hour—always an hour later than the previous day, like clockwork, in a cycle that repeats every four or five days—the first shred of cloud to glide over the valley releases a rapturous downpour, pummeling your face and causing the parched soil around you to hiss audibly. If you're lucky, it'll be a good-sized cloud, and the deluge will cool the air for the rest of the day. But more often than not, the shower is a tad stingy, and kicks up humid billows of fog that make the hours before sunset all the more unbearable. Oh, the hourlaters: boon and bane of Hainan summers, arouser and dasher of hopes, malicious temptress: how many young cowherds have your punctual dousings caused to whoop with joy, then wail with despair?

One afternoon, after the rain, Lu Beiping decided to drive his animals back to the mature rubber stands near the second bend of the creek. Lately, the heat had made the animals almost impossible to manage. They would slump down in the grass when Lu Beiping gave the order to march, then run off helter-skelter into the trees when he tried to rally them to return to the corral for the night. There wasn't a single patch of grass in the whole sweltering jungle where the cattle would settle down and graze cooperatively. Usually he didn't take them into the old groves, where the grass was too thin to sustain the herd for long; but the tall trees gave plenty of shade, and the wide orchard lanes promised cool cross-breezes. Plus, he was concerned about Maria, the pregnant heifer, who had been staggering around drunkenly and foaming at the mouth as she hauled her ponderous belly through the pitiless heat. On several occasions she'd plunked herself down by the creek and refused to budge. He worried that she'd die from heatstroke, and hoped to find a shady spot where she could rest, and maybe give birth, if the moment came. Also, he knew that the camp was almost vacant—everybody was off clearing forestland for the big Total Mobilization Agrec-Op—and it wouldn't be hard to avoid the few workers who remained. Even the slanderous rumors circulating about the "shadow-wed boy" didn't deter him, though the riddle of Han's death still gnawed at his heart. It would be difficult, of course, to revisit those leafy orchard lanes without being reminded of his old life horsing around with Fong and Chu. But in this hellish month, post-rain cool was hard to come by, and if taking advantage of it meant crossing paths with members of the prying masses—well, that was a risk he'd have to take.

Sure enough, as soon as the animals set foot in the grove they began lowing happily and hunkered down in small clusters around the recently tapped rubber trees, injecting a playful atmosphere into the solemn green geometries of the orchard. Lu Beiping fished out one of his long-neglected books—*Le Père Goriot*, in the Fu Lei translation—and started to read, but before long the pages were damp with his own sweat. He remembered his harmonica, also long neglected, and dug it out of the bottom of his bag. But after a few warm-up chords his music practice was cut short by a sudden commotion among the cattle, prompted by a faint noise somewhere off in the trees.

He cocked his head, listening, waiting for the sound to repeat itself, but there was nothing to hear amid the cicadas' usual racket. The cattle, though, were stirring excitedly, bumping and jostling against one another as they crowded off in the direction from which the noise had come. Soon, however, they lost interest, and hanging their heads they moseyed listlessly back into the shade. Whatever had caught their interest had moved on, apparently.

It must be some wild animal, Lu Beiping thought. Shortly afterward, a familiar, unpleasant odor began seeping through the air, a distinctly human smell that one noticed frequently in the groves, which Lu Beiping had happily forgotten about during his long sojourn in the wilderness. Lu Beiping guessed that it was a mixture of stale sweat, the sour tang of congealed rubbermilk, and the odor of the manure used to fertilize the groves. Wherever the scent was strong one saw an abundance of flies and roaches, and almost never wild animals. Sure enough, in a matter of minutes a big, bottle-green fly appeared—this was a species Lu Beiping hadn't seen much of in the jungle—and began batting insistently at Lu Beiping's nose, defying his attempts to wave it away and making him lose his place repeatedly. Sighing, Lu Beiping put down the book. Then he noticed that the cattle were stirring again, crowding toward the same spot at the edge of the grove, toward the source of whatever sound (movement? smell?) had caught their attention earlier.

Feeling suspicious, Lu Beiping stood up and strode over to Alyosha. Then he noticed, through the windbreak of lace pines that bordered the grove, a wild, weedy clearing lying in thick shade, looking strangely out of place amid the uniform tracts of rubber forest.

Peering through a net of vines, Lu Beiping made out of a swath of star groundsel dotted with yellow cottonball-like flowers, surrounded by tall stands of henfeather and fishreek, two of the cattle's favorite varieties of grass. What a pleasant surprise, Lu Beiping thought. In the early August heat, a lush, shady grazing spot like this was a godsend. No wonder the animals were so excited.

—Alyosha! Andrei! Natasha! Lu Beiping cried, summoning the animals. Look at all that tasty groundsel! Look, henfeather and fishreek! Go on, eat it!

A strange thing happened. The animals trooped through the windbreak and then halted at the edge of the clearing, where they stood stock still, gazing hesitantly out at the verdant jungle grass.

—What's wrong? Go on!

Lu Beiping whacked Alyosha's spotted rump with the thin branch he used as a switch. But Alyosha, to his surprise, began lowing shrilly, and soon the others joined in, their anxious cries echoing sharply in the silence of the forest.

(To this day, Lu Beiping told Tsung, the cattle's behavior remains a mystery to me. What did they see? What did they sense? No amount of prodding or yelling could convince them to go into that clearing.

Normally, at the sight of such delectable grass they'd have charged in and fought over it like mad. But this time they'd clearly made up their minds. They wouldn't touch it.)

Lu Beiping strode through the pines and out into the waist-high grass, where he stood, pondering.

This was a wild, overgrown field bordered on three sides by mature rubber forest and on the fourth by the lace pine wind-break. At the far end of the clearing, the pool formed by the creek's second bend glinted through the trees. Surrounded as it was by cultivated forestland, the clearing appeared strikingly man-made. It must have been planted with rubber trees once, then allowed to go fallow. Recalling that the plantation's groves were numbered, Lu Beiping counted them off as best he could remember: Sector 8, Sector 9, Sector 10 . . . the stand on the far side of the creek was Sector 12, so this must be Sector 11. Now, protruding here and there from the tall grass, Lu Beiping noticed the stumps of dead rubber trees. Had this sector been destroyed by a typhoon? Or burnt down in a forest fire? Puzzling over this, he stood gazing up at the blue rectangle of sky visible through the treetops, through which a single scarlet snakecloud had begun slowly to unwind.

The shrill moans of the cattle echoing in the trees made this place seem all the more desolate. Lu Beiping thought of the other weedy clearing, the one in which he had encountered Smudge, and an eerie premonition slithered up into his chest, filling him with dread.

The cattle began jostling and fussing again, and Lu Beiping stiffened in alarm. This time, he heard the noise:

Leeleelooloowah! . . . Leeleelooloowaaaaaaaaaah! . . .

Someone, hidden among the trees on the meadow's far side, directly beneath that crimson twist of snakecloud, was making weird, low-pitched, yodeling cries, quiet but piercing, at times lazy sounding, at other times sharp and urgent. The cattle pricked up their ears again. Then, before Lu Beiping knew what was happening, Alyosha had gone trotting off along the edge of the clearing in the direction of the cries, lowing merrily and drawing the whole herd after him.

—Hey! Lu Beiping yelled indignantly. Alyosha! Stop it! Get back here! What are you doing? Peter! . . . Judas! . . . *Stop it!*

(Years later, describing this scene to Tsung, Lu Beiping said: It never crossed my mind that cattle, like humans, could experience a crisis of loyalty. I didn't know it at the time, but those animals were being torn between two opposing allegiances.)

Suddenly Alyosha stopped, then turned and looked at Lu Beiping with a look of nervousness and reluctance on his mottled brown face. Lu Beiping could hear him snorting in agitation. Noticing their leader's hesitation, the rest of the herd halted mid-rush and stood, their heads swishing like a field of windmills, awaiting the signal to continue.

Leeleelooloowah! . . . Leeleelooloowaaaaaaaaaah! . . .

The ululating cry, which sounded to Lu Beiping's ears like a swine call, echoed again in the forest, this time louder, more brazen. Alyosha's snorts crescendoed to a shrill bugling:

Ngaugh—AUUGH! Ngaugh—AUUGH!

With a decisive toss of the head, Alyosha cast off his new master, and the whole herd rumbled away from Lu Beiping like an army of battle wagons.

Lu Beiping shuddered. Far off, at the edge of the clearing, he saw a thin, dark figure emerge from the trees. Lu Beiping heard the man laugh, then saw him reach out an arm and beckon with one finger.

—Friend Lu! he called. Come here!

By now the man was surrounded by a sea of bobbing bovine heads, which made his silhouette seem even more sinister. Lu Beiping was reminded of the night before, when he'd peered into the corral by the light of the lantern and fancied he saw, as if through the gates of the underworld, an army of horned demons.

The man was none other than the cattle's former master, Gaffer Kam—Kambugger.

Steeling himself, Lu Beiping strode toward the old man, who stood motionless amid the tall grass.

—Come, the Gaffer repeated mysteriously. Come here, friend Lu.

The cattle crowded round the old man, cocking their heads and lowing affectionately. Glancing back, Lu Beiping noticed with a pang of sorrow that of the entire herd, only Maria hadn't betrayed him. Huge-bellied, she lingered a good distance behind him, remaining in the shade of the pine trees.

—Gaffer! Was that you taunting the cattle with that weird call?

—Wasn't me, the Gaffer said, shaking his head, an inscrutable look on his dark, leathery face. Must've been a haunt, friend. A ghost brought you here. The spirits are doing your business.

—Quit playing around, Gaffer. Tell me, did you follow me here? Did you follow me and the cattle?

—Heh. Mercy me, friend Lu.

The Gaffer pointed into the grass.

—Take a look, right here . . . Hey! Stripey!—the Gaffer barked at Alyosha, calling him by his old name—settle down! You too, Shitbelly!

Instantly the cattle grew docile. Lu Beiping's eyes followed the man's outstretched arm, but the grass lay in deep shadow, and he saw nothing but the gold globes of the groundsel flowers glittering in the low sunlight.

—Stop screwing with me, said Lu Beiping, raising his voice. You can't scare me with that crap.

The Gaffer exploded into a fit of high-pitched laughter.

—Can't *scare* you, eh? Can't *scare* you? If it wasn't a haunt that brought you here, how'd you manage to find this place? Do you know where we are? Only a ghost would dare bring you here!

The Gaffer ogled him meaningfully.

—This is Han's grave! Your ghost wife brought you here, friend Lu, sure as shingles.

He padded gingerly through the flowers, reached down to pull aside a clump of leaves, then yelped, sprang back, lost his balance, and plopped down in the grass.

—Heavens above! he cried, his face white as a sheet. This place is witched! It's gone—where is it? Where's her grave marker?

In the slanting sunlight, beneath the yellow, glinting flowers, Lu Beiping made out a small weed-covered mound; then, in front of it, a shallow notch in the soil. Off in the trees the creek whispered hoarsely.

Lu Beiping's scalp prickled. Could it be true? Was this really Han's grave? As he wondered this, the Gaffer grabbed his arm and yanked him back away from the mound, then hissed:

—Go on, boy. Get out of here.

Feeling the Gaffer's gaunt fingers dig into his forearm, Lu Beiping remembered the talon-like grip of Mrs. Kau, and with a shudder of revulsion he wrenched free of the old man, turned, and gave him an angry shove.

—Damn it, Kambugger! What are you trying to do?

—Kambugger? The man's eyebrows jumped once in surprise, then he narrowed his eyes and gave Lu Beiping a conspiratorial smile. Heh! Sounds like you've been jollying around with Jade's folk.

—Get the *hell* away from me, you creep!

Knowing that the Gaffer was just an insecure bully and that such people were easily cowed, Lu Beiping advanced on him, waving a fist.

—Listen, Gaffer, if you don't stop talking shit I'm going to break your nose.

—Mercy me! the Gaffer cried. Mercy, mercy me! Come back here, I've got something else to tell you. This place is witched, son. Coming here has crossed the both of us.

Reluctantly, Lu Beiping followed him into the stand of lace pines and listened skeptically while the Gaffer confided in a hushed, urgent voice:

—You think I'm just giving you a hard time? You think I'm feeding you horseshit? Lu, you saw what the animals did. The critters wouldn't dare set foot in this place if every devil in Hell were driving them. Isn't that right?

Lu Beiping gazed silently at his turncoat cattle. It was true—even now, while flirting with their old master, the cattle had never planted their hooves directly in the grass of the waste clearing, but skirted it assiduously, remaining always in the trees. It was as if this place truly were marked off by some kind of invisible boundary.

—Look, the Gaffer went on, you see how of all these groves, just this place is grown over with fishreek grass? Fishreek grows just in one place, you know where that is? Where there's been a burning. This grove got burned down, no two ways about it. You can even see the stumps. Everyone knows cattle like fishreek, but here they don't dare take a nip of it. You see that, right?

—Yes, Lu Beiping replied nonchalantly, you're right, they wouldn't eat it. So what?

—Mercy me, boy! The Gaffer blinked theatrically. You have to understand! When I saw there was a clearing near Sector 10, I drove the beasts here, just like you did. It gave me the chills, seeing them not eat that grass. Then I saw it was Han's grave! Old folks say, cattle like to eat grass that grows on graves. Grave grass grows thick. But they won't go near graves where the dead don't rest easy. Take it from an old hand, friend—cattle won't graze on balegrass!

Balegrass. It was true, he had seen the cattle behave this way before: Once or twice, after the herd had cropped down an entire hillside, he'd noticed a single, conspicuous clump of lush green grass that they had left mysteriously untouched. Could it be, Lu Beiping wondered uneasily, that some baleful presence inhabited those stands of grass?

—Gaffer, Lu Beiping said, lowering his voice: Seriously, how did you know I'd bring the cattle here today?

—I didn't know, *she* knew! *She* brought you here, your ghost wife! Heh!—once more a note of frenzy entered the Gaffer's voice—Sky's my witness, friend Lu, sure as there are gods above and demons below! The foreman put me on grove maintenance duty after the hourlater, and I thought I'd come over to check on Choi's grove. Heh! . . . Choi's gone off who knows where, but I'll be damned if I didn't just cross paths with a haunt!

—What? Where's Choi's grove?

—Right here, son, this is it! The Gaffer grinned salaciously as he pointed at Sector 12. It's getting dark, too bad Choi's not around!

Lu Beiping's heart sank a foot deeper. First a haunted clearing, a mysterious forest fire, and an unmarked grave . . . and now, Choi. *Han.* Han was everywhere. Clearly the same dark thread wove all these things together. *Han—she was crossed, alright.* Choi's whispered words echoed once more in Lu Beiping's skull.

Dusk was approaching. Lu Beiping listened to the sound of Mudclaw Creek rushing over the rocks, and suddenly the forest seemed very quiet. It was time to drive the cattle home. They were lowing impatiently, and when Lu Beiping turned to round them up the Gaffer had vanished like a wraith into the trees. For the first time in weeks, he heard the clanging of the afternoon work bell.

Gwong . . . Gwong . . . Gwong . . . Gwong . . . Gwong . . .

As Lu Beiping drove the herd back toward his hut, he began to fret about his meat. Those two pounds of pork jowl and assorted scraps, permeating the valley with their alluring scent, were a summons to every wild animal on Mudkettle Mountain. Last night he'd been startled awake by a boar attempting to butt its way through the hut's flimsy wicker wall, and he'd managed to scare it off with his flashlight, meanwhile cursing himself for having foregone the flintlock rifle. If he'd had a gun, he might have bagged himself a prize whose gamy aroma would have had every Loi hunter in a ten-mile radius sniffing the air. No sooner had he fallen back to sleep than he was jolted awake again by a soft scuffling sound directly above him, like someone creeping stealthily across the roof. Ducking through the mosquito net he beheld a small, swarthy head hanging upside-down in the window, which disappeared immediately at the sound of him cursing in surprise, followed by a crackle of fleeing footsteps through the thatch. Running outside, he trained his flashlight on the roof and saw a gaggle of macaques hanging from the tree overhead, shrieking

and making fists at him. As they scampered off into the canopy, he
smelled the aroma of pork wafting from inside the hut and knew that
those two pounds of meat brining in the stew pot were to blame. He'd
been told that the monkeys of Mudkettle Mountain had long ago fled
before the muskets of the Loi, retreating along the Mo-Sius toward
Tomb Creek. Had his redolent treasure lured the Monkey King's min-
ions all the way from their grotto in the Mountain of Fruit and Flowers? (This was the first time during his stay on Mudkettle Mountain
that he'd crossed paths with his primate cousins.) Then, the following
morning, when he went out to wash his face, he noticed the cursive
signatures of snakes scribbled in the lime-filled drainage ditch and
knew that a delegation from the serpent kingdom had paid him a
visit as well. Next to the ditch lay a segment of dark, mottled skin,
as thick around as his wrist, which had once belonged to a black lyre
snake. Snakes were attracted to strong scents, he knew; he'd succeeded
in catching quite a few of them coiled in clumps of aromatic jungle
grass and in wild pineapple thickets. Clearly his moat had stymied the
snakes' advance, but one hopeful lyre snake, enchanted by the aroma,
had stood vigil there all night before shedding its skin and slithering
away.

When he let out his cattle that morning, the question of how to
dispose of his reeking prize was already weighing heavily on his mind.
He wasn't sure why he'd let it brine so long instead of cooking it and
eating it immediately. Probably, in the back of his mind, he'd been
hoping to share it with Jade and Smudge. But why hadn't he taken it
up to the hollow first thing, then? What was he waiting for? In such
hot weather the meat wouldn't keep long, even cured in salt water. He
knew that he couldn't leave it in the hut, though; if he did, he'd return
to find his home overrun by greedy-nosed monkeys and wild pigs. For
a long time he lingered by the creek, planning at first to construct a
tripod of branches in the shallows and perch the pot on top, where it
would be safe from questing animals. But then he reconsidered, realizing that this arrangement would leave the meat vulnerable to vultures
paradropping out of the sky. In the end he submerged the stew pot in

a bucket of water, secured the lid with a rock, and buried the whole thing in the ashes of the fire. Water and ash would doubly insulate the scent; this improvised solution, he figured, ought to be pretty much foolproof.

But as he hiked back up the trail toward his hut, shepherding a tottering Maria past the knobbly barked gorgontree, he smelled, to his amazement—the smell of cooking meat! The unbelievable aroma cut sharply through the familiar smells of the evening jungle, causing both him and the cattle to quicken their pace, and the herd's hoof-beats filled the valley with urgent thunder.

(What a wonderful, intoxicating smell! Lu Beiping gushed to Tsung, as if, after all these years, the thought of it still made him tipsy. Never before had I smelled anything so rich, so dizzying, so magical!) Perhaps because the meat was on the point of turning, its savor heightened by a hint of gaminess, the moment the pot was heated over flames it breathed forth wonders. The aroma glittered on the evening air like shards of agate embedded in a vein of crystal; it was a powerful, startlingly pungent scent, but at the same time bright and delicate.

The pall that had hung over Lu Beiping's heart all afternoon—Han's pervasive presence, the riddle of her unmarked grave—evaporated in an instant. The trail before him quivered like a string plucked softly by the aroma's invisible fingers. All at once, a flash of understanding went off in Lu Beiping's brain.

He herded the cattle, who were now lowing excitedly, into the corral and shut the gate. Glancing over the roof of his hut in the direction of the creek, he saw a milk-white ribbon of smoke curling skyward, and he smiled knowingly. Of course. *That* was where the smell was coming from.

He bounded down the slope, his feet beating out a drum line beneath the cattle's baritone chorus. The first thing he saw when he emerged on the bank was a clean, brown silhouette facing away from him, its back covered with tangled hair, full of expectancy, ripe with premeditation. Hearing his footsteps, Jade jumped down into the water.

Clearly she'd been here for a while now, cooking and bathing, waiting for him. A wet knot of hair obscured half her face. Seen from behind, her skin had looked dark, but now that she stood in the creek her body, catching the light off the water's surface, looked pale, almost pearly.

On the stove that Lu Beiping had built on the bank out of piled stones, his stew pot was bubbling away merrily.

Lu Beiping stopped running, took a deep breath. Then, as if the meat's aroma were a conducting medium, all his courage and desire flashed forth at once.

(The first time it was her on the bank, me naked in the water, Lu Beiping told Tsung. Now, our roles were reversed: her in the water, me on the bank. So, if you were me, what would you have done?

What would I have done? Tsung said. Well, like you said before: Just go with it.

Yes. Just go with it. Just go with it.)

For a moment neither he nor Jade spoke.

—Where's Smudge? Lu Beiping asked finally.

(At the mention of Smudge, Lu Beiping told Tsung, I felt immediately at ease. I told you, that boy was my guardian spirit.)

—Where's Smudge? Jade repeated, pushing the hair out of her face and examining him with a playful light in her eyes: Is that all that's on your mind right now?

Rubbing his hands together and glancing around the gully, Lu Beiping said:

—Uh, how long have you been here cooking my meat? It smells great.

Jade burst out laughing, her brown breasts and shoulders shaking as she stood doubled over in the shallows.

—Ha! How long have I been cooking your meat? Ha!

Her whoops of laughter shattered the silence of the valley, and echoes rang faintly in the cliffs. Lu Beiping started laughing too. Their laughter became a shield, a screen, insulating them from their emotions, like a draught of strong liquor.

When Jade had finally collected herself, she looked frankly at Lu Beiping and said in a teasing voice:

—If you're the Bull Devil, like Smudge says, why don't you come in the water and prove it?

Lu Beiping remained on the shore, chuckling awkwardly.

—Come on, are you getting in, or not?

—Damn it! Lu Beiping said, a rush of hot air shooting to his skull as he kicked off his rubber boots: If I'm the Bull Devil, you're a witch! A wispwoman!

—A witch? Jade said, flicking water at him. How about a river spirit? Come on, get in the water.

—Listen, if I'm the Bull Devil, you must be a wispwoman! he said vehemently, his eyes meeting, then shrinking from her gaze as he unwound the undershirt from his head and tossed it aside: You're the shape-changing leopard woman from the Cave of Spiders! He unzipped his shorts and let them drop to the ground.

Baring his fresh, brown, sun-minted body to Jade, he strode into the water. The afternoon sun spangled the water's surface, shining so brightly it hurt his eyes. Every hair on his body stood quivering at attention, and the blood pounded in his brain.

Jade slapped playful salvos of water at him as if trying to provoke another water fight. He waded toward her. Then, amid a sea of silver light, their bodies snapped tight to one another. First Jade sprang forward, pulling him into her arms; then Lu Beiping's arms slipped around her waist and clamped her tight, squeezing so hard that she gasped for air.

—Four Eyes, she murmured in his ear, her flesh seeming to flow like liquid through his hands: Four Eyes, I've been waiting, I've been waiting for you.

Saying nothing, he closed his eyes and buried his face in her hair, in her neck, in the valley beneath her breasts, nuzzling voraciously and at random. On the bank the meat bubbled and spat; its warm, amber-and-agate fragrance rose to fill the gray vault of the valley, like lambent gold light over a temple altar.

The truth was, this was the first time Lu Beiping had ever kissed a woman, and he didn't really know now. Only after Jade had grabbed his busy head and pressed her lips directly against his did a sensation of thirst wake in his own lips, and instinct took over. The smooth stones beneath his feet and the vine-obscured sky above his head began to turn in a slow gyre.

Cold water beat against their bare stomachs and backs. Several times they slipped and almost fell into the water, but each time the creek's surface seemed to turn solid beneath them, repelling them and driving them tighter together. Jade was the first to come back to her senses, and lifting her face to his, she tugged him slowly through the water toward the shore. Her white flowered blouse and navy blue shorts lay in the tall grass, and a few broad banana leaves were spread nearby. (Only much later would Lu Beiping realize how thoroughly Jade had prepared for this adventure.) Dazed, oblivious, he staggered after her into the grass, where they toppled together in a heap. Then, jolted back to reality by the change of scene or by the chilly touch of the evening air, Lu Beiping cried out, shoved Jade away, and sat up in the grass.

—Gah! he stammered, gazing at Jade's sprawled, naked limbs as if out of a dream: What the hell am I doing? I've gone crazy!

—Me too! Jade said, sitting up eagerly and pushing the hair out of her face. Oh, Four Eyes . . . darling . . . child . . .

The first few words were murmured in a dazed tone, as if she weren't fully conscious of speaking them; but the last word was pointed, deliberate, teasing. She pounced on Lu Beiping, grabbed him by the shoulders and, shaking him viciously, fixed his fogged eyes with two bright, adamant beams of light:

—Four Eyes, I *know* what I'm doing. I'm going crazy.

Lu Beiping sat there, blinded by her eyes, pinioned in her grip. This wasn't the woman who'd lured him gently into the water. From beneath that tangled nest of hair a stranger's face gazed back at him, sunburned, ruddy, glowing with an intense light that gripped his eyes like a powerful suction cup. Those red lips, wild hair, and trembling breasts didn't belong to Jade, but to a siren, a rusalka, a shapechanging wispwoman who padded through the jungle in the form of a leopard or a tiger. And the gaze that held him was that of a wild creature: strong, placid, proud, even noble. This nobility seemed a thing borne of the wilderness itself, a wild, capricious, sovereign power. *Child . . .* As his heretical, long-dormant desires flared to life again at her teasing invitation; as his willpower melted away completely beneath the renewed heat of his interior furnace; he heard, calling from somewhere deep inside him, or out of some other, distant dimension, a voice: *I too know exactly what I'm doing. I'm going crazy.*

All these perceptions took no more than an instant to play out in Lu Beiping's mind. But in the months and years that followed he would come to realize that in this brief moment of clarity, he'd finally admitted, in a deep corner of his being, that Revolution was, in fact, inevitable. Even on the morning when he first laid eyes on Jade, sitting in the sunlit meadow above the babbling creek, his nerves had begun beating a martial rhythm in anticipation of today's fight. The ribbon had been cut, and the steamship was already sliding down the slipway toward its predestined channel.

So, in the moments that followed, the tide of battle turned dramatically on the banks of Mudclaw Creek. Goaded to anger by Jade's fingers digging into his shoulders, Lu Beiping let out a roar, like a bull enraged by the crimson cloth, and plunged toward his adversary while on all sides imaginary onlookers raised a deafening cry. (At the same time, his adversary seemed to be standing in a different dimension, waiting calmly to watch the fray.) With his hands, which he'd all but forgotten about, he attacked the breasts that swung insolently before his eyes. With his lips, which she'd taught him to use just a moment before, he rained a hail of kisses on her face, neck, and nipples. She groaned as if in pain, and as she heaved beneath Lu Beiping, the curves of her body grew supple as clay. Releasing her, he struck out downward, over the ridges of her ribs, along the bend of her hip, detouring briefly to the little valley of her navel; down, down he went, till he stood at the edge of a dark, tangled copse, and there, trembling, he stopped.

Never before had he visited this alien turf. He'd gazed at it, furtively, on prints of European oil paintings in the green years of his early adolescence; he'd yearned after it vaguely on countless parched, damp nights. Now, at last, it stood before him beckoning, a dim, shadowy threshold over which danced glimmers of a divine, riddle-like light.

He shrank back, momentarily cowed, afraid to step over that mysterious threshold. Then Jade rose and rolled over him, enveloping him like a bank of clouds.

(Women are such healthy, natural creatures, Lu Beiping would say to Tsung years afterward. Much later, after Jade and I had been together many more times, I asked her why she wanted to do it, why she wanted . . . things to be "good between us." Laughing, she said: You men are always so keen to find reasons for things. You all run around hewing and hammering, fighting and struggling, always *so that* this, *so that* that. So tell me, why were you put on earth? Can you explain to me the reason for that? After she'd said her piece she sat there quietly, still laughing to herself.)

But that's a digression. At the moment Lu Beiping lay enveloped in a thick cloudbank, at the foot of a cliff ablaze with wildflowers. Needing no reasons, brooking no arguments, Jade spread him out beneath her like a tract of dark, uncultivated wilderness. She plucked off his glasses and tossed them in the grass, and Lu Beiping, in a daze, closed his eyes. Then her fingers bit into him like flying shovels, turning the raw soil of his flesh. She cupped his face in her hands, fondling him, dandling him, calling up dim memories of his first years on earth; meanwhile spades and pickaxes broke the rocky soil of his chest, and lusty songs rang out over sun-blazed fields. She tilled his belly, rich with tribulation and toil; she tilled the muscles of his legs, which shrank and swelled; acre by acre, she tilled the virgin soil of his body, in which years of accumulated sunlight were pent; and inch by inch his growing, languishing desires, his hungers, long hidden but longing to be revealed, unfurled beneath the smiling gaze of the sun, and were illuminated.

In one downward sweep, her hands enacted a Genesis: from seed to tree, embryo to adult, primeval glacier to swaying grassland. Every pore in his skin opened wide to drink in the sweetness imparted by her touch, and the evening air prickled with the ferment of rain. The tide rumbled in the distance. Storm clouds darkened the horizon. As her shovel tugged at his burgeoning roots, his brain, soft as ripe fruit, flashed in alarm. No! he cried. Jade! But it was too late; the tempest broke, and a flash flood bore him to the edge of a breathless precipice. For a moment he stood poised over a shimmering abyss; then he leapt.

Down he plunged, through agate-banded, crystal-bright fathoms, through the impudently wafting aroma of meat.

Like a fig which, having grown ripe in the jungle's fermented evening air, at last breaks free from its milk-weeping branch and drops softly to the ground, Lu Beiping fell.

—Darling, Jade called out to him, drawing him into her arms. Darling, darling . . . oh, my darling . . .

Even at that dizzy instant Jade hadn't forgotten about the stew pot bubbling over the fire.

She eased Lu Beiping, who lay with eyes closed as if asleep, out of her lap and tiptoed over to the firepit. After extracting the thicker logs she buried the flames in ash so that the finished stew would keep warm. When she glanced back at Lu Beiping, still curled on the mat of banana leaves, he was staring at her with a wide-eyed expression of grief.

—Oh, Four Eyes . . . she laughed. You're still a child.

—Fuck you! he yelled. Fucking whore! Fucking cunt!

As these ugly words escaped his lips Lu Beiping remembered the morning after the ghost wedding, standing at the edge of the well and screaming obscenities into the quiet dawn. These words, too, were ones he'd never spoken before.

Jade rushed over and embraced him. Lu Beiping tried to push her away, but after a brief struggle she had plugged his mouth with her mouth, pinned his hands with her hands. Those strong, calloused hands, which had beaten clothes for Kingfisher, picked medicine for Smudge, and sharpened saws for Autumn, now clamped tight over the hands that Lu Beiping had used to turn the pages of Balzac and Turgenev. She drew his hands to her chest, fondling them lovingly; then she drew his arms around her waist. Before Lu Beiping's eyes the curves of her body once again blurred into a haze of warm rain.

On her skin he smelled the odor of sunlight. *Light air.* It was mixed with a very different scent, heady and female, but he recognized it immediately as the odor wafting off of his own skin when he bathed in the creek: a wild, petulant smell, like gunmetal, like hoofbeats, like the calls of Yangtze river boatmen. He started to grow short of breath.

—Fuck you! he gasped.

—Yes! she said. Do that!

—I said, *fuck* you, Jade!

—Four Eyes, I'm yours!

This time his desire was prolonged and unflagging. He learned quickly how to use his lips, tongue, and hands as weapons, how to exploit the tactical weaknesses of her eyes, ears, and neck. Where once he'd trespassed timidly, he now stormed in brashly; where once she'd torn him apart and knit him back together, he now did the tearing.

It was getting dark. The sun had sunk behind the hills, but a single slice of blood-orange light hung on one wall of the gully. A crescent moon had climbed prematurely into the sky, as if impatient for the sun's descent. They rolled back and forth between the grass and the water, locked in each other's grips like a pair of tussling leopards, their cries seeming to heighten the quiet of the evening and the brightness of the moon. Over the walls of the gully, as if from stadium bleachers, peered plump banana trees and wizened bamboo, motley clots of ferns and slender betelnut palms, vicarious participants in the spotlit fray. Even the aloof, skyward-climbing vines and the decadent, longhaired epiphytes glanced sidelong at the vehement struggle taking place on the floor of the valley below.

(Never again, Lu Beiping said to Tsung, have I experienced such giddy heights of emotion as I did on that night.)

Months later, remembering that night, Lu Beiping would recall how, as they rolled through the grass, Jade had whispered again and again in his ear: *Four Eyes, you're him, you are my Horn* . . .

This time he actually entered her. How it happened was a mystery: Had she guided him in? Or had it slipped in by accident? Had his body known what to do without him telling it and fulfilled the promise of its own accord?

And so he pressed onward into that hidden valley, into the dim otherworld into which he'd been called. His soul, trembling, began to spin, bearing him back once more to his childhood, back into the earthquake-clamor of his father's percussion practice, where an eight-year-old Lu Beiping was folding paper wishes. Once, he had made a habit of writing all the wishes that he didn't dare speak aloud on small scraps of paper and depositing them in his piggy bank, a little bobble-headed mandarin made of Foshan porcelain. He didn't have much money to put in the bank, since his parents didn't have much to give, so he filled it with wishes instead. His mother had told him that when he grew up could smash the piggy bank and use the change he'd saved up to fulfill wishes that money couldn't buy. Following his own childish logic, he concluded that if wishes were the more important thing, he ought to stockpile wishes instead. So he wished to be the inventor of the kite-powered dynamo, the twentieth century's most groundbreaking invention; he wished for the plastic tommy gun that sparked and sputtered in the hands of the boy who lived next door; he wished for a pipe like the one that jutted so gallantly from his father's lips; and he wished to be noticed by a certain girl in the other third grade class, who, when all the other girls were wearing pigtails, wore her own hair in a ponytail tied with a burgundy-colored ribbon. A little rosy-cheeked girl to whom he'd never spoken a word, though he'd secretly admired the dimples on the backs of her hands between her thumb and forefinger . . .

A spasm of light cut short these reminiscences. Through a storm of fluttering paper scraps he watched another young woman approaching. What was written on those scraps of paper? Secret wishes, or inscrutable curses? Could it be that unbeknownst to him, the course of his entire life had been governed by secret messages written on bits of folded paper? Who was that girl—was she the one who'd giggled at him the day he arrived on Mudkettle Mountain, as he searched frantically for a place to pee? With a delicate chin, a quiet voice, soft footsteps . . . and an unmarked grave? Was she his ghostly soulmate, paying him another visit from the world of shadow?

As his soul, blissful, fearful, drunk on sweetness and mystery, spiraled skyward out of the valley, propelled by that spinning force— then plunged, abruptly, back to earth—he heard, quite distinctly, the sound of porcelain shattering. It was the crash his porcelain magistrate had made when he smashed it out of spite, after his mother, as a joke, had peeked at one of his wishes. For a second the crisp report of shattering porcelain, along with his own angry shrieks and his mother's cry of surprise, echoed in the dusky valley.

A blizzard of snow-white wishes fluttered earthward.

(Of course, all of this is fanciful embroidery on the part of Tsung, the real author of this story. The only thing that Lu Beiping actually told him was this: that on that night, after he had made love to a woman for the first time, he suddenly burst into tears.)

Jade pulled Lu Beiping into her lap as Lu Beiping began bawling like a child.

—No! he cried. No, no, no! No, no, no, no, no!

—Four Eyes? Four Eyes?

—Oh, no . . . Oh, no . . .

—Oh, Four Eyes! Darling . . . dear . . .

She held him tight, shushed him, pulled her blouse over him like a blanket. But rather than subsiding, Lu Beiping's sobs grew more violent. Finally, Jade too began to grow distressed.

—Heavens. I've done wrong, haven't I? It was my fault, Four Eyes. This was all my fault.

He rolled over and buried his face in her blouse, his body convulsing with sobs. With one hand she stroked his trembling shoulders, while with the other she reached carefully for a stick and stirred the ashes of the fire. Throughout all this she had kept half her mind on the pork, which was still simmering fragrantly in the stew pot. The blackened chunks of firewood hissed, and sparks leapt in the gathering dark.

Lu Beiping lay facedown, motionless, as if asleep. A damp chill had entered the evening air, and the heat of their bodies made the air feel even colder. A thin line of crimson light still glowed faintly over the mountains. Again, in the course of one evening, his entire world had changed. And this change was likely to be even more momentous than Lu Beiping's chance discovery beneath that other crimson sunset.

Suddenly Lu Beiping rolled over, sat up, and gave a sepulchral laugh.

—So, Jade, are you my ghost wife now? I feel like I've just had *another* ghost wedding—

Jade spat reflexively, then slapped him across the lips.

—Peh! Spit on that! Bounty and bliss, Four Eyes, don't . . .

Then she pulled her hand back and studied him for a long moment. The Gaffer's insinuating remarks about Lu Beiping, when the old man came up to the hollow on Midsummer's Day, rang in her mind.

—Four Eyes . . . what do you mean by that? Are you serious, or is this just hooey talk?

While Jade gazed at him suspiciously, Lu Beiping fished his glasses out of the grass, put them on, extracted his shorts from under the banana leaves, put them on too, stooped to pick up Jade's flowered blouse and tossed it to her, still not saying a word. Then, overcome by the silliness of this silent performance, Lu Beiping gave another macabre laugh.

—Of course it's hooey talk. Hey, do you want to smell my feet? After all this talk about my smelly feet, maybe you'd like to take a sniff yourself.

He waggled a bare foot at her. Jade pushed it away and continued staring at him in silence.

An intense stillness settled over the creekbend. The all-encompassing din of the insects seemed to deepen the cobalt blue of the night sky. Slowly, Jade pulled on her blouse, then sat with an expectant air, as if waiting for Lu Beiping to go on. Lu Beiping sensed something odd in her manner.

—Jade, is something wrong? Haven't you already heard about my ghost marriage?

Jade shook her head, still gazing at him with the same look of placid, unbroken attention.

—These mosquitoes sure are getting bad, he said in an awkward attempt to break the silence. He prodded the embers with a stick, and the flames leapt back to life, thinning the cloud of mosquitoes that buzzed around their heads. Jade reached over instinctively to lift the stew pot off the flames, but the wire-wrapped handles were still burning hot, and she released them with a gasp of pain.

—Crap! Lu Beiping said, grabbing her hands and blowing on her swollen palms. Is it bad?

Then abruptly, he buried his face in her hands. Jade smiled and laughed breezily.

—It's nothing. Oh, Four Eyes . . . you're a good man, you know that?

Lu Beiping froze with his face still in her hands. Then he looked up and gave a laugh of relief. Releasing her hands, he tore a strip off of a banana leaf and, using it as a glove, lifted the perilous pot off the flames and set it on the ground. Then, in a calm, even voice, he laid out the basic outlines of his story: how he'd picked up the scrap of red paper next to the rubber grove, married the foreman's dead daughter, and been exiled to the jungle to herd the cattle. Jade listened, the firelight playing on her face as her expression changed from alarm to sympathy and back again.

—Did you . . . tell any of this to Smudge? she asked in a cautious voice when he finished his tale.

—No, said Lu Beiping, grinning at her out of the shadows. I just told him it was because of my smelly feet.

—Autumn neither?

—Nope.

—Good, Jade said, clapping her hands briskly. So Kingfisher doesn't know either. Let's keep it at smelly feet. That's all they need to know. Hey! . . .

She made a show of trying to grab his feet and sniff them, as if trying to divert attention from the uncomfortable topic at hand. After Lu Beiping had wriggled out of her grasp, she sat back and finally unearthed the fear that had been growing inside her.

—Four Eyes, this is too baleful a thing. Normally we'd do a spirit-calling, wash the dark out of you. But we can't, not now. You've got to keep your mouth shut around Kingfisher. Living like we do, it's sins like this that scare him most.

—It doesn't scare you? Lu Beiping asked. You looked pretty frightened when I told you.

—Me, scared? Jade scoffed. I'm a stonewoman, what have I got to be scared about? Hard as the life of a stonewoman, have you ever heard that saying, Four Eyes? Do you know what a stonewoman is?

—A stonewoman?

Now it was Lu Beiping's turn to gaze at her questioningly. He sat, waiting for her to go on and studying her firelit face, whose usual playful expression had been replaced by a sea-deep calm. She drew his hand into her lap, stroked it absentmindedly. As she gazed off into the middle distance, Lu Beiping watched the reflected flames dance in her pupils, sensing through her hand the waves of emotion that were passing through her. After a silent moment that seemed to last an eternity, she laughed and came back from her reverie.

—I'm a happy woman, she said, heaving a deep sigh. Looking at you, I know I've got nothing to complain about.

Lu Beiping said nothing, waiting for the door of her past to slide open and admit him. From the slope above them there came a rustling sound followed by the rasp of dislodged pebbles. Maybe those meddlesome monkeys were back, sniffing after the meat again.

—A stonewoman, that's what they called me. Where I come from, stonewoman is the meanest, dirtiest thing you could call an unmarried girl. A stonewoman is a woman that can't give birth, can't bring new life into the world, a woman with nothing down there—get my drift?—no door, no hole, no place for a man to plant his seed. A woman that can't satisfy her man, a stone-cold, deadwood, good-for-nothing woman! Oh, Four Eyes . . . Jade's voice, normally a husky alto, now sounded high-pitched and tense: Back home in my unit, I was the roll clerk, I kept track of everybody's workpoints. The Secretary, he wanted to sleep with me. I told him no. He kept trying to get me into bed, but I pushed him away every time. Finally he said, There's no woman in Kwun-chow Crossing that wouldn't jump at the chance to sleep with me. If you won't, you must be a stonewoman. But just the sight of his shit-brown teeth turned my stomach. I couldn't do it, he'd have had to kill me first. He kept on hounding me, and before long I got so desperate I found myself a husband the next village over. But no sooner had I crossed his threshold than I got word that everybody back in Kwun-chow was talking about how I was a stonewoman. His family was furious. I hadn't lived there but three days and already they were clamoring for a divorce. I had no way out. I ran back to my folks' place. My parents panicked and married me off again as quick as they could, this time to a dole coddle, a crippled old bachelor living out his days on disability money. He was so old that he couldn't even take me to bed, just hung around the house and beat me when he was angry. I was nineteen years old and a bride newly wed, but I lived like a stony old spinster, cold and barren. By now the whole town was convinced I was a stonewoman, and even I started to believe it. I had the blackest name of all the girls in the village, men turned away when they saw me on the street. And worst of all, that shit-teethed Secretary—he wasn't Secretary anymore by now, he'd been struggled down in some Movement or other—started harassing me again, found every excuse to come tap on my door. Said I'd never escape the big stick in his pants. That was the last straw. I ran off and joined the driftfolk. It was at the Kwun-chow ferryboat landing that I met Smudge's pa.

She stopped.

—What year was this? Lu Beiping asked.

—Sixty-seven, the second year of your big Revolution.

Jade's expression softened, and she laughed quietly to herself.

—I had Smudge at the end of that year. Smudge's pa, he was the first man to break the stone of this stony young stonewoman. Ha! And now just look at me with my litter of squalling whelps. Four Eyes, tell me if I'm not a lucky woman.

Now that Jade had returned to the slopes of Mudkettle Mountain, the atmosphere around the fire became lighthearted again. She picked up his notorious rainboots, sniffed them and made a face, then went over to wash them in the creek. The water burbled and clattered. He sat there, watching her. This was the first time in weeks that he'd studied her closely. Farther from the fire, with her face lost in tree-shadow, the movements of her body seemed strangely exaggerated. Early on he'd noted the ivory luster of her fingers, the creamy soles of her feet; now his gaze fell upon her wrists and earlobes, the silver shimmer of her bracelets and earrings: monstrosities never seen on women in those days. The ornaments gave off a metallic dazzle in the firelight. There was a flashy self-confidence about Jade that Lu Beiping found very arresting; she had absolutely no inhibitions. To even speak of such qualities in women in those days was taboo, but in Jade, they seemed a natural expression of her femininity. She wasn't, Lu Beiping thought, actually pretty, at least in the conventional sense, but there was something very stirring about the contours of her face, those features carved by time and hardship, by the passage of long months in the hills. In old novels, lofty cheekbones, deep eye sockets, and thick lips were the clichés used to describe mountain women. There was nothing lofty, deep, or thick about Jade's features, but they had a finely etched quality, like the red-brown woodwork of an antique sandalwood fan, simple but delicate, rough but pure. Lu Beiping caught himself unconsciously trying to estimate her age. He was twenty-one; she couldn't be more than twenty-five or twenty-six. But something about her seemed . . . not just old, but ancient.

Now the empty feeling that had opened up inside Lu Beiping after they made love began to be filled by something else. He wanted to be close to Jade, to be a part of her in a way that had nothing to do with the body. This woman, who was so utterly different from him, whose life experiences were so far removed from his own, had slipped quietly into a deep corner of his being and claimed it.

Lu Beiping sighed.

—Well, he said with a wry chuckle: You're a stonewoman, I'm a ghost husband. I guess we were meant to be together, Jade.

Jade spun around and faced him in the firelight.

—Four Eyes, I'm not your ghost wife. I'm real. There's a difference.

Throwing him a sharp look, she added:

—I'll bear you a child. What do you say?

At that Lu Beiping truly felt like the breath had been stolen from his lungs. (Those words yanked me right back to reality, Lu Beiping said to Tsung.) All of a sudden the aroma of meat wafting on the night air seemed like a nauseating reek. Lu Beiping thought: Do I love this woman? Is this really love? Is this the person who deserves my love—"my" woman? God, he thought, she wants to have a child with me! In those days it was hard to imagine a proposition more preposterous, more beyond the pale, than the one that had just issued from her lips. He thought of her "whelps," his cattle; her pipe, his books; he thought of the vast, craggy, canyon-riven landscape that separated him from her. Yes, he could follow a fateful scrap of paper into the jungle to play the specious, unconsummatable role of Han's ghost husband; but could he really, for the sake of this single, absurd caper on the banks of Mudclaw Creek, abandon his life and become someone else?

And yet, before he could think any of these things through, Jade made another, even more harrowing declaration.

—Alright, she said, pushing back her hair, her bracelet flashing in the darkness: Let's head up to the hollow. I need to tell Kingfisher and the others that we're together now, that we've made good. Now you're my man too. We need to give them a heads up.

—*What?* Lu Beiping cried. Jade, you're crazy! Now you really *have* gone crazy!

—Well, what are we going to do, then? Jade said with a chuckle that betrayed a faint hint of self-satisfaction, fanning herself and wiping the sweat of their recent exertions off her brow: I already told them I wanted to make good with you. They didn't believe me, didn't think young Stinkyfoot Four-Eyes would even go with an old lady like me! Ha!—Jade hoisted the stew pot, grinning at him jubilantly— Oh, and Four Eyes, I almost forgot to chew you out. You greedy pig, how the hell did you get your hands on this big pot of meat, and why didn't you tell us? Sky's sake, the damned thing had almost turned!

—Jade . . . you . . . I . . . Lu Beiping stammered. I got it down at camp, I was saving it for you and Smudge . . .

—There you go! All the more reason to come with me. We're so meat-thirsty up in that hollow that we're about ready to gnaw each other's thigh bones. When Stump, Kingfisher, and them get a whiff of this, they'll get down on their hands and knees and worship you like a god. Come on—she tugged at his arm—Let's go! I cooked your supper, now you'd better come up and eat it.

—Jade, you're insane! Lu Beiping yelled, shaking her off with a furious twist of his arm. I am *not* leaving this place tonight! Not if you cut off my balls and feed them to the cattle!

With that Lu Beiping turned and ran up the slope toward his hut, leaving Jade alone at the edge of the water.

Chapter 6
The Hollow

But unbeknownst to Lu Beiping, the Blue Dragonfly of Fate had already alighted and was waiting for him quietly in a corner of his hut.

As Lu Beiping rounded the Tree That Dances in the Wind and jogged furiously up the slope, he noticed that the door to his hut was open. He halted immediately, remembering that he'd gone straight down to the creek that afternoon, hadn't even set foot in his hut. Who had come here? What the hell was going on? While he hesitated, Jade, toting the stew pot, caught up with him, and together they filed cautiously through the door.

Once inside they both stopped short again. Smudge was sprawled over the log stool at the foot of the bed, fast asleep, Lu Beiping's harmonica clenched tight in one hand. As he snored his nostrils quivered. Fine droplets of sweat glistened on his naked back. Clearly, he'd been waiting here for a long time.

Lu Beiping felt his heart quicken. Had Smudge seen them? At the thought that their performance down by the creek might have had an audience, Lu Beiping's scalp prickled. (Actually, Lu Beiping said to Tsung many years later, I didn't give that kid enough credit. When I became more familiar with life up in the hollow, I realized how little difference it would've made to him. Poor thing.)

Jade, standing behind Lu Beiping, uttered a syllable of surprise.

—Bless me! Look who's here, she said, striding over to Smudge and laying a slap on his bare rump. Get up, you little lout. Do you do anything but sleep? Why didn't you give us a shout?

Smudge's eyes popped open to reveal two big, black, gleaming irises. He mumbled through the fog of sleep:

—I didn't want to trouble you and Four Eyes, Pa.

Lu Beiping's face went beet-red.

—Smudge, I . . . he stuttered, I didn't . . . I didn't realize . . .

—Hmph, Smudge snorted disdainfully, sliding the hand that held Lu Beiping's harmonica behind his back: You're a dirty son of a dog.

Lu Beiping's heart went cold. Crap, he thought. I'm done for. He stood there in dumb silence, a vein throbbing in his forehead, waiting for Smudge to come out with the inevitable, damning accusation.

—Stinkyfoot! Smudge burst out at last. You promised! Said if you didn't play for me next time you were a dirty son of a dog! And you still haven't played!

Oh, that little imp, Lu Beiping thought. He sure knows how to maneuver the grown-ups out of a sticky situation. A wave of relief washed over Lu Beiping, and he slumped back against one of the hut's central roof-posts, his body limp as a slack fiddle string.

—But Smudge, Lu Beiping said with a forced grin, this *is* next time, and we've been together for barely a minute!

Jade chuckled at that, and hoisting the stew pot she chimed in:

—Smudge, you're right. He is a dirty son of a dog. Look at this delicious pot of pork scraps he had squirreled away all for his greedy self. He hadn't even cooked it yet. It was a lucky thing I found it, or it would've gone bad!

At the word "meat" Smudge's nose twitched automatically, and he flopped off of the log stool and scrambled across the floor to the stew pot. Bringing his nose close to the warm metal, he drank in the aroma, pursing his lips; then without warning he began to giggle and weep at the same time. For a moment he sat there stupidly, wiping tears and trembling with laughter, then all at once he flew upon Lu Beiping and began pummeling him with his fists.

—Oy-yoy-yoy! he wailed. Stinkyfoot! Whyever'd you do such a sorry thing? Bad man! Pa, I'm hungry! I want meat! I want to eat—now!

The boy's hand darted out to snatch off the lid, but Jade barked at him reproachfully and he froze.

—Smudge! Did that fever addle your head? Don't you *dare* touch that meat till your uncles get a chance to eat too! Shame on you!

Three pairs of eyes came to rest on the stew pot. Its dented, smoke-blackened lid seemed to glow softly in the dim evening light.

(Years later, recounting this story to Tsung, Lu Beiping would emphasize again and again how powerful a hold this pot of meat seemed to possess over the minds of the driftfolk. Migrants living deep in the Hainan hills weren't likely to taste meat more than once or twice a year, and in the calculations of such people two pounds of pork scraps could easily outweigh a woman. For them, Lu Beiping's meat had an almost magical power.)

—Four Eyes, Jade said, turning to face Lu Beiping: Come with us. You just saw what this poor boy'll do for a bite of meat. Our bones are squealing for lack of grease up there. Why, when Stump and Kingfisher smell this stew, they'll get down on all fours and yap like dogs if you tell them to.

Lu Beiping sat down heavily on the bed and stared blankly at the stew pot.

—Think about it this way, Jade said. If you don't come, could I be so cruel as to steal this pot of stew away from you? And Smudge, tell me, would Four Eyes be so cruel as to keep this meat all to himself? Oh, and Four Eyes, I forgot to mention. Kingfisher has something he wants to talk to you about.

Lu Beiping sat on the bed, motionless, silent. Smudge thrust the harmonica under his nose and resumed his dogged petition.

—Play it, Four Eyes! he said, dancing around him impatiently: Please! You promised, or else you're a dirty son of a dog. Please! I want to eat meat, I want to hear you play the mouth harp!

(Alas, Lu Beiping sighed to Tsung, seeming almost to pride himself on his own fatalistic attitude: What else could I do? I had no other choice. Like I told you before, I knew that kid would be my undoing.)

Mother and son led the way in triumph, Smudge waving the harmonica, Jade carrying the stew pot. Feeling resigned, Lu Beiping latched the door amid the nasal complaints of the cattle and started up the trail after Jade and Smudge. The path glowed faint blue in the dappled moonlight, leading away up into darkness. That's the color of destiny, Lu Beiping thought.

When they reached the fourth bend of the creek, having crossed the meadow where Lu Beiping first encountered Jade, they waded into the water. Now Lu Beiping held the stew pot, at Jade's insistence. As they began sloshing up the creekbed, Jade grabbed Lu Beiping from behind and said to Smudge, giggling:

—Smudge, Four Eyes said he wouldn't come with us unless I cut off his balls. Shall we cut them off now? We don't want him to change his mind . . .

—Heehee! Smudge cried as he scampered through the water and pounced on Lu Beiping's leg. Pounding him and tugging at him, he said: If we cut off your balls, will you still be the Bull Devil?

Lu Beiping laughed as he tried to wriggle free of them, their struggle churning the creek into a dancing rattlesnake. Finally, feeling a bit surly, he yelled:

—Quit it, you two! You'll spill your own dinner!

The hollow was silent as a ghost town. No lamps were lit, and nobody stirred in the two dark cabins sitting catty-corner by the creek. The moon glared over the bluffs that ringed the hollow, illuminating the twisted figure of the lychee tree that loomed to one side like a door-god guarding the entranceway to a temple. As they emerged from the tunnel of branches Wildweed began to bark again, and Jade shushed him. With silent eagerness the dog ran over to sniff Lu Beiping's legs, then gamboled greedily after the stew pot.

After exchanging a glance with Smudge, Jade took the pot from Lu Beiping and proceeded to the near cabin, where she disappeared behind the protruding bulk of the hearth stove. Smudge led Lu Beiping to the other side. He tiptoed to the door, gently eased it open, peeked inside, then looked back at Lu Beiping with his tongue out in surprise.

It was pitch black inside, and silent. First Lu Beiping made out the two children sprawled on the bed; then, in the shadows near the foot of bed, he noticed two glowing specks of orange light. Stump and Autumn were sitting side by side on the floor, smoking, each holding a lit incense stick for a lighter, silent except for the hoarse gurgling of their water pipes. As Smudge pulled Lu Beiping into the cabin Autumn started to rise, but Stump tugged him back down and, pointing wordlessly with his incense stick, directed Lu Beiping's gaze to the other figure in the room.

Kingfisher sat cross-legged on a log stool, his back to the door. The gaunt ridge of his spine was barely visible in the darkness. He looked like he was meditating, or maybe just brooding. Lu Beiping remembered the frigid atmosphere around the dinner table on his first night in the hollow, and sensed that another blizzard was about to hit.

That austere, cross-legged pose, Lu Beiping thought, was an expression of Kingfisher's authority over the other hollow-dwellers. By doing daily homage to the band's dead leader, he now positioned himself as their new one.

Over in the kitchen Jade had already rekindled the fire and set the stew pot on the stove to warm. Now she lit a kerosene lantern and sashayed into the room.

—What are you boys doing here in the dark? Sitting the sevens? What happened, did somebody die?

When this sarcastic question failed to provoke a response, Jade picked up her comb from the bed and flung it across the room at Kingfisher.

—Sorry I'm late, Kingfish. I'm back, you can kill me now if you want.

The comb bounced off Kingfisher's back and skittered across the floor. Kingfisher seemed not to notice. Slowly he joined his hands in prayer, raised them to his forehead, swept them out and around in a broad downward circle, joined them at his chest again, and made a slight bow. Having formally concluded his meditation, he turned with the same deliberate slowness to face Jade. Then, in an abrupt, explosive motion, he grabbed the wicker prayer mat and hurled it against the doorframe.

—Shameless woman! he boomed. Face west, Jade, get down on your knees, and pray! Pray to your brother Horn, to the father of your son Smudge! Pray, Jade!—his voice became suddenly shrill—Pray to him, now!

Tick and Roach stirred in bed and began to whimper. Stump silenced them with a bark. Glancing sidelong at Lu Beiping, Kingfisher rubbed his arms briskly and said:

—Beg pardon, Four Eyes. The kingdom hath its mandates, the family its laws. Jade here just broke family law, and I forgot my manners.

Lu Beiping could tell by the veins bulging on Kingfisher's bald head that the man was working hard to contain his own rage. He stole an uneasy glance at Jade, trying to catch her eyes in hopes of gauging his own standing vis-à-vis Kingfisher. Jade stood off to one side, her arms folded, gazing wordlessly at Kingfisher with a bitter smile on her face while he continued to berate her:

—The first thing on your lips is *die, die, die*. Haven't you had your fill of dying? Remember what you promised Horn when you joined up with us—you said he could trust you to take care of the family. Right? You said you'd be a mother for this family of orphans. Ever since we came into the hills we've counted on you for every scrap of cloth on our backs and every ounce of rice in our bowls. I don't believe you've ever shammed out on us like this. You think you're some kind of goddess? Leaving the whole family hungry to go larking it up downmountain!

He glanced sideways at Lu Beiping again, then continued:

—Jade, I just talked to Horn through the plate sprite. The plate said *fire*, then *scatter*. When there's no fire in the hearth, the family will scatter! Smudge, this is your fault too! You . . .

Kingfisher's voice trailed off abruptly. Smudge hung his head and gave a morose sniff. Kingfisher pointed at the prayer mat and continued imprecating Smudge, but now his head was inclined slightly in the direction of the kitchen and his nose was twitching unconsciously as he spoke:

—Kneel, boy! Kneel with your Auntie and apologize to your Pa's spirit! I send you down to look for her and you disappear like a dog with a bone! You—

He stopped again, sniffing as if he were coming down with a cold. Firelight was dancing inside the hearth stove, and the aroma of stewed pork had begun to fill the room.

—Eh? All of a sudden Kingfisher's body went slack and his legs flopped out limply in front of him. Then his face lit up and he gave a joyful whoop: Jade! he cried. You devil!

—Ha!

Chortling triumphantly, Jade charged over and barred Kingfisher's way as he made a beeline for the kitchen.

—Hmph! she snorted, giving him a shove: Not so fast, Kingfish. First, *you* kneel.

—Quit it! Kingfisher yelled, trying to fight his way around her: Stew my balls, I've never smelled anything so good in years!

—Nope! Jade said, arching her brow. No dice! Not till you kneel down in front of Smudge's pa's shrine and apologize for what you just said to us.

Already Stump had scrambled to his feet and bounded across the cabin to the stove, where he stood, pot lid in hand, beaming down into the bubbling stew with a look of pure rapture on his face.

—Oy, yoy, yoy! he crowed. Mother heaven! Sis, where in the blazes did you cozen this big pot of meat?

Crooning like a singshow actor, Stump did a little jig of excitement in front of the stove while Smudge led Tick and Roach in a high-pitched, jubilant chorus:

—Meat, Auntie! We—want—meat!

Jade, who was still busy fending off Kingfisher, managed to get a grip on the bald man's ear and twisted it ferociously.

—Come on, if you won't kneel, Stump gets to tuck in first!

—Ouch! Hell! Fine, Jade, fine. When supper's over I'll kneel till the sun comes up, if that's what you want.

—That's not good enough, Kingfisher. I want you to get down on your knees right now—she pulled Lu Beiping to her side and tapped her toe on the prayer mat Kingfisher had thrown against the door—in front of Four Eyes! It was him that brought us this lovely supper tonight. And did you say a word of thanks? No! You just lit into all of us and started cussing up a storm—

—Jade! Lu Beiping snapped: Enough, okay? Kingfisher, don't listen to her, I don't want you to kneel for me.

He struggled free from her grip, and immediately Jade sprang aside and danced three paces over to the kitchen, where she positioned herself in front of the stew pot and stood shielding it like a sacred flame while clacking a chopstick loudly against the rims of the enamel dinner bowls:

—Supper's served! she yelled. Wash up and come eat!

Wildweed contributed his own barking voice to the chaos, and soon the whole cabin was aglow with light and merriment. Kingfisher threw an arm around his pale young rescuer and squeezed him so hard that his shoulder hurt.

—You're a fine lad, Four Eyes, he said, laughing. A right, fine lad!

For the first time in his life Lu Beiping discovered that it was possible to get drunk off of meat. *Meat drunk*, he'd often heard the plantation workers say, but he'd always assumed it was a joke. Now it became clear to him what a powerful intoxicant meat really could be.

(In the highlands, eating meat was a ritual act, Lu Beiping explained years later to Tsung. Even in the Agrecorps camps, where everyone "ate of out the magistrate's hand," you could count on one hand the number of times a year a pig was slaughtered, and such occasions became raucous holidays. Needless to say, breaking meatfast was an even more hallowed observance in the remote wilds of Mudkettle Mountain.)

Tonight, after the initial uproar subsided, Kingfisher, Stump, and Autumn proceeded to the edge of the creek to wash their faces and hands and then returned to the lodge, still shirtless but wearing checkered waistcloths that provided the bare minimum in the way of coverage. The kids frolicked at Jade's knees as she bustled in the kitchen, and Smudge kept pestering Lu Beiping to teach him the harmonica. In the blink of an eye Jade had cleared the long, low dinner table of its clutter of knives, cane wicker, work sleeves, and half-finished sandals, whipped together an assortment of vegetable appetizers, and brought out a big pot of yam porridge that had been cooling since morning. Meanwhile Kingfisher took charge of ladling out portions of yam beer into individual drinking bowls.

In the center of the table sat the pot of stewed pork, like an offering to the gods, browned and gleaming. The meat filled the room with its ambiguous odor, part savory aroma, part noxious reek.

Stump was eager to dig in, but Kingfisher checked him. Now, despite the scene he'd just made, Kingfisher took the time to pull several sticks of mosquito incense from under the mattress, light them in the hearth stove, and stick them in the brazier in front of the altar that occupied the alcove next to the door. As Lu Beiping watched Kingfisher, he made out in the shadows of the alcove a small shrine with a wooden memorial tablet—that must belong to Horn, Smudge's dad—and an unassuming porcelain statue of Kwan-Yin.

Kingfisher didn't kneel to pray; instead, he took one of the beer bowls and sprinkled a few drops in the dirt before the shrine, then clasped his hands and bowed, muttering:

—Sup first, brother. Sup first.

From the far side of the table Autumn gave Lu Beiping, by way of acknowledgment, a knowing smile.

Then the meal commenced, and Jade's chopsticks immediately took on the role of guardian spirit of the meat. In a heartbeat the three kids fell upon the stew pot, but Jade parried their chopsticks deftly, deposited several pieces of meat and veggies into each kid's bowl, then waved them away from the grown-ups' table. The two little ones retreated to the small table near the hearth stove, but Smudge lingered for a moment, appealing to Lu Beiping for aid, before Jade gave him a decisive slap on the rump and he slunk off, pouting, to join the others. At that point Stump's chopsticks darted out too, but Jade deflected them and said with a smile:

—Not yet, boys. I have a big piece of news to share with you all before we start supper.

Lu Beiping tensed. The dog was nosing around hopefully under the table, and he fingered its scruff in an attempt to hide his own unease, bracing himself for the harrowing announcement that was soon to follow. He surveyed the three men sitting around the table, certain that he was in a highly dangerous situation. It's a trap! a voice cried out inside him. Run, it's a trap!

Now Jade took their bowls and began portioning out the meat piece by piece. When this was done she lifted her beer bowl to Four Eyes, then, noticing that his was empty, said abruptly:

—Hey! Where's your beer?

A moment before, when no one was looking, Lu Beiping had furtively poured his beer back into the serving bowl.

—Every man's a king when he's got meat and wine, but without them, we're no better than swine! Kingfisher boomed, now in very high spirits. Four Eyes, we might not be kings, but we're not swine either. Jade, pour our guest a drink.

—Guest? Jade said as she refilled Lu Beiping's bowl. Kingfisher, would a guest bring us such a precious gift? Raising her bowl to Lu Beiping again, she said: Four Eyes, Kingfisher just thanked the spirits for our meal. But tonight, with my first drink, I want to offer my thanks to *you*.

—Stop it! Lu Beiping blurted out. Are you crazy?

Lu Beiping cringed in embarrassment when he heard these words come out of his mouth. (Trust me to find exactly the wrong thing to say in every situation, he said to Tsung. I blame it on the yam beer. First I made the mistake of calling Kingfisher Smudge's pa, and now . . .)

—Crazy? Jade said with a cryptic smile. We're all crazy around here. So, as I was saying, let's drink to Four Eyes. First he saved Smudge's life, and now he's made us all kings for a night—she laughed, then turned and grinned at Lu Beiping—You can see, Four Eyes, we've all gone crazy over your meat.

—Ha! Kingfisher hooted. I'll drink to that!

Stump and Kingfisher guffawed, clacked bowls with Lu Beiping, downed their drinks without looking to see whether he'd followed suit, and promptly began stuffing their mouths with pork. Autumn ate with quiet focus, chewing each mouthful carefully before swallowing.

—Bull Devil! Smudge chipped in from the table next to the stove: I'm crazy for your meat too! Then he came running over, waving his bowl above his head and giggling giddily: I'm—crazy—for your—meat! I'm—crazy—for your—meat!

—Smudge! Jade yelled. Don't interrupt the grown-ups! Then, seeing Kingfisher's expression darken, she added quickly: Kingfish, you ought to thank me too, you know. If it wasn't for me, this whole of pot of meat would've spoiled.

—Eh? Is that so?

Kingfisher, red-faced from athletic eating, swiveled around to look at Lu Beiping, evidently pleased to have found an opening for conversation with the bespectacled city boy. Lu Beiping chuckled self-effacingly.

—It's true. My unit slaughtered a pig at the pre-campaign rally, and my friends saved me my ration. I'd been brining it so it would keep longer, thinking I'd share it with you guys. But it was hot out, and the cattle were hard to manage, and I never had the time to bring it up to the hollow. Jade's right, if she hadn't found it and cooked it today, it might've gone bad by the time I got back from work.

—Small wonder it tastes a trifle like stinky feet, Stump said, and the whole room erupted into laughter.

—Right on! Kingfisher chortled, slurping beer. That must be what gives it that kick. Toe grease!

—Peh! Mind your tongues! Jade said, shaking with laughter. You'll make me lose my appetite!

—All the better, then there'll be more for Four Eyes.

Kingfisher deposited another heap of veggies on Lu Beiping's plate while urging him to *eat, eat* through a mouthful of pork.

—Where I come from, Kingfisher said, addressing the room, every time a couple gets hitched the groom's family serves pork chitterlings for good luck. The groom's mother has always got to remind the kitchen helpers not to wash them too clean—there needs to be some stink left for that savor to reach heaven, bring glory to the whole family. Eat, Four Eyes, eat.

Lu Beiping was beginning to feel dizzy. His tightly wound nerves had relaxed, and he was now in a very good mood. Obviously it wasn't an effect of the alcohol, as throughout the whole meal he'd been careful not to let more than a few drops of yam beer pass between his lips. But eating rich, fatty pork on an empty stomach was like pouring water into a hot, dry kettle; at the first drop of fat his stomach gurgled tumultuously and an ammoniac flavor rushed up into his nose, making his sinuses tingle and his head spin. It was intoxicating. Yes, he thought, you really can get drunk on meat. He smelled the same odor on Stump's and Kingfisher's breath when they belched, and he noticed that their eyes had acquired a drifty, glazed-over look. Jade was no longer so vigilant with her chopsticks, and every leap of her eyebrows and toss of her hair betrayed the disinhibiting effects of the meat.

Only Autumn's manner remained unchanged. Throughout all this he ate serenely and with great focus, gazing now at Jade, now at Lu Beiping, and occasionally turning around to glance at Smudge. He chewed his meat as if he were sucking the juice out of every fiber, savoring some flavor the rest of them couldn't taste. But Lu Beiping didn't have long to ponder what this flavor might be before Jade jerked him rudely back to the present. As a second helping of pork made its way around the table and the remaining yam beer was pressed on everyone in turn, Jade slapped her forehead and exclaimed:

—Heavens above, I was so busy stuffing myself that I forgot to tell you my news! Gentlemen, guess what: Today, I made good with Four Eyes. Kingfish, you bet me I couldn't get him? Well, I did.

Just like that, as if it were the most ordinary thing in the world, Jade dropped the bomb that Lu Beiping feared would bring the mountains crashing down on his head. Kingfisher's red-veined eyes widened, and he looked at Lu Beiping, then at Jade, with a broad smile on his face.

—Eh? Is that so?

—Uh . . . Jade? Lu Beiping said, beginning to panic.

—You'd better believe it! Jade said, taking advantage of the giddy atmosphere to snake an arm around Lu Beiping and give him a hearty squeeze. So, from now on, Four Eyes isn't a guest here. You all had better treat him good.

—Oy, cheers to that! Stump rumbled, raising his beer bowl.

Kingfisher gazed at Lu Beiping for a few seconds, and it seemed to Lu Beiping that a shadow passed behind his eyes. Then, in a cheerful voice, he announced:

—Well, no wonder Jade prayed the eights for you, Four Eyes. She's a good woman, no? Let's drink—to her!

Lu Beiping was thoroughly dazed. Even Autumn's smile from across the table took him by surprise. The mood was still mirthful; the sky hadn't fallen, the ocean hadn't risen to swallow the land. Amid the haze of meat-drunkenness and actual drunkenness, Jade's announcement had seemed like the most natural thing in the world. (Later, it would occur to Lu Beiping that even the tipsy atmosphere that night had been of conscious design. Like cooking the meat and spreading the palm leaves, this evening of boozy revelry was a deliberate step toward a well-thought-out end. Jade was nothing if not practical, Lu Beiping reflected to Tsung, years afterward. Even in the most uncertain terrain her feet instinctively picked out a level road.)

Chuckling awkwardly, Lu Beiping wracked his brains for something to say and once again alighted on the most tactless thing possible.

—Have some more! he said, gesturing grandly at the almost-empty pot as if he were now the master of the house.

Another jug of yam beer, its seal freshly broken, arrived at the table, ferried over from the kitchen by Smudge. Later on Lu Beiping would learn that the driftfolk made this beer in their own stills, which explained why it didn't have the same foul, stomach-turning odor as the rotgut the hands drank down at camp. While the grown-ups pressed more beer on one another, Smudge planted himself directly in front of Lu Beiping and thrust the harmonica in his face again.

—Play, Bull Devil!

For once Kingfisher didn't silence the boy. Instead he toasted Lu Beiping and said to Smudge while giving Stump a playful shove:

—Doesn't your uncle Stump have an old Teochew dulcimer lying around here somewhere? Why don't you run and get it. Stump, looks like you'll have a music-playing partner from now on!

—I don't want to listen to Stump's dulcimer tonight, Jade said. Four Eyes, why don't you give us a tune?

—Aye, said Stump, wagging his head. I'm not in the musicking mood just now. Play for us, Four Eyes.

Pushing Lu Beiping from behind, Smudge cried out:

—Come on, play! You promised, Bull Devil! Or else you're a dirty son of a dog.

Autumn took the harmonica from Smudge, wiped the boy's greasy fingerprints off of its silver surface, and examined it meticulously before handing it to Lu Beiping. Swaying, Lu Beiping got to his feet.

The moon had risen early that night, and by now it had disappeared behind the hills. With the harmonica cradled in his hands like an infant, Lu Beiping coaxed forth the bright, plaintive strains of "Red River Valley," meanwhile laying out the rest of the program in his head: "Troika," "Katyusha," "The Deep Blue Sea," "Moscow Nights." These were songs that most young people in those days knew by heart, all of them from *Two Hundred World Folk Songs*, and most of them Russian. The musical gifts he'd inherited from his father were on full display tonight as he marshaled arpeggios, glissandos, and pitch-bends to mimic the sounds of a full orchestra. These sounds, he thought to himself, must seem to the hollow-dwellers as beautiful and otherworldly as a choir of angels. But no sooner had he launched into the opening phrase of "Troika," sweeping in one breath to the keening, querulous high note, than he stopped, sat down, and fell into a stupor. Meat drunk. His stomach juices, unable to digest such rich food, had fermented like yeast and spread alcohol throughout his bloodstream. Though he remained aware of what was going on around him, he felt himself slipping off into a dream-like half sleep. At some point Stump had hauled out his dusty old dulcimer, set it up on the table, and started plinking away while Kingfisher and Jade stood arm in arm, swaying and singing West Canton river shanties. Smudge, Tick, and Roach pranced around on the bed, giggling and crowing with delight. Foggily Lu Beiping noticed that someone had taken the harmonica out of his hands and, looking up, he found himself staring into a pair of deliquescent eyes. It was Autumn. Only much later would Lu Beiping realize that Autumn, even more than Jade, perhaps, was grateful for the entrance of this new member into their household, and had his interests at heart.

When he woke the next day Lu Beiping would dimly recall that later that night, after the music was over and Kingfisher and Stump had downed another big bowl of yam beer, the two men had built a bonfire in the yard and competed to climb the lychee tree, scrambling up opposite sides of the trunk as they vied to be the first to grab the topmost branch of its bare, twisted crown.

Just as the night sky began to pale, long before the sun would clear the walls of the hollow, Lu Beiping was jolted awake by the rasp of a saw. He sat up, and realizing that the scrape of sawteeth wasn't the lowing of his cattle, he immediately broke into a sweat. Staring up into the patched mosquito net that hung over the bed, he wondered: Where am I? Why am I lying here? Then fragments of the previous day's adventures surfaced in his memory, and scene by scene the story reassembled itself, dim and distant, like memories from a past century. He chuckled. This was the same feeling he'd had the morning after the ghost wedding, after spending a night vomiting up the gallon of yam beer he'd been forced to consume the evening before. No, not quite. It wasn't exactly the same. That felt unreal; this was real. And far stranger. The ghost wedding had had an absurd, nightmarish quality, but last night's events, though no less absurd, were like the plot of a vivid, fascinating dream that brought him a faint thrill to recall.

His mind was a wild jumble of emotions, scrambling every which way like a kudzu vine across a mountainside.

Smudge, Tick, and Roach lay curled in bed next to him, three grimy monkeys fast asleep. The bed opposite them must be Jade's, he thought. But when he pulled back the mosquito net he saw that it was empty. He rolled out of bed, fumbled for his glasses, and hurried to the door, where he collided head-on with Jade, just returned from the forest with a basket of freshly picked amaranth leaves, who had heard him stirring inside the lodge and was on her way in to wish him good morning.

—Aren't *you* in a hurry! Got someplace you need to be?

—Uh, yes, actually, Lu Beiping stammered, circling the room in search of his undershirt. I can't believe it, I forgot all about the cattle! I've got to get back down to my hut right now.

—What's the rush? Wait till Kingfisher and Stump are done sawing, then we'll all eat breakfast together. On hot summer days like these they try to get in as much work as they can in the morning cool, before the sun climbs high. We've got plenty of leftover veggies, we got so carried away with the meat and beer last night that we barely ate any of them!

In this eager rush of solicitous patter Lu Beiping sensed a slight awkwardness on Jade's part. Well, he thought with an inward chuckle, this was, after all, his first day as a "man of the house."

—How about Autumn? Where's he?

—Gone tree-scouting. These days they split up the work, Autumn finds the timber, Stump and Kingfish fell it and hew it.

Jade gave Lu Beiping a sharp look.

—Care to talk with me for just a minute? You look like you're about to bust a nerve, you're so eager to get out of here.

—I can't stay. I've got to let the cattle out. It's late.

He found his undershirt, put it on, and strode out the door. Jade hurried after him.

—Come back for supper tonight!

—I can't!

Without looking back Lu Beiping walked briskly across the pebble beach that bordered the string of pools. Kingfisher, perched on the woodcutting frame beneath the lychee tree, yelled something at him, but he was too far away to hear clearly. Lu Beiping acknowledged him with a wave and waded into the creek. As he entered the shady tunnel of branches he heard Jade, standing on the bank, call out teasingly:

—Four Eyes, you homesick for dole food? Eat with us from now on!

It was cool in the tunnel. The lingering after-odor of meat and yam beer was now replaced by the familiar morning smell of the jungle, that odd, fishy smell that reminded him of semen. If you sniffed hard enough at this time of day you could detect even the body odors of long-dead dinosaurs—but no matter how hard he tried to refocus his attention, that semeny odor remained strong in his nostrils, a mocking reminder of recent developments. Crazy, he thought. Jade's cooking has gone to my head. Laughing to himself, he reflected that those two pounds of half-turned pork had become his passport into the hidden nation of the hollow-dwellers. From now on, he suspected, he would be doing a lot more dining "off the registers."

The thought made him smile, but at the same time it set off a deep current of melancholy within him.

The water was chilly. In the rush to leave his hut last night he'd forgotten to put on his boots and had hiked up to the hollow wearing only his "commando" sandals. He fancied himself a fairly rugged forester by now, but he'd never gotten used to walking barefoot in the jungle. The creek was shallow but icy cold, and after wading a short distance his feet began to go numb. It was with good reason that the grove hands had warned him against "jungle chills." *Drink more yam-mings*, Kingfisher had said to him last night as he pushed another cup of yam beer on him: *Liquor's hot-natured. I can tell you've got a heavy shadow lying over you. You ought to drink more, son.* Suddenly it struck Lu Beiping that he hadn't vomited last night; he should have, after all that meat and beer. Maybe Jade and Kingfisher's "light air" had driven off the shadows, kept him from getting sick. He laughed again. As he turned these things over in his mind, he kept returning to the same image: Jade curled in his arms, like a sleeping wildcat. What a thought! A four-eyed city boy, embracing a leopard-woman. Was a leopard a creature of shadow? he wondered. Surely it was. He pictured himself striding through the jungle with a were-leopard at his side, a herd of cattle at his back, a ghost husband commanding a host of horned demons. Ha! The Devil himself would give him a wide berth.

Oh, what a bunch of nonsense. A few months in the jungle and his brain was already full to bursting with light air and shadow air, haunts and weirds. What if—the thought occurred to him suddenly—what if the spirit world were a place anyone could visit, if one went far enough? In a way, Han's ghost *was* leading him into another world. He shuddered. Han, it always came back to Han: vexing, omnipresent, impalpable Han. By now, just thinking about her made him queasy. The clearer her face grew in his imagination, the more he saw through it to something sinister lurking behind, like looking too long at a piece of carrion and noticing maggots crawling beneath the skin. No, he wouldn't reach out and touch that rotting flesh; he'd do his best to steer clear of it, though it might be too late. For it now seemed that Han dogged his every step, that her spirit had seeped through every inch of his being. There was no way to be alone any more. He remembered yesterday's encounter in the abandoned grove, thought of the Gaffer, the "balegrass," the unmarked grave . . . No, it didn't bear thinking on.

Then, as he stared off into the light that spangled the water's surface where the creek curved away into the trees, another thought occurred to him. Hadn't Han, his imaginary "ghost wife," brought him a real woman, Jade, summoned her out of the hazy otherworld of the jungle? From Han to Jade, from fiction to fact, from haunted rubber grove to palm-shaded creek bank: Hadn't one led naturally to the other? God, enough of these bizarre fantasies. Shaking his head, he brushed aside a fat fern that trailed over the creek and saw, on the steep slope opposite him, a swath of myrtle flowers flaming orange in the mist. In autumn those myrtle bushes, whose flowers the locals called "maidengolds," bore clusters of purplish-black berries whose mouthpuckering sweetness was like sunlight on the tongue, and whose juices left one's lips purple for hours afterward. Maidengolds liked to grow on sun-facing slopes; maybe they, like liquor, were "hot-natured." Damn it! Here he was, spinning Kingfisheresque sophistries again. He gave a loud, macabre laugh, and as his laughter echoed in the valley the orange flowers in the shadowy undergrowth winked at him through the mist.

At that, his melancholy finally began to lift.

As he emerged into the sunlight, Lu Beiping noticed with a start that there was a human figure standing high above him on the slope. He squinted through the mist and saw that it was Autumn. He must have heard me laugh just now, Lu Beiping thought. From down here Autumn's thin silhouette looked like a scrap of black cloth caught on the crown of the bluff. As Autumn picked his way downward through the bushes, Lu Beiping noticed that he had a short-handled machete hanging at his side. Autumn, who had seen Lu Beiping first, raised a hand in greeting, then turned and scrabbled backward down the slope on his hands and knees. When he reached the bottom, he bounded up onto a low overhang, leapt clean over the water, and landed on the opposite bank, where he swayed for a second, windmilling his arms, before succumbing to his own momentum and toppling head first into the grass.

Lu Beiping rushed up the slope to give him a hand, but Autumn was already on his feet, striding toward Lu Beiping with a grin on his face. He was wet from head to toe, like he'd just been dragged out of a lake. Dewdrops glistened on his bare upper body, and his roughspun shorts were soaked.

—Wow, Lu Beiping said, unable to hide his admiration: You're a real acrobat!

—Can't not be, Autumn said, wiping sweat from his brow: Living the way we do. And today I've got twice the usual vim, thanks to your meat.

—My meat? Lu Beiping asked with a chuckle. What was so magical about my meat? You all made it out to be some kind of gift from the gods.

—It sure was! Didn't you see Kingfisher?

Autumn clasped his hands and aped Kingfisher's bow and his muttered prayer. Then he straightened quickly and said in a serious voice:

—No, I shouldn't. Kingfisher always says, honor the spirits, but don't get too friendly with them.

Lu Beiping noticed that Autumn's manner became more lively whenever they were alone together. Up in the hollow he always wore an absent expression; or maybe his dark features were just hard to read. Now his face, which was quite well-proportioned, had a sunny, open aspect.

—Is meat really that hard to come by up here? Lu Beiping asked. I see wild pigs and rabbit deer running all over the place. Don't you have a gun?

—We can't do that. If we want meat, we have to buy it at the Whitesands market when we haul our lumber down to the purchasing station. But it's a long way, and half the time the meat goes bad on the road.

Autumn licked his lips as if still savoring last night's meal.

—Kingfisher says, Tam-chow hill men can chase hogs and shoot deer all they want. But not us. We're outsiders. Felling trees is enough hurt on the land. If we killed too, that'd bring ruin on us.

—Good god, how'd you end up with all these rules?

—Never mind that. Listen, friend—Autumn changed the subject, pointing excitedly at the mountain ridge that loomed over them—when Kingfisher gets word of this, he'll drink a dozen cups to celebrate! On the far side of that slope, there are mountain valleys that nobody around here dares set foot in. They're steep and viney and swampy, and folks say they're haunted too, full of spooks and treeweirds. These past few days I finally got up the nerve to explore them, and you'll not believe the kind of timber I found. Red lauan, silkwood, pearlwood, flowering pear . . . and other queer trees I don't even know the names of!

—Really? And you didn't run into any . . . spooks?

Lu Beiping smiled wryly, remembering the eerie thoughts he'd entertained just a moment before while wading down the creek.

—No spooks, but plenty of snakes. I've never seen so many snakes in one place! And plants that make your skin itch, lacquer bushes and blood kudzu and such. But look—he pointed at his wooden bracelet and the sopping-wet cloth tied around his waist—I've got my snakes-bane bracelet, soaked my waistcloth in sulfur water, even smeared my skin with orpiment wine. Kingfisher taught me all this. Whenever I go upmountain I bring a flask of hillflower wine infused with orpiment, to rub on my skin. Snakes don't like orpiment, and the liquor keeps your skin from itching. Here, can you smell it?

Autumn leaned toward Lu Beiping. Sure enough, a faint, alcoholic fragrance wafted off of his skin. Lu Beiping wrinkled his nose and laughed.

—Is that good against shadow air too? You said Kingfisher thinks you've got the shadow of death on you or something . . .

Autumn's face darkened.

—There you go again, breaking laws. Careful, you don't want to cross yourself.

—Oh, give me a break! How many laws do you people have? See you later, Autumn, I've got to let the cattle out. They've been waiting for me all night.

Autumn looked at him in surprise, his face hardening into a stiff mask of disappointment. Clearly Autumn had wanted to keep talking. The clear morning air was a fine stimulant for conversation, but the mention of sins and laws had instantly drained Lu Beiping's enthusiasm. As he walked away Lu Beiping felt crestfallen, regretting that he'd spoken so rashly and secretly hoping that Autumn would find some new topic to break the silence, bridge the reopened gulf between them. He'd had so much on his mind lately that he really did need someone to talk to.

But Autumn said nothing. There was no second chance, no bridge. Once more his face had the same look of unmitigated gloom that Lu Beiping was used to seeing him wear up in the hollow.

After walking a short distance Lu Beiping looked back and saw Autumn still standing at the edge of the creek, gazing up at the ridge. Lu Beiping waved but got no response. Weighed down with a fresh load of melancholy, Lu Beiping turned and jogged onward up the slope.

Soon he heard the faint lows of the cattle emanating from the far side of the hill. When he reached the top of the rise he turned and looked back again. Autumn was now wading into the creek, his paper-thin silhouette infusing the whole scene with an air of coldness and desolation. Strange man, Lu Beiping thought. Strange people. He could almost reach out and touch Autumn's brittle, injured pride hanging palpably in the air over the valley.

—Oy, Four Eyes! You don't wit what this is? This is some grave business, I'll warrant.

That evening, as he counted the cattle, Lu Beiping noticed that the reek of manure in the corral had grown unbearably strong. He concluded that it was time for a corral cleaning, and wondered whether he should go down to camp and tell them now. The grove maintenance crews were responsible for cleaning the corral, and when the time came they'd send up a team of men to shovel out the manure-caked straw and haul it down to the groves to spread as fertilizer. But at the moment Lu Beiping had no desire to be seen at camp, or to behold the foreman's blunt, ugly countenance. Just as he'd begun debating this question Lu Beiping looked up and saw another set of blunt, ugly features hanging in the doorway, just below the lintel.

It was Stump. His broad cheeks gleamed with sweat as he stood stooped in the doorway, looking like some kind of primeval ape-man. In one hand he held a charred wooden board. Lu Beiping listened as Stump, panting, recounted a story whose gist became clear only slowly as Lu Beiping's ear grew accustomed to Stump's thick accent. Jade had sent him. Two days ago, Stump said, he'd followed Mudclaw Creek down this side of the mountain in hopes of scouting out a new path by which to ship their timber to market. Not far from Lu Beiping's hut, he'd seen a strange sight. A shifty-looking young man had been standing on a stony beach by the creek, burning a bundle of paper notes. After he finished burning the notes he'd stuck this wooden board straight up in the stones and set fire to it too. Hearing Stump sloshing down the creek toward him, the man had looked around wildly and then hightailed it into the trees.

—What did he look like? Lu Beiping asked.

—He weren't tall. Wore a soldier's hat, soldier's shoes.

Soldier's hat and shoes? Lu Beiping's stomach lurched. Home-made, guano-green military caps and canvas army shoes were the latest fashion among the re-eds. Lu Beiping inspected the board. Half of it had been burnt away, and on the badly singed remaining half he saw something scrawled in ink, though he couldn't make out the characters. A premonition budded in his brain, but he furrowed his brow and, shaking his head, said:

—Nope, I've never seen this thing. I have no idea who it was.

Stump had taken the board back up to the hollow, and Kingfisher, after brooding on the matter for two days, had finally decided to invite Lu Beiping for supper in order to get his opinion on it. That was the original reason for Jade's visit yesterday. But when the meat appeared, all was forgotten. As Lu Beiping was leaving the hollow that morning, Kingfisher had remembered this pressing matter and yelled to him as he waded into the creek, but Lu Beiping hadn't heard. Then, as evening drew near, Jade had prevailed upon Stump to trek down to Lu Beiping's hut and urge him to join them again for supper. Stump mustn't take no for answer, Jade said. If Lu Beiping didn't come, Kingfisher might get suspicious.

—What Jade told you in confidence I don't wit, the huge man said hesitantly as he stooped to negotiate the vines that hung in the entrance to the creek-tunnel: But she bade me tell you, when you're with Kingfisher, be mindful what you say.

Lu Beiping waded up the creek in silence. If secrecy was so important, why had Jade entrusted this message to Stump? His heart started beating faster. Off in the trees, some nameless jungle bird repeated an insistent, two-note song.

—Where are you from, Stump? Lu Beiping said finally, when the silence had begun to grow oppressive.

—Old Hill.

—Old Hill? Which Old Hill?

—Oy, you don't wit Old Hill? Home and hearth of the Kings of the South, where their bones lie buried. Famous men've been there. Han Feizi, Justice Bao too.

—What? Lu Beiping said reflexively. Han Feizi? Can't be. You mean Han Yu. He was exiled to the South during the Tang Dynasty. Han Feizi was from way back in ancient times.

—I mean Han Xin, Han Xin of the Song, same as Han Feizi, no?

Lu Beiping grimaced and changed the subject.

—So . . . you and Kingfisher aren't from the same part of the province, right? When'd you leave home?

—Year of the frog, month of the dog. Been earning underground coin a long time now, couldn't keep my belly greased doing dole work. Nay thing in the supper bowls but northwest wind. I'm a strong man, I'd fain use my arms but there was nay work to do. So I hied me down to the river, started helping folk haul sand. Magistrates call that capitalism, I say, do I look like a capitalist? But they were keen to struggle me down, same as they struggled the gentry.

A vein stood out on Stump's thick neck. He blew his nose into his hand and flung the snot in the water.

—Let's not speak of this.

The rest of the way to the hollow there was no sound but the sloshing of their footsteps.

Much to Lu Beiping's surprise, the atmosphere was as cheerful as before. The whole clan had gathered around the low dinner table, ready to dig in, eager for Stump and Lu Beiping to arrive. As usual Jade reigned over the rowdy scene; here was the "den mother" in her natural element. Last night she had pulled a devious trick and skimmed off a few scraps of pork before serving the stew, and now the vegetable dishes that crowded the table wafted savory reminders of yesterday's feast. Where there's meat there's godliness, Autumn would later say to him; this was a hallowed truth among the driftfolk. When Lu Beiping came into the lodge Smudge was squatting at the foot of the bed, tooting randomly on his harmonica to the squealing delight of the little ones, while Kingfisher sat at the table fingering his own bald pate and needling Jade with salacious remarks. When Lu Beiping entered, Kingfisher's eyes brightened immediately, and he greeted the young man with a playful leap of the eyebrows and an audible tap on his own skull. Only Autumn seemed indifferent to his arrival, and acknowledged Lu Beiping with the slightest of nods before returning his attention to his sooty bamboo water pipe.

Stump tossed the burnt board aside before walking into the lodge. As he reached for a supper bowl Kingfisher—not Jade, Lu Beiping noted with mild surprise—barked at him to go wash his hands.

—Stump! he said. Don't you dare come in here after touching that filthy thing. Four Eyes, you go wash your hands too.

Jade caught Lu Beiping's eye, as if to say, This time you had better do as he says.

Laughing inwardly, Lu Beiping followed Stump outside and knelt to wash his hands in the pool. Such was his fate; he was now a hollow-dweller in his own right, and must bow before Kingfisher's authority.

When he went back into the lodge Kingfisher immediately asked about the board. Lu Beiping, remembering the veiled admonition that Jade had conveyed to him via Stump, denied all knowledge of it.

—So . . . Kingfisher said slowly, gazing up at the ceiling with his shoulders hunched, the whites of his upturned eyes looking unnaturally large: You really have no idea who it was, eh, Four Eyes? This is a queer matter, for sure. What could that young man in army clothes have done that'd send him running into the jungle to burn paper money? And why'd he burn that board too?

—I told you, Jade cut in from over by the hearth stove: It must have been one of the Tam-chow tribesfolk setting a fire to flush wild hogs. It's not worth sweating about, Kingfish.

—Then why'd he turn tail and run when he heard Stump coming? Doesn't sound like a hill man to me.

—I bet he thought Stump was me, Lu Beiping said quickly. All the hill folk on this side of the mountain know me by sight. Not long ago I almost lost my foot in one of their hog traps, and afterward I had it out with them and told them never to hunt hogs in my area again.

Kingfisher stared at him for several seconds, as if weighing his words, then said:

—Maybe what you say is true. But the whole business still strikes me as a mite shadowy. Mark my words, Four Eyes: We can rile ruffians and tribesfolk all we want, but we can't afford to make enemies with the spirits. Eat, lad, eat.

With the matter temporarily closed, joviality reigned over the dinner table once more. Jade yakked and guffawed, spinning the conversation in circles around her. Autumn fed himself silently, heedless of the others, while Stump, as usual, ate like it might be his last meal. Smudge slurped amaranth soup as noisily as possible, kicking Lu Beiping from time to time beneath the table. Once Jade leaned over, a devilish grin on her face, and deposited a big chunk of pork in Lu Beiping's bowl, then returned her attentions to her own bowl of soup, throwing Lu Beiping a honeyed glance over the rim. Lu Beiping noticed that before Kingfisher lifted his chopsticks, he once again turned toward the shrine in the alcove by the door and murmured a quiet prayer.

These folks, Lu Beiping thought, are the most uninhibited, yet at the same time the most cautious, people I've ever met.

There was a brief rain shower after dinner, then night fell, and it was time to extinguish the lamps. Smudge and the two little ones pestered Lu Beiping to play the harmonica, but by the end of the second song all three had plopped wearily onto the bed and drifted off to sleep, their small bodies curled together like cooked shrimp in a pot. During dinner Kingfisher had announced that he'd pulled a muscle sawing, and afterward Jade went with him into the big lodge to firecup his back. Lu Beiping heard Stump call out mockingly: Strained your back, eh, Kingfish? Careful not to strain your pecker too! Lu Beiping wondered whether this was one of the usual stratagems by which the three men managed to share one woman. By the precedent he himself had set, he ought to have left right after dinner so that he could be in his own hut by nightfall, but Smudge had nagged him relentlessly, and after a pointed glance from Jade he decided not to press the issue. He was already eating "off the registers"; he might as well sleep there too.

He straightened out the jumbled bodies of the children so that there was enough room for him in the bed, pulled down the mosquito net, dimmed the lamp, then took a bamboo dipper to the pool behind the lodge in order to wash his face.

A dash of rain turns July into November, one of the handbooks they'd been issued before departing for Hainan had advised. It was true—nothing dispelled the summer fug better than a light rainfall in the evening. The water splashing over Lu Beiping's skin was a delicious sensation in the cool night air. As he stood by the pool's edge, stretching his back and humming to himself, he heard a sudden movement behind him and tensed. Before he could turn to look a pair of soft arms had circled his waist.

It was Jade, of course.

—Selfish boy, she said, her voice purring like a gentle breeze over his ear: Enjoying yourself out here without a thought to anyone else.

—Selfish? Lu Beiping said, looking at the wrists crossed over his navel. He glanced back at her, laid one hand lightly on her forearm. You think I'm being selfish, Jade?

—Yes, Jade said. You've been avoiding me.

—Really? He laid his other hand on her other arm, then said hesitantly: Uh, Jade, weren't you going to . . . massage Kingfisher's back, or something?

—Is this bothering you? she asked, squeezing his waist and chuckling. You know, it was Kingfish who sent me here to keep you company. He said that that meat supper made his back feel better!

—*Kingfisher* sent you? Lu Beiping asked in amazement. Surely *that* must be against your laws.

—Against our laws? Jade's voice betrayed her own surprise as well. I wanted to make good with you, and Kingfisher and the others agreed. Kingfish always says: What's law in the valley isn't law on the mountain. Living and loving, bearing and sowing, none of that's against our laws. Death is the only crime, the only sin. Life is light; death is shadow. Only through sowing life can we make the light grow, push back the mountain's shadows. That's what Kingfisher says. You get me, Four Eyes?

—Not at all, Lu Beiping said, thinking: These people sure have some strange laws.

—You really don't get me? We're all in this together, Four Eyes. Man and woman, scraping by whatever way we can. What's wrong with that? Love is no sin—only killing, lying, wasting is sin. So Kingfisher says. You still don't get me?

—Nope, said Lu Beiping, laughing. So . . . we're all in this together, you say? Does that include me?

—Stop playing the idiot, Jade said, slapping his lips playfully. Then she laid her cheek on his shoulder and began running her hands over his body, caressing his chest, his sides, his stomach, and on down.

—Don't, Lu Beiping whispered, grabbing her wrists: We'll wake up the little ones, and they'll see.

Jade laughed.

—So what? We've got no secrets around here. You can't hide from the sun. What's a mother to care if her child sees the flesh he's born of?

—Can't hide from the sun? What's that supposed to mean?

By this point Lu Beiping was already rather aroused, and was just making pointless patter.

—What do you think it means, stupid? she said, pinching him on the side. The sun sees everything. You, me, the pups. Every little bit of us. What's to be ashamed of? Me and the men, when we sleep together we never hide it from the little ones. Once Kingfisher caught Smudge spying on us and gave him a good licking, said: You can watch the grown-ups in bed all you want, but spying—*that* isn't allowed!

Another lesson in Kingfisherist philosophy, Lu Beiping thought. Another dose of mumbo-jumbo. Jade slipped her hands into his shorts and discovered his present state of excitement.

—Mercy me! I've found your horn, Bull Devil.

—My horn? Am I your Horn, Jade?

Jade laughed.

—Sure. Just for tonight.

Lu Beiping closed his eyes, breathing heavily. Then he turned and, straining with all his might, hoisted Jade off her feet and heaved her into the pool.

—Take that! You can't hide from the moon, Jade!

Lu Beiping took off his shorts and tossed them into the water, then, as Jade shed her thin cotton blouse, waded in toward the silver silhouette swimming on the pool's moonlit surface.

—Ha! You're stronger than I thought! Jade called out, laughing.

Chapter 7
The Flood

Lu Beiping pulled the burnt board out of the tall grass and flung it at the Gaffer's feet. The old man hopped back with a yelp of dismay.

—Ruin and balefire! Where'd you find this accursed thing? the Gaffer hissed, probing Lu Beiping with his perennially bloodshot eyes.

Lu Beiping chewed his lip and said nothing.

—You know what this is? This is Han's grave marker! What used to mark her grave over in that weedy patch! The Gaffer gestured in the direction of the waste clearing at the edge of the rubber grove, then spluttered a voluminous stream of questions: How'd you get your hands on that? Why's it all burnt up? Bless me, boy, were they telling the truth when they said you're kin to shadow? I'll bet your dead sweetheart showed up in a dream and told you where—Fah! Get! Go on!

The Gaffer swatted away a pair of cows that had moseyed over to show their affection, then laughed at Lu Beiping.

—Friend Lu, seems you and our foreman's daughter were tight as cane twine a few lives back.

Lu Beiping, having heard what he'd come to hear, turned and walked away without saying a word. The Gaffer followed close behind, spewing *Friend Lu*s, but Lu Beiping ignored him and hollered to Alyosha. He was eager to be gone from this blighted place.

—*Leeleelooloowaaaaaaaaaaaaaaaaaah!*

The Gaffer, loitering undeterred in the trees behind Lu Beiping, let out one of his ululating swine calls, and the herd rumbled to a halt like a bulldozer with a broken starter. Lu Beiping stood there fuming as the cattle appealed to him with bewildered lows.

159

—Looks like you could still learn a few tricks from an old codger like me, the Gaffer said, sidling over to Lu Beiping, dangling the board at arm's length between thumb and forefinger. And don't forget this, young master Lu! You can leave me behind, but you can't leave your own wife's grave-marker!

He dropped the board at Lu Beiping's feet. Lu Beiping stared at it expressionlessly.

—Shut your foul mouth, Gaffer.

—You think my mouth's any cleaner than that bale-crossed thing? the Gaffer said, peering sidelong at Lu Beiping as he continued to needle him: You think you can toss me aside like an old yam chip? Wring the juices out of me and then just chuck me in the ditch? Mercy me! After all the hard knocks I've been through, I'm not going to let you spill a bucketful of your own bad air on my head and then just walk away.

The Gaffer glared up at Lu Beiping, his arms folded, his leathery chin jutting out defiantly. Lu Beiping stared back at him, wiped a drop of the Gaffer's spittle off of his cheek. Then he told the old cowherd the story of the board, how a young man wearing an army cap and fatigues had burnt it and left it by the creek near his hut. He left out the part about Stump.

—So, Lu Beiping said, Who do you think that guy was?

—It was Wing, the old man replied without hesitation.

Lu Beiping's chest went hollow. It was just as he suspected. Guano-green fatigues were Wing's signature outfit; he was never seen in public wearing anything else.

—Pardon me for being frank, the Gaffer said with a broad smile that revealed a row of smoke-blackened teeth: But this is all plain as day to me. You married his sister, of course he's going to burn you her grave marker, that's the sign over her door. That way your souls can find each other. She won't stand in his way anymore now. You set him free!

Lu Beiping looked back and forth between the feverishly gesticulating Gaffer and the burnt board lying at his feet. He chuckled drily. Then, without warning, he erupted into a fit of crazed laughter.

—Ha! *I* set him free?

He spat on the board, kicked it, jumped on it, trampled it, all the while laughing wildly and cursing at the top of his lungs:

—Wing! You motherfucker! Fuck your mother's goddam fucking *cunt!*

The Gaffer, frightened by this irrational outburst, grabbed Lu Beiping's arm and threw an anxious glance in the direction of camp.

—Lu! Shhh! Quit it! Has a devil got into you? Quiet down!

Lu Beiping slumped down at the foot of a rubber tree and stared blankly at the burnt grave marker, cradling his forehead in his hands. He wondered in what previous life he'd had the misfortune to get tangled up in this filthy, unfathomable affair. The more he resigned himself to whole thing, the more he tried to keep Han at a healthy mental distance, the tighter she clung to him, like a glop of day-old, congealed rubbermilk.

The trees gazed down at him with their wizened old faces, weeping tears of latex from their lumpy knife scars. The cicadas abraded his ears. Once more he smelled the foul odor of human influence, the combined reek of sweat, old rubbermilk, and manure that always pervaded the rubber groves. The Gaffer leaned down to inspect the grave marker, jabbing a finger at the near-illegible characters as he read off laboriously the words written on the charred oaken tablet: *Our . . . beloved . . . daughter . . .* Then, lowering his tarry teeth to Lu Beiping's ear, he whispered:

—That's the foreman's handwriting. I'll bet this goes deep, my friend.

—What? Lu Beiping said quickly, looking up at him. What did you say?

—Nothing! the Gaffer said, stiffening and waving a hand in denial. I don't know a thing!

Lu Beiping stared at him.

—Gaffer, *I'm* not a dry old yam chip either.

—Don't ask me, boy! Ask Choi.

—Choi? This is Choi's grove we're in right now, isn't it?

No sooner had this question escaped his lips than a crackling flurry of footsteps through the underbrush stole the breath from both his and the Gaffer's lungs. Turning to look, they saw a familiar female figure hustling off down one of the orchard lanes, latex bucket in hand, her rubber boots squawking loudly as she fled. Choi—who was, indeed, responsible for tapping this grove—had heard them talking, crept over, hidden behind a rubber tree, and listened in on most of their conversation.

—Well! the Gaffer cried, If it isn't Choi, the light of my eyes! Affecting the mincing croon of a singshow actor, he sang out after her: *Halt, fair princess! Why—hie—you—hence? Won't you honor this pooooor, pooooor wretch with a glance?*

Lu Beiping scrambled to his feet and hurried after Choi.

—Choi! Wait! Stop!

Without looking back Choi quickened her pace, crackling and squawking through the underbrush as fast as her clumsy rubber boots and heavy pail would permit her.

Lu Beiping stopped, fell into his grade-school relay-runner's crouch, then bounded forward at a full sprint, catching up with her in a matter of seconds. Choi whirled around to face him, panting, her large breasts heaving visibly beneath her latex-spattered, sweat-darkened work suit. Her face, which like many rubber tappers' was unusually pale from working a mostly nocturnal schedule, was now even paler from fright, and her lovely almond eyes spat flames at him.

—Lu Beiping, she yelled: If you take one more step, I'll pour this pail of rubbermilk over your head!

Lu Beiping halted, gasping for air.

—You . . . you were eavesdropping on our conversation! Just tell me—

—Go to hell! she shrieked. Don't corner me, city kitten! You—you—if you'd tasted half an ounce of salt in your life, you'd be terrified your children'll be born without assholes! You think that just because you've been ghost-married into the foreman's family, you can storm around like you own this place and hound me to death?

You shit-licking pissant! You miserable little kinkiller! I hope you die bleeding in the dirt!

Choi turned and walked away, cursing and huffing, her pail thumping at her side. Lu Beiping stood staring after her, thunderstruck.

. . . honor this pooooor, pooooor wretch with a glance! Behind him the Gaffer's voice echoed mockingly in the trees.

The stench of the corral battered the clouds, crushing Mudkettle Mountain beneath its stomach-turning weight. The creek gurgled fetidly, like a case of the runs; the birds darted pell-mell, driven from their nests by the manure's ammoniac reek; even the buzzing of the cicadas had lost its usual insolent tone, and now sounded like the hoarse weeping of a princess fallen from favor. Fat, mildew-spotted rainclouds jostled in the sky, plugging the valleys like big clay jugs, within which the odor of cowshit bubbled and stewed, thick, choking, and unbearable. Only the cattle seemed lighthearted today, lowing amiably as they nibbled grass down by the creek, pleased, no doubt, that the humans had finally taken it upon themselves to clean their filthy abode.

The day before, Lu Beiping had ventured into camp to summon the maintenance crew to haul out the manure. Today he'd been awoken from an early afternoon nap by a hubbub of voices on the hill above the banana grove where he'd been sleeping, and rushing up the slope he discovered to his shock that the foreman himself was leading the team. This was the first time during his tenure as cowherd that he'd encountered his "father-in-law" here in the jungle. The foreman, a giant by Southern standards, seemed to tower over Lu Beiping's hut as he stood joking loudly with one of the hands, his presence lending the whole scene an oppressive air. Among the milling bodies Lu Beiping immediately picked out his new brother by ghost marriage, the honorable princeling Wing, his jaunty green cap cocked conspicuously on his head. And sashaying along in the crowd behind him Lu Beiping saw, to his even greater surprise, his former girlfriend, Fong.

What were all these people doing here? Lu Beiping had assumed that everybody was off on "campaign," burning down rainforest in a neighboring county. Why had they all appeared at once on his home turf? Wing greeted him with a nod, then took off his hat and fanned himself with it while muttering about the heat. Fong sauntered out of the trees, a pair of empty wicker cargo baskets dangling from her shoulder yoke, and looked around with an impassive air, pretending not to notice Lu Beiping. A few of the hands hectored him good-naturedly. He glanced furtively toward the back of the crowd and saw the Gaffer perched atop one of the tongues of the oxcart, leering at him. This particular array of people, turning out en masse to clean his corral, seemed uncomfortably like a show of force.

The foreman swept his gaze around Lu Beiping's campsite, noting every detail. He even lifted the lid off of his frypan and peered inside, smiling.

—How've you been holding up, son? the foreman called over to him.

—Fine, Lu Beiping answered nonchalantly as he led a group of workers up the hill toward the corral. I'm getting used to it.

—Glad to hear it, the foreman said, falling in alongside him and cracking his big knuckles as he spoke. If you've got any problems or questions, report them immediately to the unit.

Fong, who seemed put out that he hadn't acknowledged her, jounced her yoke as she walked up the trail so that her empty baskets slithered audibly through the bushes. Lu Beiping laughed and whistled to himself, ignoring her.

—So, the foreman went on, trying to seem casual: Some weather we've had, eh? Been too hot in the mountains for the cattle? Seems you like to graze the animals a lot down in Sector 12.

Lu Beiping's heart skipped a beat. Sector 12—that was Choi's sector, the grove next to the waste clearing where Han lay buried. He saw that the foreman was underlining the real reason for his visit, and answered airily:

—Yep, it's been hot as the blazes up here. For some reason the cattle love to go down to that grove for their afternoon nap.

Lu Beiping glanced over at Wing. The boy looked away immediately. Obviously, he had something to hide.

On his visit to camp yesterday Lu Beiping had meant to seek out Wing and press him for details about the burnt board. But the place had been dead quiet, empty except for one lone worker snoozing in the latex-collection station. He'd even entertained the idea of knocking on Choi's door and demanding more information about the mysterious grove, but then he'd thought better of it, knowing that this would probably incite a tantrum that would draw unwanted attention to the matter. Now, seeing Wing so obviously flustered, Lu Beiping felt his curiosity flare once more, and he made a snap decision. Amid the uproar that ensued when the first group of workers waded into the mire, Lu Beiping kicked the burnt board out of the clump of weeds next to the corral gate where he'd tossed it yesterday upon returning from camp, and nudged it with his toe into the middle of the trail. Then he waited, eager to see how Wing would perform in the next act of this drama.

—Bless me, this is good, ripe manure! the foreman exclaimed, his eyes glowing as he raked aside the straw to reveal the black layer of fertilizer glittering beneath. Slipping back into his accustomed role, he began singing Lu Beiping's praises: Looks like I chose the right man for this job! You're no slacker, not like some folks I know—he threw a barbed glance in the direction of the Gaffer—who're always keen to cut corners. Look at these fine beds of straw you've laid. This is the best batch of fertilizer we've had in years!

Lu Beiping smiled. He knew that the foreman's compliments were sincere. Ever since he started on as cowherd he'd been particularly diligent about spreading fresh straw, mostly because he cared for the animals and wanted to keep their living quarters pleasant. Maintaining herds of cattle for the sake of their manure was a "high-yield strategy" employed by many of the region's rubber plantations, whose heavily tapped trees relied on frequent doses of fertilizer to recover from hard use and replenish their milk reserves. As a consequence, a plantation's "manure yield" was often invoked as an indicator of its overall productivity. It was no surprise, therefore, that the foreman was so vocal in his praise as he stirred the rich, dark manure.

—Aw, this place reeks! Fong complained, pinching her nose against the smell. What a stinking pile of shit you've left us with, Lu!

She laughed loudly, pleased with this sidelong insult, then, when no one else joined in, she fell silent and buried her nose in her handkerchief, hacking and muttering to herself. Lu Beiping, standing at the edge of the corral, chuckled.

—Hey, Fong! he called over to her. Don't forget what the Chairman said: Cowshit is the perfume of the class-conscious woman! I think you should use that line tonight when you make your self-critique to Sergeant Fook.

Fong spluttered and went red.

—Good for you, embracing revolutionary aesthetics! Lu Beiping pressed on remorselessly. Nobody can ever accuse you of harboring petty bourgeois sentiments!

—Hmph! Fong retorted, rolling her eyes: You ought to practice what you preach!

—Oh, really? said Lu Beiping, cocking his head. And what exactly do I practice?

Fong turned her shapely buttocks to him and flounced off toward the corral.

Lu Beiping pretended like he didn't give a damn, but the truth was, he still cared far too much.

—Listen to you two! the foreman chimed in, laughing from within the press of bodies now swarming into the corral: A woman warrior and a surly cowpoke, quarreling like an old married couple!

At that moment Wing, not to be outdone, plunged his hoe into the manure and began heaving with militant vigor, applying to his own skin and to the workers standing around him a liberal spattering of revolutionary makeup. Soon his arms and legs had acquired a thick coat of mossy green.

The air was heavy with the stench of manure. The crew labored in silence, their bloodshot eyes glittering pungently above the shirts and waistcloths they had tied as facemasks over their noses and mouths. Lu Beiping alone waded into the morass undaunted, stomping through the manure with no protection except his ignominious rubber boots, barking orders to his comrades as they evacuated his slimy bounty bucket by bucket. As they worked, the contents of the corral formed a mounting gray-green hillock in the Gaffer's oxcart.

The corral was a little over half empty when Lu Beiping heard a hoarse yell of surprise from over by the corral gate.

—Mother heaven! It's a curse! It's witched!

Lu Beiping smiled. The Gaffer had entered right on cue, and was playing his part admirably. The oxcart creaked back a few paces, then the old man hopped down, picked up the burnt grave marker, and held it up, crowing theatrically:

—Mercy, Lu! This baleful thing of yours was blocking the wheel of my cart!

The manure-hauling team halted, stupefied, amid the roiling stink. But before anyone could bat an eye the foreman was standing right in front of the Gaffer and upbraiding him in a voice an octave higher than usual.

—You, you, you . . . Kam! What the hell are you playing at?

The crowd craned their necks to watch, and a hush fell over the corral. The Gaffer tossed the "baleful thing" into the grass and, turning to Lu Beiping, cried out:

—You, Lu! What the hell are *you* playing at?

Lu Beiping stumped over in his manure-caked boots, picked up the board, examined it, and turned to the foreman.

—Sir, do you know what this is?

The foreman's face went pale. Lu Beiping, pressing the offensive, turned to Wing.

—Wing, do you have any idea what this thing is?

—I . . . Of course not!

Wing skipped back as if on scorched feet, waving his hands.

—That goddam thing is witched! the Gaffer burst out, stealing a glance at Lu Beiping. That trail was clear but a moment ago, then that filthy piece of wood popped out of nowhere, right in front of my cart, like a ghost put it there!

—What filthy piece of wood? What's going on? Fong asked innocently, squeezing to the front of the crowd.

—Enough of this bullshit! the foreman snapped. He grabbed the board from Lu Beiping and flung it into a nearby thicket, then exploded at the Gaffer: You, Kam, you lousy troublemaker! Quit playing tricks! After a good day's manure haul you go messing around and sabotaging revolutionary production! Don't you . . . don't you ever forget . . . don't you ever forget class struggle! Long live the Revolution! Long live Chairman Mao!

The Gaffer squawked in continuous protest over the foreman's shouts, so that nobody could tell exactly what the foreman was condemning. The last thing the onlookers heard was a string of *balefires!* and *mercy mes!* from the Gaffer as the old man stamped his feet and appealed to Lu Beiping for aid.

— . . . balefire! Mercy me, Lu, *you* know I don't have the slightest clue what that goddam thing is! Tell him, son! On my honor, I swear!

—Your honor? the foreman said with a scornful laugh. Kam, don't play me for a fool. You think I was born yesterday? You think I don't know what's under your pants? I know just how long your dick is and the color of your shit—as the foreman's invective took on a vulgar tint, the workers standing around them began to chuckle quietly—so don't be sly with me! I assign you to mind the cattle and you gripe the light out of the day, then I call you back and you do nothing but slink around meddling and pissmongering! For better or worse, I'm the captain of this unit! Are you trying to undermine my authority? You think I don't know what rotten juices you've got sloshing around in your bones? Listen, Gaffer, you'd better be careful what noises you make with that limp little tongue. There's not an ant or a cricket on this whole mountain that can cross me and get away with it!

It was clear to all who listened that this was a general warning, not intended for the Gaffer alone.

Lu Beiping stood to one side, expressionless, laughing inwardly. The angrier the foreman got, the more he smelled a rat. Obviously this tirade was meant, above all, as an admonition to him. Yet it only served to stoke his rebellious impulses. He hadn't expected a confrontation with the foreman so soon, and this was clearly a sign that he was hot on the trail. Of what, though? He wanted desperately to know.

In the midst of the foreman's outburst Lu Beiping had noticed Wing slip to the back of the crowd, where he lingered, throwing furtive glances at Lu Beiping through the gaps between the workers' bodies. Whenever Lu Beiping looked in his direction his gaze darted quickly away. Lu Beiping smiled grimly to himself. Whatever secret lay behind that burnt grave marker, Wing was the key, the breach, the chink in the foreman's armor. As he began spreading a new bed of straw for Maria in the corner of the corral, he decided upon a fresh course of action.

Turning his back on the Gaffer, who continued shrilling his agonized self-defense, the foreman bellowed to the assembled workers:

—What are you all standing around for? Come on, pick up those buckets, keep moving! Once the cart's full, everyone take a pail of fertilizer down to his own grove!

Before long the corral was clean. The stench that had saturated the forest thinned to a faint suggestion of pungency wafting among the evening mists. As the workers trooped noisily after the foreman down to the creek to wash themselves, Lu Beiping peeled off and doubled back to his hut, where he found Fong leaning against the doorframe, her hands resting on her hoe, eyeing him warily.

—Lu, can we talk for just a second?

—Sure. What's up?

—I know you must really hate me by now. And if so, I totally understand—

—Just tell me what's on your mind, Fong.

—Okay, Fong said, shifting her weight with a willowy bend at the hip that did not escape Lu Beiping's attention. Here's what's on my mind. I know you're sort of part of the foreman's family now. But really, Lu, you shouldn't poke your nose into their business.

—What business? Lu Beiping asked, furrowing his brow. What business of theirs am I poking my nose into?

—I don't know, she said slowly, gazing up at him. But . . . I know that they care. A lot.

—Care? About what?

—It's not my business! Think about it, Lu. I'm going now.

As the crowd surged back up the slope, Fong hooked her hoe through the handle of her manure pail, hoisted it over her shoulder, and walked away with laborious, swaying steps. Lu Beiping noticed that she'd abstained from washing like the others; below her rolled-up cuffs, her shapely calves were still spattered with manure. He laughed to himself, remembering that it was now the custom among the most "progressive" re-eds not to wash away the evidence of the day's labors, but to leave their bodies dirty in order to prove the purity of their thoughts. A good spattering of filth was a badge of merit, not to be disposed of lightly.

As the foreman shouldered his towering manure bucket and led the staggering troops away from the corral, Lu Beiping slipped into the trees on the pretext of rounding up his cattle. He wasn't interested in lingering among the departing hands and nattering polite good-byes. *Peeeeeeee-ter!* he yelled. *Al-yooooosha!* The empty forest thrummed with echoes. He could still hear the Gaffer's oxcart squeaking sullenly far off in the trees, as if giving voice to the old man's resentment, overlaid with the sonorous shouts of the foreman, who seemed launched into high spirits by the sight of the quivering, gray-green monument to his unit's productive capacity. Now, from far down the dusk-reddened trail Lu Beiping heard the foreman leading the workers in a chorus of Red Book songs: *We! Are—the—chil—dren! Of all—the lands—between—the seas! And—yet—our—will—is—oooooooone!*

But the afternoon's intrigues were not yet over.

(Years later, Lu Beiping would wonder aloud to Tsung whether those months spent alone in the jungle, in a life that managed to be grindingly monotonous at the same time that it was filled with strange adventures, had inflated his curiosity to dangerous proportions. At the time, he said, I was almost shocked by the intensity of my own desire to provoke. It makes me shudder just a bit to remember what came next.)

As the sun sank low and the column of workers wound its way down the valley, Lu Beiping herded the animals into the corral, grabbed his machete, and, scrambling over the creekside bluffs in a series of shortcuts well known to him, arrived in a matter of minutes at the second bend of the creek. As he sloshed up out of the shallows, Wing, who had arrived moments before with his manure pail, turned to look, and when he saw Lu Beiping his eyes goggled so wide they looked in danger of falling out.

—Hey there, Wing! Lu Beiping said. Isn't this a coincidence?

—What . . . what are you trying to do? Wing stammered, his eyes glued to Lu Beiping's machete. He had removed his hat reflexively and now held it clenched in one hand, as if he might somehow defend himself with it. Lu Beiping, trying hard to keep from laughing, took a deep breath and announced dramatically:

—Don't be scared, Wing. I know what you did.

—What are you talking about? Wing said in a defiant voice, retreating a few paces.

—That burnt piece of wood the Gaffer made such a scene about. That was your sister's grave marker, right? It was you who slunk up into the hills and burnt it by the creek next to my hut—right?

Lu Beiping stiffened the muscles in his cheeks to keep from laughing at the hilarious expression on Wing's face.

—And that jungle fire. It was you who set it, right? You were the one I saw mucking around near the pool during that fire that almost burned down Sector 12. Right? Tomorrow afternoon, Wing, one hour before sunset, I want you to be waiting right here at this spot. I've got a few more questions to ask you. Don't forget!

Lu Beiping spun on his heel and walked off into the forest. Soon his silhouette had melted into a nearby stand of banana trees. Wing, speechless from shock, stood rooted to the spot.

✺

The next day, in the early afternoon, the wind picked up. At first Lu Beiping didn't pay it any mind, assuming it to be the harbinger of a routine summer thundershower. Yesterday's corral cleaning had left the air heavy and rank, and he'd been hoping for a nice, big rainstorm to deliver him from the lingering stench. When he woke up he saw gray clouds massing in the sky, and rejoicing that they were in for a good dousing he immediately set about mustering the cattle so that they could get in some grazing before the hourlater hit. The animals, however, were sluggish and unresponsive, probably none too pleased to be roused from their freshly cleaned beds. He gave Alyosha a few whacks on the rump, was answered by a groan of protest from Maria. Maybe today, he thought, her time might finally arrive.

But no sooner had they forded the creek than the sky grew alarmingly dark, as if night had fallen prematurely. The cattle began lowing in fright. When Lu Beiping looked up he could barely make out the mountain through the fog, and now he heard, far off in the distance, a faint disturbance in the air, a low, muffled rumble. Then without any warning the rain came ripping down, pounding the hillside so hard that the ground seemed to tremble beneath his feet. With a panicked shout he tried to rally the cattle, hoping to get them home quickly, but they stood motionless, petrified by the sudden, stiff onslaught of wind. A moment later he could see and feel nothing but hard darts of rain as the downpour wrapped him in a howling hood. He crouched down reflexively, afraid to move; then before he knew what had hit him a powerful gust of wind had knocked him off balance and slammed him facedown into the dirt.

The animals crashed off in all directions. Two terrified bulls came close to trampling him as they veered off into the trees.

Good god! Nature had forgotten her manners. It was still summer, and typhoon season usually didn't arrive till autumn. And normally the approach of a typhoon would be signaled by a long prefatory period of drizzling rain. But this time there'd been no warning signs;

the sky had just opened up in a fit of unpremeditated wrath. There'd been no lightning, no thunder—a silent dog has the deadliest bite, the locals said, and surely a lightningless thunderstorm was a thing to be feared. Lu Beiping felt like the ground beneath his feet was being twisted and sucked upward by a giant suction cup. He struggled to his feet, bounded forward a few steps, then flattened himself against the ground so as not to be blown over again. He yelled for Alyosha, but the wind swallowed his voice. The cattle had disappeared. All he could see were dark boils of fog twisting and whipping toward him like Mudkettle Mountain's famous snakeclouds. Water slapped over him in solid chunks, and as the tempest rose to a fever pitch the entire mountain seemed in danger of being ripped free from the soil and yanked upward into the sky.

Where water goes, wind follows, he remembered—in the mountains, during a typhoon, the wind would writhe its way along the watercourses before blowing out into open land. He needed to get out of the creek valley fast, needed to find refuge from the wind. But his glasses were drenched and he couldn't see a thing. He took them off, only to find that the sky had turned black as midnight and the world around him had been reduced to a wavering haze. He had no way to get his bearings. The only thing he could hear besides the eerie wailing of the wind was the rapid thudding of his own heart. Gripping his machete in one hand, he unwound his sopping undershirt from his head and wriggled into it, for the raindrops, not to mention the windborne pellets of grit, were biting like knife points into his skin. He crawled forward on hands and knees, head turned away from the wind, seeing nothing, feeling like time had stopped and the entire universe had collapsed into a single, vast scream. He paused for a moment, panting, then, taking advantage of a brief lull in the wind, he scrambled to his feet and ran forward as fast as he could. There was no path. He was completely lost. Relying solely on intuition, he plunged onward through the brush in what he hoped was the right direction, until he staggered to a halt in front of a huge, dark rock that loomed abruptly out of the haze.

The rock moved. Lu Beiping almost fainted from fright. Then he got a grip on himself and, peering through the rain, saw that it was a cow—Maria! She lay slumped on the ground, her huge belly bulging. When she saw him her nostrils flared and she opened her mouth, but no sound came—the roar of the tempest had long ago superseded all sounds that any human or animal was capable of making.

—Maria! It's you! he cried, throwing his arms around her as if embracing a long-lost relative. Now, with his head up close to hers, he could hear her groaning faintly, and the thought flashed through his mind that she might be going into labor. He gave a shout of dismay and, panicking once more, saw through the drive of rain that they were sitting on an exposed windward slope. If the calf were born out here in this cold trough of rain, it would freeze to death in its first moments on earth. Just as this thought occurred to him the wind picked up again, ripping through the trees like a titan's saw.

—Come on! Lu Beiping shouted. We can't stay here! Maria, get up!

Wiping water from his face, Lu Beiping tugged on the rope that trailed from Maria's nose ring while hollering to her at the top of his lungs.

She struggled, swaying, to her feet, and as she did so the wooden clapper that hung around her neck gave a few hollow knocks. Then she collapsed again under the force of the wind. No! Lu Beiping cried. Move, Maria! Move! The wind subsided for a moment, and Lu Beiping yanked on the rope with all his might, shoving and tugging at the ponderous bulk of her body. She managed another few swaying steps, then toppled back into the dirt and began lowing in anguish, her shrill moans knifing through the howling curtain of rain.

Crap, Lu Beiping thought, it's about to happen. Her eyes were bloodshot, and the muscles of her belly were twitching. She really was about to give birth.

The *tock-tock-tock* of the wooden clapper resounded in the wind. This clapper was one of two improvised cowbells that he'd carved several weeks ago out of a chunk of solid heartwood, one for Alyosha, the lead bull, and the other for Maria, so that he could track her down if she wandered off into the forest alone. (When I made that clapper, Lu Beiping said to Tsung, I had no idea that it would save Maria's life—and the life of her calf—and mine!)

With Lu Beiping tugging at the rope and pushing the pregnant heifer, they inched forward together through the rain, tottering a few steps, resting, then tottering a few more. As they lurched through a grove of wild banana trees overshadowed by a high bluff, Maria's legs went limp and she crumpled into a pool of mud, where she lay and refused to move any farther. Just then Lu Beiping heard a loud ripping sound above him, and looking up he saw all the trees in the grove lose their tops to a single, scything gust of wind. For a moment whirling leaves and branches filled the air, then the foliage, reduced to confetti by the churning gale, scattered like a flock of birds. Seconds later, from the far side of the bluff, there came a series of wrenching cracks that sounded very much like a wooden structure being twisted off of its foundations.

He sprang to his feet. That was his hut! Sure enough, he'd built the hut and corral too close to the water; a channel for water was a channel for wind. But at least he knew where he was now—somehow, he couldn't guess how, he'd gotten turned around and headed in the opposite direction from the one in which he'd set out that morning. He thought he'd been following Mudclaw Creek out toward the valley bottom, but here he was, back on the slope near his hut, in the banana grove from which Smudge and Jade had watched him bathe, having crossed the creek without even realizing it. How the heck had that happened?

But before he had a chance to regain his senses, the howling of the wind was drowned out by the roar of water. He stiffened in panic. No—was that the sound of a flash flood? He glanced down at Mudclaw Creek through the headless trunks of the banana trees and saw that the stream, once a thin, clear rivulet, was now rushing in a wide, muddy torrent, the water racing in turbid swells around the roots of the trees. The water was already rising swiftly, advancing right up into the banana grove.

Now, finally, there came a deafening crash of thunder.

For a brief moment lightning illuminated his surroundings, and Lu Beiping looked around and assessed his position. Here beneath the bluff they were shielded from the full force of the wind, and it wasn't a bad spot for Maria to rest. She looked exhausted. After collapsing into the mud she'd just lain there quietly, her eyes closed, her nostrils flapping and foaming. Now, spooked by the boom of thunder, she raised her voice again in a shrill, urgent bellow.

Mopping water out of his eyes, Lu Beiping watched the rain slap down on Maria's twitching flank and felt like his heart had sprung a rent, cracked open, and fallen into a thousand pieces.

It was completely dark now. The wind still howled in his ears, but it had slackened a bit, and the rain had diminished to a steady drizzle. Now, from high up on the mountainside, he heard, faintly but distinctly, that strange, low-pitched, sepulchral wail, the sound of the Child Crying from Beyond the Grave, piercing the darkness for a split second. He pricked up his ears, but he heard nothing more. The sound was gone, like the fleeting glimmer of a marsh light: a trick of the brain, an aural hallucination.

His hands and feet were freezing. He shuddered involuntarily, yielding to a tremor that welled up from the depths of his soul. The wind had slapped him silly, and for a long time he'd been oblivious of the cold, numb to the passage of time and even to the fear of death, conscious of nothing but the storm's endless, pitch-black, silent roar, a primordial chaos where sight, touch, and hearing were all rendered irrelevant. Now the sky was somehow both darker and clearer; he wiped off his glasses, which he still held clenched in one hand, put them on, surveyed his surroundings, and, as his wits returned to him, felt the hair rise on the back of his neck. Yards away from him lay a massive boulder, fallen seemingly out of nowhere, riddled with cracks. If he had been lying just a little bit to the left, he'd now be a fine powder coating the bottom of that rock.

It was cold. Bone-chillingly, brain-numbingly cold. In the hills the temperature always dropped dramatically after sunset, and now, drenched, wind battered, and completely in the open, Lu Beiping felt like his clothes had turned into a carapace of ice, and a numb feeling was already seeping outward from the pit of his stomach. He thought of cuddling up to Maria for warmth, but when he touched her he found her hide cold as a snake's skin. He let his mouth fall open and permitted his teeth to chatter while his whole body convulsed from the cold.

What was he going to do about Maria? He didn't know the first thing about helping cattle give birth. *Animals are animals*, the Gaffer had said, *they squeeze out their young faster than you take a shit*. But it seemed like Maria had been twitching forever, and still there was no sign of the calf. And her cries were growing fainter, the foam around her nostrils growing thicker and thicker . . .

No sooner had that awful thought crossed his mind than another, even worse possibility transfixed him. Already the racing torrent had climbed halfway up the slope, and muddy water swirled around the trunks of banana trees standing not ten yards away from the foot of the bluff. He knew how quickly mountain streams rose during a typhoon; in no time at all, he and Maria would be submerged.

He sprang to his feet. Get up! he shouted at Maria. Get up, we've got to get out of here! He yelled at her, pushed, pulled, yanked on the rope, but Maria just tossed her head, summoning a few feeble *tock*s from the clapper, her body's huge bulk remaining still as a rock. As they struggled, the rain began pelting down again. Wide-eyed, Lu Beiping gazed down at the dark, glinting water that was steadily gobbling up their last few feet of earth. He wanted to run, but Maria, lying on the ground wracked by painful spasms, was unable to take even a single step.

Right at that moment she began lowing again, her anguished bellows growing shorter, higher pitched, more breathless. The clapper clacked loudly as she swung her head forcefully, seeming to strain inward with all her muscles. But she was exhausted; gradually her moans of pain, along with the knocks of the clapper, grew weak and irregular, then expired in darkness.

The water churned up the slope steadily, insatiably. He couldn't just lie here, waiting for death to claim him. But Maria . . . the thought of having to leave her made Lu Beiping sink into despair.

The awful fear that had consumed Lu Beiping during his first few nights in the jungle now seeped out of the darkness, paralyzing him once more. The end of life, the simple fact of death, lay before him, its features plain. The wind railed on in endless, pointless fury. The slope on which they sat was a sinking vessel, soon to slip down irrevocably beneath the waves. The bluff behind him offered no path of escape, not even a single, withered tree branch to which he could cling. The time to abandon ship had passed long ago.

The water kept rising. Pale, phosphorescent flashes trembled in the sky, briefly illuminating the dark contours of the hills. Really? he thought. Was he really going to sit patiently on this hillside and wait for the waters of death to close over him? All of a sudden the tune to the one of the Red Book songs, which he and the other re-ed boys used to belt out together half-ironically, sprang into his mind, and at the top of his lungs he shouted those Immortal Words into the darkness as if they were profanities: *I'll fight—to my—last BREATH! You'll nev—er see—me YIELD! Let the can—nons RING! Let the bul—lets SING! I'll MEET my DEATH on the BA—TTLE—FIELD!* He could barely hear his own voice over the keening wind, but singing helped drive away the chill and the fear, and he thought jokingly to himself: Damn, if I really am going to meet my death out here, I wish there were some fireworks, at least.

The sky above him erupted in light.

—Ha! he cried, scrambling to his feet as the thunder rolled over him. That's more like it! Waving his fist at the pitch-black sky, he jumped up and down, yelling: Come on! Let's have another! Do it again!

Again the sky lit up with a deafening boom.

—Yes, yes! he shouted, tearing his shirt off and waving it hysterically like a flag in the face of encroaching darkness: Is that all you've got? Come on, do one more, blow me to bits!

As if in answer to his challenge, a bone-shaking, ear-shattering, eye-searing explosion of thunder and lightning enveloped the entire valley. Light caromed off the mountains, and Lu Beiping danced in the afterglow, exulting and sobbing, teetering at the peak of ecstasy and despair. On all sides the thunder rolled away from him in waves, pulsing and reverberating, drumming in accompaniment.

(I believe, Lu Beiping said to Tsung years later: I believe, I really do, that when a human life is pushed to its limits, there is a critical threshold where light and shadow, the human world and the spirit world, meet, and we can converse with the divine. As sure as my name is Lu Beiping, I believe that.)

But then the thunder ended as abruptly as it began, plunging Lu Beiping once more into darkness and silence.

This truly was the silence that heralded death. The sound of the wind and rain receded far into the distance, and the wilderness became a dark void, engulfing him. In his wild raving he'd forgotten the world, forgotten even about Maria—had it not been for the knocking of the clapper, she'd have been nothing more than a lifeless black stone. Now, the world had forgotten him.

Emptied, exhausted, he slumped to the cold, wet earth.

After a span of time—he had no idea how long—he heard an odd noise layered in faintly with the wind and rain. What was this? Were his ears playing tricks on him again? Was this the music of the dead, drifting over the border from the land beyond? No. It was a real sound: soft, intermittent, prodding insistently at his hearing. Was it the sound of his lost cattle rustling through the undergrowth as they found their way back to their master? He had no idea what had become of the rest of the herd. Had Alyosha, Judas, Peter, and all the others been swept away by the flood?

Slosh . . . slosh . . . slosh . . . It was water. Someone was sloshing through the water. Now he barely made out, through the veil of rain, a figure half-wading, half-swimming through the swollen river, heading directly toward the spot where he and Maria lay.

Was it the foreman? During typhoon season the cattle's welfare was one of foreman's most pressing concerns. Suddenly he remembered his date with Wing, the showdown he'd planned, and now missed, with his stammering brother-in-law. Could it be Wing, maybe?

He gave another deep shudder. Through the slanting rain he discerned the faint firefly-glow of a lantern, winking in and out of sight, drawing steadily nearer.

—Four Eyes! . . . Four Eyes! . . .

A hoarse voice drifted up to him out of the darkness. Maria stirred at the sound, her clapper clacking with excitement. There was no mistaking it—that voice belonged to Jade.

He felt like he'd emerged from the darkness after death back into the sunlit world of the living.

Once more Lu Beiping rushed over to Jade and embraced her at the water's edge. He opened his mouth to cry but no sound came out, and silent tears streamed down his cheeks.

—Oh, Four Eyes, Jade said, laughing gently while wiping the tear-streaked mud from his face: Careful, you'll put the lantern out.

Jade held an old barn lantern, its flame guttering low. Wet hair spilled down one side of her face. She was soaked from head to toe, but her body was warm from exertion. She grinned, panting breathlessly.

—That was some storm. The thunder just about deafened me. Four Eyes, it's a good thing your cow was wearing that clapper, sometimes dumb wood's a sight smarter than a human being. If it wasn't for that knocking sound I don't think I'd ever have found you, and you might've been washed away by the flood.

The rain was still coming down. The wind picked up again briefly, and the piece of "dumb wood" hanging around Maria's neck gave a couple of faint *tocks*.

—Is everybody okay? Lu Beiping said when he finally regained his senses. How are Smudge and Kingfisher and the others?

—Doing fine. The hollow kept us safe. We lost a few trees, but the bluffs break the wind. Kingfisher was worried for you, said it was a lousy idea to build your hut so close to the water. Is it all gone? I didn't see a single log or roof beam on the way over here. I was afraid you'd gotten blown away with it!

As Jade spoke, gesturing animatedly, Maria asserted her presence with an agonized groan.

—Four Eyes, good heavens!

Before Lu Beiping could explain the situation, Jade's eyes alighted on Maria's belly and went wide with disbelief.

—She's pregnant, Jade gasped as she cast the light of her lantern over the dark mass of the cow's body. It's the middle of a typhoon and she's about to give birth! Why didn't you say something?

She reached out a hand to touch Maria's flank, then pulled it away reflexively.

—She's cold as death! You idiot! How's she ever going to give birth if it's this cold?

Lu Beiping opened his mouth to speak, but Jade cut him off again.

—Don't even think about it! We can't move her. She's dying, she's having trouble squeezing out her own flesh. She needs to stay here and rest.

—But, but . . . Lu Beiping stammered, and pointed to the racing water, which had already risen another two feet.

The rain had thinned to a drizzle. In the lantern's dim glow Jade's face was a mask of fury and indignation. Holding the lantern aloft, she cast its light first over the encroaching water, then over Maria, then up into the darkness above her—the flame wriggled like a glowworm against the sky's infinite blackness—then finally along the bluff that rose up behind them.

—Damn it! she exclaimed. Don't mind the water! Fire's what we need. Fire'll keep us alive!

Lu Beiping furrowed his brow, puzzled by this. Was this another of Kingfisher's weird superstitions?

Jade handed him the lantern, crouched down and ran her hands over Maria's squirming belly, then wiped the lather from her nostrils. Looking up at Lu Beiping, she said:

—There's still hope. Build a fire. She needs warmth. She needs her strength back so she can push out the calf.

—But . . . Lu Beiping protested, There's no time! Look at the water! See how fast it's rising? We've got to get out of here, quick!

—I told you, don't worry about the water! Jade snapped. Did you even hear me? We need a fire! She needs warmth, safety! Get that? You men don't have a clue.

—What the hell are you talking about? Lu Beiping burst out. The whole world's a soaking mess, and you want me to start a fire? Look at this—he thrust a finger upward at the sky, which was still steadily dripping water—everything's drenched! Where are we going to find dry wood? It'd take a magician to start a fire in this rain!

—I don't believe it, Jade said, her eyes flashing. Wait here.

Jade snatched the lantern and disappeared into the darkness. When the speck of light slipped behind the bluff, the night seemed to grow so cold and still that it might freeze around him. The rain had stopped, the hurrying eddies had slowed their pace; above him the dark forms of the mountains huddled together like a band of giants fomenting some savage plot. He stroked Maria's flank. It was frigid. She made no sound. Except for an occasional twitch, she lay lifeless as a pile of stones.

In no time Jade was back, carrying an armful of glistening leaves and twigs. She threw them down, then turned and vanished again into the night. The next time she appeared she was holding a charred tree branch, felled by lightning in some previous thunderstorm. When she laid it down Lu Beiping was surprised to hear it give off a brittle rustle, and he saw that the leaves were dry.

—Take a gander at that, you four-eyed sissy.

With all four eyes Lu Beiping stared in amazement. Jade brushed the wet hair out of her face and grinned triumphantly.

—I dug it out of a crack in the rocks. A roof of stone'll keep anything dry. Where there's wet, there's dry, and when there's dryness at hand, there's no need to fear the wet. That's the law of the living. You got me, Four Eyes?

(There was something magical about the fire they built that night, Lu Beiping would say to Tsung years later. If it hadn't been for the lantern she'd borne unextinguished through the storm, if it hadn't been for the dry kindling she'd conjured out of the wet forest, there'd have been no flame, no fire, no way to quell the fury of the flood. That woman was superhuman. Do you believe me? Well, no matter— believe what you want!)

—Quit standing around! Jade barked. Help me get this fire started.

Borrowing the barn lantern's feeble flame, they managed to get the firewood burning. Sure enough, the crackling flames lit from the few dry branches soon sucked in the wet leaves, crumpling them and desiccating them. As the flames mounted, humid billows of smoke enveloped Jade and Lu Beiping, turning the floodwater-encircled slope into an island of warmth.

Fire is life; that was another law of the living. As Lu Beiping hacked and wheezed, Maria let out a long bellow, and soon the fog-shrouded hills echoed with her vigorous cries.

Ngauugh—AUUUUUGH! . . . Ngauugh—AUUUUUGH!

Jade busied herself at the fireside, tying a knot in one panel of her blouse and using it to ferry dripping mouthfuls of silty water to the cow's lips. Till then, Maria's eyes had been closed; now they popped open, glistening like a pair of sleigh bells, and she lapped at the water with a quiet moan of happiness. Jade warmed her hands by the fire, then began rubbing them slowly up and down the cow's twitching flank.

Lu Beiping laid a hand on her shoulder and pointed wordlessly down the slope.

The floodwater now swirled not six feet from where they stood. Dark swells raced through the ring of firelight, and through them tumbled the jagged shapes of severed branches borne downward on the swift current.

Jade, still mopping rain from her face, stared at the water with enmity building in her eyes.

—Ruin and balefire! she cried out at last, flinging an accusatory finger at the water. I curse you! What kind of evil demon harries a mother about to give birth! I curse you, curse you right on back to hell! When I'm done with you, you won't dare show your face in front of your daddy the Devil!

Muttering under her breath, Jade gathered a hissing handful of ash and, leaning down, scattered it in a line between the fire and the advancing flood, as if forbidding the spirits of the water to pass over this boundary. Then she turned, grabbed a burning stick out of the flames, held it aloft over the black, churning torrent and, drawing a fiery symbol in the air, she danced and called out in a keening singsong:

—Iron, woodsbane! Water, flamesbane! Mother Heaven, Father Earth! We honor your laws, but you should too! Dragons, devils, serpents, specters—how dare you get in the way of a mother bringing new life into the world? Rainfather! Wind-sisters! Gods in heaven, have mercy on us! Open your eyes!

Lu Beiping stared at her, speechless, utterly taken aback by this frenzied, leaping, chanting performance. Finally Jade clasped her hands in prayer, bowed once toward the water, and then fell to her knees.

—Gods, demons, spirits! she cried out, knocking her forehead against the ground: I curse you, I damn you, I pray to you, I beg you!

Then Lu Beiping followed suit, and got down on his knees.

The firelight illuminated their paired silhouettes: two tiny human beings supplicating a vast, watery darkness. Forks of lightning flickered soundless and fitful in the sky, as if the heavens had spent all their strength in the preceding maelstrom. As they knelt, a succession of bright, abstract figures played silently across the black canvas of the night.

Once again Maria's wooden cowbell rang out crisply: *Tock!* . . . *Tock!* . . . *Tock-tock!* . . . *Tock-tock!* . . . Kneeling by the water, Lu Beiping stared wide-eyed at the trail of ashes strewn on the ground before him—for amid the peals of the clapper, it seemed like a miracle had occurred: *Strange*, he thought . . . the advancing floodwater, as if heeding a divine command, appeared to have halted just short of the line of ash. And when Jade came to the end of her incantation, they both turned and gave a simultaneous cry of surprise: There in the firelight, as if it had fallen out of the sky, stood another living being: a calf, its body covered in fine, curly hairs like a lamb or doe, sopping wet, already teetering unsteadily on its own delicate legs. Behind it Maria lay wet and gleaming, licking with quiet focus at her calf's bloodstained pelt. Seeing Jade and Lu Beiping, she tossed her head and gave a jubilant bellow, and the clapper hanging around her neck sounded a brisk tattoo in reply.

Ngauugh—AUUUUUGH!

Tock-tock, tock-tock!

Ngauugh—AUUUUUGH!

Tock-tock, tock-tock!

—Maria! Lu Beiping gasped. Wow! You really . . . He rushed over and threw his arms around her, squeezing her big, gallant head, then gave her a hearty shake before reaching out to stroke her calf. But Maria drew the line at that, and standing up immediately she placed the mountain of her body between Lu Beiping and her child.

—Ha! Sorry, Maria! I know, I know . . .

Lu Beiping clapped his hands in admiration. The flames danced. Then abruptly, he lurched over to Jade and pulled her into his embrace. All over the valley of her bosom his kisses opened like wildflowers.

—You're crazy, Jade murmured, laughing and pushing him away.

—Crazy . . . Lu Beiping repeated. Of course I'm crazy!

Then he was transfixed by a bolt of desire stronger than any he'd felt before, and a sea like the one Jade had held at bay rose up and washed over everything. He grabbed her, hoisted her, laughing, off her feet, and crammed his lips against hers, cutting off her laughter.

Flames lapped at the tranquil silhouettes of Maria and her newborn calf, lying side by side.

He laid Jade down on the fire-warmed earth, then took off her blouse, whose fabric was still twisted and knotted. When the whites of her breasts showed in the firelight he stopped, tilting his head to one side, and smiled, admiring those soft, cream-colored hills, the curls of her pubic hair glinting. He made a goofy face at her, then, without hurry, he pulled off his own drenched shorts.

All around them, the dark forms of the trees stood at attention. Naked, Jade lay on a flat rock near the fire, gazing at him silently, her eyes half-closed.

—I missed you, Bull Devil, she said finally.

—You missed me? Really?

—Of course, silly. Does that surprise you, that somebody else was thinking of you out there in the wind and rain?

—What's there to miss about a four-eyed sissy like me?

—A lot, Jade said, smiling as she reached to pluck the glasses off of his face: Like your Horn.

She grabbed him, grinning playfully. He drew closer to her, feeling exalted, like a towering banyan.

—Four Eyes, you really are my Horn.

—Your Horn? Really? Forever?

—What do you mean, forever?

—Okay, just for now.

Already this had become their secret code language, an affectionate nonsense whose meaning was immaterial. But now, at the end of this long, windblown day, Lu Beiping truly felt, as their bodies joined once more, that his books, his education, his future, everything, had melted away in the embrace of this wild mountain woman. For the sake of that tiny speck of light borne to him out of the boundless darkness, he'd cross oceans for her sake, walk through fire. (At that moment, Lu Beiping said to Tsung many years later, I thought I might never part from this woman again, for all the rest of my life.)

The flames of the dying fire rose and fell like small, bright blades, sharp yet intangible. For a moment the scudding clouds parted to reveal a slice of silver-dusted sky, then they closed, piling thick again, and the fresh scent of rain filled the night air.

—We'd better be careful, Jade said, panting: The storm might not be done yet.

—I don't care. *I'm* not done yet!

—Alright, hurry up!

Lu Beiping laughed joyously, and renewed his efforts.

The calf lay curled against its mother's breast, sucking milk with its diminutive lips. Maria lay like a mountain, happy and at peace, gazing down at the rush and tumble of the humans below.

The peals of the wooden clapper rocked gently on the wind, and finally the floodwaters began to ebb.

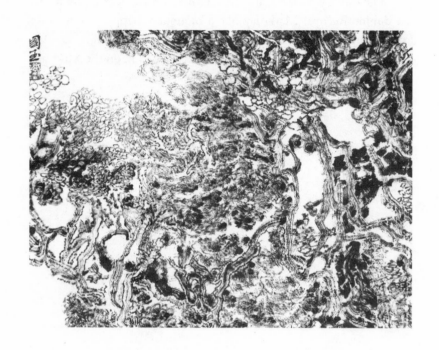

Chapter 8
The Ancient Tablet

Mudkettle Mountain was a mess.

What greeted Lu Beiping's eyes the next morning was a disaster scene: All plants of any appreciable size on either side of Mud-claw Creek—prickly cane, kudzu brakes, wild banana trees—had been sheared off uniformly at the height of a human head, leaving a forest of cockeyed stubs thumbing randomly at the sky. His campsite looked like it had been carpet-bombed, the beams of his hut scattered like pickup sticks, his cot relocated to the creek, his frypan hung from a tree branch, and all his other possessions—clothes, books, water bucket, harmonica, alarm clock, radio—strewn over the hillside for hundreds of yards around. The corral was a naked, muddy pit out of which a few lonely palings protruded, and the rest of the logs that had fenced in the cattle were nowhere to be seen. Of the cattle themselves there had been, naturally, no news since last night. When the sun rose and Lu Beiping parted ways with Jade, he'd led Maria and her calf back to the devastated campsite, glanced toward The Tree That Dances in the Wind, and stood gazing at it in astonishment.

The gorgontree, alone among its neighbors, had not toppled or been decapitated, and most of its branches had even survived intact. But the motley array of creepers and epiphytes that once coated the tree trunk had been stripped away as if by a giant magnet, and in their place jutted an odd collection of shrapnel: rock shards, wood splinters, even fragments of brick and roof tile blown up from the valley bottom, embedded in the bare wood like knives in dough. When Lu Beiping had first set up camp in the jungle, he'd tried to carve a message for posterity in the tree trunk and failed miserably; his machete, bouncing off the hard, knobbly wood, had flown out of his hand and landed a few yards away. The storm's wrath, it seemed, had turned the sturdiest hardwood into clay, the smallest piece of debris into a deadly bullet. In fact, it was in just this manner that the notorious wanderer, Judas, had perished; later Lu Beiping would find him lying in a ditch on the far side of the mountain, a pebble lodged in his forehead. It was no surprise, then, that the local radio station had crowned "Typhoon Number Five" with so many frightening titles: an Unprecedented Calamity, a Tragedy of Vast Proportions, a Naturally Occurring Nuclear Explosion Rivaled Only by the Atomic Power of Mao Zedong Thought. That day, as he wandered through the gap-toothed forest wearing tattered clothing, hunting for his cattle, Lu Beiping discovered strange abominations at every turn: a pair of gigantic trees, their trunks unbroken but wrapped together like braided pastry; a boulder the size of an oxcart hanging in a hammock of vines over a steep ravine; ramrod-straight boulevards running through what was once impenetrable brush. Volcanic wasteland, atomic fallout, war, blight, plague—though he'd never witnessed any of these forms of devastation, he figured they couldn't be much worse than this.

Dark rain clouds still brooded in the sky. Hollering for his cattle, Lu Beiping heard, faintly at first, their answering lows drifting up from hill and valley. As he followed their voices he found himself once again crossing the low, sloping ridge where he'd first met Jade. As always Mudkettle Mountain loomed imposingly over the landscape, but now the green bowl of the mountain, swaddled in strips of cloud, showed patches of lighter color where the wind had reversed the leaves, and here and there he saw downed trees and severed branches. He could now tell that the lows of the cattle were mostly emanating from the high mountain bowl—the "high valley," the driftfolk called it; this was the "kettle" that gave the mountain its name—which, he recalled, was accessible only by a steep path leading up from behind the driftfolk camp. How the cattle had managed to find their way to this remote refuge, a place even the wild swine couldn't penetrate, was a mystery to him.

The "tunnel of branches" was a tunnel no longer, its roof of foliage ripped away by the wind, and the slopes to either side strewn with wreckage. When Lu Beiping waded up out of the mire that had once been the creek, Smudge was waiting for him on the bank, Wildweed growling at his side. Gazing into the hollow, Lu Beiping gaped in surprise.

Both of the thatched lodges were completely undamaged. The wood-cutting frame nailed to the lychee tree at the foot of the bluff had been blown slightly askew, but the entire exposed area between it and the hollow mouth remained miraculously undisturbed, the huts trim and tidy, the ground clear, the chickens still milling, as if this place had been a haven of tranquility at the eye of the storm, protected by a divine hand.

—I hate you, said Smudge, pouting. I'll not mind you nay more! He looked away from Lu Beiping, pretending to ignore him, and made no move to quiet the dog.

—Nay mind me? I don't believe it, Lu Beiping said, giving Smudge's ear a playful pinch. Tell me, Smudge, what have I done to deserve your hatred?

—Now all you care about's my Pa, not me! Smudge harrumphed. Last night Pa didn't sweat a drop about me, just hied on down the mountain looking for you, and wouldn't let me come with! Lousy Bull Devil!

—Oh, Smudge, Lu Beiping said with a grin: You know too much for your own good!

At that moment Jade emerged from behind the lodge, her hands green with amaranth-pickling juice. Laughing, she said:

—Looking for your animals? Autumn was fretting about them the moment he woke up. Must be something in the air this morning—first your cattle come running up here, then you. Did you smell the porridge I'm cooking?

—Four Eyes isn't looking for the kine, Pa, he's looking for you! You think I don't wit—

—I know you know, you little rascal, Jade said, slapping Smudge on the rump. Why don't you call Four Eyes Pa from now on? He can be your pa now.

—I won't! Four Eyes isn't my pa! He's a dirty son of a dog! Smudge said, wrinkling his nose at Lu Beiping. Then he stalked away sullenly with Wildweed trotting at his heels.

Lu Beiping started to lay a cautioning hand on Jade's shoulder, then he stopped, his arm frozen mid-reach, something about this gesture feeling too oddly spouse-like.

—Oof, Lu Beiping said. Don't joke about that. I'd rather he not call me "pa."

—You sure? Jade said with a teasing smile. What should he call you, then? Oof? He-eyyyy, Oof! How's it going, Oof? I love you, Uncle Oof!

—Shhh! A little quieter! You'll piss off Kingfisher and Stump!

Sticking his machete in the dirt outside the door of the smaller lodge, Lu Beiping gazed up incredulously at the stoutly built structure, at the thatch roof woven from tidy grass plaits, and marveled at the strange selectivity with which the storm had vented its fury.

—Piss me off? What about?

Kingfisher's bald dome popped up over the crest of the roof, causing Lu Beiping to go beet-red and splutter in surprise.

—Take care what you say around here, Four Eyes, Kingfisher said with a fey laugh. Nothing's private. Good thing I sent Jade down to look for you last night, eh? An old lover owes it to his den mother to keep an eye out for the new favorite. Isn't that right, Stump?

Stump's hearty chortle emanated from the far side of the roof.

Kingfisher and Stump had been lying on the roof of the lodge, hidden from Lu Beiping's sight, mending thatch. Now Stump's sweat-gleaming, guileless face appeared next to Kingfisher's, and joining in the banter he burbled jovially to Lu Beiping:

—Wind ran off with a few knots of thatch, that's all. She'll be shipshape by breakfast time. Care to share a cup with us, Four Eyes?

Heard you and Jade were up all night birthing a babe. Heh! Tiresome work, nay?

More guffaws all around. This time Jade joined in too, her loud laughter pealing over the others', and Lu Beiping felt some of his own awkwardness dissolve. He asked:

—Have you seen my cattle? They ran off last night, and I think they somehow made their way up into the valley above here.

—That's what we were just discussing, Kingfisher replied. Your beasts have been keening all night. Talk about horned demons and hidden serpents—I think every demon on the mountain joined in the chorus! Autumn went up there first thing this morning, said he feared your horned demons wouldn't stand a chance against the biggest hidden serpent of them all.

—Autumn said what? Lu Beiping couldn't believe his ears. "Horned demons and hidden serpents" was a catchphrase that in those days referred to society's bad elements—capitalists, vagrants, troublemakers; in short, people like Jade, Kingfisher, and Stump. On Kingfisher's lips, however, the phrase had an obvious, added layer of meaning.

—Say! You don't wit? Stump interjected. 'Course, as long as she's happy, she keeps hidden. Let's hope it stays that way!

When Lu Beiping's puzzled expression didn't go away, Kingfisher laughed and said:

—Don't tell me you don't know about her, boy? That's where she lives—the high valley! It was her that kept us safe during the storm. Why else'd we be spared? You don't suppose the wind just lost its appetite when it passed through here? No water-demon or wind-devil would dare defy her will!

Lu Beiping knew that he was back in Kingfisher territory, the land of sins and laws. Certain that he would break some taboo if he said anything more, he picked up his machete and called over to Smudge:

—Hey, Smudge! Want to come with me up to the high valley to look for your Uncle Autumn?

—*That* one can't go, Kingfisher said immediately. She'll smell the darkness on him from a mile off.

Smudge made a face at Lu Beiping behind Kingfisher's back. Now Jade came hurrying over, carrying a dripping, brownish-yellow rag. This strip of cloth, she explained, had been soaked in sulfur water, and he was to wear it around his waist to ward off evil. Lu Beiping said nothing. Sensing his skepticism, Jade took off her "snakesbane" bracelet and put it on him too.

—Be careful, she said. She's not to be messed with, that creature. There's room in her belly for you and every one of your cattle.

Stump came over to Lu Beiping and began describing the route he was to take up into the high valley. As he tied the wet rag around his waist, Lu Beiping caught a whiff of its noxious odor and imagined for a moment that he could actually smell the darkness wafting down from the Snakeweird's lair.

Skirting the log-soaking pool and following the thin rivulet that trickled down the stone ledges on the far side of the hollow, Lu Beiping climbed upward toward the looming central bowl of Mudkettle Mountain. He knew that the source of this rivulet was a pool high in the valley whose waters fed all the streams of the Mudkettle and which, according to legend, was formed by an underground spring bubbling up from the ocean itself. The Sea's Eye, the locals called it. He wondered if the tall, dark bluffs ringing this valley had shielded the drift-folk during the storm, creating a natural windbreak. But the wind, he remembered clearly, had been swirling and erratic, never coming from just one direction. Why, then, had their hideout been spared? It was a mystery. He thought again of the legendary serpent, the Snakeweird, and a cold feeling gathered in his chest. He threw back his head and hollered to the cattle. This time he heard a response, faint but clear; he could even tell that the answering low belonged to Alyosha, because of the knocks of the wooden clapper punctuating it. On the slope above him a clump of myrtle burned orange against the sullen gray sky. He wondered: How had these flowers survived the typhoon? Would the spirits of Mudkettle Mountain protect something as insignificant as a flower? If so, this place must be swarming with them!

Walking and musing, he soon arrived at a small pond, and suddenly Autumn was standing before him, wet from head to toe, as if he'd just emerged from the water. Lu Beiping shuddered in surprise. Outlined against the dark shapes of the trees, Autumn's long, gaunt face looked unusually pale, and red scratches from bushwhacking crisscrossed his bare torso.

—Sheesh, Autumn, Lu Beiping said after he'd recovered from the shock of Autumn's sudden appearance: I thought for a moment you were a ghost. I didn't hear a thing, you just popped out of nowhere!

Autumn grimaced at that, then chuckled.

—I was beginning to think you'd never come, friend. Don't worry about the cattle just now. I have something to show you.

—Right now? Can't it wait a few minutes? I thought you said you'd help me round up the herd.

—I did, said Autumn, smiling. And I was hoping you'd do me a favor in return. Come along, follow me.

—No, it has to be later, Lu Beiping said, coming to halt. I need to find the animals now.

Autumn's face stiffened.

—You're a good cowherd. Alright, fine then. Those critters of yours must have magic powers, wending their way up here in the midst of that roaring storm. Look—Autumn pointed at the scratches on his torso—I couldn't get in there without the prickly cane nearly tearing me to bits. How they squeezed through with those big, mountainous bodies I can't guess.

—Gosh, Lu Beiping said, beginning to feel anxious: What are we going to do, then? You think that even if we find them they won't be able to get back out through the prickly cane?

—Don't fret, Autumn said placidly. Now that their master's here things'll be easier. I tried calling them myself but they wouldn't listen—mercy, that made me mad! Best not to go up there ourselves, you just stand here and holler for them, they'll recognize your voice and come out to meet you. They found their way in, they can find their way out.

There was something else Lu Beiping wanted to ask, but he checked himself, afraid that he might hurt Autumn's feelings again with some thoughtless verbal misstep. Wordlessly he followed Autumn along a freshly cut path through the tall grass, skirting the edge of the pool, crossing a patch of wild forestland, and finally arriving at a thick cluster of bushes out of which rose the twisting, needle-tufted limbs of two horsetail pines.

—Look at this, Autumn said.

Lu Beiping stiffened in surprise. Beneath the bushes, half-dug out of the mud but still covered in dry pine needles, lay a large tablet of blue-black stone. The top corner of the tablet, which must have protruded from the soil, was green with moss and severely worn by the elements.

—What the—? This is what you wanted to show me? Lu Beiping fought back a reflexive rush of fear at the sight of what appeared to be another lost gravestone. What is it? he asked nervously. What's this doing out here in the wilderness? How'd you find it?

—Noticed those two horsetails, Autumn said, wiping sweat from his face with one end of his waistcloth, his voice growing more animated as he spoke: Scouting timber's given me a keen pair of eyes. Pines like that don't usually grow around here, Mudkettle Mountain has too wet of a climate. Soon as I saw them I knew they'd been planted, and a long time ago, by the look of them. And why would pines be planted in a wild place like this? I knew there must be a story—then I discovered this tablet, and lo and behold, it vindicated my suspicions!

Lu Beiping noticed that when Autumn grew excited his speech took on an odd formality, his cadence and choice of words becoming much different than normal. As Autumn spoke he leaned down and brushed the pine needles off of the tablet.

—I've studied it long, but this thing—it's lost on a rude woodsman like me. I'd hoped, if it wasn't too much trouble . . .

He looked up at Lu Beiping and laughed awkwardly.

—Can you . . . read it for me?

Lu Beiping leaned down and examined the tablet. A pair of coiling dragons writhed across the worn surface; it looked like a genuine relic. Between them was a dense grid of carved characters, now almost illegible on the pockmarked stone. Lu Beiping read off the blocky seal-style heading, then deciphered, haltingly, the inscription that followed in classical script:

MEMORIAL UPON THE CONQUEST OF THE LOI

This Record set in Stone by . . . Minister of Taxes and Rev . . .

. . . for though the Isle's four Prefectures have long fallen under Celestial Rule, the barbarian Loi, who abide in curious Dwellings deep in these hundredfold Vales, nevertheless wheeled free as Vultures in the Sky, and made war upon His Subjects, inflicting great slaughter thereupon, which state of affairs persisted until the first of Eighthmonth in the year Cel. VIII Ter. IV . . .

. . . did excuse themselves, saying it were vain to exhaust His Legions upon so treacherous and wild a Land; and invoking the doctrine that the Wise Ruler Governeth Not the Distant to justify their own Ease and Indolence, did continually neglect their Duties as Administrators of His Justice and Guardians of His Peace . . .

. . . whereupon the Son of Heaven did declare, that inasmuch as His Will and the Will of Heaven are one, and desirous that His People be better served, and that His Realm remain forever Unified and Indivisible, as it rightly ought to be, it would please Him to send a Force numbering thirty thousand against the savage Loi who dare defy His Might, that in three years' time all might bow before Him . . .

. . . grain ripening in the fields, yet we laid siege to their Strongholds, denying them Nutriment; the Weather favored us, our Soldiers fought valiantly, and the People came to our aid, there being no truer sign that Heaven despiseth the wickedness of the Loi . . . in a mere two months Victory was accomplished, and His Sagaciousness was greatly pleased . . .

. . . already the Loi of Chopfoot Valley in Man Cheong, of Sevenmill Valley in Tam-chow, and of divers other Vales, submit taxes unto the Realm, render their labor thereunto, study letters, and comprehend the One True Tongue . . .

. . . of His Grace the Shenwu Emperor, may His Years be fruitful and numberless, who aweth without Force, who humbleth without Threat of Punishment, whose Word is the Will of Heaven; He hath caused to be erected this Stile, on first of Firstmonth in the year Cel. IX Ter. I, that every passing Generation, even unto the end of Time, shall be instructed as to His Greatness.

As Lu Beiping stammered out the faded inscription, he noticed that Autumn had pulled a small notebook out of the folds of his waistcloth and begun following along, drawing his finger across the page, soft syllables of awe and surprise escaping his lips as Lu Beiping pronounced the glyphs he'd attempted to record. Clearly Autumn had been poring over this tablet for a long time.

When Lu Beiping had finished laboring through the final, convoluted sentence, he looked up and saw that Autumn's eyes were brimming with tears. Seeing Lu Beiping's look of surprise, Autumn turned his head away quickly, wiped the tears from his eyes, and laughed.

—Autumn, Lu Beiping asked with an uncomfortable chuckle: Are you okay? Does this old tablet mean something special to you?

—No use weeping for what's dead and gone, eh? Autumn said with a grim laugh. Then he added: I'm moved that you helped me read that stone. You sure know a lot of figures. If someday I can claim to have half the learning you've got, I'll be a happy man.

A shadow of regret or unease passed across Autumn's face. Then he asked Lu Beiping:

—Can you tell what year it was carved?

—During the Ming Dynasty, I think. Somewhere in there it mentioned the emperor's reign-name, didn't it?

Lu Beiping searched the tablet again, running his fingers over the worn surface.

—I always contended that people lived in our hollow back in ancient times, Autumn said. But Kingfisher'd have none of it. That lightning-struck lychee tree looks like it was planted, it's got a human feel. Kingfisher said I'm too full of shadow, said I'll call up the shades of the long-ago dead, talking like that.

Autumn paused, his mouth half open, as if struggling to find the right words. Then he chuckled bitterly and said:

—"The wise ruler governeth not the distant"—couldn't be more true, what the tablet said. Mudkettle Mountain was always a place of refuge, it seems. It's got a good land-lay. Good place to dodge ruin, hide from the magistrates.

—Not so successfully, Lu Beiping said, fingering the stone. Doesn't it say that they besieged the natives here for two months, cut off their food supply? I think Kingfisher's right to worry about calling up the shades of the dead. Hundreds of years ago here, the emperor's troops were killing people right and left. It was a massacre.

The two young men stood gazing at the stone for a long time while the wind rustled the pine branches above them. Behind them a string of bubbles rose out of the depths of the pool, as if the water itself were sighing in sympathy.

Autumn seems like a completely different person right now, Lu Beiping thought. Just as this unprepossessing little pond, with the memorial tablet nearby, seemed vested with a powerful aura of history, so the tablet, the black notebook in Autumn's hands, the entire adventure of bushwhacking into this remote valley and decoding a record of centuries past, seemed utterly out of place in the world they lived in today, like an episode from some grand old tale. It was all so incongruous, yet it kindled in Lu Beiping a feeling of warmth that he hadn't experienced in a long time.

—Autumn, Lu Beiping said, I had no idea you were a man of letters.

—A man of letters? Autumn scoffed. A boor, a crude peasant— deaf and dumb.

—Oh, come on. I think you're only pretending to be deaf and dumb, Lu Beiping said, glancing at the little black book. Then, grinning, he asked: Hey, can I see that notebook? I want to read whatever secrets you've got hidden in there.

The question was meant more as friendly banter than as a serious request, and Lu Beiping didn't really expect Autumn to reveal the contents of the book. In those days private journals were a sensitive subject; they were a liability, they were dangerous goods.

—You really want to see it? Autumn asked. To Lu Beiping's surprise he actually seemed to entertain the idea, fanning the notebook's pages for a moment with a sheepish expression on his face. Then he said: Oh, you city kids are such jokers. Aren't you in a hurry to find your cattle? Here I've gone and distracted you from your real business.

Lu Beiping sprang to his feet.

—Yes, you're right! I almost forgot about them while we were puzzling over that old stone!

He grabbed his machete and was about to run off into the trees when Autumn laid a hand on his shoulder, holding him back.

—You're a hot-blooded savage just like us, he said with a twinkle of laughter in his narrowed eyes. Four Eyes, I wouldn't . . . wait, I can't call you that. What's your real name? I don't suppose people down there call you "Stinkyfoot."

—Oh . . . of course! . . . My name's Lu Beiping, Lu Beiping said with an awkward grin, conscious of the fact that none of the drift-folk, even Jade, knew his real name.

—I'll call you Bei, then. I don't imagine anyone else calls you that. Ordinarily you go by "Lu" or "Ping," I'd guess.

—You're right, Lu Beiping chuckled. It was true: Except for the diehard junior-high-school comrades with whom he'd raided the locked-up library, nobody had ever called him "Bei" as a nickname.

—What about you, then? he asked Autumn.

Autumn curled his lips.

—Nameless shall the wanderer forever remain. You've been calling me Autumn, no?

Suddenly a loud bovine moan shattered the quiet. Seeing the look of anxiety that flashed across Lu Beiping's face, Autumn said:

—Like I said before, no need for you to go blundering around in there and getting all cut up like I did. Just stand here and holler. This bowl is real echoey, your critters'll hear your calls for sure and find their own paths out of that viney maze. Better than you ferreting around in there and trying to hunt them down one by one.

—I should just stand right here? And shout?

—You can sit if you want.

—What if not all the animals find their way out?

—Don't worry, Autumn said, waving the notebook: You helped me fill in the blanks in that inscription, I'll guarantee your cattle for you. If any are missing, I'll go in there with you and help you track them down one by one.

—So . . . alright, then! Lu Beiping turned toward the mountain, squared his shoulders, then glanced at Autumn, feeling a little embarrassed. He drew a deep breath, opened his mouth to shout, then burst into laughter. I can't do this, he said. This feels like a performance. I've never done cattle calls in front of another person.

Autumn grinned.

—I won't watch, then. Just pretend I don't exist.

Like a child, he turned his back to Lu Beiping, covering his mouth with his notebook to keep from laughing.

Then abruptly Lu Beiping, keying his voice as high as it would go, let out a long, piercing yell, his voice sailing out like a knife blade thrown into the sky.

—Al-YOOOOOOOOO-sha! PEEEEEEEE-ter! A-LEEEEEEEEE-xei! Come OUT, come OUT, wherever you AAAAAARE!

Autumn clamped his hands over his ears and grinned, bobbing his head enthusiastically.

—What a voice! A man who speaks like thunder!

Lu Beiping ignored him and kept shouting, his cheeks turning bright red, the veins standing out in his neck. Now he imitated one of the Gaffer's swine calls:

—LeeleelooloWAAAAAAHHHH!

Echoes danced among the peaks. Autumn joined in:

—LeeleelooloWAAHHH! LeeleelooloWAAAAAAHHHHHHH!

They took turns doing cattle calls, one watching while the other yelled, trying to outdo each other like a pair of elementary school boys competing at hoop-and-stick games in some schoolyard long ago. Lu Beiping had heard that shouting at the top of one's lungs is a powerful way to unlock one's inner strength; he'd even read somewhere that Japanese samurai-in-training and cadets at West Point received special instruction in yelling technique.

—Wow! he said, turning to Autumn. It sure feels liberating to shout like this.

—It's true. My dad once told me, the ancients had a special art of yelling. They called it . . . what was the word? Yes—"caeloclamation." "Then did he make a great caeloclamation, and lo, the gods harkened to his voice." Isn't that from some poem or other?

Lu Beiping glanced over at Autumn, whose expression was now exuberant. It felt great to give such free rein to his emotions. He hadn't done so in a long, long time.

When he caught sight of the first pair of horns glinting in the green depths of the forest, which soon gathered around it the large, cantering body of a bull—Alexei!—Lu Beiping actually jumped for joy. And when his feet hit the ground, he looked up and saw—

Autumn still stood facing into the wind, yodeling up at the encircling cliffs. But now his voice sounded stiff and mechanical, and rivers of tears ran down his gaunt, dark cheeks.

—Autumn . . . are you okay?

—*Lee-lee-loo-loo-WAAAAAAAAAAAAHHHHHH!*

Clearly, something Lu Beiping said had once again touched a nerve.

Autumn's tactic proved to be a good one. In barely half an hour's time they were surrounded by an undulating sea of horned heads. One by one the animals reported to Lu Beiping, then meandered over to the pond to nibble the tall grass that grew nearby. Lu Beiping and Autumn stood on either side of the tablet, belting an occasional cattle call into the mountains and then returning their attentions to the inscription on the stone, comparing it character by character with the copied version in Autumn's notebook. At the moment Lu Beiping held the little black book, whose pages were brittle and yellowed with age.

—Who's Li Shutong? he asked as he flipped through the notebook. There didn't seem to be anything unusual about it; in those days every bookish youngster had his own "confidential" journal full of famous quotations, lines of poetry, lists of good adjectives, and so forth. Autumn's handwriting was blocky and laborious, every character looking like it had been copied from a crib sheet, and in fact he had devoted several pages to practicing hardpoint calligraphy, the letters now indecipherable where the cheap ink had run. But almost all of the poetry that he'd copied out had the same heading: "Lyrics by Li Shutong"—song lyrics, Lu Beiping guessed.

—You haven't heard of Li Shutong? Autumn said, bringing his head close enough to Lu Beiping's that he could make out the tracks of wind-dried tears still visible on Autumn's cheeks. I don't know much about him. My dad told me he was a monk, a very learned monk.

—A learned monk? Are there such things? Lu Beiping scoffed. The impression of monks he'd gotten from his history textbooks was not a good one. He read one of the poems:

May Promenade
by Li Shutong

The silks of the revelers flutter and dance
       Caressed by a gossamer breeze,
While gusts of springtime blossoms whirl
       'Round these painted gaieties:
Pearblossom, rapeblossom gold as the sun,
       Wild mustard and green willowflower,
Then the oriole cries, and the revelers depart
       As the bell tolls the day's last hour.

—What do you think? Autumn asked excitedly.

—Doesn't do much for me, Lu Beiping replied, then immediately regretted it. He knew now that it was at times like these that Autumn was at his most vulnerable. Hastily he added: I mean, this is just the lyrics, I'd need to hear the tune to get the full effect. Here, let me read another!

September Scene
by Li Shutong

A lone sail skims the lake,
       Twinkling against the blue;
The pavilion's slender spire
       Obscures the moon from view;
How many honeyed glances
Behind the willow branches
       Have tendered promises that proved untrue?

The mountain gazes down,
    Its dark brow coyly bent;
Pink clouds hurry by
    In blushing dishevelment;
The night wind, softly humming,
Hints at autumn's coming,
    And flowers nod their blooms in assent.

—Hmm! Well . . . this one's interesting! Lu Beiping said, hemming and hawing as he wracked his brain for something complimentary to say. That line about the honeyed glances is really nice. But . . . this doesn't seem like a poem a monk would write!

Already the excitement had faded from Autumn's face. He made no reply, then turned and continued hollering up into the steep-walled valley.

—*Leeleelooloo-WAAAAAHHHH!*

Crap, Lu Beiping thought. He decided to shut up, and lowering his head he fanned the pages in search of another poem. Then suddenly, with a cry of amazement, he stopped.

—Whoa! Who wrote this? This calligraphy is incredible!

Autumn turned to look at Lu Beiping, a shudder of cold pride passing through his eyes. Biting off the words one by one, he said:

—My dad wrote that.

—Your dad? Lu Beiping's heart lurched when Autumn's eyes met his. He knew now that he'd struck the source of Autumn's melancholy, the place where all those tears had come from. Unable to hold Autumn's gaze, he looked down and began to read the lines written in that vigorous hand:

Stanzas Written to the Tune of "A Golden Thread"

How do you fare, Wu fourth-sired?
If ever you regain the long-desired
    Sun-warmed earth

That gave you birth,
Could you bear to think on all that has since transpired?
Long is your road, with none to ease your woe:
Your children still young, your house in poverty mired;
Dim is the memory of the last cup we shared
In a leafy plum bower long ago;
Sad victim of Fate! Prey to men of lesser worth—
To liars and traitors who at each turn conspired
To lay you low;
Now all you know
Are the moaning winds of the frigid north.

But take heart, and do not beat your breast;
How many who are to Earth's edges pressed
Enjoy the company
Of their own family,
Your own flesh and blood by your side—truly, you are blessed!
Not so I, doomed forever to spill
Bitter tears for my lost love, and dwell as a guest
Beneath borrowed eaves, drifting, alone—
But O, I do not envy you the winter's chill.
Think on staunch Baoxu, who at last did free
His captive homeland, when Time put to the test
The oath he swore to fulfill,
His wild hope, cherished still
While others despaired—by these stanzas, remember me.

The poem continued on the following page, but already a thick, choking gloom had fallen over Lu Beiping, and he stopped, unable to go on. He couldn't bring himself to look up and confront Autumn's tears again, so he just sat there, staring at the lines of brusquely written fountain-pen characters crowding the yellowed page. The handwriting was brisk and forceful, the pen nib biting into the paper hard enough to draw blood. For a long time Lu Beiping stared in silence at the poem, then at last he looked up, met Autumn's eyes, and said slowly, holding out his right hand:

—Autumn . . . I'm sorry.

A look of confusion and panic passed briefly across Autumn's face; then he took Lu Beiping's hand with both of his and gripped it for a long time, gazing at him. There were no tears in his eyes now, but his jaw was clenched tight and Lu Beiping could see the muscles working beneath his skin and as he ground his teeth.

—Autumn, Lu Beiping said, hesitant: Who wrote this poem? Was it your dad?

Autumn said nothing.

—Autumn, won't you tell me something about yourself?

Autumn let go of his hand.

The pool exhaled another long stream of bubbles. The cloud-streaked mountains loomed imposingly on all sides, but the leisurely munching of the cattle created an atmosphere of ease and quiet. Autumn gave another few listless cattle calls, then turned back to Lu Beiping and said with a wan smile:

—There'll be plenty of time later for telling stories, Bei. You know, every one of us driftfolk has so many stories to tell that we could sit by the fireside and jaw for a week straight and barely scratch the surface. If you don't believe me, ask Jade, Kingfisher, or Stump. Come on, it's getting late, if any of your cattle haven't found their way out yet, then we might really have to go in and hunt for them. Count them, let's see!

Thrown for a loop by the abrupt change in Autumn's manner, Lu Beiping leapt to his feet and cried out:

—Autumn, you can't just leave me hanging! Did your dad really write that poem? It's so powerful, I want to write it down myself!

Autumn dusted the pine needles off of his thighs, took the notebook from Lu Beiping, and tucked it carefully under his waistcloth. Lu Beiping guessed that he'd sewn a hidden pocket in there specifically to hold that little book.

—No, he didn't write it. Such art was beyond my father. He copied it down for me the night I left, the night I ran off to join the driftfolk. He told me a famous Qing magistrate wrote that poem for a friend of his who'd been exiled to a distant frontier. He said that that poem saved his friend's life.

—Huh? So is your father—

—*Was*, not is. Count your cattle, let's go.

Without another word Autumn strode out of the grove where the tablet lay, went around the pond, and started up the trail leading into the high valley. Lu Beiping stood there for a moment, dazed, unable to keep pace with the erratic turns of Autumn's mood. What a strange character—you never knew whether he was going to laugh or cry. Feeling nonplussed, he ran after Autumn, pausing for a moment to belt another cattle call up into the mountains.

—*Leeleelooloo-WAAAAAAHHHHHHH!*

The reassembled herd now lazed on the gentle slope above the pool, having sated themselves on the tall grass. Lu Beiping walked among the cattle, counting heads, then suddenly he heard Autumn shout from farther up the trail—

—Bei! Can you tell which cow that is, calling high up in the valley?

Lu Beiping cocked his head and listened.

. . . *auuugh—ngauuugh! Ngauh! Ngg—AUUUGH! Tock-tock, tock-tock!*

Sure enough, he heard a series of faint lows, growing shorter and sharper, as if in mounting alarm, interspersed with the knocks of a wooden clapper. Lu Beiping cried out in dismay. It was Alyosha! He'd heard him calling first thing that morning, but there'd been no sign of him when the herd regrouped—and he was, after all, their leader. Lu Beiping rushed after Autumn, his heart thudding. He'd carved that wooden cowbell for Alyosha first, before Maria's, because he so often led the herd. God, what had happened to him? Was he tangled in some thick net of vines, or trapped in a steep ravine, unable to climb out?

—Wait! Autumn shouted. Did Jade give you a brimstone rag? He walked over to Lu Beiping and tugged gently at the T-shirt that Lu Beiping had tied around his waist, saying: You ought to put your shirt on so your tender skin doesn't get all cut up like mine. And make sure your rag belt's on the outside, so the smell can get out.

208

Lifting one apron of his waistcloth, he added solemnly:

—It's dangerous up there, she's not to be taken lightly. Whenever I'm not wearing this cloth I let it soak in a jug full of brimstone water. Trust me, it works.

Once more a chill gathered in Lu Beiping's chest. Alyosha's cries had ceased, but as they hiked up into the high valley the day seemed to grow dim. It was still early afternoon by Lu Beiping's reckoning, but the jungle canopy above them was growing denser, shutting out the light. And so Lu Beiping, following Autumn along a path visible only to him, ventured at last into the dark wilds at the heart of Mudkettle Mountain.

God, this truly was a primeval wilderness. A forest? More like a sylvan fortress, a maze of vertiginous ramparts formed by thick nets of creepers hanging all the way from the treetops to the ground. The path, if it could be called a path, involved burrowing through nests of thorny vines, clambering over the massive knuckles of aerial roots, teetering over dark chasms on bridges of fallen trees, slip-sliding down sheer slopes while clinging to elephantine shafts of bamboo that grew out at sharp angles from the hillsides. Relying on the keen sense of direction that Autumn had cultivated over the course of many tree-scouting expeditions, they navigated a circuitous route into the inky depths of the jungle. From afar, the bowl of Mudkettle Mountain just looked like a big, dark semicircle, but once inside, Lu Beiping saw that it was a world unto itself, a maze of crisscrossing ravines, winding ridges, and mountain streams leaping down precipitous slopes. It was just like Autumn said, when they stood at the mouth of the valley their cattle calls had resounded throughout the bowl, but now, deep inside the labyrinth, even their loudest cries were muffled as if by a thick blanket. Hollering at the top their lungs, they would be answered by no more than a fitful scattering of echoes, then once again the valley would be awash with sound, the aggregate roar of wind, running water, and the calls of animals and insects inundating their ears. By now it was already dark as night, and the chinks of sunlight high up in the canopy were like stars studding a black firmament.

Lu Beiping's heart was in his throat. Without Autumn's help he wouldn't have had a prayer of finding his way in this place. This was bona fide wilderness, a true virgin rainforest; by comparison the tracts of jungle down by Mudclaw Creek through which he was accustomed to roam must be nothing more than secondary, tertiary, even quaternary-growth forest! Autumn relieved him of his machete, now merely an encumbrance; he needed both hands free to meet the many demands for climbing, crawling, groping, and burrowing that the jungle imposed on him. In the company of the other re-eds Lu Beiping fancied himself a mountain man, but now, forced to navigate a real mountain wilderness, he was once more a clueless, very out-of-place city kid, utterly dependent on Autumn's help.

—Hey, Autumn, can we rest for a bit? Lu Beiping panted, half-leaning on, half-hanging from a large woody vine that dangled between two sky-eclipsing trees, daunted by the prospect of pressing farther into this interminable darkness. Autumn, who seemed keyed up into a state of nervous excitement, stopped, tilted his head to one side, and murmured absently:

—Strange. I could've sworn from the sound of it this morning that your bull was calling from right at this spot.

—Autumn, do you come in here every morning when you scout timber? Lu Beiping asked, mopping his brow.

—Where else? Autumn replied with a rare smile of pride. I know every nook and cranny of this valley.

—It's so dark in here. Don't you get scared?

In the thick tangle of vines behind Autumn's back Lu Beiping thought he saw a slithering movement, and reflexively fingered his sulfur-soaked belt.

—Sure, I'm scared. When I'm afraid of her, I sing.

—You sing? Lu Beiping asked with sudden interest. I didn't know you sang, Autumn. What songs do you sing?

—The ones by Li Shutong which you just read. My dad taught me them when I was little.

The expression on Autumn's sweat-streaked face was now easy and cheerful. There was no vestige left of his earlier gloom.

—Your dad taught you to sing songs written by a monk? Lu Beiping asked, his curiosity whetted by this interesting discovery. Can you sing one for me now?

No sooner had the question escaped his lips than Autumn's quiet, reedy voice began piping in the shadows: *The silks—of the re-ve-lers flutter and dance, ca-ressed—by a goss-amer breeze . . .*

—Nice! You've got a good ear, you know that? I like it, it's in three-four time . . . *oom-pa-pa, oom-pa-pa* . . . The percussionist's son, true to form, started clapping out the rhythm beneath Autumn's melody. You know, Lu Beiping added, my dad told me that these days, no orchestra can play anything in three-four. It's illegal.

—What's three-four? Autumn asked, his pupils glittering in the darkness. Bei, what does your father do?

—You haven't heard of three-four time? You know, a waltz, like when men and women used to dance together? Lu Beiping struck the pose of a ballroom dancer, then laughed and explained: My dad used to play percussion in a Western-style orchestra. With violins and trumpets and all that stuff. He's the one who stands in the back, snoozing and waiting for the moment when he's supposed to hit the bass drum or clack the little wooden fish heads. It's kind of a menial job.

—How could you say that about your own father? Autumn exclaimed, laughing despite himself, and Lu Beiping laughed too. It seemed that in that moment, both the faintly patronizing air that Lu Beiping couldn't help adopting whenever he talked with Autumn, and Autumn's own slightly guarded manner, evaporated, and they were on an even footing at last. Coming into a wild place like this, Lu Beiping noticed, had the effect of drawing people closer together.

In the midst of their laughter, Autumn's face stiffened in the shadows, and drawing close to Lu Beiping he put a finger to his lips, shushing him. A moment later Lu Beiping heard a strange sound far off in the jungle. He grabbed Autumn's hand instinctively.

It was a deep, distant, muffled rumble, like a roll of thunder in a neighboring valley, an upswell of sound so vast it seemed almost silent, and at the same time to emanate from the earth itself. Immediately Lu Beiping remembered the roar that had preceded the typhoon, that weird, borborygmic perturbation that had seemed to rise up out of the forest floor and envelop the entire valley. Listen! Autumn hissed in his ear. Then, with a fearful shudder, Lu Beiping heard it: the Child Crying from Beyond the Grave, the hoarse wail of a ghostly infant—as sudden as the flash of foam on the water when a cormorant stoops for its prey, and just as fleeting. Then, just when Lu Beiping began to doubt his ears, a different cry, clear and unmistakable, pierced the silence. God, no! That was Alyosha! This wasn't his usual gallant trumpeting; it was a weak, strangled moan, as if a heavy object were crushing his throat, accompanied by the fitful knocking of the clapper. The moans continued for a brief while, then faded from hearing.

A hush fell over the forest. Then, after a long interval, a blood-curdling, high-pitched bovine wail knifed through the air, setting the earth ashiver and reverberating in the treetops:

Ngauuuugh—AAAAAAUUUUUUUUGGGGGHGHHHHHH!

The echoes leapt upward through the canopy and were gone. So was the rumbling sound, the voice of the Crying Child, leaving behind a silence that seemed older than the earth itself, larger than all of Mudkettle Mountain, a terrible thing to hear.

Lu Beiping was now covered in sweat. He slumped limply on Autumn's shoulder. Supporting him with one hand, Autumn gripped the front apron of his waistcloth in the other and brandished it before him like a shield or flag, his eyes darting in every direction. Yes, Lu Beiping thought, his mind in tumult—it had to be it, it had to be *her* . . . Looking down, he noticed the bulge of Autumn's genitals visible through the man's damp running shorts. Strange, he thought: Out here in the jungle, Autumn showed a bold, masculine side that contrasted sharply with the passive, shrinking manner he adopted around Kingfisher and Jade.

The jungle fell back into its usual cacophonous silence, the all-encompassing din of wind, water, and insects. Coming back to his senses, Lu Beiping released Autumn's hand and said in an urgent whisper:

—Autumn, let's go. Alyosha's done for. He must have been killed by . . .

Autumn clamped his hand over Lu Beiping's mouth, stifling the word *Snakeweird* before it could escape his lips, and commanded him with a withering look to remain silent. It was clear to Lu Beiping that now, of all times, in this place, of all places, he must be mindful not to violate any . . . laws.

—Wait here, Autumn said quietly, crouching down. I'm going to go take a look.

—No! Lu Beiping said, frightened. I'm coming with you.

Stooping, he followed Autumn through a labyrinth of red-leafed kudzu vines, his eyes locked on the white-checkered waistcloth flexing intermittently among the leaves ahead of him. With cautious steps they mounted the nearest ridge, then picked their way down into an even darker, more densely forested valley.

Even here a few bars of sunlight pierced the gloom, filtering down through the branches of half a dozen huge trees with trunks as wide across as a man's arm span. They stood like a congress of thunderheads, each tree a forest, a fiefdom, a nation unto itself. All over their trunks, in the teeming shade, writhed the big, woody tentacles of epiphytic plants—either vines or roots, it was hard to tell—encasing their wide torsos like nets. As Lu Beiping followed Autumn down the slope, slip-sliding through thick mats of decomposing leaves, the trees loomed over him like titanic idols crowned with clouds, their stern, dark gazes weighing upon him.

Nothing stirred here; the valley was utterly silent. Beneath the trees Lu Beiping noticed a small pool or mire, its surface almost completely covered by decaying leaves, and here and there water glinted through the black leaf-carpet, the light tinged with a rainbow sheen as if over many years the pool had accumulated a thick film of oil. No plants grew in this fallow ground, and the fallen branches that jutted through the leaves were coated with a glistening layer of rot. There was no sign that any living soul had ever passed through here, no footprints, no pawmarks, no slither trails to mark the passage of man or beast. There was only the pungent odor of decaying leaves, a sour, stifling scent that clotted his nostrils, heightening the sense that this was all a strange dream. Now that they'd crossed the ridge, it was clear that the rumbling sound, the shriek of the "infant," and the cry of the dying bull had all emanated from this noisome, otherworldly place. Autumn and Lu Beiping traded a look of surprise. Once again Lu Beiping remembered the "baleglen," the weird phantom valley that he'd stumbled into and then never been able to find again.

—That . . . pool, Lu Beiping asked in a low voice: Does anything . . . live down there, you think?

Autumn shook his head.

—No, he whispered, and gestured up at the mountains that ringed the valley: It's just a little pond. There's a stone marker near here, I recall, which some surveyors planted during the years of the Republic. This marks the spot where three county lines cross, right here at the heart of Mudkettle Mountain.

He glanced hurriedly around the shadow-thronged forest, then muttered:

—Queer. Did we catch the ague? Kingfisher said the year Smudge's dad got smudged, there was an awful run of fever in these parts. They say the vapors are strong back in these valleys, you'll have the fits before you know it, and start hearing things . . .

—What's that? Lu Beiping said suddenly, pointing at a spot beneath one of the trees where an odd color stood out against the black-brown leaves. It was too dark in the shade to see the object clearly; they walked quickly toward it, then Lu Beiping stopped, a raw mixture of dread, grief, and awe rising in his throat. He bit his lip, choking back a cry of astonishment, and tears began rolling down his cheeks.

At the foot of the tree, half-covered by rotting leaves, lay a wooden clapper—the cowbell he'd carved for Alyosha. And next to the cowbell, beneath the leaves, he saw a small, dark pool of fresh blood.

Once more a great silence descended upon them, engulfing the entire forest. Autumn stood there for a moment, staring at the bloody cowbell, then he sank to his knees, and brought his forehead again and again to the ground.

Chapter 9
Amaranthine Rosewood

It was evening by the time they made it back to the hollow. When they reached the pool they found the cattle still lazing among the trees, waiting for their master, joined recently by a few stragglers who'd picked their way down out of other mountain valleys. Lu Beiping counted heads and found none missing except for Alyosha and the inveterate wanderer Judas, who was known to saunter innocently back to camp after days spent peregrinating alone through the hills. The cattle seemed to understand intuitively what had happened, for when Lu Beiping approached, bearing Alyosha's cowbell, they rose immediately at the familiar knocking sound and crowded round him in their eagerness to sniff the bell, shouldering one another out of the way as each brought its nose to the wood in turn in a gesture eerily similar to a kiss. The sight so moved Lu Beiping that he told Autumn he wanted to sit for a while and keep the grieving cattle company, and handing him the cowbell he instructed him to go on ahead. But as soon as Autumn set off down the trail the cattle rose in sudden agitation and, spurning their master, followed Autumn and the tock-tock-tocking clapper all the way down to the hollow.

Kingfisher, Stump, and the three children sat by the log-soaking pool behind the cabins, waiting for them. Clearly they too had heard the bull's dying wail and guessed what misfortune had befallen Alyosha in the high valley. When Autumn and Lu Beiping descended the stone steps at the back of the hollow, Jade strode out from behind the hearth stove and hurried over to meet them, clapping her hands briskly.

—Good, glad to see nothing happened to these two. As long as the humans are safe, we ought to count ourselves lucky. Four Eyes, won't you stay and drink another cup with Kingfisher tonight? Wait till you smell supper, I stewed up some wild monkeyheads with sour cabbage, it's to die for—

This blithe chatter, clearly intended to dispel the sober atmosphere, had the opposite effect when Jade uttered this last unfortunate phrase. Glancing nervously at Kingfisher, she prattled on:

—Kingfish and Stump were just scolding me, saying I shouldn't've let a city boy like you go up into the valley by yourself. If anything had happened to you, we'd—

Kingfisher glared at her, and the "den mother" fell silent. Quickly Lu Beiping herded the animals to the slope on the far side of the pool, where he found Maria and her calf, whom he'd tethered to one of the corner posts of his hut that morning, resting on a pile of fresh-cut hay next to a wooden basin filled with water. Jade must have gone down earlier that afternoon and fetched them. The hay was a salad of different-lengthed pieces of grass, like pig feed, and Lu Beiping guessed that this was the work of Smudge and the little ones. Maria had eaten her fill and now lay sprawled in the pile of hay, a jumble of teats and legs, while her calf drank milk placidly. As Lu Beiping approached, Maria hailed him, trumpeting a long, warm note of greeting.

Once he'd gotten the animals settled he returned to the pool behind the lodge, washed his face, and collected himself. When he stood up he glanced over at the cabin and froze. Behind the hearth stove and the supper table, in the dim interior of the lodge, the entire family knelt in prayer. In the shuddering lamplight Lu Beiping made out Alyosha's cowbell placed fastidiously on the altar next to Smudge's dad's name tablet and the white porcelain Kwan-Yin. Kingfisher, clasping three incense sticks, muttered and led the assembled clan in a series of prostrations. Watching this, Lu Beiping had the distinct feeling that he'd been excluded. Whether this was intentional or not he couldn't say—but today even he, no great believer in spirits, would've happily knelt and said a prayer for Alyosha. (Before long, Lu Beiping would learn that this sense of foreboding he felt had been quite on the mark.)

The mood at dinner was still somber, and he continued to feel like an outsider. Wordlessly Jade arranged the dishes that she'd sweated over all day, and wordlessly the others took their seats at the table. The bowl of beer, which had been placed on the altar as an offering, disappeared into the kitchen after Kingfisher spilled two ladlefuls for Horn. Jade filled their bowls with yam porridge, and the whole gang slurped diligently at the tasteless gruel. Nobody was dying for Jade's stewed mushrooms tonight, and the redolent dish, which normally would have required protection by Jade's nimble chopsticks, drew little attention except from the goggle-eyed youngsters. The atmosphere was sepulchral. Never before, dining "off the registers," had Lu Beiping seen the driftfolk so unenthusiastic about food. He ventured a glance at Autumn, but as soon as the man set foot in the lodge he'd reverted to his usual rag-doll passivity, and didn't acknowledge him. Weirdly, even Jade, who'd greeted them so gregariously when they entered the hollow, now looked despondent; once in a while she deposited a pinch of mushrooms in Lu Beiping's bowl and threw him a mournful look. Smudge, sitting next to Lu Beiping, affected an expression of grown-up seriousness, but kept kicking him from time to time beneath the table with one of his small bare feet. Lu Beiping stole a glance at him, but the boy's face remained impassive. Only when Kingfisher ducked outside to blow his nose did Smudge bring his lips to Lu Beiping's ear and alert him in an urgent whisper:

—Foreman and Kambugger came looking for you this afternoon!

Instantly Lu Beiping grasped the gravity of the situation. If Alyosha's suspicious death—or any other of many possible reasons—had brought a doler "magistrate" up into the hollow, Kingfisher and the others would be counting their prayer beads and contemplating a suitable retribution.

Sure enough, the moment Kingfisher stepped back through the door he cleared his throat and said:

—Four Eyes, have you eaten your fill? I fear you must be hungry after a long day upmountain.

His tone was gentle, but Lu Beiping detected a smoldering edge to his voice. Everybody drank porridge for a few silent seconds, then Kingfisher lit his water pipe, took a couple of drags, and began speaking in earnest.

—Been a long time since I checked an almanac, so I can't say whether this is a fair day or ill. Yesterday a storm more fearsome than any I've ever seen blows through here, Jade frets about you all day, turns out you're well, and on top of that your cow bears a babe overnight. Where there's new life, there's light, light that can push back the vile shadows of this world.

Kingfisher spoke slowly, puffing smoke between sentences. The whole family listened with held breath as their chieftain worked through his spiritual calculus. Stump chose now, of all times, to lurch up off the bed and steer his massive frame, hunched over like a shrimp, around the others and in the direction of the door. Kingfisher glowered at him. Stump stammered:

—I . . . I need to take a shit.

Jade snorted, barely suppressing a laugh. Smudge was not so successful and broke into giggles. Tick, sensing an opening, piped up in a tittering voice:

—I need to take a shit too!

Kingfisher blanched, grabbed a porridge bowl, and hurled it squarely at Smudge.

—A blight on you, you miserable little cur! You hungry for a whipping? How many ounces do you think you count for around here? You—

Kingfisher raised the big bamboo pipe and was about to strike Smudge when Jade rushed over and planted herself between them, shielding her son. Kingfisher shoved her out of the way, raised the pipe again, and this time a black stream of tobacco juice arced out of the barrel, splattering all over the table and turning their dinner into a tarry mess. Momentarily dazed, Kingfisher lowered his pipe. Then, seeing Smudge's obstinate face still staring up at him without a hint of shame or deference, half-formed syllables of protest working their way around the boy's gritted teeth, Kingfisher's anger flared again and he lifted the pipe once more. This time, though, it was Lu Beiping who stopped him, his hand shooting out to grab the pipe.

—Kingfisher! If you're angry, take it out on me, okay? Lu Beiping said, fixing him with a level gaze. I know you have something to say to me. Just say it, then you can punish Smudge if you still want to.

The tension in the room subsided. Stump, who had had the poor fortune to set off this bout of mayhem, slunk back to the table and sat, red-faced and squirming, as if his bottom had sprouted needles. Autumn, sitting next to him, gave Lu Beiping a wink. Jade, leaning over the table to clean up the contents of the overturned porridge bowl, gazed into the pot of squid-ink soup to which her stewed mushrooms had been reduced, and muttered:

—God, Kingfisher, what a mess. If you like shit soup, I'll remember that for next time.

Then she slapped her lips and said no more. Lu Beiping smiled to himself, thinking: That woman simply cannot keep her mouth shut.

—You're right, Four Eyes, Kingfisher said, wiping the look of embarrassment off of his face and reining the conversation back to the subject at hand: You're a strong man, I see you've got grit. So I'm going to tell this to you straight. Things have been real odd on Mud-kettle Mountain lately. First, that young man comes slinking up here burning paper money. Then the storm comes, then the flood. Today the gods that live up on the mountain got angry, no mistaking it, and *she* showed herself, and a cow got smudged. Or could it be that *I'm* in the wrong—that *I* riled her, cursing you with her name in broad daylight before you headed up into the high valley?

Kingfisher spoke quietly now, and a note of melancholy entered his voice as he went on:

—We who live on this mountain, starting back with Smudge's pa, Horn, we've always known that when we fell timber, we've got to take care not to cut the land's veins. The Tam-chow hill men, Lam-ko tribesfolk, and Loi and Hmong hunters we've met in these parts have warned us, time and time again, that half the ley lines on this island cross right here under Mudkettle Mountain, and that no matter what we do, we can't afford to rile the wyrm-demon that lives up in that bowl. They say she comes and goes through that pool, the Sea's Eye, that funnels straight out to sea. That's how she comes up from her godly dwelling place. The year he fell into shadow, Smudge's pa saw her skin up in the valley and didn't know to pray, so when he went up onto the mountain on Midsummer he got squashed beneath a falling tree. Midsummer—he didn't know Midsummer's her sacred day! Never, never wake the snake air on Midsummer!

Kingfisher put his nose to the water pipe, discovered it was already empty, and handed it to Jade. He continued:

—These past couple years we've had no trouble from her. Yesterday, when that fierce wind blew through, it didn't do a speck of harm to us, here in the hollow. You can bet it was her blessing that kept us safe. Why, then, did she get angry today, why'd she show herself to us and gobble up your bull like a sweetpaste morsel? In my forty-five years I've heard plenty of tales of dogs, pigs, and chickens getting swallowed by snakes, but I've never, not once, heard tell of a snake big enough to swallow a bull. If this isn't the work of a wyrm, a dragon, a thousand-year-old snake-spirit—then what is it? Horned demons and hidden serpents—what the ancients meant by that, I know all too well!

Kingfisher's speech had cast a chill over the room. Borrowing the light from Stump's pipe he lit three incense sticks, walked over to the altar, and looking upward traced some sort of symbol in the air, then he bowed, muttered something beneath his breath, and planted the burning sticks in the small censer before Alyosha's clapper. Everybody in the room watched Kingfisher's motions in reverent silence, as if he were a priest performing last rites at a gravesite.

This guy, Lu Beiping thought, really is like some kind of evil priest. He's the grand shaman of Mudkettle Mountain.

Outside, from the direction of the other lodge, came the sound of a door banging in the wind. Kingfisher sighed and returned to the table.

—I've always said, we driftfolk, our lives are twigs in Heaven's palm. We can't afford to get on the bad side of evil people, but more than anything we can't afford to get on the spirits' bad side. I don't know what we did to warrant their anger, such that she bestirred herself up there in the mountain's belly. Four Eyes—now Kingfisher fixed Lu Beiping with a dark, searching gaze—here's what I think. All this queer stuff started happening right about the time you first came up to the hollow. If you, if you . . . if you're the villain who's going to bring down ruin on our poor heads . . . then, please! Tell us!

As Kingfisher's speech mounted toward its climax Lu Beiping had risen, ready to make his testimony, expecting Kingfisher to call him to account. But to Lu Beiping's surprise this jeremiad culminated in a humble plea, then ended abruptly. He opened his mouth to speak, but before he could say anything Kingfisher rubbed his hands together briskly and said:

—That's enough for tonight. Stump, go take your shit.

Then he turned, grabbed his water pipe, and without one look at Lu Beiping he strode out the door.

Lu Beiping was flabbergasted. Jade leaned over to say something to him, but he pushed her away roughly. Outside the moon shone bright, bathing the hills in the same cool, limpid light that he remembered from his first night in the hollow. Why hadn't Kingfisher once mentioned the foreman's visit? As he puzzled over this, Autumn went to the door, glanced back at Lu Beiping, and beckoned him to follow.

Three bamboo cots stood in a row, set off by thatch-and-bamboo screens. Autumn's was nestled in the far corner and looked slightly more fastidiously cared for than the others, the only additions being a hand-sewn pillow and an old, ratty blanket that covered half the bed. Kingfisher's and Stump's cots were bare except for a jumble of waistcloths and shirts that probably served as bedclothes when the nights got cold, and for pillows each had a single thick log of bamboo, their surfaces worn to a smooth sheen like the water pipe that leaned against Jade's bed.

This was the first time that Lu Beiping had set foot inside the second, larger lodge that huddled against the base of the bluff. Outside in the moonlight he saw Kingfisher sitting alone under the lychee tree, nursing his water pipe, the flame winking in the darkness beneath the tree's black silhouette. Stump had gone off to "salute the wind," as they called it—there being no latrines in the hollow, all ablutions were performed guerilla-style. It was said that Stump had the remarkable ability of returning from such missions carrying a clutch of partridge eggs or half a dozen frogs tied to a string. Who knew what succulent prize he'd bring back this evening. As Lu Beiping walked into the lodge, nerves still ajitter from Kingfisher's menacing speech, he hesitated at the door, asking:

—Is it . . . okay for a guest to come in here? That doesn't violate your laws?

Autumn lit the small kerosene lamp at the head of the bed and said with a gentle laugh:

—You, a guest? You're Jade's new Horn.

—Autumn! said Lu Beiping, marching through the door with a stricken expression on his face: Come on, don't joke around. Are you trying to humiliate me too?

—Oh . . . no! Of course not! Autumn said hastily, seeing Lu Beiping's look of chagrin. Four Eyes . . . Bei, you misunderstood me. I only wanted for you to come and keep me company, so we can talk a bit, ease ourselves. Here, sit down.

A log stool sat next to the cot. Probably Autumn perched on it and used the cot as a desk when he practiced calligraphy. Lu Beiping took the seat and looked around. On one corner of the cot lay a wooden crate that had once held soap at a "doler" supply co-op, now serving as Autumn's footlocker. On top of the crate sat the black notebook and an enamelware cup blazoned with the red slogan of a bygone campaign, out of which protruded a toothbrush tucked in a rolled-up washcloth. On the mud wall at the head of the bed hung two tree branches crowned with dry leaves, looking grand but somewhat incongruous.

—Though . . . you really are a guest, truth be told, Autumn said, rubbing his hands with an awkward chuckle. And look, I don't even have a cup of tea to offer you.

Lu Beiping opened his mouth, searching for something to say, then pointed at the branches.

—What are those? Why did you hang them there?

—Those are flowering pear branches, Autumn replied automatically.

—Flowering pear? What's that? Are they . . . to ward off evil?

—There you go again, Autumn said, then he went on, leaving Lu Beiping's question unanswered: How do you scholars call it?—he gestured at the wicker outer wall against which the cot nestled—My chilly hermitage. Chilly indeed, look, when it rains the water comes right through this wall. It gets downright cold.

Lu Beiping said nothing, staring levelly at Autumn, then glanced again at the branches. He sensed that Autumn was concealing something behind this pointless patter.

—Bei, Autumn said with a humorless laugh, You come in here and rather than asking why Kingfisher got so angry at you, you ask me about those old dead branches?

A sly smile crept across Lu Beiping's lips, and he continued to stare at the branches mounted on the mud wall. He wasn't going to let Autumn slither away so easily.

—You're a hard one to please, Autumn sighed at last, then his deliquescent eyes locked with Lu Beiping's and he said in a tone that was suddenly fierce:

—Fine, I'll tell you. Those branches have to do with my dad. This afternoon you kept asking about him and I wouldn't answer. Now, I will. What do you want to know?

Lu Beiping gazed back at him. What a strange, moody man; his emotions were like warm and cold fronts blowing back and forth across the map of his face. Lu Beiping laughed.

—Autumn, who do you think I am? One of those "down with counterrevolutionaries" types? You think I'm going to demand to see your papers?

—More or less.

Once more Autumn's expression became downcast. Lu Beiping, still looking at the branches, asked:

—So, what are you willing to tell me?

—My dad's dead, Autumn said abruptly. Whole family's dead. Every one of them. They buried them alive, dug them up again, then cooked them and ate them. Even the organs.

—What?

Lu Beiping sprang to his feet as if he'd been burned.

—Autumn, are you kidding me? Is this the truth?

Autumn's face was pale in the lamplight. He smiled grimly as he gazed at Lu Beiping.

—Would I lie to you, Bei? You wanted to know the whole story behind those branches, didn't you?

Lu Beiping's shock contrasted sharply with Autumn's cool tone. He watched the moonlight creep under the bamboo door like a spreading pool of blood, and remembered the dark slick he'd seen under the carpet of leaves up in that dusky forest at the heart of the high valley.

(Years later, repeating the story of Autumn's family to Tsung, Lu Beiping still couldn't contain his horror. Even today the wave of cannibalism that swept through the backcountry of Guangxi province during the Cultural Revolution has the air of an unbelievable tall tale. But it was in a manner strangely calm and devoid of emotion that Autumn laid out to Lu Beiping the details that follow.)

Late one night, in the autumn of sixty-eight, Autumn's father burst into his mother-in-law's house, where his son lay in hiding, and escorted him secretly to the edge of the village. He told him that he must leave town immediately, leave the province, find work as an off-register laborer, anything, and in no case should he come back, particularly if the harvest was bad. The next day Autumn's father was arrested by the local militia. Shortly afterward the vigilantes broke into Autumn's aunt's house and took away his mother and two sisters too. A Special Agricultural Workers' Tribunal was convened; Autumn's family was tried and denounced; the villagers pushed them into a freshly dug hole, buried them under six feet of earth, and, once they had suffocated to death, dug their bodies out and . . .

—But why, why . . . why would they bury them first, before they . . .

Lu Beiping choked on the word "ate," unable to form that awful syllable.

—I didn't learn the reason till years after I ran away, Autumn said, staring at the ground. I was told that in those days there were different popular ways of eating human flesh. Roasting people, burying people alive and then stewing them . . . they said that that gave the meat different flavors—

—Stop! Stop!

Moonlight lay like frost on the ground outside, burning so coldly that Lu Beiping had to avert his eyes.

—Your dad . . . your father, what did he do? Lu Beiping asked, still curious for details even after this dreadful revelation.

—He was an elementary school teacher. He taught at the village school in Tung Ling, where we lived.

—Where's Tung Ling?

—In Guangxi. Lots of famous men came from Tung Ling, back in the day.

—Why'd they want to kill your father? What crime could an elementary school teacher possibly be guilty of?

—They said my dad was gentry, a landlord. My whole family came from a long line of local noblemen. Back then they were always fixing to . . . what was it, first it was Tearing up Capitalism by the Roots, then it was Exterminate . . . Exterminate All . . .

—Horned Demons and Hidden Serpents.

Lu Beiping shuddered as he supplied the phrase.

—I don't know much about my granddad, except that he was a learned man, lived in Lau-chow City, and died long before I was born. But I know that way back, my father's people were one of the most distinguished families in Tung Ling. By the time of the Republic they'd already come down in the world.

Lu Beiping said nothing, studied Autumn's face silently in the lamplight. Those weather-worn, sun-darkened features, upon closer inspection, had a clarity of contour that hinted at Autumn's literate upbringing. No wonder Kingfisher and the others always said that Autumn wasn't meant to dine at the driftfolk table. No wonder Autumn loved to scribble in that notebook, had memorized poetry by Li Shutong, knew so much arcane lore beyond Lu Beiping's ken . . .

Lu Beiping gazed at the branches hanging on the wall, truly wanting to know the whole story.

—These branches, Autumn said, taking them down from the wall, a note of excitement entering his voice: They're from two different kinds of flowering pear tree I found when I was scouting timber. Folks around here call trees with this kind of leaf "yellow flowering pear," and this other kind "red flowering pear." It's good wood for making furniture—some of the best, they say. But Bei, have you ever heard of amaranthine rosewood?

Lu Beiping shook his head. More and more he was discovering that Autumn inhabited a very different world from him, full of things of which he was ignorant.

Autumn spread his palms and opened his mouth, but said nothing. It seemed as if he hadn't spoken of these things in a long time, and needed to dust off another register of speech more appropriate to the topic at hand. Later, whenever discussing such lofty matters with Lu Beiping, Autumn always began in this groping, tongue-tied manner.

—Amaranthine rosewood . . . Autumn said, gazing down at the branches, the leaves rustling crisply as he rolled them between his fingers: How can I . . . put words to such a thing? My dad said, true amaranthine rosewood trees have long gone extinct from this world. Already in the days of the Ming and Qing emperors it was hard to find them, even in Jiaozhi, even in their native reaches beyond the South Sea. Jiaozhi's what they used to call Vietnam. My dad said they grew so slow, amaranthine rosewood trees, that no tree younger than a hundred years old was fit to be hewn.

Autumn spread his palms again and went on, gesticulating as he spoke:

—Nowadays, red camphorwood's held to be the finest of woods. But in the Qing court ledgers, amaranthine rosewood was priced at twice, three times, ten times the price of red camphor! Unbelievable, no? So, starting in the time of Kangxi and Qianlong, it was illegal for anyone outside the imperial house to own amaranthine rosewood furniture, and any pieces the commoners owned the emperor bought back. Later on plenty of vain, self-glorious officials and merchants got in the habit of claiming that their own furniture, camphorwood, teak, mahogany pieces and the like, was amaranthine. Ah, those base creatures—what did they know from amaranthine rosewood?

Lu Beiping gazed at Autumn in mild surprise. *Base creatures.* How strange it was to hear a backwoods drifter like Autumn dismiss in such lofty terms the worldly pretensions of the human race.

Autumn looked up at Lu Beiping, his eyes shining.

—I kid you not, Bei, my family owned three pieces of amaranthine rosewood furniture. A censer, an armchair, and a desk. My dad told me that one of my long-ago ancestors brought them down with him from the Forbidden City when he was demoted to the prefectship of the Jiaozhi Commandery. When I was a boy, my family's fortunes were thin as pot likker, but my dad cherished those rosewood pieces like there was nothing more precious in this world. Me and my sisters, only on our birthdays and New Years would he grant us to sit in that rosewood chair. And every student in my dad's classes knew that whoever got the best marks, at the end of the semester my dad would invite him over to his house to sit in the Master's Greatchair and eat a bowl of sweet dumplings in longan coulis.

As Autumn got deeper into his story his speech grew swifter and more self-assured. Now, abruptly, his tone changed:

—Then came the Movement. First thing they did was confiscate my family's rosewood furniture, said it was evidence that my dad had monarchist leanings. Then they arrested my dad and put the chair itself on trial, like they'd seen in that movie, *The Case of the Landlord's Armchair*. After the struggle meeting was over, they told my dad to light a match and set fire to the rosewood furniture he'd inherited from his ancestors.

—What happened? Did he burn them?

—Burn them? Autumn laughed bitterly. You've got to understand, Bei—amaranthine rosewood doesn't burn! They used up a mountain of firewood trying to burn that furniture, but in the end that desk and chair just sat there, black and gleaming, on top of a huge heap of charcoal. My dad rushed into the ashes, threw his arms around the red-hot rosewood chair and wept, saying: You people go ahead and burn me too! Then the villagers crowded round with hoes and hatchets, hacked up that unburnable rosewood furniture, then took the pieces and threw them in the Ebonwater.

All this Autumn said with unusual calm, as if he were telling someone else's story.

—Thing is, amaranthine rosewood doesn't float either. When they saw those pieces of black wood piled in the shallows like hunks of iron, not floating or getting carried away by the current, the villagers said they were witched, and wouldn't dare touch them anymore.

Lu Beiping stole a glance at Autumn. Now his friend's emotions were beginning to show on his moonlit features.

—I was still working in the fields at that point. The Movement had just started, they hadn't yet killed or eaten anybody. I wanted to go to the river in the middle of the night and haul out the pieces of wood, but my dad urged me not to. He said, If that wood sees the light of day, it'll just die another death. There in the river, it's got some life to it yet. Leave it be.

Autumn's voice was rising now, carried upward on a swell of emotion. Lu Beiping, fingering one of the pearwood leaves, decided to change the subject.

—So . . . you said that people often mistake camphorwood and mahogany for amaranthine rosewood. How do you know that these pearwood branches are true amaranthine? That's what you think it is, right?

—Here, take a look. Folks here call both of these flowering pear, but they're not at all the same kind of wood.

Autumn handed him both branches, and Lu Beiping examined them in the lamplight. Sure enough, the leaves were quite dissimilar. One kind was pointy, the other was round, and they both had different textures.

—The one with the round leaves, that's yellow flowering pear. It's a precious wood too, they call it amber rosewood, but you won't find it anywhere on Mudkettle Mountain. This one, though—Autumn shook the pointy-leafed branch, which gave off a crisp, metallic rustle—this is from a rare tree alright. It's mighty old, with small leaves, and so covered in creepers it was hard to tell what kind it was. Bei, I've explored every nook and cranny of this mountain, but it wasn't till yesterday that I found this red flowering pear tree. Old as the gods, it was—oh, what a tree!

Autumn opened his notebook and flipped to a page where he'd sketched a map of Mudkettle Mountain.

—It's fearful hard to get up there. You have to climb up over this treacherous pass—Autumn indicated a spot on the map, and as he spoke his voice was now charged with excitement—My dad said there's three kinds of amaranthine rosewood. The censer we had was starry amaranthine, the chair was cockblood amaranthine, and the desk was rippled amaranthine. Rippled amaranthine rosewood's sometimes called amaranthine pearwood, and that's what you're looking at, people here call it red flowering pear. The grain's wavy on every side, that's how you can tell. See?

Lu Beiping took the pointy-leafed branch and turned it over in his hands. The wood was a deep reddish purple, and just as Autumn said the grain was wavy no matter how you turned it. The dense, rippled growth rings glittered a faint, dull gold. Small as the branch was, it weighed heavy in his hand, as if it were cast out of metal. The thin, sharp leaves had already dried out, but they were quite thick and had a jade-like luster. The joints where each twig budded off from the branch were firm as knobs of solder. The wood was pliable but tough; it must have been hard to break off.

—What do you think? A rare thing, no?

Autumn took the branch and hung it carefully back on the wall, then stood for a moment, his head tilted to one side, admiring it. He laughed quietly to himself.

—I'm certain of it, that red flowering pear tree is amaranthine pearwood. Amaranthine rosewood trees haven't gone extinct—sky's my witness, it's not true! And I've had the luck to see one!

A thin line of sweat shone on Autumn's right temple, its faint glimmer outlining the dark contour of his face. Autumn had sunk deep into his world of rosewood. As if no one else were present he muttered to himself:

—One amaranthine tree on all of Mudkettle Mountain . . . and I found it!

A slanting shaft of moonlight lay across the floor.

—Good heavens, why have I been prattling on like this? Autumn said with a chuckle. I'd only meant to sit a minute, give you a chance to rest, hear what's new with you.

He threw a glance out the door and said in a hushed voice:

—Did that scare you, what Kingfisher said?

—Scare me? It's just you people's taboos, Lu Beiping replied nonchalantly, his mind still on other things. I'm not really one of you. Kingfisher can't do anything to me.

—Yes, Autumn said, smiling grimly: But you're Jade's man. You and her made good, that makes you as much her man as Kingfisher and Stump.

Lu Beiping turned quickly to look at Autumn.

—What, and you're not?

—Nope, Autumn said simply.

—How come?

—Can't rightly say, Autumn said, curling his lip and looking at the floor. I don't fancy being her man, that's all. I'm just . . . like she says, I'm her adopted kid brother. Her ward, her houseboy.

—Her *houseboy*? Lu Beiping stood up abruptly, outraged at this blatant display of self-scorn: Autumn, how can you say that about yourself? You sweat as hard as anybody else around here. Why do you pretend like you're some kind of slave?

These words brought a fresh glimmer of tears to Autumn's eyes. Seeing that he'd struck a nerve, Lu Beiping pressed on, vowing that tonight he'd peel aside every protective layer that concealed the sorrow at Autumn's core.

—Autumn, I know you've got a lot of things weighing on you. Don't be so tough on yourself. If you want to cry, just let yourself cry! Let it all out, then stand up and face the world like a man! I just hate to see you shuffling around here so subserviently in front of King-fisher and Stump!

Autumn wiped his eyes.

—Bei, he said, it's been years since I cried in front of another person. But it seems that every time I talk to you, something just brings the tears streaming out.

Lu Beiping felt a slight lurch in his chest. Both of them sat there for a while, saying nothing, while Lu Beiping studied Autumn's face in the wavering lamplight. A pair of tear-tracks gleamed on his dark, hollow cheeks. As he looked at them, Lu Beiping felt as if their light had reached deep inside him and plucked a string that had long lain silent.

—Autumn . . . Lu Beiping stood up, preparing to take his leave. Then he stopped with a cry of surprise: What the . . . ! Smudge?

The big dome of Smudge's head was framed in the window. The thatch shutter propped on its bamboo rod obscured half of his impish grin.

—You little devil, Lu Beiping said. Have you been eavesdropping on us?

Smudge threw a backward glance around the clearing, probably to make sure that Kingfisher hadn't moved from the foot of the tree, then went around to the door and strode ostentatiously into the room.

—Hmph! So many friends you've got now, Four Eyes! Why don't you talk with me nay more?

—Oh, don't be silly, Lu Beiping said, giving the boy a tap on the forehead. You'd better be careful, Smudge. You know what they say, children who eavesdrop will never grow up.

—I don't want to grow up, Smudge retorted. Four Eyes, that Kambugger's an evil bastard. He came up with your foreman this afternoon looking for the kine, my Pa she greeted him nice, the foreman looked plenty happy, then just ere they left, Kambugger said something to Kingfisher that made his face go all grave.

Autumn caught Lu Beiping's eye and gave him a knowing grimace.

—That old shrimp. What harm can he do you?

—Gentlemen, Lu Beiping said, narrowing his eyes and affecting a look of frosty menace: Kambugger may be an evil bastard, but I can be an evil bastard too.

Autumn stared at him in surprise. Smudge giggled.

—Show me, show me! Smudge cried, and running over he snatched the glasses off of Lu Beiping's face then clambered up onto Autumn's cot. Lu Beiping grabbed Smudge, but Autumn took the glasses and hid them from Lu Beiping, and soon all three of them had collapsed in a tangled heap on the bed.

In the midst of this there came a loud *bang* from the direction of the other cabin, followed by Jade and Kingfisher's voices shouting over each other.

Autumn, Lu Beiping, and Smudge ran to the window. Outside, the lychee tree stood like a paralyzed monster, its frozen limbs splayed in the moonlight. The sounds of muffled argument began again, and as they competed with each other the voices grew louder and higher pitched.

—Kingfisher, Jade said sharply, a beseeching note in her voice:
You can't do this. If you make him leave, I'll leave.

—You'll leave? You *want* to leave? You wouldn't dare!

There was another *bang*, followed immediately by the rumbling of
a deep voice. Kingfisher hollered:

—Stump! Don't you try to play the peacekeeper! She won't let
him go, you won't let her go—then, fine! I'll go! Is that what you want?

—Calm down, Kingfish, calm down! Stump burbled. 'Tis all but
hooey and hearsay. Whose word do you trust more, his or mine? I—

—He doesn't trust anyone! Jade interjected shrilly. Nobody but
his own self! And his goddam spirits!

Whap! There was the sharp smack of flesh on flesh, and Jade
shrieked:

—Kingfisher! You *dare* hit me! You *dare*!

The two little ones, who had just woken up, added their wails to
the uproar, and a multilayered clamor of voices and noises ensued.

—I'll give you one better, you rotten, low-down, motherfucking
piece of *shit*!

Thock! Swissssh! THUNK-tock-tock-tock . . .

From the sound of it, dipper, broom, and cowbell had been
hurled in quick succession.

—Mercy, woman! Peace, peace! Hit me all you want, just don't
curse the spirits!

Suddenly they all fell silent.

Autumn was standing in the doorway.

—Quit fighting, you all. He's gone.

Outside they heard the splashing tumult of the herd's departure,
like a bulldozer rolling down the creekbed. While they were busy
fighting, Lu Beiping had mustered his cattle and, leading Maria and
her calf on a rope, slipped away into the moon-dappled forest.

—Four Eyes! Kingfisher roared. Halt! He rushed out the door,
jumped onto a pile of logs near the head of the creek, and shouted
after Lu Beiping: Hear me out, son! I've got one question for you!
Then you can leave!

The sloshing footsteps quickened. Obviously Lu Beiping was in no mood to stick around. Kingfisher, growing more flustered, bellowed desperately into the trees:

—Four Eyes! Kambugger said you're not clean! Tell me straight, what did you do to get sent up into the mountains? What did he mean by that, not clean?

—Peh! Jade spat in his ear. You've got some nerve, asking him a question like that. Is Kambugger clean? There's nothing that man loves better than to stick his dick up a cow's asshole. What right's he got to judge who's clean? Hmph! You and him are quite the pair.

Now Jade turned and shouted into the forest:

—Four Eyes! Wait up! I'm coming with—

A heavy male hand yanked her back. Jade stumbled and sat down heavily on the rocks.

—Four Eyes! she wailed at the top of her lungs: Four Eyes! Please! Then she broke down and sobbed.

Chapter 10
Cockfight

Lu Beiping's new hut and corral had traded places: The corral now bordered on the creek; the hut nestled in the shade of the trees. The roof thatch was now reinforced with strips of bamboo, the timbers of the frame were nailed together with metal staples, and the kitchen was equipped with a real lime-and-clay hearth stove—the whole setup, as Chu quipped to Lu Beiping while the workers gathered their tools at the end of the day, was a fitting headquarters for the Cattle Commander. Gosh, he said with a sly smile: Do you suppose the foreman hopes you'll integrate? Or maybe that's what you had in mind, to spend the rest of your life up here on Mudkettle Mountain making revolution? Lu Beiping studied his friend's sun-browned face, feeling an overwhelming sense of remove that even the phrase "overwhelming sense of remove" wasn't strong enough to capture. Even their language was of two different worlds; he'd almost forgotten about "integration," "making revolution," and all the rest of the re-ed lingo. Fate had consigned them to separate dimensions. Being flung to the far side of an ever-widening gulf between him and his old life and all his old friends wasn't something he'd have chosen voluntarily, but at this point, returning to the old way of things wasn't something he'd do voluntarily either. Wow, he thought, I really have become a citizen of the shadow world.

The foreman himself had led the work team into the jungle to rebuild Lu Beiping's ruined campsite. Typhoon Number Five had thrown the entire Agrecorps into chaos, and even the epic cross-battalion land-reclamation campaign currently in progress had been blown to the winds, as the troops massed at the work site several counties over scattered back to their own units. Lu Beiping didn't know it at the time, but "Big Number Five" had dealt a near-mortal blow to Hainan Island's rubber industry. Over the past two years the endless string of Operations and Campaigns aimed at accelerating rubber production had, literally, worn the orchards to the breaking point, and when the typhoon tore through the groves, the overworked trees, their midriffs whittled thin by the knives of overeager tappers, split clean in two as if snipped by divine scissors. The newly planted groves, where the planters had sacrificed windbreak acreage in order to inflate production statistics, were in the sorriest state of all. Whirling into these defenseless stands, the wind had wrought murderous havoc, bending the young, breaking the old, beheading the tall, ripping the short clean from the soil. Almost without exception the stands of four-year-old saplings, all of them nearing rubber-bearing age, had been rendered useless, and the new groves were now wastelands of naked stumps. Needless to say, the flash floods had taken a vicious toll on the livestock and on the human inhabitants of the camps as well. On a neighboring plantation a squad of sixteen re-ed girls who'd called themselves the Steel Swineherds had been swept away and never seen again.

As the foreman told all this to Lu Beiping, his eyes grew red and he began to tear up. This was the first time Lu Beiping had ever seen the foreman cry. (And it wouldn't be the last, he added to Tsung.)

In the silence that followed Lu Beiping reported his own losses to the foreman. Judas, the scrawny old bull with the spotted back, had run off alone in search of shelter and been killed by a windborne stone in a gully on the far side of the ridge. And Alyosha, the lead bull with the mottled brown hide, had led the herd up into the bowl of Mudkettle Mountain, where they'd all weathered the storm safely except for Alyosha, who . . . disappeared.

—Disappeared? the foreman asked, noticing the odd catch in Lu Beiping's voice. How?

—Well, the migrant woodcutters who live up there told me . . . Lu Beiping began falteringly. They told me Alyosha was . . . eaten.

By a giant snake. That lives up on the mountain. All I found was the wooden cowbell I made for him, lying on the forest floor.

Lu Beiping felt tears burning in his own eyes. He said nothing else about what he and Autumn had seen and heard up in the high valley.

—A giant snake? the foreman said, a look of amazement flashing briefly across his swarthy face. You mean the Snakeweird of Mud-kettle Mountain? You're kidding me.

Overhearing their conversation, the workers who'd been busy hammering and thatching laid their tools aside and crowded round.

—I'll be damned! Friend Lu saw the Snakeweird! Did you hear that? It ate a whole—

—Nonsense! boomed the foreman. Get back to work!

Amid the faces of the workers, Lu Beiping picked out the fat moon-cheeks of Sergeant Fook. Both Fong and the foreman's son, however, were absent today.

In its most basic outlines Lu Beiping told the foreman the story of how Maria had given birth overnight at the height of the storm. As usual he didn't mention Jade. When he finished, the foreman laid a brawny arm across Lu Beiping's shoulders and gave him a hearty squeeze.

—Well done, son, well done, said the foreman, still wiping his nose. Don't fret about that brown bull. We gained one, we lost one, it equals out. You know, thanks to the diligent job you've done with the cattle, our unit had the fewest livestock losses of the entire battalion! If *he'd* been in charge—the foreman gestured at the Gaffer, who was busy tinkering with the oxcart—I fear we'd have lost the entire herd. You're a real hero, Lu. I'm going to recommend you for a medal.

—I don't want a medal, Lu Beiping said quietly.

The foreman tightened his grip painfully on Lu Beiping's shoulder.

—What was it you called that bull who got killed by the stone? Judas? Ha! What queer names you come up with. No loss at all, as far as I'm concerned—it was about time that old coot bit the dust. And we'd already planned to slaughter one of the animals, throw a big ration supp to celebrate our unit's successful weathering of the typhoon. We all need a little extra grease in our bellies to make up for the hard times we've just been through.

Once again the foreman had quite a bit to say to Lu Beiping. This time, though, Lu Beiping sensed no insincerity in his words.

He freed himself gently from the foreman's grip, went over to the newly built corral and busied himself laying a bed of fresh straw for Maria and her calf. The foreman turned and started rallying a group of men to go over the ridge and butcher Judas's corpse, so that the entire team could haul down the meat when the day's work was done. And he didn't forget to lead the others to the site of the old corral and bucket away what manure remained—when it came to Production, that all-important matter, the foreman's stance was never ambiguous.

As Lu Beiping gazed from afar at the foreman's bear-like figure, he felt, suddenly and surprisingly, a great deal less antipathy for his "father-in-law." Perhaps it was because of those earnest tears he'd shed over the damage wreaked by the typhoon, the loss of human life.

—Well done, son, well done! Chu crowed, leering at him from the crest of the roof where he lay belly down, tying bundles of thatch.

Fook, perched atop the Gaffer's oxcart, chipped in:

—Yeah, Lu, you're a real hero!

Once again the creek's babbling filled the night, and Lu Beiping couldn't sleep.

The hut had a clean, new-house smell, the grassy scent of new thatch mixing pleasantly with the odor of freshly spread lime in the drainage ditch. The cattle, too, seemed satisfied with their new creek-side quarters; after a short spell of trumpeting and jostling they settled down for the night, and from time to time Lu Beiping heard them ruminating sleepily in the corral, like a bunch of old monks yawning in a monastery. It had been a tiring day. After entertaining visitors from dawn till dusk, he was thoroughly exhausted, and expected to fall asleep as soon as his head hit the pillow. Maybe he was suffering from that lofty-sounding malady the scholars of old complained of in books—the "pacing sickness." Ha, Lu Beiping thought, laughing to himself: A new house and a new bed have turned me from a mountain man into a poet.

He remembered the year he got downcountried, lying in his bunk on the steamship bound for Hainan Island and listening to the water whispering under the hull. But after a short while the sound of water seemed to be coming not from beneath his pillow, but from over his head, as if waves were washing back and forth across the roof of the hut.

In the darkness before him he watched the oxcart of Chance, in which he lay captive, creak to a halt at a fork in the road. The typhoon had changed everything, and yet at the same time it had changed nothing at all. What if he were to leave, pull out now? Would that make everything change for real? Up in the hollow, he and Kingfisher had had a bitter and probably irreversible falling out. He didn't really belong in the world of the driftfolk, had never really belonged there. Autumn was right that he was now "Jade's man," but Jade had had many men, and he was just one passing stranger who had stumbled into her arms. To leave her now made a kind of sense, both emotional and practical. He had feelings for her, it was true, and not just of the sexual kind; but would he really, for Jade's sake, for the sake of a woman *like* Jade, throw away his own tiny life in this godforsaken mountain backwater? As far as things down at camp were concerned, it was the whole silly affair with Han that had gotten him exiled here to begin with. Whether she'd died from malaria, been murdered, fallen off a cliff, been eaten by wild pigs—what was it to him? Wasn't all this just a game of make-believe? It was starting to seem pointless to dirty his stockings wading through this swamp of bad juju and foul intrigue. By happy coincidence, the typhoon had swept away his fateful date with Wing; why not take this as a chance to turn over a new leaf—he'd finally proved himself as a cowherd, made a respectable showing in the arena of corral counts and manure yields—and retire honorably while his fortunes were running high? He could request a new assignment, invent some excuse to get transferred back to camp, and the parade of absurdities that had been the past four months would vanish like dust into the wind.

The water rang loud in his ears. Swollen by the runoff from the surrounding mountains, Mudclaw Creek had gone from a tinkling rivulet to a gong battered by a Loi tribesman at a raucous holiday festival.

Three nights ago, up in the hollow, he'd also stayed awake listening to the water. Probably no one except the kids had slept that night. As he was driving the cattle down the creek earlier that evening, Lu Beiping had sworn a solemn oath never to go back. But Autumn—not Jade—had waylaid him, popping out of the trees halfway down the tunnel of branches (how did he manage to find his way through the jungle in utter darkness?) and stood before him in the ankle-deep water, blocking his way. Where are you going? he asked breathlessly, his dark figure almost invisible in the shadows. Your hut's gone, your corral's gone. Maybe you'll be fine sleeping outside with your cattle, but if you do, it might not be long till *we* don't have a roof over our heads. Autumn spoke unusually quickly and articulately. Lu Beiping stood, silent and obstinate, surrounded by his cattle. Bei, Autumn said, you know how flighty Jade can be. If you leave . . . His voice fell off abruptly, then he said: Please, Bei, I beg you. Won't you come back? Please?

At that moment, for some inexplicable reason, Autumn seemed to possess a kind of authority over him.

So Autumn hollered to the cattle, and Lu Beiping had no choice but to turn around and march back up to the hollow. All night Jade sat huddled behind the hearth stove, sobbing, refusing to see any of them. Kingfisher and Stump nursed their water pipes beneath the lychee tree. Autumn and Lu Beiping sat on the far side of the creek among the sleeping cattle, listening to the water, waiting for morning to come.

Autumn shouldn't have held me back, Lu Beiping thought to himself. And I shouldn't have given in. I should have stood by my decision.

Rolling over in bed in his newly rebuilt hut, Lu Beiping remembered the other time the babbling water had kept him awake all night, right after meeting Smudge, during his first few weeks in the jungle. Smudge was the second scrap of red paper that Fate had flung at his feet. Now, maybe, he was due for a third . . .

The odor of lime and the scent of dry grass mingled in the night air. *Watch as Man builds his towers, watch as his towers crumble* . . . It was a line from some old play—which one, Lu Beiping couldn't remember—lamenting the impermanence of all human endeavors. Now that his castle had been rebuilt, was it time to pass it on to a new owner?

Jade's face floated before him in the darkness. It was just as he remembered it from their first meeting in the sunlit meadow: shiny, mica-like earrings dangling from her ears; thick, sun-reddened braids spilling into her lap. Perched on a log, a hand-rolled cigarette burning between her fingers, like a gypsy woman out of a Russian novel. Or no—maybe he'd only imagined her that way. Was it just his own imagination that made this woman seem so powerfully alluring? He pictured two leopards wrestling by the water, thought of the leopard-riding wispwoman, the water-witch; he remembered the eerie incantation that she uttered in the firelight on the night of the typhoon. It dawned on him that every time they'd . . . "done it," it had been by the water. Water, water, always water. Was water their destiny? Was it a supernatural sign, a mystic premonition? How did it fit in with Kingfisher's system of spirits, sins, and laws? They said that Lu Beiping had too much darkness in him, too much "shadow air." So which of the five elements was he missing? Did he need water, or fire? Iron, or wood? *Iron woodsbane, water flamesbane* . . . which realm did "it" belong to, water or fire? God, enough now. This was getting too bizarre.

The water seemed to grow quieter, and the racket of insects swelled to fill the silence. A pair of birdcalls, clear and melodious, sounded far off in the forest, somewhere behind the grove of fragrant agarwood trees that grew near his campsite. A rising call here,

answered by a falling call there: long short, long short, *keeeeeeee—oooh,
keeeeeeee—oooh* . . . A mating call, perhaps? *Kwan, kwan, call the ospreys from
the river isle* . . .

Making good, Jade called it. *I made good with Four Eyes.* What did
that mean, exactly? Was "good" the same thing as love? Probably not.
Ever since the fourth grade, when he and his soccer-playing pals had
traded furtive whispers about the girl who sat next to him in class, he'd
constructed a towering edifice of fantasies around that word, love.
Now, he had "made good" with Jade—but did he love her? Did she
love him? He couldn't say. In any event, the thing between him and her
was very different from what he'd imagined love would be like.

He rolled over again. All these torrid imaginings had given him
an erection, and he was beginning to feel hot and uncomfortable. He
thought: Maybe that's all "making good" was—"doing it." In Jade and
Kingfisher's world, "it" wasn't shameful. It wasn't a sin, it wasn't taboo.
Bearing and sowing, sharing sympathy with other living beings, none
of that was sin, Kingfisher had said. Jade had even told him that when
she and the men slept together, they didn't hide it from the kids. For
them, "making good" was good, pure and simple; it was a bright, natural thing, like the sunlight or the mountain air. For all its strangeness,
the driftfolk way of thinking had a wholesome simplicity that made
the tight-laced pieties of his own world, and the dark perversions that
they concealed, seem all the more absurd. In the beginning he'd been
convinced that the tangled web of relationships that bound him, Jade,
and her men together was freakish, aberrant, morally wrong. But what
was right, then? Who decided what was moral? Did the morals of the
outside world have jurisdiction over Jade and Kingfisher's tiny province of light and shadow, superstitions and taboos? Were the morals
of the mountain required to bend knee to the morals of the valley?
At this thought a spacious feeling opened up inside him, and he felt
as if he were standing on a distant star, gazing down at the dust and
tumult of the human world. In that square inch of dust, "it"—the
"it" of lofty Love and lowly lust, all tangled together—was a hallowed
mystery at the same time that it was a filthy taboo. But in Jade's world

it was a simple fact of daily life, like the water in the creek, running sometimes fast, sometimes slow, sometimes clear, sometimes turbid, but always there, always flowing, unremarkable.

The sound of the creek hypnotized him. No wonder the sages of old liked to meditate by the water. As he sank halfway into dream, he watched his own silhouette step free of his body and walk, undulating amid the babbling of the water, toward the threshold of life and death, where it paused, hesitant, wavering at the border of that unseen land. The shadow husband. He'd married a ghost, a very real and very complicated woman, Han, had ventured into these otherworldly hills that were her home, and in the process he'd gained a real woman, Jade, who was just a shadow in the daylit world, an outcast, nameless, invisible. It was his destiny, it seemed, to walk a path that ran along the frontier between light and shadow. Whether it was a game of make-believe no longer mattered—he must still walk the path. For by playing this absurd role that Chance had assigned him, he could sample the flavors of life pushed to various extremes, could pursue in these strings of accidents and coincidences a hidden meaning that, though elusive, was not at all accidental. Though the weight of the sunlight, the heft of the damp air, and the fullness of surprise often knocked him off balance. Fate seemed bent upon harrying him toward some impossible outer limit, flipping him back and forth faster and faster between different roles, rushing him straight from inception to apex. Now, a typhoon had swept through the land like an all-erasing Biblical flood. Could it be that now, when it seemed like everything was about to begin, his story was actually nearing its end?

He woke up with a start.

The silhouette had turned and was walking back from that hazy threshold. Yes, it was him, it was his own shadow. But now it stopped, as if reluctant to return to his body, and stood there, gazing back at him.

His shadow chuckled. No, this wasn't a dream at all.

He sprang out of bed. In the pale light of dawn he saw a figure standing in the doorway.

It was Autumn. As usual he was drenched with dew. Laughing, he said:

—Did I wake you? Were you having a bad dream?

—What . . . how . . . how long have you been here? Lu Beiping stammered, still heavy with sleep.

—It's early yet. You should sleep more. I'll leave.

—Why'd you come? Is something wrong?

—Nope. I'm just an early bird. I have to get up before sunrise to scout the day's timber, clear the ground, cut a trail to haul out the wood. I figured I'd stop by and take a gander at your new abode.

Autumn's voice sounded clear and refreshing, like the dew. Now fully awake, Lu Beiping noticed a pool of water in the dirt outside the door and figured that Autumn must have been standing there for a while. Autumn propped his machete against the doorframe. He wore no shirt, as was his habit, and his red-and-white checkered Teochew waistcloth was sopping wet.

—Sit down, Lu Beiping said, yawning and stretching. You're soaked!

—*Sleep, sleep but a minute more, for it is such bitterness to wake . . .* Autumn intoned as he sat down on the log stool next to the bed. I'm sorry, I spoiled your sweet dreams.

—My sweet dreams? Lu Beiping said, leaning back against the windowsill: More like sour dreams. Kind of fishy, he added with a shrug and a laugh, remembering "it."

Autumn winked.

—Fishy dreams? Fishy how?

—Hard to explain. Dreams can't be put into words, right? If they could, they wouldn't be dreams. Lu Beiping glanced at Autumn, then changed the subject: Autumn, he said, you're a man of many faces, you know that?

—Many faces? How, pray tell? Faces are a lot easier to describe than dreams.

—Well, when it's just you and me, it's all "pray tell" and "sweet dreams," Li Shutong and amarawhatsis rosewood. You've got a lot to say, lots of secrets. But when you're around Kingfisher and Jade, you're as silent as a stick of wood. An old, fallen log that's being chewed up by insects, rotting from the inside.

—That's a good description, Autumn said placidly.

—But then, when you're around Jade and Smudge, you come to life again. You start sprouting timid little green fronds, quaking and quivering in the light of the—

Autumn jumped up from the stool and gave Lu Beiping a shove.

—Hell with you and your little green fronds! he said, wrestling Lu Beiping back onto the bed and pinning him there. I'll show you quaking and quivering!

—Hey, quit it! Lu Beiping gasped. I wasn't serious! I was just giving you a hard time.

Down in the corral the cattle stirred and moaned, dismayed at the muffled sounds of struggle emanating from the hut.

—Hmph, Autumn snorted as he released Lu Beiping: When Jade's around, *you're* the one quivering—

—Let's talk about something else, Lu Beiping interrupted. What was that poem you recited when you came in? Was it Li Shutong?

Autumn didn't answer. Stooping, he surveyed the hut, grabbed the flashlight that lay in one corner and cast its beam over the new stove, the brown satchel that lay nearby spilling its cargo of contraband novels onto the floor. He picked one up, fanned the pages, and chuckled.

—I believe this is the first time I've ever crossed your threshold, Bei. If I'd known earlier, I'd have borrowed a few books.

Laying down the book, he asked:

—What do you like to read, besides Alexei and Dmitri and all that? Do you like the ancients? The poets?

—Well, Lu Beiping replied, I'm not such a fan of sonnets. Seven-seven-seven, five-five-five, all those chockablock syllables like cubes of beancurd—he watched a misty sunbeam inch its way around the half-closed door, filling the hut with the light tang of morning jungle air, and feeling a faint thrill at the antiquated oddness of this scene, of enthusing about esoteric literary pursuits on a clear morning in the wilderness, he went on excitedly: But lyrics, I love those! Long, galloping lines—da, da-da, da-da, da-dum! Da-da-da dum! Those have got verve, vitality!

Lu Beiping stopped short, listening to the sound of his own dramatic cadences echoing in the rafters.

—So whose lyrics do you like? Autumn asked, his eyes glittering.

—Xin Qiji, Lu Beiping replied immediately. *At least yon hills are pleasing to mine eye, and I fancy they think the same of me . . . O, that those men of old still walked the earth, if only that they might envy my bacchanal!* Isn't that great?

For a moment Autumn stared at Lu Beiping with his mouth half-open, as if this sudden outburst of poetic enthusiasm had tapped a spring of deep feeling inside him. Then he heaved a sigh and plunked down on the log stool.

—Bei, he said, you really are much younger than me. My Xin Qiji-ing days are long over, I fear.

Lu Beiping smiled at this eccentric yet eloquent turn of phrase.

—So, who do you like? Lu Beiping asked with a quick look at his friend, sensing that something in this exchange had touched one of Autumn's sensitive spots.

—Nara Singde. That's who I was reciting when I walked in.

—Nara Singde, Lu Beiping repeated. Sounds like a European name to me.

It was now obvious to Lu Beiping that he'd stumbled across another sprig of amaranthine rosewood. Autumn's world was filled with things that to him must always seem distant and strange. With a wan smile, Autumn said:

—My dad taught me his poetry when I was little. He's also sometimes called Nara Jungjo, he was a famous Manchu lyricist. He wrote a book called *Drinkwater Airs*—lovely name, isn't it? It was my dad's favorite.

Autumn paused, his palms spread open, as if once again self-consciously adjusting his mode of speech. Then he began chanting in a soft voice:

Drunk, I lie among the army tents
Watching the starry heavens shake;
The howling of wolves assaults my sense
And the rushing river prevents
Me, even in dreams, from darkening the door
Of the home I did forsake—
Sleep, sleep but a minute more,
For it is such bitterness to wake.

—What do you think? Do you like it? Just like this scene right now, you waking in the wilderness, next to a river. Pity, though, that what's been disturbing your dreams isn't the howling of wolves but the mooing of the cattle.

Indeed, at that moment the cattle were lowing impatiently in the corral. Both of them laughed. Lu Beiping said:

—I love it, it's a great poem. Can you recite another?

By winding valley and crooked track
We march through the mountains, northward bound;
The lights of our fires bejewel the black,
Glittering like stars all 'round;
With pent-up rage and savage spite
The wind declaims its sorrow all night,
Arresting my spirit's homeward flight—
In my arbor, I knew not this awful sound.

—That's from Nara's "Song of Long Yearning," Autumn said. You like it too?

—"Song of Long Yearning!" Wow! A sudden, inexplicable excitement came over Lu Beiping, and he sprang up from the bed and threw open the door, letting in a blaze of mist-clotted sunlight that wreathed him in a hazy glow. Giving Autumn a playful shove that nearly tipped him off of the log stool, Lu Beiping cried: Alright, Autumn, you win! I don't know a fraction of the stuff you do. Li Shutong, Nara Singde

. . . I think you must be one of those gentleman hermits, living alone here in the mountains since ancient times!

—A gentleman hermit? Autumn said with a dry chuckle. Not a bit. Just a beggar, scraping by the only way I can. So, he went on, the way my dad tells it, Nara Singde read that poem you saw in my diary the other day, by Gu Zhenguan, and he was so moved he wept, and swore he'd rescue his friend's friend who'd been sentenced to exile on a far-off frontier.

—What? Whose friend? I'm confused.

—Said he'd rescue Gu Zhenguan's friend, Wu Zhaoji, who'd had a pass of bad luck and been punished unjustly. Autumn paused for a moment, lost in thought. Right, he said, I remember now. My dad said Nara's father, a lord named Mingzhu, was the Grand Tutor, a very influential man at court. Nara begged his father to help, and his father got the Emperor to step in on Nara's behalf and save his friend's friend from the trouble he was in.

—Wow! So this Nara Singde was a powerful man.

—He was the Grand Tutor's eldest son, yes. What you'd nowadays call a cadre brat. Oh . . . Autumn sighed, and said in a voice tinged with melancholy: You wouldn't hear that kind of story these days. A friend saving a friend on account of a poem he wrote. That sort of thing only happened in olden times.

—Autumn!

Lu Beiping slapped the bed and sat back down again, gazing in awe at this waistcloth-clad "beggar" whose brain was an encyclopedia of classical lore. The subtle air of erudition that Lu Beiping sometimes caught wafting off of Autumn not only surprised him, but moved him deeply.

—Oh . . . Lu Beiping sighed, and said without thinking: Too bad I'm not Nara Singde.

Autumn studied him for a long moment. Toward the end of it, his lips began to tremble slightly.

—Bei, it's enough . . . just to hear you say that.

Then he stood up quickly, as if trying to hide something.

—I ought to go, he said, and leaned over to pick up his machete. Lu Beiping rushed around and tried to block his way as he made for the door.

—Autumn, don't go! Let's talk some more, eh? Lu Beiping said, trying his best to express coherently and casually the swarm of thoughts that had just rushed into his head. Things have been crazy lately, there's been a lot of stuff bothering me. And now you're the only person on this whole mountain who I can talk to.

There was a slight hitch in Autumn's stride, but he kept on walking. Once he was outside he turned and looked back at Lu Beiping with a devious grin.

—That's not so. What about Jade? Oh—he added with careful nonchalance—I forgot to tell you, Jade's sick. She hasn't eaten for two or three days. Stump and Kingfisher gave her herbs, but it's no help. You ought to come see her.

—What? Lu Beiping exclaimed. She's sick? With what? Is it serious?

—See? Autumn said with a sour look. She's got a hold on your heart yet. If she saw the look on your face just now, I'll bet she'd get better right away. You ought to go.

—No way, Lu Beiping said, leaning on the doorframe. Not if Kingfisher's there. I don't want to see that man's face.

—That's where you're in the wrong, Bei, Autumn said, his voice suddenly stern. You oughtn't to bear a grudge against Kingfisher. He comes on fierce sometimes, but he's gentle inside. His heartwater runs clear. He means best for all of us—for you too.

—For me? How?

—I don't know. But I trust his judgment. He can tell you're . . . in some kind of trouble.

—What do you mean? What . . . Lu Beiping began, then he stopped himself. Autumn didn't answer. Instead, he brandished his machete at Lu Beiping and called out: Bei, ready your blade! I challenge you! Then he danced up into the bushes that grew on the hillside above the hut, assumed a fighter's squat, and started whirling his machete back and forth from hand to hand in a show of martial legerdemain. *Thwack! Thwack! Thwack!* With confident, dexterous motions, Autumn dodged, parried, slashed, and harried the imaginary opponents that flanked him on all sides, scything the leaves of the bushes into an emerald confetti that sparkled with dew as it fluttered to the ground.

Lu Beiping stared in astonishment. Autumn, thoroughly engrossed in his make-pretend showdown with the surrounding vegetation, swung his machete in faster and faster circles till it became a silver blur.

What a weird guy, Lu Beiping thought. He was every bit the gentleman hermit, an eccentric outcast with a story to tell.

Through the morning mist the faint clang of the work bell drifted up from camp, barely audible and carrying a hint of melancholy. It had been a long time since Lu Beiping had heard that sound.

—What's up? Lu Beiping demanded. Chu, what's going on?

Chu wouldn't give him the time of day.

In the heat of the September afternoon Lu Beiping had, as usual, driven the herd to the old groves near the second bend of the creek, only to find that his shady haven had been reduced to a ragtag posse of disheveled trees leaning at drunken angles. He hollered the animals into a decimated grove rimmed by a lace pine windbreak, set them free to graze, and ducked away for a quick visit to camp. Of the latex collection station that had once stood at the trailhead nothing remained but a few forlorn studs. Skylights had been ripped in the roofs of almost all the cookhouses that surrounded the workers' quarters, and everywhere Lu Beiping looked he saw ragged cowlicks of torn thatch, exposed beams, and shattered roof tiles blanketing the ground. Yet the camp's atmosphere was bustling and festive, like a village in the wake of a market fair. Children milled impatiently near the mess hall, holding an assortment of bowls and pots in which to receive their share of celebratory beef—Judas's meat, carried down from the gully where he met his end. Those workers who had families were busy repairing the damage to their cookhouses, and the camp resounded with the calls of men shouting from roof to roof as they mended thatch. Lu Beiping, clomping into town in his big black boots, drew surprisingly little attention; normally, the return of the foreman's "ghost son-in-law" would have set off waves of whispers and stares. From behind the hutch that housed the blackboard gazette Lu Beiping heard the sonorous voice of the foreman, probably leading a political training session for Party members, reading aloud a report from the *Agrecorps Daily Dispatch* with all the soulful gravity of a funeral oration. As he walked toward the old warehouse that served as the re-ed dormitory he saw that the building had lost much of its tiled roof, and the open spaces had been covered with tarpaper. The few re-eds he met greeted him perfunctorily, then hurried back into the dorm. Puzzled by this, Lu Beiping went into his old room and found Chu lying stomach-down on his cot, elbows propped on the wooden crate he used as a footlocker, writing something. He didn't look up when Lu Beiping walked in, just kept scribbling away with sullen determination.

Too familiar with Chu's moods to risk bothering him, Lu Beiping opened his rattan chest, which Chu had pushed into the far corner, and fished out two shirts and a few more books. As he tidied the chest's contents Chu continued to ignore him, and finally Lu Beiping's irritation got the better of him.

—Well, fuck you too! he snapped. How about, "How are you doing?" How about, "I'm so glad you came back to see me after you almost got killed in the biggest fucking storm of the century!" Come on, what's up? Wipe that sad-puppy look off your face and dignify my presence with a hello, or at least some eye contact, okay? Why don't we start with that?

Chu stopped writing. He threw a lazy glance in Lu Beiping's direction, but did not reply.

—Chu, what's going *on* around here?

—Why don't you ask your pal the foreman? Maybe he can give you a straight answer.

—Just tell me, alright?

—No wonder you're out of the loop, since you spend all your time up there on the mountain communing with nature like some kind of holy man. Lost to the world and all that shit, unconcerned with earthly affairs—the more agitated Chu became, the further he spun off into flights of verbal fancy, till finally, getting a grip on himself, he cut to the chase—Okay, here's the deal. A man came from the Re-education Office in Canton yesterday. It's official, there's going to be a personnel call for trainees and students.

—A personnel call? Lu Beiping said, still uncomprehending.

—You're kidding me! Chu burst out. Have you drunk some kind of magical elixir and forgotten about all your worldly cares? Then he explained in a slow, sneering tone: It's a *personnel call*. For *trainees*—and *students*. A chance to get your ass, and your registration status, transferred back to the city. Do you get it? Or is your head still in the clouds?

Lu Beiping sprang up as if his feet had been burned.

—Really? How? Who? Who's getting transferred? To where? How's it work?

—*That's* what you should ask your father-in-law, Chu fumed. There's a provincial quota. There aren't many spots per unit, and they were supposed to be reserved for students like us who originally had urban registration status. But as soon as word got out the foreman pulled a fast one, said that anyone could apply as long as they've shown a strong commitment to local grassroots integration. So now only students who've "integrated themselves successfully" here on Hainan are eligible. They just announced it in meeting. In order to be considered, every re-ed needs to write an Integration Statement.

—An Integration Statement? Lu Beiping said with an incredulous laugh. So that's why you're acting like such a sourpuss? You're working on your Integration Statement?

Chu glared at him tragically.

—You laugh. Of course, everyone wants to go back to the city— integration my ass! But in order to be considered for the personnel call, you need to express your commitment to integrate in the countryside. It's right there in black and white, they've got you by the balls. If you don't make the cut, you'll have no hope of ever getting back to the city—Chu flung down his pen—all because of your goddam father-in-law! What a jerk!

—Hey, go easy on my old man, Lu Beiping joked, pulling a grave face. So that's what the meeting this morning was all about? This personnel call business?

—Of course not. That was just a footnote. The fate of our lives doesn't mean shit to that man—Chu glanced out the window, then lowered his voice—You know what they were going on about, in the meeting? "We must raise awareness of the national outlook! We must pursue local integration with an eye to the national outlook!" A typhoon blows this place to hell, and they're still blathering on about how great the "national outlook" is.

Chu thrust the sheet of paper at Lu Beiping.

—Come on, Balzac, help me out here. Write me a few good lines.

—Screw you. I've left behind all worldly cares, remember? I'm going to do my best not to get embroiled in this business.

—You don't want to go home? Sure, suit yourself. One less piglet at the tits.

—Who said I don't want to go home? Lu Beiping said quickly. (In those days, Lu explained to Tsung, most re-eds had resigned themselves to lives frittered away in a remote backwater, had almost given up hope of returning to the comforts of the city. Who, offered even the faintest glimmer of such a possibility, wouldn't flail for it like a drowning man for the rope, ready to seize it for himself even if it meant abandoning his comrades to the depths?) Still, Lu Beiping did his best to appear nonchalant, adding: All I meant was that I'd rather not get involved in writing pledges and statements and stuff. Better to not put anything on paper. I'll just let my actions speak for themselves.

—Wow, so you're really not going in for the personnel call? Chu asked incredulously. Then, giving Lu Beiping a meaningful look, he added: If I were you, though, I'd put some thought to your future. You can't spend the rest of your life holed up on Mudkettle Mountain, living as a kept man—

—A what? Lu Beiping said, stiffening. Chu, what kind of bullshit—

—I know nothing, Chu said drily. But there have been . . . rumors to that effect.

—What rumors? Who says? Lu Beiping sprang up from the bed. Chu pulled him back down, grinning.

—Hey, don't panic. It's nothing. But you should be careful, your old friend Gaffer Kam has got a very loose tongue. Right after you came into camp he showed up here at the dorm and gave us all a detailed intelligence report.

—Fucking Kambugger! Lu Beiping burst out angrily, while secretly feeling terrified. Chu picked up his ink-spattered paper and began grumping to himself like a man with a toothache:

—"If I am given the chance to return to the city I will do so with the vigorous aim to deepen my local grassroots integration here on Hainan and thereby advance the solemn glory of the . . ." Oh, fuck this! Come on, you can do this so much better than I can! Just write me two sentences. Please?

Just then there was a loud commotion outside the window.

—Ration supp! Ration supp! Everyone get your beef!

Chu leapt up, grabbed an enamel basin, and rushed out the door, where he almost collided head-on with a visitor who at that very moment was rushing in.

—Oh, it's you! Sorry! Uh . . . welcome! Chu backed into the room, his manner turned mincingly cordial: Come in! I wasn't expecting to be graced by your presence.

The visitor giggled.

—Graced by my presence? Oh, I'm nobody special. But I hear our famous recluse is back from the mountains. I was just down at the mess hall, so I thought I'd pick up his share of beef and pay back a favor I owe him.

In walked Fong. Lu Beiping went slack-jawed with surprise. She was carrying a tin lunchbox filled with chopped raw beef. Recalling how he'd picked up her allotment of pork scraps and frozen fish at the last ration supp, back when they were squadmates—how long ago that seemed!—he sneered:

—Fancy your thinking of me, after all this time.

Then, realizing that this remark had the wrong ring to it, he added, tacking hastily:

—Why didn't you pick up Chu's portion as well, since you knew you were coming up here?

—Heh! Chu cut in, chuckling obsequiously: Are you serious? Even the big man Fook doesn't get this kind of treatment. I wouldn't dare presume. Then, flashing a look of distaste at Fong, he asked her: So, have you written your integration statement yet?

—Oh, I gave it to Sergeant Fook a while ago, Fong responded airily. Those things are a piece of cake to write.

—A piece of cake? Ah, I see . . . Chu studied her for a few seconds, then winked at Lu Beiping. Alright, I'll leave you two alone to talk. Time to go get my beef.

Chu hurried off, snapping his fingers twice at Lu Beiping as he went out the door.

The midafternoon sun threw a patchwork of shifting shadows on the concrete floor. Lu Beiping accepted the tin of meat from Fong, feeling the atmosphere in the room harden into awkwardness. This room was a strange place to him now—it didn't feel like home, not when he stood in the doorway it didn't, not even when he sat down on his own bed. If this exchange were happening in his hut he certainly wouldn't have felt so at a loss for words, so lacking in self-confidence. Their "romantic history" was like a hard shell that he couldn't get back inside of, and he felt foolish trying to stir the waters of their old friendship, standing here wracking his brains for something to say with a rigid smile clinging to his cheeks.

—So . . . he brought out finally, wanting to kill himself: How have you been?

—Much terrible! she crowed, imitating the voice of a Japanese soldier in a war flick, then burst into loud laughter. Lu, I'll bet that during that typhoon, you weren't thinking about me at all, right? But out at the reclamation site, sitting awake in our tents, what we girls talked about most was how tough it must be for you, all alone up on Mudkettle Mountain.

—Well, I appreciate your concern, Lu Beiping said, his face relaxing as the awkward moment dissipated. You're right, it was pretty tough.

In brief he told her how he weathered the storm and the flood and helped Maria give birth to her calf. Naturally, he once more omitted the story's most important character, Jade. When he got to the part about Maria, Fong giggled and said:

—Foreman Kau mentioned that. He said you had to learn on the spot how to be a midwife!

—The foreman told you that? Lu Beiping asked, suddenly suspicious. Fong . . . there must be some other reason you came to see me.

Fong glanced out the window; then, abandoning all pretense of casual conversation, she got straight to the point:

—Wing knows you're back. He just came to see me.

—Wing? Wing came to see you? Lu Beiping said, a shiver of alarm running through his whole body as he remembered his long-forgotten date with the foreman's son. What did he want? Why'd he come looking for you?

—He said you stood him up. He said that on the day of the typhoon he waited in Sector 4, just like you asked him to, till the creek started to rise and he got trapped on the other side in the wind and rain. He said he almost drowned.

—Good god, Lu Beiping said, taken aback: So . . . why didn't he come to see me himself? Why'd he pull you into this?

—He knew you and I . . . Fong curled her lip, then gave a sniff of laughter. Wing said that his dad asked him to ask me to tell you . . . that you should put it behind you. That thing. Between you and him.

—What thing? Me and who? Lu Beiping asked, feigning innocence. The image of the burnt grave marker flashed through this mind, and he wondered why the foreman, acting through his son, no less, would delegate Fong to settle up this mysterious affair between them. Why was Han's grave marker such a sensitive topic that it necessitated all this subterfuge?

—Lu, Fong sighed: I feel sorry for you, getting tangled up in this weird witchy stuff. I told you already, you really shouldn't pry into their business.

—What business am I prying into, for god's sake? Lu Beiping burst out. Fong, do *you* know what it is? Why's it such a big deal that he has to appoint *you* as a go-between?

—I don't know, Fong said coldly. And I don't want to know. What's it matter to me? God, Lu, you just don't know when to stop. You know, I could just fold my arms and look on while you blunder around and get yourself into a world of trouble. This is their home, their turf! Do you think that you're really some kind of son-in-law to the Kaus now, that you have a right to know every last detail of their lives? Lu, I . . . sheesh, what's the point?

Fong spun on her heel and walked out the door. Then, looking back at him, she tossed her hair and said with a winsome smile:

—I've changed a lot these past few months. But you—you're the same as ever. I guess retreating into a life of contemplation hasn't made you any less of a stubborn jerk.

Lu Beiping's gaze wandered to the tin of beef while he waited for her to finish.

—Alright, Fong said, I won't bother you anymore.

She walked back inside, deftly tipped the meat into a large enamel jar that was sitting nearby, then strode back out, carrying her lunchbox. When she was just outside the door she paused again.

—And you really should write that integration statement. This personnel call is going to be super competitive. Don't pretend like it doesn't matter to you.

Fong hurried away, and once more Lu Beiping took note of the stirring contours of her backside. The afternoon work bell began to ring, sharp and forceful, its tintinnabulating knells settling like a fog over Mudkettle Mountain. As if it were not a rusty rail struck with a hammer, but the tolling of a palace gong.

And he knew it was the foreman who held the hammer.

As he drove the cattle back into the hills, Lu Beiping had a jar of salted raw beef weighing down his satchel and a fresh mystery pressing on his mind. Halfway up the trail Choi had cornered him and thrust a faded blue blouse into his hands. It was, or rather had been, aquamarine blue, which in those parts was often called "teasey blue"—a cheap, flashy color that was one of the few bright hues available to Cantonese country women in that puritanical age. Bringing her lips close to Lu Beiping's ear, Choi said in an urgent whisper: *Han was wearing this the day she died.* Lu Beiping started as if he'd been nicked by a knife. Choi had found the shirt lying at the edge of her grove—it wasn't true what they said, Han hadn't died of malaria. She'd drowned herself, naked, in the creek. Choi was the only one who saw her. The teasey blue blouse was a gift from her brother, Wing. Wing and Han, it turned out, had been sleeping together. But why she drowned herself Choi didn't know. That year there'd been a malaria epidemic and lots of people had died, so this gave the Kaus a convenient cover. Where'd they bury her? Lu Beiping had the presence of mind to ask, even in his state of shock. Was it in the clearing next to Sector 12? Yes, that's the place, that used to be Sector 11. It burned down in a grove fire not long after Han was buried.

Tugging his satchel open, Choi stuffed the blouse inside and said: Keep this, hide it. I fear I'm in danger now. Then, having concluded her breathless story, she slipped off into the twilit forest.

Thus, in this sudden and totally unexpected fashion, the riddle of Han's death unfolded itself in front of Lu Beiping. The familiar bend of the creek, the little trail winding between the trees, now seemed inhabited by an eerie, sinister presence. While the daylight lasted Lu Beiping took a detour through Sector 12 and drove the cattle along the edge of the waste clearing. Already the fast-growing stands of hen-feather grass had completely obscured the gravesite. As he forded the creek he noted that right where it passed near the abandoned grove it did, in fact, widen into a little pool. He remembered the "baleglen" and the jungle fire that nobody owned up to; probably Wing, burning some kind of secret offering here, had let the fire get out of hand and started the blaze by accident. Was this pool the very place where Han had died? The cattle, blissfully ignorant of its dark history, sloshed one after another into the shallow pool in their eagerness to shed the day's heat. Even swollen in the wake of the typhoon, the water barely reached their stomachs. Gripped by a sudden, Kingfisheresque fear of calling down some terrible stroke of bad luck on his head, Lu Beiping hollered loudly to the cattle while a cold dread began to uncoil inside him.

His voice echoed in the treetops. Lu Beiping clenched the satchel tightly under his arm, not daring to look at its contents.

He knew that he'd walked into a minefield. The charred grave marker meant nothing to him, he could've thrown it away and not given it a second thought. But this blouse was different: It was a bond between him and Han, a physical legacy that tied them together, alive with memories, fraught with secrets. It was a keepsake. With such a thing in his possession, Lu Beiping couldn't laugh off his link with Han as pure fiction, couldn't pretend that the death of this poor country girl had no purchase on his soul. Maybe even, to make amends for the blatant way in which her death had been covered up, he owed something to her, bore her some kind of responsibility. And after Fong's visit on Wing's behalf this afternoon, he could hear, all too clearly, the approaching footsteps of the living.

That evening, for some reason, he found himself once more wading up the creekbed toward the hollow. Was it because the jar of beef in his satchel made him think of Jade, made him worry for her health? Or was it because his ghost wife's eerie bequest was weighing so heavily on his mind? In any case, it was the combined pull of these two very different women that tugged his feet toward the driftfolk camp that night.

After Wildweed announced Lu Beiping's arrival, a butt-naked Smudge came splashing down the creek to meet him.

—Four Eyes! he cried. I won, I won! Pa said you'd nay ever come again, but I bet her a bowl of meat stew, and you've come! I won, I really won!

—Who taught you to gamble with food? Lu Beiping said with a wry chuckle, his mood lightening instantly at the sight of the boy. Taking the jar of beef out of his satchel, he said: Look, you're in luck. Here's meat for your stew. It's beef. It's from that bull that got killed by a stone in the storm.

With a squeal of triumph Smudge snatched the jar from Lu Beiping and went galloping back up the creek, his small feet churning up a rainstorm.

—Pa lost! I won! Aieeeeeee!

Watching the boy bounding up the stream like a little brown fawn toward the mouth of the hollow, Lu Beiping thought: Smudge really is my guardian spirit. As he was approaching the driftfolk camp he'd begun to feel apprehensive, not sure what kind of attitude he should adopt as he set foot, once more, in this place he'd sworn so firmly to leave. With Smudge's intervention, everything became much more straightforward.

The hollow was unusually quiet. As he crossed the pebble beach only Wildweed and a small gaggle of chicks came out to meet him. The hoary old rooster strutting on the opposite bank sized him up from afar, reminding him of the first evening he'd set foot in the hollow, driving his herd of cattle into this clucking, yapping other-world hidden in the hills.

Smudge's big round head poked out of the front door of the near lodge, and he waved to Lu Beiping, indicating with a curl of his lips that someone was inside.

Lu Beiping strode through the door and saw Jade lying with her back to him on the bed. She had all her clothes on and no blanket covering her, and appeared to be asleep. It was cold inside and the room was a dusty mess, with hats, waistcloths, sandals, comb, and water pipe strewn all over the beds and floor. There wasn't even a fire flickering in the hearth stove in the kitchen nook at the far end of the lodge, as there usually was.

The jar of beef sat on the trestle table like an idol, its fresh, pungent odor filling the room.

—Where is everybody? he said, addressing the empty cabin. It seems like nobody's around!

—Uncle Stump's taken Tick and Roach into the woods to pick medicine for Pa, Smudge supplied helpfully. Uncle Autumn and Kingfisher, they've gone up into the high valley to look for that rosewood tree Autumn's forever talking about. As for me—Smudge gave Lu Beiping a tactful wink—I ought to go finish gathering firewood.

Smudge and Wildweed trotted out the door. Lu Beiping was about to go to Jade's bedside when it occurred to him that she might not really be asleep, and instead he tiptoed over to the table and sat down gingerly on one of the log stools.

A slanting beam of twilight divided the room into two zones, one of light, the other of shadow.

—Nobody here? Jade said softly in the darkness, a mocking edge to her voice. What about me, Four Eyes? Or have I always been nobody to you?

Lu Beiping could tell from her voice that Jade was fighting back laughter, but her black silhouette on the bed remained motionless. Seized by a devilish impulse, Lu Beiping marched over to the bed and laid a forceful slap on her hindquarters.

—Hey, I thought you were sick. Sick as a dog, right? Autumn told me you weren't yourself.

The touch of Lu Beiping's palm proved a very effective cure. Jade rolled over and pounced on Lu Beiping, then slapped him twice across the lips.

—Wise-ass. Who'd Autumn say I was, then? Chairman Mao? Yama, King of Hell? Oop—shame on me! Listen to me talk!

She threw back her disheveled hair, looking perfectly radiant, and held his gaze for several seconds, her mica earrings shimmering in the darkness.

—Do I seem myself? Maybe just a little bit?

A faint light glowed on the curves of her hips and shoulders, on the rounded tip of her chin. Lu Beiping took all this in, his eyes wide with astonishment.

—So . . . you're not sick?

Jade exploded into a full-body fit of laughter.

—Of course not! It was just my time of the month, that's all. But I kept putting on like I was really sick, till even *I* starting thinking it was real. Ha!

—You were just pretending? Good god!

She chortled uproariously, kicking her legs and rolling from side to side on the bed. Jade's wildly boomeranging mood left Lu Beiping feeling a bit nonplussed, but he was still relieved to see her feeling so well.

—Jade, I can't believe you'd fake everybody out like that, Lu Beiping said with a sigh, drawing her into his arms and running a hand through her hair. Autumn said you hadn't eaten anything for days. You had me scared.

These words summoned an instant flood of tears from Jade. She didn't wipe them away, just let the tears roll down her cheeks while her body convulsed with sobs.

—Four Eyes, she said, lying half-sick like this, all these days . . . what I wanted most of all was to hear you say that.

Lu Beiping hugged her tighter. This woman who once seemed to tower over him like a cliff now trembled in his arms like a fallen leaf.

—Four Eyes . . . She pushed him away, and now a harsh light burned in her eyes: Do you really want to know why I wanted to make good with you? Have you ever wondered why?

Lu Beiping shook his head with a bitter smile of amazement. Everything that had befallen him since coming into the hills flashed in a jumbled sequence through his mind, and an ocean of feeling welled up inside him.

—I've been thinking about that a lot, lying here, Jade said, wiping a hand across her face and smearing the snot and tears on the bedframe beneath her. Me and Kingfisher and Stump, when we sleep together, we do it because we need to. It's part of life, it's how we pass the days. With you it's different, though. I wanted to make good with you because I wanted you, that's all, because I liked you, from the bottom of my heart, it didn't have a thing to do with needing things or getting by. But now—she gestured at the dusty chaos that surrounded her—look at this. Without you here, the days just didn't seem worth living.

As she spoke Lu Beiping felt a lump growing in his throat. He hung his head. Then he looked up again and finally summoned the nerve to say the words he'd been rehearsing in his mind for the past several days.

—Jade, you and me . . . I've been thinking about us too. And I'm starting to think . . . I just can't see a future, between us.

He imagined that these words would trigger another torrent of tears, but to his surprise Jade said simply:

—I know.

She slid quietly off the bed, walked over to the stove, lit the fire, put on water to boil, emptied his jar of beef into the frypan, put the lid on, tidied some things. Then, turning to look at him again, she said in a gentle voice:

—I guessed that's what you were thinking. The thing is, I don't want a future. You men, you live half your lives in the future. You're forever scurrying around, hunting for reasons, doing this so that that, that so that this. Herding cows, hewing timber, fighting for this, struggling against that . . . all so that you'll be a little bit better off in the future. But what about now? Why don't you just live the day you've got right now?

—Now? Lu Beiping said. He glanced around at the mosquito-netted beds, the thatched ceiling. He remembered the other thing that had been bothering him, and felt a sharp pang of worry.

—Jade, he said, laughing: You're a philosopher, you know that?

—A whatafer? I'm a keep-house-afer. I do my best to turn this place into a home. Some folks have got homes, others make no home into a home—as Jade spoke her hands were in eight places at once, octopus-like, transforming the volcanic disorder of the room into a shining vision of tidiness—I wanted to be with you because I wanted to be with you. I wanted to make good with you, and you did too, and that was good. There was no other reason. No other good reason, no other reason worth talking about. Right?

She reached under the bed, picked up her comb, and tossed it in Lu Beiping's direction.

—Comb your hair, will you? You look like you just escaped from a labor camp.

When he didn't move to pick it up she walked over, grabbed the comb herself, and went to work on Lu Beiping's rumpled hair.

—I like to see you looking smart, like that fine young scholar gentleman I met in the meadow, who greeted people—she mimicked the slight bend at the waist he made when they first met—like this.

—Fuck you!

Lu Beiping gave Jade a shove that sent her tottering back a few steps. Jade burst out laughing.

—Ha! Bull Devil! Smudge is right about you. Come on, Bull Devil, if you're so strong, hit me!—she threw open her flowered blouse and rushed at Lu Beiping, her breasts swinging brazenly: Hit away, Bull Devil! Lay 'em right here!

—Whoa, whoa . . . Lu Beiping stammered, then broke into laughter as well, overcome by Jade's ridiculous antics. Ha! Alright, then! he cried. Take this!

He raised a fist, feigning the wind-up for a punch. Jade dodged to one side, retreated a few steps . . .

. . . then Kingfisher, chortling, bounded through the door, and Jade backed directly into his arms. Lu Beiping's face went crimson as Kingfisher made a show of fondling Jade's breasts, beaming like some kind of lecherous Buddha.

—Ha, ha, ha! Look at her, Four Eyes! She's looking pretty chipper now!

Jade struggled free, slapped Kingfisher in the face, then pulled her blouse over her chest and scurried over to the kitchen. Kingfisher gazed around the transformed interior of the cabin, then turned to Lu Beiping and said with a grin:

—Couldn't ask for a better doctor, Four Eyes! You cured her, sure enough. And you cured us too.

—Smells a wonder in here! Stump announced, thrusting his swarthy head through the door while the three children swarmed in noisily ahead of him, Smudge's voice shrilling over the others:

—Meat tonight! Meat, meat, meat! Pa, you owe me a bowl of beef stew!

—Quiet! Stump boomed, swatting the kids aside as he trundled over to greet Lu Beiping: We smelled that smell way up on the mountain, we did, and sussed it was Four Eyes come to share his supper with us. Looks like your meat worked a miracle for our sis—he glanced at Jade's still half-open blouse and licked his teeth—I do believe she's come out of her fast.

The aroma of beef filled the room, making the cabin feel warm and cozy. Smiling but saying nothing, Jade went about her business at the stove, her motions deft, her blouse still hanging open, as was her habit when she was in a good mood. Stump's and Kingfisher's gazes flitted constantly to her breasts as they made small talk with Lu Beiping, shooting the breeze as if nothing had happened.

Suddenly a golden light bloomed through the cabin—Autumn, who'd slipped quietly into the room while they were talking, had lit the storm lantern that hung from one of the central posts.

In his hands Autumn held a big white rooster, its legs kicking the air defiantly as he twisted its wings behind its back. As usual he greeted Lu Beiping with a lively glance, then said to Kingfisher:

—Let's make it a twofer tonight. On top of Four Eyes' meat—ha! It's always Four Eyes' meat, isn't it?—let's finish this sorry bastard and cook him up, make a feast out of him to spare him getting pecked to bits.

As he held the bird aloft, it let out an admonishing shriek and launched a spattering stream of shit onto the floor.

—Put it down, Autumn! Jade cried, rushing over from the stove: Please, put it down!

Autumn refused to let go of the bird. Jade turned to Lu Beiping and said:

—It wasn't us you saved, coming up here tonight—it was this rooster! These filthy, meat-hungry men have had their eyes on my Australian white for days. We lost a hen in the storm, so we had to join the two nests of chicks at either end of the hollow and let the hen who nests by the creek mother them all. But the roosters aren't too pleased, they've been pecking each other bloody trying to win favor with the hen. Kingfish and them have been fixing to kill the widower to grease their stomachs. Poor thing, he lost his lady, and now you heartless people want to turn a rooster's sorrow into a man's supper. Four Eyes—Jade chuckled—if you hadn't brought us this jar of beef today, I doubt my Australian white could've dodged the knife.

Lu Beiping laughed. Turning to Autumn, he said:

—I feel like the Emperor all of a sudden. Alright, if it's up to me—I pardon him!

—Pardon him! Stump and Kingfisher hooted. Aye, pardon him!

Smudge grabbed the rooster and was about to release him outside when Kingfisher said:

—Wait! I've got an idea.

Everybody fell silent, nervous that they'd once more run afoul of one of Kingfisher's taboos. But Kingfisher smiled, glanced sidelong at Lu Beiping, then, speaking slowly, addressed the other two men:

—They say that in this world, the winners are the kings and the losers are the outlaws. Right? Let's let these two roosters fight it out fair and square—Kingfisher drew a deep breath through his nose, savoring the aroma of beef—We've got meat tonight, that means we'll have beer too. Eh, den mother? I say, let's have a feast and a cockfight. Let 'em fight to their hearts' content. We'll eat our beef and watch them settle their score.

—Oy, oy oy! Smudge and Stump clamored in unison, rattling up a jubilant ruckus on a clay bowl and water pipe: Cockfight! Cockfight!

Autumn pinched Lu Beiping from behind and tried to catch his eye. But Lu Beiping was distracted by Jade, bustling merrily and cracking jokes as she readied the trestle table to be carried outside, and didn't respond.

—Four Eyes, Jade quipped, giving him a meaningful look: They say saving a man's life'll put you in grace for ten lives down. Maybe saving a chicken's life will at least charm some of the shadows off you, bring you a spell of good luck.

Lu Beiping's heart sank. He remembered the dark secret still bundled in his satchel, lying in a clump of grass next to his hut.

Sunset comes late to the high mountains. Was that a line from a poem, or a pretty phrase that had just popped into his head? In any case it had been nearly dark when he'd encountered Choi down in the rubber groves, but after lingering for a while in the orchard and then hiking halfway up the mountain, the sun still hung like an egg yolk at the rim of the sky. No snakeclouds writhed in the heavens as they usually did at this hour; the sky was clear, a sheet of freshly washed satin shot through with shimmering greens and blues.

The supper table sat beneath the charred lychee tree, and Jade presided over young and old in a dinner as momentously rowdy as a holiday banquet. As usual Kingfisher inaugurated the meal with a bundle of smoking incense sticks and a prayer to Horn, then a steaming pot of poached beef was ferried from kitchen to table, accompanied by a big bowl of yam beer. Given any hodgepodge of ingredients, Jade was able, relying on intuition alone, it seemed, to whip up a mouthwatering spread of novelties. (Years later, entertaining guests at business dinners, Lu Beiping would always order Sichuanese poached beef in hopes of recapturing the glory of that meal. But even at the best restaurants it fell miserably short of Jade's simple but delicious version of the dish: the beef blanched just-so, sliced just-so, dipped in a sauce of ginger, scallions, and crushed garlic whose flavor was ever so sweet, fresh, and uncomplicated.) After Jade had cut the beef into wafer-thin slices, rolled them with her chopsticks, and run them through a bowl of oil and a bowl of sauce, she piled them on steaming mounds of rice to be proffered, one by one, to the salivating mouths arrayed around the table. When she was done she ducked back into the cabin for a handful of rice bran, tossed it in the air while clucking loudly, and an army of chicks led by a big, hobbling white hen swarmed in for the kill.

Lu Beiping couldn't help watching her, her figure silvered by the waning light, her blouse still hanging open, her breasts swinging with the motions of her limbs. The low sun stretched and skewed the shadows so that Jade, arm aloft, baiting the chickens, cast the silhouette of a slender, dancing crane. What a woman, Lu Beiping thought; as far as he was concerned, this was true beauty.

Immediately the dusty earth beneath the dinner table became a fairground for chickenkind. The two families of chicks were easy to distinguish by the shapes of their bodies and the different colors of their feathers. A brawny young Man Cheong rooster, sporting a dapper suit of red-and-white plumage, patrolled a short distance away from the milling crowd, saving his strength to beat back at a moment's notice any intruder who dared provoke him or threaten his flock.

Kingfisher, having finished off his first bowl of yam beer, shouted through a mouthful of beef:

—Smudge! Let out the Australian!

Thumping on their water pipes, Autumn and Stump joined in the chorus:

—Let him out! Let out the white rooster!

Kingfisher leaned over and said to Lu Beiping:

—Four Eyes, care to place a bet? Where I come from, we like to stake big money on cockfights.

—Sorry, Lu Beiping said, laughing: I can't. I don't know the rules.

—No gambling allowed! Jade cut in. If you want to bet something, bet your own damn selves.

Just as they were speaking, the old Australian rooster alighted in their midst like a flash of white lightning, igniting mayhem among the fowl and excitement among the humans. Wings outstretched, he advanced through the frightened mob of chicks, then rushed at the usurper with a bloodcurdling screech. The two roosters drew their bodies taut and stood for a moment in a quivering stand-off: red against white, young against old, native-born against foreign inter-loper. Then they lunged, pecked, kicked, flapped, twisting themselves into a ball of claws and wings, raising clouds of dust and a shrill, murderous clamor. The chicks swarmed over to join the fray, darting in between the fighters to snatch morsels of food, their milling bodies and twittering voices adding to the chaos. The hen, however, didn't seem the least bit concerned, strutting about with a queenly air and occasionally herding the chicks to the side and shielding them with her wings, then returning to pecking the crumbs of bran as if this violent showdown had nothing to do with her. As they fought she clucked quietly to herself, either praising the combatants or lamenting the whole foolish affair.

Everybody watched, rapt. Kids and grown-ups alike took sides, egging on their favorites:

—Come on, whitey!

—Tear him up, Man Cheong!

In the midst of all this Lu Beiping noticed that Jade, after por-tioning out the beef for the others, had taken none for herself, just sat sipping a bowl of porridge with a few bits of pickled cabbage floating on the surface.

—Jade, he asked, why aren't you eating any meat?

Smudge, pricking up his ears, interjected:

—Pa lost it to me! She'd wagered you'd not come, and I won her next meat supper.

—Then take mine, Lu Beiping said, raking up the beef in his bowl and offering it to her: I already had some when they handed it out at camp.

Jade waved aside his chopsticks and said, her eyes shining:

—I'm not eating meat. I've been sick, remember? I haven't got an appetite for . . .

In the middle of her sentence Kingfisher slammed his beer bowl down on the table and roared, red-faced:

—Smudge! Quit stirring the goddam cinders! You here to watch a cockfight or to pat your own chilly little butt? Sit down and eat your food, or else give it to the chickens!

Lu Beiping laughed inwardly and caught a knowing glance that Autumn gave him from across the table. Jade got up hastily and snatched away Kingfisher's beer bowl.

—You're drunk again, toothless baboon. Mind your tongue and finish your supper.

Then Stump was on his knees, moaning in dismay:

—Oy, yoy, yoy! My Man Cheong!

On the plain of battle a victor had emerged. At the start the lusty Man Cheong had pressed a vicious offensive, pecking up a fluttering storm of white feathers, and the old Australian didn't appear to stand much of a chance, just hung back as if hoping his opponent would exhaust himself, stealing an occasional peck between the other's attacks. But after a few bouts the tide had turned. The watchers sat with heads lowered, silent, intent, and now amid the clouds of dust and the swirl of red and white feathers they discerned a fine spray of blood flecking the ground.

—First blood! Kingfisher cried triumphantly. Looks like my old Aussie's the king of the hill! Finish him off, whitey!

Tail-feathers quivering, eyes bloodshot, the two roosters halted and stood in a glaring face-off. Then they flew at each other and renewed their duel with fresh venom. Blood droplets spattered the white rooster's breast; white feathers matted the red rooster's bare neck. While the hen clucked to herself off to one side, the two fighters launched into the final, fatal round.

—Ha! Kingfisher guffawed, slapping Stump on the shoulder: So much for your pretty young Man Cheong, eh? Looks like old ginger's stronger than new.

The roosters pulled back from each other for a moment, and in a flash Jade was in the middle of the ring, scooping up the doomed red-and-white rooster in one hand.

—That's enough, boys! Any more and we'll have a murder on our hands.

—Put him down! Kingfisher barked, after a moment of stunned silence. What's gotten into your head, Jade? Killing a rooster's the whole reason we're having this cockfight!

He spat, then muttered to himself:

—A murder on our hands. It's a *chicken*, for shit's sake.

Jade snorted with laughter, then passed the rooster to Autumn and strutted toward Kingfisher with her bare breasts thrust out, smiling coyly.

—Kingfisher. I can tell the kind of balefire you've got burning in your head right now. *I'm* the hen in your eyes—right? You want a fight? You fight. You and Stump are always jealous of me, just like those two roosters are jealous of that hen—she tossed her shoulders and gave a harsh laugh—so why don't you men have it out? I think *that's* the kind of cockfight you're hankering for.

—Damn right! said Kingfisher. He slapped his forehead and leapt to his feet, sending chicks twittering and scurrying in all directions. On your feet, Stump! Hen's orders.

Meanwhile Lu Beiping too had sprung up from the table. Seeing this, Kingfisher grinned at him and pushed him back into his seat, then, wiping sauce from his face, he said:

—This has got nothing to do with you, Four Eyes. This is me and Stump's turf. We're going to have us a little boxing match to see whether old ginger really is stronger than new.

Chuckling, Stump assumed a spread-legged fighter's crouch and said:

—Wit my stance, Kingfish? Been a long time since I played at fisticuffs.

—Ha! Fighting stances and everything! Jade cried, applauding. Okay, boys, ready, set . . . but no blood now, alright? . . . fight!

—Fight! Fight! Autumn and the kids chanted.

The mountains trembled. The two men stripped off the checkered waistcloths that they wore for politeness' sake whenever Lu Beiping was around and stood facing each other with legs akimbo, in the state of nature to which they were accustomed. Squatting down, they planted their hands on each other's shoulders, their dark, sinewy arms spanning the space between them like parallel iron bridges. Then they began trying to push each other over in a contest of strength, muscles quivering, genitals dangling, like a pair of gorillas grappling for supremacy. Just as the tension in the air grew so thick that it seemed in danger of exploding, they fell apart with a gasp and staggered backward, and then the fight began in earnest: Out came tiger claws, crane palms, and mantis kicks, a fearsome bestiary of fists and feet whirling back and forth across the packed earth. The sun had already set, and in the darkness, through the lingering smoke from the hearth stove, the two figures danced, twisted, and flew, the black silhouettes of the trees and dim shapes of the mountains seeming to spin around them.

Lu Beiping watched, his breath taken away. All throughout the cockfight he'd had the feeling that this evening's pageant was somehow directed at him, that regardless of whether Kingfisher or Stump won this contest, he was at its center. But weirdly, he now felt liberated, his mind at ease. He thought about Kingfisher's superstitions, about the play of light and shadow. From the bright outer world he'd fallen into this dark, hidden place at the earth's edge; sometimes he'd truly felt as if he were walking downward toward the heart of the Land of Shadow. But now he was unsure. Which place was light, and which was dark? Which was the underworld he was trying to escape from, and which was the sunlit world he wished he could escape to? Watching the whirlwind of punches and kicks, he sat and wondered, utterly confused.

Chapter 11
Torches

To his shock Lu Beiping pushed open the door of his hut and found Jade sitting on the bed, her face deathly pale.

—What happened? It was Jade, not he, who asked. Four Eyes, are you alright? Look at you, you're . . .

Bloody cuts crisscrossed Lu Beiping's face and upper body. Breathlessly, he said:

—Into some deep shit.

—You're in trouble? Jade said, stiffening in alarm. Bounty and bliss, Four Eyes, you look like you've seen a ghost!

—*You* look like you've seen a ghost, Lu Beiping said. Why are you so pale? Is there something wrong up in the hollow?

For a moment the two of them faced each other, breathing heavily, saying nothing. Lu Beiping turned and set his satchel down on the floor, took out an array of bottles and jars: soy sauce, salt, oil, vinegar, kerosene. Trying his best to stay calm, he slunk over to the kitchen, ladled water into a bowl, and handed it to Jade, saying:

—Here, drink some water first. Then we can talk . . .

The turning of the seasons had changed the face of Mudkettle Mountain. In cool late autumn the rubber trees were at peak productivity, and those trees of rubber-bearing age that had survived the ravages of the typhoon had become wet nurses for the Revolution, forced daily to wring out Selfless Contributions to the "war effort." In those days people were always making Selfless Contributions—on Labor Day, on Party Day, on National Day; to the Anti-Reactionary Campaign, to the Movement Against Outmoded Thinking, to the all-important cause of Promulgating the Party Line. With so few trees and so many Self-less Contributions, the cattle and the groves formed a vicious feedback loop, and the entire unit's hopes for meeting their quotas rested on increased manure yields. Before, a manure-hauling team came only once every other month, and now the corral was cleaned almost weekly. Even the foreman, obedient soldier that he was, complained that they'd gone beyond sitting next to the nest and waiting for the hen to lay; now they were killing the hen for the sake of the eggs. Needless to say, after a rosy round of study sessions to Raise Awareness of the National Out-look, the grand pan-Agrecorps land reclamation campaign roared back into full swing, and all Tam-chow County marched to the tooting of bugles and the waving of crimson flags. Now manure-nannying became Lu Beiping's full-time job—the cattle needed to eat more in order to shit more, and ever more straw was needed to turn the results into fer-tilizer. Every day Lu Beiping and his animals peregrinated across the mountainside chasing every last rumor of grass, and every night Lu Beiping hurried back and forth from the corral carrying mountains of fresh straw for bedding. The days of the carefree Turgenev-reading cowherd were over; the demands of the job were getting overbearing, and Lu Beiping was feeling a bit run ragged.

And the worst of it was, more manure hauls meant more chances for the foreman to show up on his doorstep. The world of Mud-kettle Mountain and the world outside were beginning to get tangled together.

The first tangling agent was Gaffer Kam. These past few months Lu Beiping had all but forgotten about the Gaffer's "petty capital-ist" side business selling black-market tobacco, and he hadn't put any thought to how the driftfolk had been filling their pipes—he remem-bered Stump mentioning that sometimes they'd dry papaya leaves, cut them into strips, and smoke them. But now, called upon to drive the oxcart up the mountain every week, the Gaffer, sensing a business opportunity, rekindled his relationship with the driftfolk, selling them tobacco and household goods procured downmountain. In those days one needed ration stamps to buy cigarettes and other daily necessities, so the Gaffer cut a deal with the driftfolk, picking up their lumber at fixed drop-off points around the mountain and trading them tobacco, soap, and rice paper in exchange. For the driftfolk this was a practical means of survival, and the Gaffer was just taking advantage of it to reap a little profit; but in those days, had they been caught, it would've been seen as a towering crime. Though up till now the Gaffer had no idea that Lu Beiping and the "vagrants from Whitesands" enjoyed more than a passing acquaintance, after a few trips up to the hollow he sensed that something was up. Always keen to gather dirt on other people and to keep his own dirt from falling into others' hands, the Gaffer began sniffing around, alert to every possible speck of dirt— this was the special talent that those mistrustful times had bestowed upon him. At an unlucky moment Lu Beiping, on his way up to the hollow, bumped into the Gaffer on his way down, and it was the old man, goaded by suspicion and by his own guilty conscience, who would call down the first winds of the storm to follow.

Lu Beiping threw a handful of cold water on his face and tried to steady his nerves. Guessing the reason for Jade's visit, he asked:

—So, did Kambugger come up to the hollow today?

Jade nodded and sighed, then changed the subject quickly:

—Four Eyes, tell me first what kind of trouble you're in.

—Don't worry about that old bastard, Lu Beiping said, dusting off his hands. Then he announced in a solemn voice: Jade, I don't mean to scare you, but today I saw the foreman . . .

—What foreman? Whose foreman?

—Foreman Kau, who heads my unit. He's the Party Secretary down in the village.

—The Party Secretary?

—I told you, he's the one whose daughter's ghost I was forced to marry.

—Four Eyes! Jade cried. But that's the very same reason I came looking for you! That baleful business.

They sat for a moment in silence, listening to the chattering of the creek.

The Gaffer might not have seemed worth worrying about to Lu Beiping, but these past few days the foreman's constant advances had been very much on his mind.

There were lots of smiles, lots of talk. Friend Lu this and Friend Lu that. He'd laud Lu Beiping for taking such good care of the cattle, praise him for producing so much fertilizer; then, after a bunch of platitudes about Revolutionary Production and Lu Beiping's Selfless Contributions thereto, he'd ask if he'd put any thought to the personnel call. Had Lu Beiping handed in his integration statement yet? Choi always said that Lu Beiping was the hardiest of the Canton re-eds, and thought it unfair that he, the foreman, had given Lu Beiping such a tough job! Choi mentioned that she always saw Lu Beiping driving the cattle toward Sector 12—the grazing's great there in summer, but it must be getting thin now, no? Friend Lu, you think life's hard up on the mountain, you've got no notion how tough things can get down at camp. Why, if you get bored or lonesome you can always go shoot the breeze with those migrants from Whitesands. But at camp, sometimes I feel like there's not a single soul I can talk to . . .

Except him, of course. But in all this talk, never once did the foreman mention Han. It was as if all their patter were dancing delicately around their fictive bond of kinship, though Han's name was never mentioned explicitly. Yet, another name came up again and again: Choi. Intentionally or not, the foreman's talk always looped back to Choi.

That afternoon, while the cattle were feeding, Lu Beiping had slipped away for a quick trip to the supply co-op to trade in his sugar, kerosene, and soap stamps before they expired. On the way back, taking a shortcut across the creek, he heard, coming from the rubber grove on the opposite bank, a fit of breathless giggles. He paused, noting that this was Choi's sector. Peering through the lacepine windbreak on the far side of the creek he almost cried out in surprise: Lying in the grass, their bodies tangled together, were the foreman, buck naked, and Choi, wearing only her shirt.

Rumors abounded that Choi (and others) had begotten "wildborn" children with various men in the village—or managed not to beget them by various means—and it was common enough for lovers, unable to consummate their desires at camp, to do so on the forest floor. But Lu Beiping could tell that this thing between Choi and the foreman was not a typical chapter in the grove's colorful erotic history. Could it be that Choi, in her careless gossip, had let slip some card she shouldn't have revealed, then, fearing retribution from the foreman, tossed Han's blouse into Lu Beiping's lap like a burning cattail-leaf fan—after which the foreman, hot on the scent, had tried to silence her with the trump card he held in his pants? Or had Choi and the foreman been sleeping together from the start, and as their affair deepened Choi realized that the blouse was a piece of dry kindling ready to ignite, at which point she unloaded it on Lu Beiping so that it wouldn't endanger her? In any event, it was now clear to Lu Beiping why Choi, after giving him the shirt, had avoided him like the plague. In those days sex could be, among other things, a powerful tool for sealing lips.

Suppressed laughter and lewd whispers echoed softly in the dusky quiet of the grove.

Afraid that they'd recognize him, Lu Beiping beat a hasty retreat, cutting through a thicket of thorny vines and then bushwhacking home with his heart in his throat.

—Heavens, and I thought you were in *real* trouble! Jade laughed after Lu Beiping described his near encounter with Choi and the foreman. Four Eyes, good thing you wear glasses, otherwise you'd have swollen eyeballs right now. I was afraid you'd seen a ghost, and it turns out you just got a pretty eyeful of someone else's backside.

—Jade, you don't understand, I . . .

But Jade cut him off. Gathering herself up, she adopted a serious tone:

—Four Eyes, listen to me, this time Kambugger fouled things up even worse. Oh . . . Heaven have mercy on us!

Lu Beiping bit his lip, swallowing the information about Han's blouse that he was about to reveal to her.

—Kambugger? Screw him. What trouble can he make?

—What trouble? Jade seized his shoulder, her voice trembling: He . . . he told Kingfisher everything about you! Down to the last little detail. How you got ghost-married, how you're the boss's shadow-kin . . .

—Didn't he already tell Kingfisher? Lu Beiping said, still disdainful. I thought this would be old news by now.

—Mercy! You *still* don't get it! Last time he just said you "weren't clean," and you saw the kind of storm that brought down! Kingfish figured you'd probably gotten into some trouble with the law and sent up here for punishment. You know how fearful Kingfish is about ghosts and powers—you can imagine the scene when Kambugger told him about that bale-crossed stuff! This is real trouble!

The seriousness of the situation began to dawn on Lu Beiping. He thanked his lucky stars that he'd had the tact not to tell Jade about Han's blouse.

—And today . . . Jade laid a hand on her chest, steadying herself. Stump went up the mountain and . . . You need to come up. You . . . you need to come up with me this evening, Jade stammered.

—Why this evening? Lu Beiping asked suspiciously.

—Four Eyes! Jade exclaimed, her voice sounding hollow and choked: How can you not understand?

Lu Beiping stared at her quizzically, with no notion of the terrifying revelation that was soon to follow.

—Four Eyes, I . . . Jade began, blinking back tears. She buried her face in her hands, then said: For almost three months now, I've been . . .

Understanding struck Lu Beiping like a lightning bolt. He took a step back from her, gazing at the slight swell of her belly, then grabbed her by the shoulder and shook her.

—Jade, what? Tell me!

—Last . . . when I was pretending like I was sick, I knew already. But I didn't want to tell you . . . She gave a teary snort of laughter: I told you I was going to bear you a pup, didn't I? I told you . . .

—No! Lu Beiping cried, cutting her off; then he turned and began pacing furiously around the room like a donkey that had just thrown off the reins.

Jade stopped crying, collected herself, and gazed coldly at Lu Beiping's antic silhouette.

—Always the same, she muttered to herself. And *I'm* the one that has to bear the kid.

Then she rushed over to Lu Beiping and threw her arms around him, whimpering:

—Four Eyes, you've *got* to come up with me tonight. Kingfisher, he, he . . . he wants to kill our child!

Jade laid her head on his shoulder and began to bawl.

Lu Beiping shook free of her, then stalked over and slumped down on the bed. Gazing up into the darkness above the rafters, he burst out:

—Goddam, motherfucking, son of a—!

Time was a net closing slowly around him, cold, mindless, unstoppable.

Smudge and Autumn met them at the top of the creek.

—Don't go in the cabin, Autumn said quietly, his face a mask of melancholy. Come with me.

It was dark now. A bright crescent moon illuminated an eerily familiar scene: The crude trestle table sat in the yard beneath the lychee tree, just like on the night of the cockfight, and the combined brood of chicks pecked feed beneath the table alongside the hen and the two roosters, who were minding their own business, having coexisted harmoniously for some time. But the mood was not at all like the other night. The whole family sat around the table sipping gruel in silence. Stump and Kingfisher, who had finished their shares of the big bowl of vegetable porridge that Jade prepared before going down to find Lu Beiping, gestured with their chopsticks at an empty log, inviting Lu Beiping to sit. Autumn and Smudge returned to their places and their unfinished suppers, which they slurped without looking up. Jade strode over to the cabin, returned with a kerosene lantern, and said with forced cheer, as if this were any other night:

—Four Eyes, care for a bowl of porridge?

—Have some food first, Kingfisher mumbled.

Jade hung the lantern from a branch. The wooden frame nailed to the base of the tree threw a long, angular, black shadow, like the shadow of a gallows, heightening the sense that they had all gathered to witness the passing of some kind of judgment. Lu Beiping, who hadn't eaten yet, felt suddenly ravenous, and without thinking twice he drank down his bowl of porridge, finishing it in a few gulps.

Smudge began to fill him another bowl, but Kingfisher stopped him short with a stern gaze.

Stump and Autumn lit their pipes from the lantern's flame and sat back down, gurgling smoke.

Now that he had a little food in his stomach, Lu Beiping felt like he ought to say something, not just sit here like an animal waiting to be slaughtered. Armed with a better knowledge of Kingfisher's temperament, he said calmly:

—Kingfisher, I heard there's something you wanted to talk to me about. Tell me what's on your mind.

Kingfisher closed his eyes, his face stiff, as if suppressing some powerful feeling welling up inside him. Then he opened them and said in a soft voice:

—Stump, bring over that barrel. Show Four Eyes what's inside.

Stump picked up a slack-hooped wooden barrel that sat at the foot of the tree and carried it over to the table, muttering:

—Look in, Four Eyes.

In the moonlight, the mouth of the barrel yawned like a cave. Perplexed and beginning to grow anxious, Lu Beiping peeked in, straining to see whatever this terrible thing was that they wanted to show him.

Then Kingfisher stalked over and kicked the barrel on its side, causing the thing it held to spill out in several pieces on the ground. At first Lu Beiping couldn't tell what it was; then he stepped back in shock, goose pimples rising all over his skin. It was a snake—no, it wasn't a snake; it was a huge, sagging, greyish-black snakeskin, the great tube of it bundled and kinked, bigger around than the barrel itself.

The kids started to wail.

—Stump's been crossed, Jade broke in from one side. He saw her two days in a row, up in the high valley. This is what real trouble looks like, Four Eyes. There's evil brewing around here—

—You need to shut your mouth and let other folks do the talking for once! Kingfisher barked, cutting her off. A whole lot you know about the difference between good and evil!

Then he addressed Lu Beiping, punctuating the air with his water pipe:

—Stump ran afoul of the spirits. Thank the powers she's moved on, or else . . .

—I didn't see her, just heard her, Stump burbled quietly. Whole mountain quaked up a mighty thunder, and I got so cold I certained I was feverish. Gave me a real fright. Then just this morn I saw that thing hanging all over the trees and the ground. Soon as I saw it, I got down and prayed . . .

Coiled on the ground, the massive, scaly skin glimmered faintly in the moonlight.

—It's not just Stump who's been crossed, *all* of us've been crossed! Kingfisher burst out, whirling around to face Lu Beiping: In the old days they said, when the holy leocore appears, bounty'll shower upon the year . . . but when we first showed up on Mudkettle Mountain, folks told us never, never to rile the Snakeweird, said if she ever showed herself, ruin would rain down on man and beast! When Smudge's pa went into the high valley on Midsummer, he saw her skin and didn't pray, and the next day a falling tree crushed the life out of him. Horn shouldered the ruin on all of our parts. Horn, he . . .

Kingfisher clasped his hands automatically, turned and bowed three times toward the dark valley, then whipped around again and said:

—Four Eyes, tonight, I want you to stand up! Stand up and face the spirits! Stand up and face Horn!

Lu Beiping glanced at Jade, then, obediently, stood up.

—Good, said Kingfisher gruffly. I like that you're the honest kind who'll answer for what he's done. Stump, ready?

Stump sprang up and before Lu Beiping could react, the big man had grabbed both of his arms, yanked them behind his back, twisted them, hooked one arm around his neck and wrenched his head down.

—Wha . . . what are you doing? Lu Beiping gasped, struggling with all his might. But he couldn't move; his hands, arms, neck, and head were all clamped in a steel vise.

It was pointless to resist the mighty bronze golem that was Stump. What shocked Lu Beiping most of all, though, was that nobody seemed surprised or panicked by these developments. Even Jade, Autumn, and Smudge gazed on solemn and expressionless, as if all this had been arranged in advance.

Kingfisher strode over to Lu Beiping, clasped his hands together respectfully, and said with a forbidding frown:

—Four Eyes, we're putting you to some trouble because you did the same to us. Tonight I need to ask you to endure a little pain of the flesh. First Stump'll tie you to the tree, then I want to make a couple things clear to you.

—You . . . Lu Beiping threw an imploring glance at Jade. Kingfisher leveled his gaze on her, and she hung her head. Unable to resist, Lu Beiping let Stump steer him limply toward the tree, where Stump bound his hands behind his back to the wooden frame. Fighting down the terror that was welling up inside him, he stood motionless and waited to hear what Kingfisher had to say.

The tabletop gleamed ghastly white in the moonlight, like a polished cleaver. The moon-dappled shadows cast by the lychee tree seemed to darken, enfolding both him and Kingfisher. Kingfisher gazed at him in silence, then nodded.

—You're a good man, Four Eyes, you've got some grit after all.

Then abruptly his voice leapt the octave:

—But I was right the first time, wanting to drive you out of here! Witchy stuff's been going on right and left since you first set foot on this mountain. If Kambugger hadn't told us the whole story this morning, I fear you'd've dragged the whole lot of us to an early death! Peh!—Kingfisher spat over his shoulder, remembering his own taboo, then rubbed his lips—Four Eyes, why'd you try to hoodwink us? Tell me! Why?

Lu Beiping chewed on his lower lip. He knew there was nothing he could say.

—Stinky feet—hmph! That's a pretty story! Said you got sent up here on account of your stinky feet . . . Then Kingfisher, realizing that this unlofty topic had spoiled the gravity of his speech, threw a quick, barbed glance over at Jade and barked: Don't you dare laugh!

Jade lowered her head, her lips twisted into a smile. Lu Beiping, though, couldn't restrain himself, and let slip a snicker.

—Why, I'll—!

Now Kingfisher was thoroughly incensed. Cursing, he leaned down and whisked out from underneath the table a crude bullwhip braided from flattened lengths of shad cane, which he'd fashioned just that afternoon. With an earsplitting crack he brought it down on the tabletop, causing the two toddlers to erupt in wails of terror. Then, heedless of the scene he'd just caused, he advanced on Lu Beiping, shaking the whip.

—You laugh, Four Eyes? You won't have an ounce of laughter left in you by the end of tonight! Now it makes sense, all that shadowy business. That boy running up here burning spirit money, that burnt up wooden grave marker, it was all on account of you. A ghost husband, tricking your way into our family—you have any idea how much poison air you've brought in amongst us? You could've been the bane of us all, driven us and everything our brother built down into the dark place!

Kingfisher heaved a sigh, then went on:

—Us driftfolk, our lives are cheap, we can't afford to rile powers of any sort. We ran away from our homes and families because we fear the government, and you come up here with a doler magistrate sniffing your heels. A foreman's kin! And ghost kin, at that! Hah!—Kingfisher chuckled grimly—We're haunt-fearing folk, and here you are, wedded to shadow, with a real demon hounding your steps. Mercy, now the bad vapor's so thick here that the gods themselves are stirring and taking notice! That means light and shadow are tipping out of balance, and just one end can come of that—bloody ruin!

The wind had picked up. Moonlight flickered ambiguously on the slopes above them, like the faint shadows of remorse that were now passing over Kingfisher's face. Softening his tone, he went on:

—Tonight, Four Eyes, we need you to shed a little blood. Only blood can push back the dark now. This is for your good too. Once your blood's been seen, you'll be free of the bale that's clung to you. Blood's the only thing that'll wash the sin off you now. So, I beg you, friend . . . forgive this indignity.

Lu Beiping stared at the silver band of Kingfisher's whip coiled in the moonlight. There was no begging for mercy. He'd muddled his way into this den of outlaws, and now he must be judged according to their own peculiar logic. He closed his eyes and waited for the whip to fall, anticipating the thorny bite of splintered bamboo.

—Kingfisher! Jade cried, standing up abruptly. Autumn grabbed her and pulled her back down. Then Kingfisher exchanged a glance with Stump, and the big man, chuckling, bounded over and seized Jade as well.

—Pardon, sis, Stump said as he pinioned her limbs.

—Holy hell, Stump! What are you trying to do?

Jade kicked and cursed, but she too was helpless against Stump's steel-caliper biceps. As she wriggled futilely, Stump bound her hands behind her back and tied her to the other end of the woodcutting frame.

—Pa! Smudge cried. He stood frozen to the spot, hugging the two sobbing toddlers in his arms, eyes locked on Kingfisher's crimson, sweat-streaked face, afraid to make even the slightest move. Flexing the whip, Kingfisher walked over to Jade, who was still cursing up a storm, and bowing to her with his hands clasped in front of him, he slipped into the dramatic cadences of a Cantonese singshow player:

—I beg your forgiveness, my lady! Tonight I've got to spill a drop of your blood too. You knew Four Eyes's story . . . yet you pledged to make good with him . . . and brought him in amongst us! His poison has seeped into your bones too. You've got to give up some of your blood as well, to save us all from ruin—

—You shit-eating pig, Kingfisher! Jade wailed, struggling against her bonds. I've known all along the kind of foul juices you and Stump've got sloshing in your bellies!

—Kingfisher, Lu Beiping cut in from the other side of the wooden frame, Just whip me, okay? I'm the one responsible for all this bale and poison. Shouldn't my blood be enough?

—Fine!

Before the sentence was out of Lu Beiping's mouth the whip came arcing out—*crack!*—and a bright red welt shot across Lu Beiping's upper arm and chest, blood beading at the places where the thorns had caught. The kids started to scream. Kingfisher roared:

—Quiet! Tonight I've got to be the ugly one!

Crack!

—And don't any of you dare stop me!

Crack!

At first Lu Beiping gritted his teeth, trying his best to bear the pain. Then, when at last it exceeded his endurance, he gave a long moan, and suddenly began cursing at the top of his lungs in Mandarin:

—Fuck you, Kingfisher! Fuck both of you! You filthy, fucking vagrants! Miserable illiterate redneck trash! Fuck you all to hell!

Crack!

—You and Stump are just paying me back because you're jealous! This isn't about the spirits, this is about *you!*

—That's right, curse me, boy, curse me! Of course I'm paying you back!—as his rage got the better of him, Kingfisher began lashing Lu Beiping double-time, passing the whip back and forth from hand to hand—Listen to him, Stump! Cussing us out in high speech like a damn northerner! Come on, your turn!

Stump took the whip and without a word started raining a storm of lashes down on Lu Beiping's neck and shoulders.

It was now all too clear that these two brutish men had seized this moment to unleash upon the pale city boy three months' worth of pent-up anger, which even their sparring match on the night of the cockfight hadn't fully vented—and to reclaim their fiery village pride in a blood-spattered frenzy. In every lash, Lu Beiping felt the hard bones of their resentment. He swore and sobbed till his throat grew hoarse, and before long his voice couldn't be heard over the crack of the whip.

Jade, however, was wailing ever more stridently:

—Shame on you! Conniving to beat up an innocent student! Beat me, Kingfisher, beat me to death! You want to beat somebody, beat me!

Red-eyed with fury, Kingfisher grabbed the whip from Stump and wheeled around to face her.

—Alright, here goes, you filthy whore!

Crack!

—You *dare* call me a whore! Jade shrieked, her hair streaming as she struggled, kicking over the table and spattering Kingfisher with a spray of porridge from cascading bowls. Kingfisher stood frozen for a moment, caught off guard, and Jade, pressing the offensive, spat on him and yelled: I *knew* you were a pair of black-hearted bastards! You were just looking for an excuse to murder my child! You . . .

But now there was no stopping Kingfisher. Her rebuke had only inflamed his lust for vengeance, and he continued lashing her with mounting viciousness.

Crack!

—Damn right! I'm going to snuff out that shadowborn whelp growing in your belly!

Crack!

—Keep you from squeezing out another devil spawn like Smudge, to drag us all to hell!

Panting raggedly, Kingfisher held the whip aloft, about to lay a vindictive stroke directly across the bulge of Jade's abdomen. But

Autumn, who'd been standing off to one side sheltering the children, rushed over with one hand outstretched and blocked the whip as it fell. The thorny rope landed squarely on Autumn's shoulder, but he managed to grab its end and then, gripping it, gave Kingfisher a shove that sent him tottering backward and left Autumn holding the whip.

—Enough, Kingfisher! Enough!

—What? Autumn? Kingfisher stammered, aghast. You dare get in my way!

—Kingfisher, Autumn said slowly, brandishing the weapon: Listen to me. All these years I've believed you with your talk of light and darkness. You said loving and bearing life is wholesome, full of light, said only killing and harming living beings was evil. I believe all that. Tonight it's clear you and Stump set a trap to kill Jade's babe— tell me, is that good, or ill? Boon, or bale?

Kingfisher stood frozen, the power of speech stolen from him. Autumn waved the whip in the air and said to both Stump and Kingfisher:

—So. Have I got my point across, or do I need to spill some of your blood too?

—Fie! Stump bellowed, then he rushed straight at Autumn and tried to grab the whip. But a well-placed punch from Autumn knocked him off balance and sent him sprawling into the dust.

—Why, you . . . you . . . Kingfisher stuttered, astonished at this show of fiery self-confidence from his normally listless companion.

—Kingfisher, Autumn commanded, You try to control everything and everybody with those laws of yours. But you've got to remember that they apply to you too!

Kingfisher grabbed his water pipe and was about to strike Autumn out of spite when Smudge, Tick, and Roach stampeded over and grabbed him by the legs, howling beseechingly at their uncle.

The giant snakeskin lay strewn across the yard, trampled to a muddy hash.

The crescent moon hung in the lychee tree's bare branches, a spotlight illuminating the raucous farce below. Pipes, bowls, log stools, and the overturned table lay scattered across the ground like stage props, while high above them the dark forms of the mountains huddled shoulder to shoulder, watching intently—perhaps discerning in the poses of the actors a hidden truth that they alone could read, having watched this same pageant repeat itself act after act since time immemorial. A cold wind blew, carrying a foretaste of winter. Mudclaw Creek burbled on incessantly, seeming always on the verge of spitting out some shocking revelation.

But Kingfisher was exhausted. His body sagged, and he staggered a few paces toward the lodge, then he lost his footing and fell to his knees. Bowing his head toward the dark bowl of the mountain, he cried out, tears streaming down his face:

—Horn! Please! What's right? Where's the light? Help me! I don't understand . . .

A bellyache bird was singing in the trees. *Bellllll-ly ache! Bellllll-ly ache!* it cried, complaining of abdominal discomfort in a clear Man Cheong accent. Farther down in the valley, a water rail answered: *Ooo-ah . . . ooo-ah . . . ooo-ah . . .* a desolate, imploring cry that was enough to send shivers down the back of any human listener. A laughingthrush, which the locals called a "gigglebird," gushed its melodious but rather moronic-sounding stream of questions: *Really—really—really? You sure? You sure? You really sure?* while a cumber wren down by the creek announced: *Chewed it! Chewed it!*, reporting matter-of-factly on its latest meal of watercumber flowers.

The first thing to return to Lu Beiping through the heavy delirium was not the pain, but his sense of hearing. Listening to the clamor of evening birdsong, he couldn't tell if it was night or day, whether he was lying in bed or floating in the clouds. The bright, clear cries of the birds were like knives stabbing at his dulled nerves. Then he felt the searing pain in his body, and he groaned. *Are you awake?* he heard a soft voice calling through the fog. He opened his eyes, but the effort was too much, and before he could make out the speaker's form his eyelids slipped closed again. Was it the pain, or the fatigue? Or pain and fatigue dueling inside him? The pain that blazed all over his body every time he tried to move goaded him toward wakefulness, but exhaustion was a bottomless pit into which his budding consciousness slowly sank, till it was completely subsumed.

Or rather, the topmost layer of his consciousness was awake; he felt the brush of a hand gently bathing his wounds. The lightest touch on his wounds was piercing agony, making him grimace, groan, hyperventilate, cry out; but deeper down, he was still asleep, deeply, sweetly asleep, unable to raise up even the faintest, most diaphanous tendril of motivation or desire. Sometimes pain pushed exhaustion into the background, and the sensations of his skin, ears, and tongue became acute: He was thirsty, cried out *Water* . . . Someone put something cool against his lips, and liquid comfort suffused his body. But more often fatigue toppled the pain, engulfed it, drowned it. He felt someone picking the thorns out of his wounds, every movement of the pin triggering a reflexive twitch, but the spasms of pain were like the rocking of a terrible cradle, each one compounding the pain of the last while simultaneously easing him down into the boundless, bottomless darkness of sleep.

Too tired. A scrap of red paper had unleashed on him such a teeming crowd of absurdities that his narrow window of experience was filled to the bursting point, strained to the breaking point. It was all just too much. Never mind that the weeks of "selfless contributions" and "manure nannying" had already squeezed his endurance dry, wrung out every last drop of the flamboyantly competitive spirit that he usually mustered to meet such challenges. This pain was a vacation: a breath in a loud, relentless march, a desperately needed white space on a canvas cluttered with colors. Would that everything had already come to pass, that nothing more would ever happen, that he could just call it quits, hang up his hat, and slip away.

How could he be so cruel . . . Lu Beiping heard a voice choked with pity speaking close beside him, so close that he could reach out and touch the person who spoke. He strained to open his eyes, say something, curse the pain or make a wisecrack. But the effort drained his last reserves of energy in the battle between pain and fatigue, and he gave up. His muscles went slack, and he drifted off to sleep.

He slept all day. Sometimes a bad dream or a stab of pain jerked him awake, but his wakefulness was no different from sleep, his eyes unseeing, his consciousness a blank. The birds sang, then the forest fell silent; night fell, then dawn came. Lu Beiping didn't know how deeply he slept, or for how long. He didn't know who'd stripped off his blood-crusted clothes, cleaned and bathed his wounds, picked the splinters out of his skin. He didn't know who'd untied him from the wooden frame beneath the lychee tree and carried him down the creek and over the ridge to his hut. And of course he didn't know, would never know, that his "vacation in pain" had created, for another person, a vacation in affection—a sudden and unlooked-for chance to leap across worlds that stood in the way, and gently, leisurely, unreservedly give succor to one long-fretted-for, give care to one long-admired, offer tears of sympathy and murmurs of concern. Such that in a dark corner of his heart he thanked Heaven for the act of violence that gave him this opportunity.

Unconsciousness can be a form of bliss; and ignorance is often the clearest, most self-conscious excuse.

Lu Beiping lay on his bed with only a waistcloth for covering, his sleeping, pain-wracked body twisted into one laughable pose after another. He didn't know that the poultices spread on his wounds were made from fresh herbs picked in the mountains, chewed till they were soft and then crushed to a paste, spread, then washed off, then spread again. He didn't know that his hut had been cleaned, his water jug refilled, didn't know that his cattle had been let out to graze, their corral bedded with fresh straw. And he didn't know how much his caregiver rejoiced in the fact that he didn't know. Lightly, busily, joyously he tripped across the mountainside, dispensing his many duties, not even neglecting to haul Kambugger's regular shipments of timber down Mudclaw Creek to the places they'd arranged. Every evening he sat by Lu Beiping's bedside in the light of the lantern, listening to his friend's breathing grow more and more tranquil, letting his own cares flow freely over that pitiful figure. Never before had his days passed so easily, with such natural order, such a reliable sense of satisfaction. All day he savored the not-knowing that made all this possible, indulged it, saved it, stretched it, diluted it, preserved it for lean days in the future. If only nobody ever knew—even him? Or except him? He didn't know . . .

It was the racket of birdsong as the birds returned to their roosts in the evening that dragged Lu Beiping's consciousness up out of the chasm of sleep. First he heard the birds calling, then he felt the pain. Birdcalls stabbed at his eardrums, and pain lanced through his limbs. Now he might have the strength to lift his lids; the blood had returned to his chest, vigor had reentered his muscles. But he didn't want to open his eyes and emerge from the darkness.

A strange feeling, a sensation of warmth mixed with soreness, spread out slowly over his body. Bathing in this feeling, he thought half consciously: Is someone changing my bandages? Who is it? Whose fingertips would be so light, so careful, each touch containing miles of unspoken meaning? Was it Jade? Even in half sleep he tensed at the thought of her. But he was happy to linger longer in this womb-like darkness, for the hands that tended him had slid away from his wounds and begun to massage him. The touch of the palms against his skin was a complex, many-layered sensation: gentle and caring, every brush of the fingertips conveying meticulous restraint; pitying and compassionate, the hollows of the palms radiating warmth; faintly mocking, a light caress suggesting the arch of an eyebrow; full of love, every stroke trembling as if with a slight charge of electricity. No, this wasn't Jade. Jade's fingers would be more dexterous than these, but less careful. Or had that bloody nightmare changed everything? Maybe. Only Jade would cherish him, protect him like this. The shallows of his mind were beginning to clear, though the depths were still murky. Secretly, conspiratorially, he arched his body to drink in that sensation, like naked soil absorbing sun and rainfall, letting the desires awoken by that remarkable touch lap freely over him, warm, rosy, and radiant.

As the warm feeling slid off of his cheeks and down along his neck, he began to laugh quietly inside. His caregiver's caresses had changed from hands to lips, and he heard the barely audible sound of shallow, withheld breath. When the spot of warmth hesitated on the inside of his thigh, sending a rush of heat up into his groin, then alighted on his penis, immediately giving him an erection, he knew he couldn't feign sleep any longer. He opened his eyes, casting around for some lewd joke to say to Jade. Then he saw the figure bent over him in bed and sat up, thunderstruck.

—Oh my god . . . Autumn?

Autumn's hands flew away from him, and he stood frozen in place by the bedside, his face turned bright crimson, unable to look directly at Lu Beiping.

—Autumn . . . what are you doing?

For a moment Lu Beiping truly didn't understand. But now the pain brought on by his sharp movement exploded all over his body, and grimacing he tried to lie back down on the pillow.

Autumn rushed over and reached out a hand to help him. But now the touch of his fingers was repellent as snakeskin, and Lu Beiping pushed him away with a cry of anger.

—Don't touch me! Get away from me!

Autumn tottered back a few steps. Then he turned and, without a word, opened the door and slipped out.

Lu Beiping slumped stiffly against the bamboo wall.

The sunset glowed gold, still clamorous with birdsong. A few sunbeams slanted through the hut, full of glittering motes of sawdust drifting down from the rafters. The cattle complained quietly. On top of the water jug next to the bed sat Lu Beiping's washbasin, inside it a liquidy paste of pulverized herbs. For a moment he wasn't sure where he was, then he saw sitting on the stove the enamel jar that he'd used to carry his beef up from camp, and the events of the past few weeks flooded back to him.

The door opened again, and Autumn leaned in and muttered without looking at him:

—Cattle've grazed already. Medicine's in the basin, don't forget to put it on again this evening.

Then he left.

Listening to Autumn's hurried footsteps dwindle downhill toward the creek, Lu Beiping didn't know what he'd just seen or done. Both the dreamlike warmth and the chill of his own rejection of Autumn clung stiffly to his skin. Then pain burst over him once more, knifing deep into his shoulders and back. He was cold, wanted to get up and walk around, but found that there wasn't an ounce of strength left in his body. He was too weak to sit up straight, and lying back down was going to be a trial.

Easing himself down on the bed while groaning and cursing, he noticed Smudge's big head poking through the door, a look of seasoned sympathy on the boy's face as he gazed at Lu Beiping with his large black eyes.

—Smudge?

Smudge walked in, carrying a scrap-wood basket that contained a bowl of porridge, a bowl of greens, and a handful of fat, medicinal-looking leaves. Cocking his head and affecting a tone of matronly concern, he said:

—How're your hurts? Have you got everything you need? Kingfisher bade me bring you this basket—I swear, it was Kingfisher told me to.

Lu Beiping twisted his head to one side, as if just hearing Kingfisher's name uttered aloud was painful to him.

—How's Jade? How's your pa?

—Pa's well, Smudge said cheerily. Uncle Autumn saved her from the worst of it. You got hurt bad, Pa just got a couple lashes. Do you wit what's troubling Uncle Autumn, though? I saw him crying on his way back up the mountain, and he didn't stop nor say hello.

Lu Beiping hung his head and said nothing. Smudge stared at him.

—I don't know, Lu Beiping said. I just . . .

He shook his head and sighed.

—I really don't know.

A vacation in pain—what a strange kind of vacation!

He had a fever now, and he could do nothing but lie in bed drifting in and out of sleep, frittering away the daylight hours. Jade came. Hugged him and sobbed uncontrollably, repeated *how awful* and *you poor thing*, wiped a lot of snot and tears on the edge of the bedframe. Lu Beiping wanted to reassure her, make light of the whole thing, but the sight of her belly always stopped him short. That rising bulge sent a chill through his heart, renewed all the recent trauma and made him reluctant to think too deeply about either the past or the future.

Kingfisher and Stump came too. The trio of little monkeys trooped with them down the mountain, and their loud antics relieved some of the awkwardness. Kingfisher brought poultices of freshly crushed herbs and ministered to Lu Beiping with the deftness of an old village healer. Stump took a small glass bottle out of his wicker hip-pouch, saying it contained a special tincture that he'd made himself using dried gecko skins and hillflower rice wine, and made Lu Beiping drink it to replenish his voids. Lu Beiping lay with his head bent away from them on the pillow, saying nothing, while Kingfisher filled the silence—not one word of apology, just a constant gruff patter as he read Lu Beiping's wrists and tongue: *A month for the bones, a fortnight for the flesh, a week for the skin. Don't fret, son, soon as the bile comes out you'll feel better.* As he was about to leave, Kingfisher patted his shoulder, where the welt left by the whip's first bite still throbbed, and said:

—You're a good man, Four Eyes. You've got grit.

—You said that already, Kingfisher.

But what made him feel worst of all were not the uncomfortable topics that lay unbroached between him and the two men, but the constant, quiet sounds of activity he heard in the mornings and evenings outside the hut.

Every morning Autumn came down the mountain and let out the cattle for him, then herded them back after the day's grazing, counted them and bedded the corral with fresh straw. All this he seemed to do in his off-hours, between timber-scouting and lumber-hauling trips for Kingfisher. Several times Lu Beiping woke to find a bowl of freshly crushed herbs sitting on the wooden stopper of the water jug, along with bottles of mercurochrome and gentian violet and a small roll of fresh bandages. He knew Autumn came into the hut whenever he was asleep, and that he must have bought these "magistrate's medicines" on his trips downmountain to sell wood. He also guessed that Autumn was the one who delivered Jade's bowls of porridge and soup. At first he thought it was Smudge who placed the baskets on the jug for him to find when he awoke, then he realized it couldn't be so, it was too much of a coincidence for Smudge to arrive only when he happened to be asleep. And if it were Smudge, the boy would certainly have pestered him until he was awake.

The silence was the most painful thing of all. Through the thin bamboo wall he heard plenty of movement, plenty of noise—but there were no words.

As his injuries healed, Lu Beiping grew apprehensive, unsure how to face down the ever-more-awkward wall of silence that was building between him and Autumn. Lying in bed, listening to the oppressive sound of Autumn's diligent labors, he felt as if the scant wicker barrier that separated them had been slathered over with mud, then covered with ice, growing thicker, colder, heavier, even acquiring a thin crust of animosity. Maybe animosity was too strong a word. The initial silence had simply gathered inertia till it was impossible to find words to break it, till it hung palpably around him, wintry and all-enveloping. After a few more days, when his wounds were almost healed and strength had returned to his limbs, the bowls of herbs and baskets of food began to be dropped quietly on his doorstep, not placed on the water jug. Lu Beiping would wait tactfully till the end of the evening, when the rustling of straw had ceased, then pad out the door, stretch his back—the deep cut on his waist still ached just a bit—then sigh, lean down, pick up his unclaimed dinner, take it back into his hut, and eat it without appetite or relish.

On the day when Lu Beiping felt well enough to manage his daily cowherd duties again, he gauged the number of days that had probably passed and guessed that he was due for another visit from the manure-hauling team. He resolved to tell Autumn that he shouldn't come tomorrow, but he put it off all evening, at a loss for how to begin the conversation. Finally, when he heard the corral's thick wooden gate clunk closed, he steeled himself and pushed open the door. Autumn turned his back to him and walked quickly downhill toward the stream. Lu Beiping rushed out a few paces and shouted Autumn's name, but Autumn didn't answer, and without looking back he bounded across the creek rocks and vanished into the forest.

The next day, Autumn didn't come.

Early winter was Hainan's rainy season. An intermittent drizzle, like the plum rains of the lower Yangtze, dragged on for several sullen, gray weeks, till his hut's brand new thatched roof dripped like a sponge, making for cold nights between damp blankets and mold-spotted clothes. Every day Smudge delivered light meals that Jade had prepared, and sometimes Lu Beiping drove his cattle up through the rain to the hollow, where he watched Jade bustle ponderously about and bantered politely with Stump and Kingfisher. It was as if nothing had happened. The only difference was that he rarely saw Autumn, and didn't ask after him. The days dribbled on just like the rain, predictable, endless, listless.

Tonight, after laying the cattle's bedding, Lu Beiping sat beneath the lantern, leafing through his long-untouched books, peeling the wet pages apart from one another. His harmonica, which he hadn't played for weeks, was beginning to rust. He remembered Han's blouse, stuffed into a crack in the rocks down by the creek—maybe the fabric had already disintegrated in the rain. He thought of Jade's swollen belly, concealing his own ignominious flesh. There was no reason, apart from the protests of his own conscience, that he couldn't let that tacky blue blouse fall apart into rags, let Han fade back into the realm of fiction and rumor from whence she came. But whether he liked it or not, the child in Jade's belly would soon emerge into the world, bawling and kicking and impossible to deny or erase. He still had a lot of life left to live; how would he, now a father-to-be (just thinking those words made his heart race) manage the entire thing? Two women, one in daylight, one in darkness, had laid a dual curse upon his head—and now he had to contend with another, even more ambiguous, player, Autumn, that inscrutable entanglement, that unwanted complication; the whole situation was unutterably mysterious, yet he couldn't just wave it away. God . . . here was one absurdity piled on top of another, at the foot of an even greater absurdity. Kingfisher said he had grit, but did he have enough to handle all of this?

As he mused on these questions, he heard, through the pattering of rain on the banana leaves outside, the crunch of approaching footsteps. Pushing open the shutter and peering down into the darkness, he saw the glow of a hurricane lantern wavering up the slope from the creek. Who was this? It must be Jade. Or Autumn, maybe?

Without waiting for a knock Lu Beiping opened the door for the visitor, then backed away stammering as the man walked into the room. Never would he have expected that at this late hour, in the middle of a rainstorm, Kingfisher would decide to pay him a visit.

Wordlessly Kingfisher took off his broad-brimmed palm-leaf hat and shook it dry just inside the door, then he sat down on a log stool and began rolling a cigarette. Lu Beiping watched the beads of water on Kingfisher's back glitter in the lamplight. Finally he said:

—You don't come around here often, Kingfisher.

—You're well? Kingfisher asked after several silent puffs on his cigarette.

Lu Beiping understood that Kingfisher meant his injuries, and answered with a curt affirmative, then fell back into silence. Kingfisher breathed out a cloud of smoke, then got right to the point.

—Horn came to me in a dream last night. You were standing next to him. Gave me a scare, that did. Finally I decided I needed to come down here myself to tell you . . . that you ought to leave.

—What? Why? Lu Beiping asked, stiffening, conscious again of the lingering ache of his wounds. Why should I leave?

—This hasn't got anything to do that evil stuff Kambugger told me about, Kingfisher said, rubbing his hands together: Your blood's been seen, you're square with them now.

Square with *them*—catching Kingfisher's drift, Lu Beiping smiled.

—I'm talking about Jade's babe. No, don't get me wrong—what I mean is, no matter whether the child makes it or not, you still ought to leave.

Lu Beiping stared in confusion at Kingfisher's smoke-shrouded face. Kingfisher took a long drag, breathed it out in a series of shallow exhalations, then heaved a sigh.

—By rights the child should be yours. That's fate, no getting around it. It was fate that you got marooned up here in the mountains, and it was fate that we took you in.

Kingfisher sat for a moment with his head lowered, lost in thought. Then, raising his voice slightly, he said:

—But your fate isn't to meet your end with us, Four Eyes! And if on account of that pup in Jade's belly you joined us for good, got pulled in for good . . . that'd be your end, I fear.

Lu Beiping gaped at him in surprise, slowly puzzling out the logic beneath Kingfisher's mysterious circumlocutions.

—I've tied my brow in a knot lately, thinking about these things. And I think that our days aren't long here on Mudkettle Mountain. I've got a hunch that some great ruin's fixing to fall on us, swallow us all up, man and babe alike—Kingfisher paused, listening to the bugs gnawing at the rafters, then pointed upward and heaved another sigh—When we lose the balance, when light and shadow get tipped out of true, then god knows the kind of awful things that'll start taking shape around us, god knows what kind of calamity'll descend on our heads.

Every one of Kingfisher's sighs raised a chill wind and pulled the darkness in a step closer, Lu Beiping thought. Outside, the rain wept on and on. Kingfisher blew a long wisp of smoke.

—Go, Four Eyes. Get far away from us, however you can. We drift-folk, we're the ass of the world, we're the people who've been pushed to the farthest ends of the earth, all the way to the edge of the sky. What do you find at the edge of the sky? Gods, spirits. And what do you find at the ends of the earth? Haunts and demons. We folks who keep company with gods and demons, our lives are cheap, and hard. Four Eyes, you wouldn't last.

By now Kingfisher's cigarette had burned so short that the flame was singeing his fingertips. Oblivious of it, he took a last drag and said softly:

—I know that in all her life the two men Jade's loved most are Horn, and you. I told her, Four Eyes is a good man, but I don't want him to become like Smudge's pa. I don't want him to become Horn's brother.

Kingfisher stood up. He picked up the lantern.

—Kingfisher! Wait!

As Kingfisher made to leave, Lu Beiping was seized by a sudden impulse. He now felt as if he'd gained some new insight into this strange man, that amid Kingfisher's tangled web of mysticism he'd detected a gleam of something else: human sympathy, a sense of compassion for the whole foolhardy human race, even a kind of wisdom. He was overcome with an urge to tell Kingfisher about Han's blouse, to spill the dark secret bottled in his chest, reveal everything. His lips trembled, but he fought back the impulse. Then, remembering what Autumn said about Kingfisher, he asked:

—I wanted to know, Kingfisher . . . why did you, why'd a clear-hearted man like you, go off and join the driftfolk, go all the way to the ends of the earth and the edge of the sky?

Kingfisher stood in the doorway, his bald head almost touching the lintel. He said with a frosty smile:

—They said I was a godmonger, a peddler of superstition. Strug-gled me till I was red from head to foot and they were all blue in the face. I'm not a godmonger. I'm just afraid. For years now I've been afraid—yet I don't know what it is I'm afraid of.

Picking up his hat, he said:

—Truth is, it wasn't so much that I offended them as that they offended me. So I left.

Then Kingfisher turned, and did exactly that.

Lu Beiping rushed out the door into the mist and rain and the all-encompassing forest night and stood there, watching Kingfisher's lantern and palm-leaf hat dwindle into the darkness.

Then he went back into his hut and sat for a while in silence, listening to the cattle ruminating in the corral. He thought about Kingfisher's final words—about this "them," different from that *them*—and laughed.

But now "they" were closing in on all sides, and Lu Beiping was starting to feel cornered and helpless.

The next afternoon the manure-haulers came. This time the foreman brought along a team of tappers in addition to the grove maintenance crew. Normally tappers didn't take part in manure hauls, but now, in this time of Selfless Contributions, nothing was outside the bounds of possibility. Yet when Choi hopped down off of the Gaffer's oxcart and began tittering and cackling as if she owned the place, while the foreman strolled alongside her punctuating her monologue with genial remarks, it became clear to Lu Beiping that the tappers were here because of her, and that she was here because of the foreman—that through her presence the foreman was trying to communicate something to him. As the workers shoveled, Lu Beiping tried to catch her eye, to read her real intent from even a brief glance; if she hadn't forced that "teasey blue" blouse on him, Han would've been no more than a passing fancy, a faint disturbance in the air, not worth probing into. But though the whole forest echoed with Choi's chatter, not once did she turn her head in Lu Beiping's direction. As usual the foreman showered Lu Beiping with avuncular approval, congratulating him for his first-rate work with the cattle and asking Choi in a loud voice: High-quality manure yield's the key to accelerating production, don't you agree, Choi? I think we ought to recommend our friend Lu for a medal. What do you think, does the tapping crew have an opinion?

When the manure haul was over, as Lu Beiping herded the cattle back down the mountain, he saw Sergeant Fook and Gaffer Kam coming toward him up the trail, and reeled with alarm. What were they doing walking in the direction of the hollow? The last Lu Beiping had heard, his goose-stepping former rival been reassigned to some sort of cross-divisional Working Group at battalion HQ. They waved, and when they came abreast of each other Fook stopped, gave Lu Beiping a long, appraising look, and asked point-blank: Have you handed in your integration statement yet? Foreman Kau wants to know.

—How could I hand in something I haven't written? Lu Beiping said tartly, and turned to leave. Fook called after him:

—Fong's already handed in hers!

They went their separate ways, Lu Beiping laughing quietly to himself. He realized that he hadn't seen the familiar faces of Fong, Wing, or Chu among the manure-haulers today, and remembered that on his last trip to camp Chu had informed him, with great relish, that Fong had dumped the Sergeant. When Fong brought you your beef ration, Chu said, Fook thought she'd already entered into Secret Negotiations with the Enemy!

What a ridiculous idea, Lu Beiping thought. But as he watched Fook march off into the forest alongside Gaffer Kam, a feeling of foreboding crept into his chest.

It was starting to get dark earlier now. When at last he'd bid adieu to the manure-laden workers and spread the cattle's straw for the night, he shut the gate, forded the creek, and hurried up toward the hollow. That morning Smudge had come down the mountain to tell him that Kingfisher and Stump had finally slaughtered the old white rooster. After dining on "Four Eyes's meat" so many times these past few months, the driftfolk wanted to treat Lu Beiping with their own, since today was a special occasion. All day Lu Beiping wondered what this "special occasion" might be. Was it a sacred feast day? Some sort of rite of passage? He thought of Jade's belly—did the family want to break meatfast with Four Eyes to celebrate the child's imminent arrival? Good god, he couldn't begin to imagine that harrowing day. Maybe Kingfisher wanted to bless the child by holding some kind of special ceremony.

Lately Lu Beiping and the driftfolk had entered into a spell of halcyon relations that had been all too late in coming. After the cockfight and the blood-spilling, Lu Beiping felt like he'd been initiated into their number, had been accepted, at last, as a full-fledged member of the band. Hardly once since his wounds healed had he lit his own stove; he ate "off the registers" almost every single night. At first Smudge delivered his meals to his door, then later he headed straight up the mountain after work for supper. Naturally, on his trips to camp, he took the chance to trade in his ration stamps for various household items he knew the driftfolk could use, adding a touch of "highborn living"—that was Stump's phrase—to life in the hollow. The first time the three old chimney pots ripped open a twenty-five-cent pack of Harvest cigarettes, Stump and Kingfisher pooh-poohed them as "too light in the throat," but Jade was an instant convert, declaring that never again would she gurgle smoke from a "canebat" like an opium eater on the Sam Shui waterfront. Stump chortled that Jade, puffing delicately on her cigarette with her pinky finger extended, looked like a "magistrate's wife." More like a Jap secret agent in a moving picture, Kingfisher scoffed. Tugging on Lu Beiping's arm, Smudge demanded: What's a moving picture? What's a Jap secret agent? It dawned on Lu Beiping that the kids were already of school-going age and yet had never seen, had never even heard of, a movie. From then on, after supper, Lu Beiping made a habit of sitting with the kids and telling them stories, teaching them numbers and characters, while Jade, Kingfisher, and Stump looked on with a mixture of admiration and sadness.

Yet throughout all this, Lu Beiping's relationship with Autumn continued to be strange and awkward. The more frequent his visits became, the less often he crossed paths with Autumn; the closer he grew to Kingfisher, Stump, and Jade, the further he and Autumn drifted apart. More often than not Autumn went out before sunrise and didn't return till after dark, after everybody had eaten, after the men had beguiled the evening with their pipes and Jade had finagled the children into the bath and into bed, at which point he'd mosey back into the hollow, slip into the kitchen, and help himself to a dish of cold rice and veggies and a bowl of cold soup. Autumn was usually such a limp fish that Stump and Kingfisher didn't notice anything out of the ordinary. But once or twice when, after his storytelling sessions, Lu Beiping slept in the big lodge with Jade and the kids instead of returning to his own hut for the night, the two men bumped into each other as Autumn slunk in to ladle leftovers, and didn't exchange a greeting or even a glance. Jade was surprised. What's the matter with you two? she said. Used to be you'd chatter up a storm whenever you were around each other. Now you're like a pair of chickens with their tongues cut off. Lu Beiping was the first one she asked, and he replied: I don't know, ask Autumn. Then she asked Autumn, and Autumn said: Don't ask me, ask Four Eyes. Lu Beiping's tone was light, Autumn's was grave; and this made Jade all the more suspicious. But it wasn't long before this incident faded away into the endless rain and flat light of winter. And the dynamic between him and the hollow-dwellers was changing in other subtle ways that made Lu Beiping himself surprised. At first, whenever he slept in the hollow, Jade spent the night with him; then, from time to time, she'd retire to the men's quarters to be with Stump or Kingfisher. At first she seemed reluctant to let him know, always waiting till Lu Beiping fell asleep to slip off to the other cabin. But eventually she stopped hiding it. What surprised Lu Beiping most of all was that he himself ceased to care. In daytime, herding the cattle, he would puzzle in amazement at the ease with which he'd accepted the whole arrangement.

The hollow reeked of chicken, the odor brash and pungent. When he asked, Lu Beiping learned that Kingfisher was in the kitchen tonight—that was unusual. When they sat down to eat, he asked Jade what the "special occasion" was, and Kingfisher, passing him the bowl of yam beer, said solemnly:

—Powers be praised, Four Eyes, today we got our logging license.

Logging license? That sounded odd as well.

—Aye, Stump added, got the official stamp and everything. Whitesands County rev board approved us, now we can work these hills with the government's blessing.

Grinning, Stump reached under the bamboo mat that covered Jade's bed, pulled out a thick sheet of paper, and handed it to Four Eyes. This wasn't at all the answer Lu Beiping had expected. Hadn't Kingfisher said, time and time again, that magistrates were the bane of the driftfolk, that they mustn't be seen or fettered by the law? Why would they slaughter a rooster and break out the yam beer on account of some document printed by a government committee? Puzzled, he said:

—But Autumn told me you guys already had some kind of official permit from Whitesands.

Once more Kingfisher took a deep breath, let it out in a string of shallow exhalations, then sighed.

—So it goes for us drifters. A permit like that lets you sail your ship, but it's not till you get an official government license that your ship's got an anchor. We driftfolk, we're like deep-sea sailors, one wrong tack and you're done for. When the sea gets rough, you need to head to shore and drop anchor. But as soon as your anchor hits bottom, you know it's time to set sail again.

Lu Beiping was still confused. Kingfisher chuckled.

—Don't know how else to explain it to you. You don't get it now, but you will. Drink, son, drink.

Lu Beiping noticed that Jade said very little—lately she'd been eating less, and was less talkative. Maybe it was a biological thing, an effect of the pregnancy. Lu Beiping couldn't help noticing the melancholy air that hung over the family all dinner. Every time he'd broken meatfast with the driftfolk before it had been a rare and rowdy celebration, but this meal, for some reason, felt like the Last Supper from *Bible Stories*. Even Smudge and the little ones, who normally tittered like mynahs all throughout the meal, ate in studious silence.

—Eh? Kingfisher said, chopsticks frozen in the air. Where's Autumn? What's he doing, missing out on a good meat supper?

—Running about like a crazy man, hunting for his rosewood tree, Jade answered. I left some chicken for him in the frypan. He said he prefers his food cold.

—Eating cold meat and supping cold tea! Stump exclaimed. Bless me, 'tisn't right nor proper.

Every time the brawny backwoodsman broke out one of these courtly, antique-sounding phrases, Lu Beiping wanted to laugh. Did everybody speak like that where Stump came from, or was it just his own peculiar way of talking? But this time, the grin of amusement froze on Lu Beiping's face, and his eyes widened in shock:

Everybody had stood up. Outside, the dog was barking like mad.

Wildweed had charged over to the top of the creek-tunnel and stood on the rocky bank snarling furiously. Just like on the first day when Lu Beiping had driven his cattle up into the hollow, the dog's hair-raising cries of alarm ripped through the air—

RhrhrhrhRHAWF—rhrhrhRHAWF-RHAWF!—rhrhrhRHAWF!—rhrhrhrhr . . .

Firelight glowed in the trees at the mouth of the hollow.

No wonder Wildweed was raising such a frightful clamor. Up out of the creek-tunnel marched a line of men carrying torches, the swirling of the flames and the snarling of the dog combining to make the arrival of this unusual delegation seem doubly imposing. The seven or eight bamboo torches, spewing black clouds of diesel smoke, made a particularly strong visual impression, and like stage props lent the scene an air of intentional drama. These days one didn't need a torch to light one's way through the jungle at night; there were flashlights, weatherproof storm lanterns, gas lanterns than shone bright as day. The torch was an outdated instrument, with little practical use. But each time the Chairman Issued a New Directive and the newspapers announced that the Good News Had Reached the Farthest Corners of the Nation, the front pages, perhaps taking their cue from the climactic scenes of revolutionary movies, always showed the same image: a golden river of torchlight snaking through the dark. And so the torch became a hallowed symbol of patriotism by which a new generation of radicals proclaimed their fervor. The Torch of the Revolution (Hold it High!) was a sacred thing, not to be profaned; its illumination was not of the same order as that of flashlights, gas lamps, or hurricane lanterns.

Clearly, it was in the spirit of revolutionary struggle that these visitors had come bearing torches tonight. These were Good Men Out to Spread the Word.

Flames crackled and smoke swirled along the creekbank. Wildweed kept barking furiously, but the flames had spooked him and he didn't dare attack. The blazing ring of torchlight advanced into the hollow, came to a halt before the foremost lodge, and then over the dog's yelping, snarling diatribe a chorus of voices belted out in unison the well-known passage from the Quotations:

... ALL—MISGUIDED—BELIEFS! ALL—POISONOUS— WEEDS! ALL HORNED DEMONS—AND HIDDEN— SERPENTS! MUST—BE—ROOTED—OUT! REPUDI- ATED! AND ERADICATED! THEY—MUST—NOT—BE ALLOWED—TO RUN RAMPANT! ...

Stump ran outside, then fled immediately back into the cabin at the sight of the flames. Kingfisher, however, sauntered out the door, sat down on a log and, slowly and deliberately, lit his pipe and began to smoke, storm clouds gathering on his brow. Hugging Smudge tight against his side, Lu Beiping walked out and saw, standing in the firelight at the head of the troop, his former squad leader, Fook, the impeccable patriot, holding a torch aloft in his right hand and a Little Red Book open in his left, declaiming the Chairman's words in his particularly musical Teochew-accented Mandarin. Lu Beiping's heart raced. He knew that this whole thing was directed at him; but at the same time the melodrama of it all made him want to laugh.

The Enumeration of Basic Principles turned out to be quite long, and it took the troop forever to get through it. In the flickering torch-light Lu Beiping made out a number of familiar faces along with several new ones. Surprisingly there was no sign of Kam or Choi, who were always eager for a spectacle, and among the Canton re-eds who'd joined the ranks of the torchbearers he noticed his friend Chu. But instead of a torch Chu had a big long-handled flashlight dangling around his neck, and stood at the back of the crowd waving nervously at Lu Beiping and making faces at him.

The torches crackled and showered sparks into the group, upsetting the formation and causing the readers to get out of sync. It occurred to Lu Beiping that they must've waited till they reached the mouth of the hollow to light the torches. He couldn't imagine holding those nasty, sputtering things aloft all the way up the precipitous paths through the dense forests of Mudkettle Mountain.

When they finally finished, Lu Beiping took a step forward and demanded:

—Fook, what you do think you're doing?

The torchlight illuminated the stern aspect of the Sergeant, his arm held high, his chin raised slightly as he addressed Lu Beiping, biting off the words:

—Fancy finding you here, Comrade Lu. I'm here on the authority of our local Party Line Promulgation Working Group to commence revolutionary morality education . . . upon you.

Lu Beiping winced. But he held his ground:

—Morality education? Seriously? Who approved this thing?

—*Naturally* we're here with the endorsement of the leaders of the Party Line Promulgation Working Group! Fook proclaimed, having obviously rehearsed this line.

—So . . . Kingfisher, sitting on the log, cut in coldly: What exactly do you folks want to do?

Now Jade, who'd been keeping Tick and Roach out of harm's way inside the cabin, squeezed outside and joined the others, holding one child against her shoulder, the other by the hand. Stump, however, turned quickly and went back inside the lodge. The light from the torches illuminated the half-naked, rag-clad family of migrants, Lu Beiping's glasses glittering conspicuously among them.

—You're the migrant woodcutters? Fook inquired, surveying the group. Have you got papers issued by a revolutionary board permitting you to work on this mountain?

Kingfisher and Lu Beiping exchanged a glance. Just at that moment Stump emerged from the lodge, crying:

—Aye, sure do, right here!

He held out the stamped document to the Sergeant. Fook took it and passed it to a man standing next to him whom Lu Beiping didn't recognize, probably a representative from the Working Group who'd been assigned to their unit. The man looked it over, then handed it back to Fook.

—"Whitesands County . . . Mudkettle Mountain . . . Timber Processing and . . . Contracting Collective," Fook read out awkwardly. Then, raising his voice, he said to Lu Beiping with a tinge of sarcasm: Last I remember, friend Lu, you weren't a member of this contracting collective—right? This isn't your line of work?

A few of the torchbearers broke out in giggles. His revolutionary ardor stoked by his audience's laughter, Fook pressed on:

—Look at you! A soldier of the Agricultural Reclamation Corps, eating at the same table with vagrants, sleeping in the same bed—more laughs from the crowd—what are you doing, Lu Beiping? Undertaking a personal investigation into the living conditions of the poor? Seeking re-education at the hands of the underprivileged?

Lu Beiping blanched. They were serious; clearly Fook would stop at nothing short of a complete rout. He even noticed someone standing at the back of the crowd holding a coil of rope, as if they were planning on trussing him up and bringing him to justice. He knew Kambugger must be behind this—but it couldn't be just Kambugger, no, he couldn't orchestrate a thing like this on his own.

The two bands, one in torchlight, the other in the shadows, faced each other for a long silent moment. Then Fook pointed and commanded:

—Will the female comrade please step forward?

—Who? Jade said. Though these proceedings were quite alien to her, she had remained calm throughout all this. Knowing that this strange form of address must refer to her, she set down the child and said matter-of-factly: You're talking about me?

Lu Beiping rushed around in front of Jade and thrust an angry finger at the crowd.

—What the hell do you think you're doing? If you want to make an example of me, just do it! Don't drag these people in!

Then, with a glance, Fook cued four workers, who ran over, seized Lu Beiping, and twisted his arms behind his back.

—Step forward! the men shouted at Jade. Comrade, step forward!

A scattering of voices in the crowd joined in:

—Step forward! Step forward!

One arm around Tick, the other hand resting on her belly, Jade stepped forward into the firelight. A moment later Kingfisher nudged Lu Beiping from behind with his foot, laid down his water pipe, and rose.

—May I ask your name, mister comrade sir? he said gently.

The Sergeant gave him a haughty glance and didn't reply. Kingfisher walked forward, holding out his hand.

—Please give us back our document, Kingfisher said, and the Sergeant had no choice but to hand the paper back, a faint look of embarrassment on his face. When he held the paper, Kingfisher continued: We here are a part of Whitesands County. If you comrades have got some official business with Four Eyes, I suggest you deal with it over on your side of the mountain. Jade, take the pups back inside.

—Wait! Fook cried, running around and cutting off Jade's retreat. Holding the fuming ball of flames directly over her head, he said: I'm sorry, comrade, may I inquire as to your name?

—I'm Jade, Jade said.

—Alright, Jade. I have a question for you—Fook looked straight at Lu Beiping as he said this—How long've you been pregnant?

Jade smiled humorlessly.

—You're interested in childbirth, young comrade?

A few people in the crowd laughed. Fook waved a hand in irritation and barked:

—No laughing! You've got something to say, say it!

Then he turned, lowered the torch and, tilting the flames dangerously close to Jade's body, illuminated the swell of her abdomen.

—Jade! Tell me honest, whose pup is in your belly?

—Peh! Jade spat on the ground. What a queer question to ask! It's mine. Whose else could it be? Yours?

Lu Beiping heard a snort of laughter from the crowd, obviously Chu's. He grinned.

—The insolence! Fook cried in exasperation. It's unbelievable! You too, Lu Beiping! Listen, the Working Group has gotten some interesting reports—Fook cast a glance through the ranks of the torchbearers—and tonight we want to know, we want you to clear up this mystery for us, once and for all: Who's the father of this woman's baby? Tell us!

—Tell us! Tell us! a few voices shouted in the crowd. Kingfisher and Stump exchanged an anxious glance as Lu Beiping stood there motionless, gritting his teeth, his face pale, saying nothing.

—Come on, big man! Fook said, adopting a hectoring tone: Own up to it! Everyone agrees you're a bully cowherd, but that's no excuse for you to come running up into the mountains to spread your wild oats! Do I need to tell you that? You know as well as I do that rectification of ideological outlook with regard to sexual politics is a necessary prerequisite for a progressive, ethical—

Fook stumbled over his words and stopped, gasping for breath. Then, with a cold laugh, he drove on pitilessly:

—If you've really got a pair of eggs down there, then prove it to us! Show us what's really under your pants—the crowd erupted in laughter, and Fook seized this moment to press the offensive—Who got that woman pregnant? Tell us! Who's that kid's daddy? Tell us!

—Speak! Speak! people began chanting as a wave of excitement ran through the crowd, and at that moment the stranger with the rope strode forward and cried:

—He won't talk? Then tie him up! Let the law prevail!

A few people rushed toward Lu Beiping, clamoring to lay hands on him. But just at that moment there was a loud expectorating sound and a gob of spittle landed at Fook's feet, causing Lu Beiping's would-be captors to stop short and turn their heads in astonishment. Kingfisher stood wiping his lips. He said nothing, but the anger was written clearly on his face, and his jaw muscles quivered as he gazed at the coil of rope. Then he turned to the stunned Sergeant and said to him coolly:

—I've learned a couple interesting phrases tonight. One is "show us your eggs," and the other's "let the law prevail."

—You—Fook stammered, shaking a finger at Kingfisher—don't you start muddying the waters here!

—I think they're pretty muddy already! Kingfisher burst out. Comrade, you want to see eggs? You want to see what we've been laying up here? Take a look—he gathered up Smudge, Tick, and Roach and shoved them toward the Sergeant—Here they are, all of them! You're curious what a pair of eggs looks like, don't ask Four Eyes, ask me!

Grinning wickedly, Kingfisher patted Jade's belly, then he tore off his waistcloth and stood completely naked in the firelight.

—You pissant! he roared. Here are my eggs! Now I want you to show me what's under *your* pants!

The dancing flames illuminated every inch of Kingfisher's hard, pitted body, leaving nothing to the imagination. For a moment the crowd stared in dumb silence, then they burst into laughter. Lu Beiping heard Jade giggling, and Chu cried out over the hubbub:

—Right on! Show him, Sergeant!

There was another wave of laughter. Fook stood frozen to the spot, his lips trembling, utterly at a loss for how to respond to this.

—Lowlifes! he cried at last. Low-minded . . . Sentiments!

Lu Beiping laughed to himself. *You can't hide from the sun.* "Supping sunlight" had become a weapon, had instantly cut the trumped-up majesty of the Revolutionary Torch down to size. Now the crowd had no hope of staying serious, and the Sergeant whistled again and again to no avail over a sea of whispers and giggles.

The makeshift yarn-wrapped bamboo torches crackled and fumed. People dodged sparks, and the troop had long ago fallen out of formation. Kingfisher took his time retying his waistcloth, then went on:

—The second phrase I liked was . . . "may the law prevail," that was it, right? As far as the law goes—Kingfisher waved the sheet of paper—the family hath its mandates, the nation its laws. I just told you, you're in Whitesands County right now. Who's holding a stamped, certified document issued by the Whitesands County rev board? Me. Did you ask my permission before you came marching up here with your torches and your questions and your talk of the law? No.

—Your permission? Fook spluttered. Why would I ask your permission?

Kingfisher chuckled.

—This is Whitesands soil. Whose law exactly do you think you're prevailing up here, tying up folks and hauling them away? Do *you* have a stamped, certified document issued by *your* revolutionary board? Show it to me!

For Kingfisher to have followed up his underhanded egg-baring with this swift commandeering of the moral high ground caught Fook completely off guard. With no reasonable way to parry this attack, he was about to resort to another angry tantrum when a fresh ripple of excitement passed through the crowd.

Autumn, his bare body gleaming with sweat, shouldered his way to the front of the mob. The Sergeant took a step back in surprise.

—Who are you?

—I'm the dad, he said, panting as he laid his hand on Jade's stomach. I heard you all shouting for me while I was over there chopping wood, so I came over to see what was the matter.

—What? . . . Fook gazed at him, thrown once more into confusion.

—I'm Autumn, Autumn said, wiping the sweat from his face, his dark, naked back shining in the firelight. I had to work late tonight.

—You . . . you . . . Fook looked at Lu Beiping, then back at Autumn, now thoroughly flummoxed.

—So . . . what was it you wanted? Autumn asked.

The crowd went quiet, and everybody stared at this unfamiliar actor who'd entered the drama so late and unexpectedly. Kingfisher and Stump traded a knowing smirk. In the moment of silence that followed, Jade burst into sobs and, stamping her feet, pointed at the befuddled Sergeant, howling:

—Shame and ruin! He . . . he . . . Autumn, he said our pup's a bastard!—Jade rushed at Fook and grabbed him by the collar—You piece of shit! Saying I'd mother a bastard child! I hope you eat that! I hope your children are born without assholes! Damn you to hell, slandering an innocent woman . . .

Jade raised a hand to slap him, but Kingfisher pounced on her and pulled her back. Smudge began to wail along with Jade, and soon the two little ones had joined in as well.

As the crowd fell into chaos, Lu Beiping shook free of the four baffled workers, who released him without any resistance and went over to guard Fook in case Jade flew into another rage and tried to strike him again.

Lu Beiping glanced at Autumn, feeling like he ought to say something to him. But Autumn had already turned and begun shepherding Jade and the three kids back toward the lodge.

The troop broke up and milled about in confusion. Chu squeezed through the press of bodies, wrinkled his nose at Lu Beiping and shrugged at him, then turned to Fook and said with a devious chuckle:

—Well, Sergeant, this has been very educational. On behalf of the Canton re-eds, I declare this mission a success—Fook brooded silently, his face ashen—but if I'm allowed to offer a bit of advice, we ought to put out those torches now. Some of us are starting to get blisters on our fingers.

The crowd began to disperse toward the mouth of the hollow. There was a great hissing and billowing of smoke as the torches were extinguished in the creek, and before long all that remained of the expedition were eight blackened bamboo bundles strewn across the rocky bank, like props on an empty stage.

Chapter 12
Spirit Flight

—Autumn! Wait!

The figure hurrying across the pebble beach sped up at the sound of Lu Beiping's voice as if it had received an electric shock.

—Wait up, Autumn! There's something I need to tell you!

Far down in the dark tunnel of branches, the sloshing of Autumn's footsteps continued.

Lu Beiping sprang into the shallows and rushed down the creek, splashing water as he ran. In the dappled shade ahead of him he could make out Autumn's silhouette marching onward with sullen determination. Piqued by Autumn's refusal to acknowledge him, Lu Beiping sprinted forward as fast as he could, scissoring his arms, and in a few bounds he managed to catch up with Autumn and tackled him from behind.

—Autumn! he cried bitterly, Are you trying to hide from me? Are you angry at me because I shoved you? Here!—he squeezed the struggling Autumn with all his might—How's this? We're even now!

Autumn flailed in his grip, but Lu Beiping wouldn't let go. Eventually Autumn gave up the struggle, and with a final, slight shudder his body went slack.

Lu Beiping released him. In the shadows Autumn stood with his head bowed, silent; it looked to Lu Beiping like he might be crying. Guessing how much shame Autumn must be feeling right now, Lu Beiping grabbed him by the shoulder and said:

—Autumn, I'm sorry.

Autumn brushed his hand off, turned, and stalked off down the creek without a word.

The water chattered crisply in the morning mist. Lu Beiping remembered walking home with Autumn down this same stretch of creek on the evening of his first visit to the hollow—even then, he'd sensed the brittleness of Autumn's ego and the depths of his inner loneliness. Aloof among others, Autumn always surprised Lu Beiping with his poised, articulate speech whenever they were alone together, and though his childlike earnestness and rough country manners could sometimes make him seem a bit simpleminded, as soon as they got to talking he revealed a dazzling breadth of knowledge that would have befitted a classical aristocrat. Even in their day-to-day interactions an occasional flash of virility or hint of tenderness shone through Autumn's apathetic facade. Truth be told, the intensity of Autumn's reaction to their awkward encounter had taken Lu Beiping aback. In those days, when friendship between the sexes was so rare and fraught with political baggage, it wasn't unusual for re-eds of the same sex to let off steam in brief moments of transgressive intimacy. Twice in the boys' tent during reclamation campaigns he'd been "ambushed" by older re-eds; people resisted such ambushes with varying degrees of unwillingness, and nobody took it too seriously. At most it was seen as a passing adolescent phase, and he'd never put too much thought to it. But Autumn was clearly so wounded by Lu Beiping's rejection of him that the whole thing had begun to seem rather serious.

If it hadn't been for last night's harrowing torchlit standoff, he and Autumn probably would have drifted apart till they were no more than a pair of strangers passing on the road.

—Autumn, Lu Beiping said finally: I just wanted to say thank you for—

—Don't mention it, Autumn said sharply, but nevertheless he slowed his pace.

—Where'd you go last night, after Kingfisher drove those jerks away? Lu Beiping asked, refusing to drop the subject. Jade made a big pot of ginger soup with water chestnuts to calm everyone's nerves, but when it was time to eat she couldn't find you.

Autumn walked on a little longer in silence, then said abruptly:

—I don't want you to get the wrong notion, friend. I didn't do you that favor last night so you'd be grateful to me, or so you'd take pity on me. If you think that's why I did it, you're wrong about me.

Lu Beiping was silent. He knew he'd once again run up against one of Autumn's deep-seated vulnerabilities.

They waded in silence up out of the creek, hiked through the dewy grass to the top of the meadow and sat down on the abandoned, moss-covered log where Lu Beiping had first seen Jade.

The sun hadn't yet cleared the ridge, and it was just barely light out. Autumn set off into the forest at this early hour almost every morning, so now was the only time when Lu Beiping, following the sound of Autumn's footsteps as he left the hollow, stood a chance of having a moment alone with him in which to try to rebuild their rusted-out friendship. During the long stretch of time when they hadn't been talking, Lu Beiping, walking alone through the forest, had often thought back wistfully on his friendship with Autumn and realized how irreplaceable it was. He had a whole reservoir of long-nursed peeves and cynical opinions that he needed the right person to vent to, and Autumn was the person Fate had offered up to him. And Lu Beiping missed Autumn's tales of amaranthine rosewood and gallant young poets—nobody else he knew, not Jade, not Kingfisher, certainly not Fong or Chu—had such stories to tell. But he also understood that between him and Autumn there existed a fragile boundary that, if broken, might spell destruction for them both.

The knowledge of this possibility filled Lu Beiping with dread, and also with a heady sense of excitement.

—Who was that young sergeant fellow last night? Autumn said, breaking the silence as they sat down on the log. You ought to be careful, it sure looked like they had it out for you. What was all that hullabaloo about?

—That's what I wanted to talk to you about, Autumn, Lu Beiping said, his expression more composed now: At this point, you might be the only person who can help me.

Autumn turned and gazed at him without speaking.

—You see, Lu Beiping began with a grim laugh, On the surface of it, it was probably because that guy, Fook—he was my old squad leader—thought that my old girlfriend, Fong, dumped him in order to get back together with me. But actually, my hunch is that the real reason behind it all has to do with my ghost wife, Han, the foreman's daughter, who I got tricked into marrying.

—Eh? What's all this gobbledygook? I'm lost.

Strand by strand, Lu Beiping teased apart the entire web of intrigue—the sudden appearance of Han's blouse and Choi's subsequent disappearance; the suspicious liaisons between Choi and the foreman and between Wing and his sister; Fong's visit and her stern warning; the Gaffer's unwelcome meddling, which had sparked the incident. When he reached the end of the story, Autumn sighed.

—Good heavens, Kingfisher saw right to the heart of it. I told you way back, he could tell you were in some kind of trouble. After he heard that stuff about you being ghost husband to the foreman's daughter, he said, there's got to be some secret behind this yet. Otherwise, why'd a doler magistrate send his son-in-law into the jungle to live like a hermit? That day, right after Kambugger left, Kingfisher turned to us and wailed out, This is it! We're done for! Our end's upon us!

—Really? Lu Beiping said, standing up in surprise. Kingfisher really said that?

—That's the reason he wanted . . . your blood to be seen.

More and more, it was becoming clear to Lu Beiping that behind all of Kingfisher's crude, backward mysticism there lay a deep perceptiveness about human affairs.

—Bei, Autumn said, using his nickname for the first time in weeks: Why didn't you tell me about this? Such a big thing . . . Autumn's voice carried a hint of reproach. Then he looked Lu Beiping in the eye and said: But you're right, you can't talk to Kingfisher about this now, and you'd better not tell Jade either. It'd give them too great of a shock. But don't fret. No matter what, before we weigh anchor, I'll help you get to the bottom of this.

—What? Lu Beiping said. Before you weigh anchor? The phrase sounded strangely familiar; then he remembered Kingfisher's cryptic words the night before.

Autumn stammered and looked down. Apparently he hadn't meant to let this slip. For a few moments neither of them spoke, then Autumn said:

—No reason to hide the truth from you, Bei. Ever since we got that permit from Whitesands we've been working flat-out in hopes of someday trading it in for an official, black-and-white logging license that could really protect us. Now that we've got that license in hand, we'd better weigh anchor and move on. Like Kingfisher says, a full moon can only wane. We woodsmen don't dare log a place to the point that we've upset the earth and trodden all over the magistrates' turf. This little family enterprise of ours, it would've been broken up long ago if we hadn't been so careful, taking only what we need, never pressing our luck—Autumn paused, and sighed quietly—And lately, the mountain's shown us we've gone a little too far.

—So . . . you're leaving? You're moving someplace else? Lu Beiping asked. He remembered the rainy night when Kingfisher had urged him to go, the strange atmosphere at dinner last night; everything made sense now. A wave of grief rose up inside him, and he said: Autumn, I know this is my fault. I've caused so much trouble, I've endangered you all . . .

He stared out at the hazy green expanse of the forest, suddenly overcome by melancholy. What other trouble have I caused without knowing it? he wondered. Who else have I unwittingly harmed?

The sun had risen over the treetops into a veil of mist, and a few white needles of light pierced the clouds. If this were evening, he thought, those would be blood-red snakeclouds.

They sat for a while in silence. Down in the valley the morning work bell began to toll, far-off and faint, filling Lu Beiping with a feeling of hopelessness and desolation. Autumn got up and began to walk away, then stopped, stood for a moment as if steeling himself, then looked back and said:

—Bei, I don't want to pretend like nothing's happened between us. My dad always said, it takes ten shared lives to make a shipmate. Since you came looking for me, I want you to know what's in my heart, I want you to know my true feelings about . . . our acquaintance.

Lu Beiping didn't dare look up and meet Autumn's candid, unforgiving gaze.

—I've been pondering this a long while, Autumn said, stabbing repeatedly at the soil with his machete but speaking with great calm: I've been asking myself, my wanting to make good with Bei, is that a crime? Kingfisher says, everything in this world that shares in growth and life, none of that's sin, no kind of affection between living beings ought to be a sin. But when people share great affection, isn't love the natural end of it? I don't know, Bei, I just don't know . . . Autumn's lips trembled as he spoke and the knuckles stood out on the hand that gripped the machete, but he went on in the same calm, even voice: When you told me, just now, about all the things you've had weighing on your mind since coming up onto the mountain, I wanted to take you to task for not telling me. I laid bare every little thing about myself to you, but you hid so much from me. I realized, then, that you hadn't taken our friendship as seriously as I did.

—Autumn . . .

—I've taken a liking to you, it's true. I can't say why. Or maybe you don't need a reason to like a person, only not to like them?— Autumn gave a chilly laugh—I know the world's not fair. Jade and you can love each other, Jade and Kingfisher and Stump can do the same, your foreman's blighted family can love the world sideways and even drive people to death on account of it. But I, I don't dare make my feelings known to you. I'm afraid I'm in the wrong . . .

As Autumn spoke, Lu Beiping sat on the log with his arms crossed, listening. After a while he unfolded his arms, looked up, and saw that Autumn's eyes were glittering with tears. He knew that he'd struck the steely hardness that hid at the core of Autumn's tenderness. Clearly Autumn had thought these words through many times before speaking them, but Lu Beiping had never considered any of this before. Here was this swarthy-skinned mountain man, this sinewy backwoodsman who'd educated him about Li Shutong, Nara Singde, and amaranthine rosewood, laying out the tenets of a manifesto of love that would be heresy in the eyes of civilized society. Who would have thought that love could be such a complex, exacting field of study.

—Bei, our acquaintance . . . Autumn said, looking straight at Lu Beiping, his hand still gripping the pommel of his machete: We don't have much time left. All I ask of you, is . . .

He stopped, his lips trembling. Lu Beiping sat, gazing blankly at him.

—All I ask . . . is that you accept my kindness.

Autumn's gaze, shining brightly through his tears, managed to be both imploring and imperious. Lu Beiping hung his head.

Autumn pulled his machete out of the soil and turned to leave. Suddenly Lu Beiping looked up and said:

—Autumn, don't go. Just a minute . . .

Lu Beiping brushed the dew off of the log next to him and patted it, inviting Autumn to sit down.

Hesitant, Autumn sat down at the far end of the log, planted his elbows on his knees, and buried his face in his hands.

—Okay, Lu Beiping said. Such a simple word, but so hard to say. Then, slowly, he reached over, drew Autumn toward him, and gave him a hug.

When at last the gray monsoon rains abated, Mudkettle Mountain emerged swathed in blue-green gauze. The sun, peeping through the clouds, was a painter's palette; the banks of mist that drifted through the forest at dawn were glittering prisms; the afternoon fog was tinted green, as if the color of the mountains had run; and the evening light, lancing through the mist, shone rainbow colored. The haze burned where it was thick, shimmered where it was thin, and down in the creek gully there seethed billows of pink and lavender fog, as if the wispwomen of Mudkettle Mountain were busy cooking up a sumptuous banquet of steam.

From a distance, Lu Beiping watched Jade sitting by the water.

Jade's always sitting by the water, Lu Beiping thought.

She's a wispwoman, he thought. A fey forest spirit.

It always tugged at his heart to see her like that, sitting alone by the creek.

This time it was he who was watching her in secret. He sat behind the row of broad-leafed banana trees—the same trees from behind which Jade and Smudge had watched him "supping sun," the same ones among which he'd given himself to Jade for the first time. This banana grove had a kind of magic to it; this little beach, it now seemed to him, was his destiny. Almost every time he and Jade had made love, it had been by the water. Jade told him that, by her calculations, the baby must have been conceived the night of the typhoon, during the jubilation that followed their close brush with disaster. I'm having a calf too, Jade had said, patting her stomach. I caught the breath of life from your cow, Maria. As always Jade broached this terrifying topic as if it were the most straightforward, uncomplicated thing in the world.

How long had she been here? Lu Beiping wondered. She must have been hanging out here all afternoon. She'd emptied his rain-sodden hut of its entire store of damp shirts, blankets, and pillowcases and strewn them, along with his satchel and boots, at the edge of the creek, where she was now washing them and spreading them out to dry in the sun. His whole wardrobe now adorned the slope like the colorful ribbons the Loi tribesfolk used to decorate their jugs of rice wine during the hillflower festival. Jade sat on a big, flat stone in the brilliant sunshine, her bare feet dangling right above the surface of the water, the whites of her soles reflected brightly in the stream and her flowered blouse hanging open so that, from this angle, her swollen breasts and large belly were just barely visible to him. From time to time she splashed a few handfuls of water onto the stone and pounded it into his sneakers and satchel while humming quietly to herself.

Her face gave off an aura of melancholy that hung palpably over the creek, like a thick blanket of fog.

Again she wore that placid expression, that far-gazing look that had so captured his imagination the day they met. Now, though, this look just struck Lu Beiping as chilly and remote, and made him feel even more distant from her.

He threw a stone into the water. Jade didn't react.

He threw another, larger, stone. *Plunk.* She still didn't move.

Finally he walked out from behind the banana trees.

—I knew you were watching me, Jade said without looking at him. I figured I'd let you watch, let you sate your eyes.

Like a true mountain woman she let no sound or movement in her environment escape her attention. Hands still busy with his clothes, she added:

—There's someone else with you. I could tell it was two people. Who is it? Smudge?

Clearly Jade too had been reliving their earlier encounter.

—Nope. Autumn.

Jade looked up in surprise. She glanced around the banana grove.

—But where is he?

—He went back up to the hollow, Lu Beiping said. Detecting the hint of awkwardness in his voice, Jade chuckled.

—Seems like you two got to be pretty good friends again after he saved your hide the other night. What were you doing just now, anyway?

Lu Beiping smiled deviously.

—Something important. Something I can't tell you about, just yet.

—Oh, I see! What else have you been hiding from me?

Laughing inwardly at the thought of the prank that he and Autumn had just devised, Lu Beiping reached out from behind and circled Jade with his arms.

—So kind of you to come down here and clean house for me, sister.

—Hmph! Jade slapped his wrist. Smells like you've been pickling kraut in there.

Lu Beiping withdrew his arms, laughing.

—Jade, what was that song you were singing? I couldn't hear it clearly.

—Oh, Jade said, blushing with embarrassment: Just a silly, salty driftfolk song. Not proper for the ears of a scholar-gentleman like you.

—But I'd like to hear it.

—Oh, fine, Jade said, and sang quietly: "There's nothing in this world that tastes so fine, as that pretty little thing you've got between your thighs . . ."

—Nice! That's pretty salty! Lu Beiping said, chortling at this vulgar ditty. He snaked an arm around her again, ready to initiate some mischief, but Jade beat him to it and pushed him into the creek.

Propelled by the swirling current, Lu Beiping staggered a few paces downstream, then, as he regained his footing, he heard Jade order him quietly from the riverbank:

—Take off your shorts, Four Eyes.

Again he thought back to the time when she spied on him as he was bathing in the creek. If she hadn't done that the past five months might have taken a very different course. Thinking this, he felt a pang of sadness, but he hid it with a laugh and retorted, parroting Jade's words:

—Alright, here goes. Sate your eyes.

With a tacit understanding and a kind of ritual solemnity, Jade and Lu Beiping prepared to perform—like the "Last Supper" of a few evenings ago—a Last Frolic in the Creek. Gazing intently at his naked body, Jade sauntered to the edge of the rock, murmuring:

—I want to remember your fine body, Four Eyes. I want to remember your good looks . . . your good . . .

Good again, Lu Beiping thought. Always good. He forced a laugh, and hoping to recapture the lighthearted atmosphere of the moment before, he fell back on his old tricks and started splashing water at her.

—Good heavens, Four Eyes! Jade said, recovering some of her former enthusiasm, and began kicking water at him. But just as she was about to jump into the creek Lu Beiping was struck by a sudden fear, and he rushed forward and grabbed her.

—Wait, Jade! The water's really cold. It might hurt the . . . He stopped, his tongue tying itself in a knot before he could say the word. Then he blurted out abruptly: Jade, is it true that you're leaving?

Jade stiffened in surprise and dropped the sneaker she was still holding, which went sailing off immediately on the current. Lu Beiping lunged and managed to grab it, and when he turned back to look at Jade he saw that her eyes had filled with tears.

—So it's true? Autumn must've told you? Jade said, wiping her eyes. Those men don't tell me anything. They're afraid to do anything that might shock me and hurt the baby. I *told* them, as soon as this pup's born I'm not going anywhere. Four Eyes . . . the reason I came looking for you today, is that . . . I wanted to ask you, do you want it? Do you really want this child?

—I . . . Lu Beiping stood motionless in the middle of the creek, now acutely aware of the piercing cold of the water. These mountain folk didn't waste any breath on niceties; they got right to the point. He remembered the question Autumn had put to him so baldly on that cold, clear morning not long ago.

Lu Beiping said nothing. He just hugged Jade tight to his chest, feeling like the moment he let her go the warmth in his bosom would turn to cold cinders.

The babbling song of the water hung in the evening air. The light on the bluffs, the bright green tresses of the vines, the leaves teeming in the mist—all of it seemed to be silently recounting the successive chapters of their shared story.

—I'm sorry, Four Eyes, I know I've put you in a tight spot, Jade said gently, wiping tears from her cheek. Kingfisher told me he didn't want you to get dragged into our world on account of this pup. Whether you want it or not, the babe's mine. I asked you whether you wanted it, but it's me who's bearing it. I know you men . . . Suddenly

Jade pushed him away and said in a pinched voice: I just want to know, Four Eyes . . . are you like those other men? Or are you different?

Lu Beiping stood in the shallows looking down, unable to meet her gaze. Wordlessly he stooped to put on his boxer shorts, and as he did so his tears splashed into the water.

—Jade, he said, I really don't know. I like kids. Thinking about having a kid of my own, it makes me want to shout for joy. It makes me want to cry . . .

As he said these words a shudder of emotion ran through him.

—But you don't want to be this one's pa! Right? Jade said, the ripples of light reflected on the cliffs shimmering on her face as well. It sure was frightful when those men came with torches the other night, wasn't it? Right then, I thought, if Four Eyes dares stand out in front of everybody and admit he's this child's father, I'd die for his sake! Jade stuck out her chin and gazed up at him with a wintry look in her eyes: Go, Four Eyes. Leave me. There's not one man in this world worth my dying for—there *was* but one, and he's already dead! Nothing lasts long among us driftfolk, we always drift apart in the end. Kingfisher and Stump have their own wives and children back home, you think *they'd* stroll into town with me under their arm and own up to having me as a mistress?

Lu Beiping's heart began to race as Jade contemplated this hair-raising scenario.

—Ha! she cried. You all mock me for a whore, and that's just what I am! A hen without a rooster, a wife to nobody! Someday I'm going to take my whole brood of filthy, squawking, fatherless chicks and march right back into Kwun-chow Crossing, show those folks who shamed me and took me for a stonewoman just what kind of woman I've become!

Jade laughed loudly, wildly, bitterly, all the while wiping tears. The entire gully resounded with her cries of grief, and the thrumming echoes sounded like they might lift the mountain.

◈

No one will know how many times Lu Beiping wandered back and forth between the third and fourth fingers of Mudclaw Creek that night. At first he was just searching for a missing bull. When he laid down his chopsticks at the end of dinner he rose immediately and made for the door of the lodge, announcing that he needed to track down a bull who'd gone astray late in the afternoon. Autumn volunteered to go with him, but Lu Beiping refused; Smudge wanted to come too, and got no for an answer; Kingfisher insisted that he stay a while and share a bowl of fresh herb tea, but Lu Beiping politely declined. Everyone, though, sensed the hidden accusation in Jade's words as Lu Beiping walked briskly out the door: Let him go, boys. No point in holding a man back when his spirit's already flown.

As he pulled aside the vines that hung in the mouth of the tree-tunnel, the image of Jade sitting big-bellied on the bamboo cot with a far-off look in her eyes as she spoke these words lingered in his mind. He laughed bitterly. It had been she who'd led him up this creek for the first time, wading against the current. Now, in the strange journey against the current of life that he'd embarked upon soon after that first meeting, he'd arrived at yet another fork in the path.

It had been an odd dinner. Everyone ate in solemn silence, as if consuming the grave offerings after a tomb-sweeping. Was the prospect of their imminent departure playing tricks with their mood? Maybe Jade and the men had gotten into another tiff about "weighing anchor" that afternoon; that had to be the reason, Lu Beiping told himself. Lately the hollow had been positively overflowing with bittersweet feelings. Even little Tick sensed that something was up, and asked Lu Beiping out of the blue: Four Eyes, will you still come to teach us figures?—which stung Lu Beiping's heart. Every day Kingfisher was out in the yard sweeping up wood shavings or rearranging the logs that were soaking in the pool, and during spare moments he'd pull out his carpenter tools and start hammering, sawing, planing, or whittling, making what implements Lu Beiping couldn't guess and didn't dare ask. Stump, too, had been busy these days; ginseng roots and gecko skins lay drying on every available rock, and the wild partridge eggs he'd been collecting and pickling now filled half a dozen enamel jars. Naturally Lu Beiping didn't inquire about these treasures either, knowing that the answer would probably bring tears to his eyes.

What pained Lu Beiping most, though, was the way Smudge was taking the whole thing. The boy would sit on the edge of the bed for hours on end, gazing at him with a bitterness that verged on antagonism, and every time Lu Beiping tried to engage him he responded with stony silence. Lu Beiping had a vague feeling that he owed something to Smudge, though what it was he couldn't say. Jade, bustling in the kitchen with one hand resting on her belly, was the most serene and composed of all of them. But even so her far-off gaze now seemed to Lu Beiping to have a cold, acid quality, and just the sight of her sitting alone by the creek was enough to make his heart start pounding. However, as the unspecified day of their departure drew near, Autumn seemed to leap free of melancholy, growing ever more cheerful and talkative in an odd counterpoint to the others' mounting gloom. One evening he returned from the high valley carrying a newborn rhesus monkey, bearded with a tiny white ball of fur, which he let loose inside the cabin to a storm of shrieks and laughter. Kingfisher joked that they'd be the perfect image of a merry outlaw band, traipsing from town to town with a monkey capering on a leash. Stump suggested that they put him in a pot with ginseng and liver-root and boil him for seven days and seven nights, saying that a nice, big jar of monkey paste would keep the bad vapors off of them for months to come. But to everyone's surprise Autumn let the little fellow go the next morning, all the while crowing newspaper slogans about Peaceful Coexistence, Mutual Understanding, and Freedom of Movement. Before releasing him, he even went so far as to appropriate the red ribbon from Jade's water pipe and tie it around his neck for a farewell present. The kids cried, the grown-ups griped, and Autumn just stood there grinning goofily at Lu Beiping.

Bustle and idleness, tears and laughter—all of it seemed to be circling around their impending final farewell. Even when the crowd was in high spirits a current of melancholy ran through their revelry, and the subtext was clear: When the guest departs, his cup goes cold.

But no—he knew this wasn't entirely true.

The days passed; the chopsticks rose and fell. Often there was meat in the supper bowls. Lately Lu Beiping had taken every chance he could to employ his "doler" ration stamps in the service of the driftfolk, buying sugar, crackers, soap, and other household goods that were of use to them, as well as trading his grain and cloth stamps to the workers for honey, eggs, and other minor luxuries that lent an air of opulence to the weeks leading up to the band's departure. Plum Tree brand red-braised pork and Pearl River dace, which always flew off the shelves of the supply co-op and into the eager hands of re-eds, were among the new delicacies that began to grace Jade's table almost every week.

As Lu Beiping's trips to the hollow became more frequent, his underlying nervousness began to show. Though he knew the decision to "weigh anchor" was set in stone, he hadn't dared ask about the actual date. He feared that one day he'd walk up out of the creek-tunnel to confront a lonely pile of beams and boards, and know then that Jade, Kingfisher, and the others had broken camp and drifted off like clouds in the night. So he drove his lowing legions up to the hollow at every available moment, keeping an eye on the driftfolk as if doing so might postpone the day of their departure, which was bearing down on him with the inevitability of a prison sentence. Leaving the cattle to graze on the opposite slope, he'd sit in the shade of the bluff and tell stories to the kids while trimming their hair with his manual hair clipper, trying his best to appear casual while secretly gnawed at by a deep anxiety. At dinner that evening, before Lu Beiping excused himself, Kingfisher had broken the silence with a sly chuckle, saying: So, folks, I want everyone to tell me one thing that's been different around here these days. The others paused mid-mouthful, perplexed by this, and Stump volunteered: Got so much grease in my belly lately, my shit's starting to stink. The whole table burst into laughter, and Jade said, No wonder the whitebait we've been catching in the pond over there smells like brother Stump's ass! Plucking a fish out of the serving bowl, she pressed it on Lu Beiping. He protested halfheartedly, then bowed his head and accepted it. Jade added: What's different these days? Main thing is, the bigger my belly gets, the more Four Eyes avoids me. Stump objected: But Four Eyes visits us oftener now than ever before! Lu Beiping remained mute, as if gagged by a mouthful of food. Smudge crowed: Uncle Autumn smiles and laughs all the time now! That's what's different! Autumn gave him a sharp look, then reached out his chopsticks with theatrical self-assurance and plucked the biggest piece of meat out of the serving bowl, then popped it in his mouth. Listening to the sound of chewing meat that filled the ensuing silence, Kingfisher said cryptically: What's different now is that we're all saying a lot more with our chopsticks than we are with our tongues.

Crafty old Kingfisher—he always knew how to drive a point home without bringing the hammer into contact with the nail.

Bastard! *You're* the bastard! That afternoon, when Lu Beiping drove his cattle up into the hollow, he'd found Tick, Roach, and Smudge embroiled in a bitter squalling match. Fucker! Tick shrilled at Smudge, You're a shadowborn, demon-spawn bastard! You're the son of the Snakeweird! You . . . The three kids had been fighting over a top that Lu Beiping had whittled for them out of a burl of wood. Smudge, being the oldest, had monopolized the toy, spinning it deftly with a piece of cane twine and neglecting to let his younger siblings have their turn. Roach tried to grab it, Smudge fought back, and they fell to fighting. When Lu Beiping arrived it was too late to intervene, for Kingfisher, who'd been doing carpentry work across the yard, strode over and without any preamble laid a savage slap on Smudge's cheek. Pissant! he roared. You little scum! You think you're the Emperor? Let the pups have their turn! Kingfisher smacked the boy again, then again, and Lu Beiping, unable to stand it, stepped between them and shielded Smudge. Kingfisher, he said, Don't blame Smudge indiscriminately. He's just a kid. Furious, Kingfisher responded: Just a kid? A kid can be a demon too. He's a devil's get, make no mistake . . . Kingfisher stalked away, cursing and swinging his fist. Smudge, who was inured to indiscriminate abuse, forgot about it immediately and went back to playing with the little ones. But Lu Beiping carried a heavy feeling with him all day. The hollow was no primitive paradise—it was a country unto itself, with all the accompanying codes of conduct, rigid hierarchies, and unreasoning prejudices. All this became clear to him as the driftfolk gradually admitted him into their world. But only this afternoon did it dawn on Lu Beiping that the child Jade carried—his own flesh—would, in all likelihood, suffer the same fate as Smudge if he (she?) grew up in this savage chiefdom. Another "shadowborn bastard," another "devil's get," to be slapped around according to the whims of Kingfisher and Stump . . . Lu Beiping didn't dare think further.

He followed the trail's familiar turnings, listened to the water's familiar babble. Once again, in the space of an evening, his world seemed to have changed color: the people strangers, the hollow an unfamiliar place, his own heart alien to him. The sun had set, but in its lingering glow a long snakecloud draped its ruby-red tail over the mountaintop, and he imagined for a moment that the cloud was another scrap of red paper beckoning him. But this time the message wasn't cryptic and obscure; it was plain as day. The troops had massed, the playing pieces were arrayed on the board, and what bounties he won, what disasters he called forth, were all up to him to decide.

Jade was right—lately, whenever he caught sight of her and her belly, he found himself slinking stealthily away. It scared him stiff to think of confronting the creature that lurked behind that smooth curve of flesh, and the host of unknown variables it brought into play: the responsibility of fatherhood, the burden of blood. There was nothing in this world more precious than a human life, he knew that to be true. What he didn't know, though, was whether he was unable to shoulder the role of fatherhood, or just unwilling to. Or could it be that Jade was right, that this whole absurd situation was something she'd brought on herself, and he wasn't called upon to shoulder any of it? In truth, it was for her that he'd shown the greatest concern lately.

All the "nice things" from the "doler co-op" were meant as gifts for her, and he always delivered them directly into her hands, leaving no doubt as to their significance. But in his heart he knew that he gave them to her out of guilt, and that this show of consideration just betokened his insincerity. Jade, sharp-eyed woman that she was, saw right through him; just like she said, his spirit had already flown.

In a vague way he understood where his heart was leaning, and he knew it had been leaning that way for a long time. These days, as he sought out fresh pastures for the cattle, his feet led him naturally up to the pool behind the hollow, where the broken tablet lay, and naturally Autumn would appear there too. They never arranged to meet, just chanced to be there at the same time—Autumn happened to be hauling timber out of the high valley while Lu Beiping drove the cattle up for a cool bath—and they would greet each other with a smile, needing no further explanation. After reading the tablet countless times and filling in almost all of the missing characters, it seemed like they'd barely scratched the surface of the things they had to talk about: from the mountains of Canton to the piers of Tung Ling, from uncles and aunts to Confucius and Mencius, from cane and clogs and sticky rice to fighting over jacks on the Tin Tsee Wharf. Never during these cheerful hours of conversation did Jade appear, though her shadow always hovered nearby. One day he discovered a sign that she'd passed through the area: a foraging basket, abandoned in the undergrowth not far from the tablet. A current of fear rushed through him at the sight. But what was he afraid of? It was just a basket, and nothing came of it afterward. Why, then, was he so overcome with dread? He'd accepted Autumn's affection, and Autumn knew that he was doing his best to make good on his promise. But the truth was that they were still carefully, gingerly, maintaining a degree of distance, lest some rude embarrassment shatter the happy equilibrium they'd rebuilt atop Lu Beiping's assent. The prospect of straying over that line made both of them recoil in fear.

If only he'd understood, back then . . . The thing was, there were plenty of interesting characters to befriend among the re-eds—what was he seeking in Autumn's company? Once he'd imagined that Fate, directing his footsteps into the wilds of Mudkettle Mountain, was leading him into the depths of lost time, into the distant past, reducing him to some simpler, more natural, more instinctual state. Why, then, now that he'd been reduced and simplified, did everything seem so much more complicated? Out of his bewildering old life he'd tried to escape to something true, something certain, but now that he was drawing near to it, he found himself feeling even more bewildered than before.

Enough already. Just go with it. Let everything come forth as it may, in its own time, in its own muddled, ambiguous fashion. Since Chance brought all this into being, better to place it all back into the hands of Chance, and wait for the spirits, standing by quietly in the shadows, to issue their own ruling.

But Lu Beiping's thoughts hadn't wandered far when the shrill moaning of a bull jerked him back to reality. Following the animal's voice, he descended from the fourth bend of the creek into a narrow, rocky crevice that overhung a deep ravine, at the far end of which, in the moonlight, he made out a large, shuddering shadow. Casting his flashlight beam down through the rocks, he saw that it was the white-headed bull, Peter, who he'd been hunting for fruitlessly all afternoon. Several fallen branches had rolled into the crevice and pinned the animal's front hooves, and the bull, pushing and tugging and bellowing mightily, seemed to be just a hair's breadth from shaking free. But when he looked closer, Lu Beiping sucked in his breath: If those branches, tumbling into the crevice after Peter, hadn't pinned his hooves just so, he'd have kept on sliding under his own momentum and plummeted to his death in the gorge below. Chance had come to Peter's rescue. But no! Looking even closer, Lu Beiping now saw that if he hadn't found Peter right at this moment, the struggling bull would've dislodged the woodpile and, propelled by the cascading branches, gone over the edge nonetheless. Once again Chance, crazy, capricious old Chance, had materialized in the form of Lu Beiping and, in a moment of spine-tingling serendipity, saved the sorry animal's life.

But Lu Beiping had no time to consider these mysteries, for he knew that he was also in a dangerous position. The bull might wrench free at any moment, and the ensuing avalanche might sweep Lu Beiping along with it and shatter him on the rocks at the bottom of the ravine.

He broke into a sweat, but he managed to keep his head. He shouted to Peter, and the bull calmed down a bit. Then he hooked an arm around a woody vine that dangled into the crevice, tested it to see if it could bear his weight, then reached out slowly and grabbed Peter's left horn, which was slightly longer than his right. Just one little push—god! what a close call—and the bull slipped free from the tangle of branches. Though Lu Beiping couldn't see them in the dark, he heard the thumping and thrashing as the branches came awake and bounced down the crevice toward the gorge. What just a moment ago seemed like an impregnable bulwark of wood sailed weightlessly, silently over the precipice and, after appearing to hang frozen for a split second in the light of Lu Beiping's flashlight, vanished into the black ravine.

Gone, gone, gone. That was the end of that. A gibbous moon hung in the mouth of the gully, illuminating the silent, slumbering mountains beyond.

Somehow—he had no idea how he managed it—he dragged Peter by fits and starts out of the crevice and up onto the path. They were met by the happy trumpeting of the other cattle, who were resting nearby among the trees, and for a moment the valley echoed with their deep, piping voices. Peter, the lucky survivor, rubbed his muzzle and horns against Lu Beiping and grunted affectionately. Lu Beiping laid a light, reproachful slap on Peter's brow, knowing that he, too, had just come back from a stroll along the edge of the beyond. As he regained his bearings, an odd thought occurred to him: For animals like Peter, for the dark, mindless wilderness that teemed beyond that cliff, did Chance mean anything at all? Did it even exist? He counted the cattle, found that two more were missing. He counted again and again, and the total came out different each time. He began wandering to and fro in the twilit valley, raising his voice in mounting anxiousness, not sure whether he was hunting for his stray cattle or for his own self, gone missing among the hills.

—*Leeeee-leeeee-looooo-looooo-waaaaaaaaaaaaaaaaaaaaah!!!!!!!*

Chapter 13
Night Music

At long last the daring piece of mischief that Lu Beiping and Autumn had plotted played itself out, in a way they never would have expected, as if according to some higher design.

The fourteenth typhoon of the season had just blown across Hainan Island, leaving Mudkettle Mountain hooded in yet another gray shroud of rain. It was manure-hauling day again. In addition to the foreman, who always headed up these expeditions, Kambugger, Choi, and Sergeant Fook had all made appearances recently, but Wing hadn't shown his face for many weeks now. It's time for my brother-in-law to take the stage, Lu Beiping thought. And sure enough, that afternoon Wing came tripping up the path at the head of the column, a pair of wicker scoop baskets dangling from his shoulder yoke and a big smile pasted across his face, sporting his usual green-billed cap and a spanking new, homemade Red Army uniform. As he appeared around the bend of the trail down by the gorgontree, Lu Beiping saw, to his mild amazement, that Fong was following right behind him, sashaying along in her customary manner and wearing a triumphant expression straight off of a propaganda poster. When she saw Lu Beiping she greeted him with a wave, then went back to bantering loudly with Wing. The reeking manure pile was now fodder for fascinating conversation, and all afternoon Fong chattered like a broken string of pearls while the workers sweated and heaved around them, silent props in her and Wing's jubilant two-person show.

When Lu Beiping inquired discreetly with Cigar, his former rival for Fong's affections, who was now laboring sullenly at the edge of the crowd, the elder re-ed laughed at him. You didn't hear? he said. Fong is going to integrate! Lu Beiping, figuring he meant the business with the integration statement, was puzzled by this. Integrate? he said. But isn't that old news? In a sense, Cigar replied cryptically. It's a new spin on a piece of old news. Then finally Cigar pulled the veil off the mystery, and Lu Beiping reeled with surprise. Wow! he thought. The foreman really was a man of action. Everybody in the unit already knew, and Lu Beiping had been the only one still in the dark—Wing and Fong were getting married! Marrying a local was "integration" in the purest sense of the word. And sure enough, when the first roster of re-eds accepted for the personnel call was made public, Fong's name topped the list. The foreman had made good on his contradictory promise that those who integrated locally could return to the city. Though the local she was marrying was the foreman's own son, nobody could accuse him of not standing by his word.

How Fong ended up in this happy situation was, of course, easy to trace. But Lu Beiping never would have expected that Fong, ever the high-minded progressive, would cast off Fook's rising star in favor of a loser like Wing. And it made his head spin just a little to think that he, in marrying Wing's sister's ghost, had unwittingly paved the way for Wing to marry his own ex-girlfriend.

The beginning had been pure chance, but the end was inevitable. (Really, Lu Beiping repeated to Tsung years later: You can make fun of a lot of things, but you can't make light of Chance.)

At the same moment that Lu Beiping connected these threads, he also realized that Wing and Fong's appearance among the manure haulers that day was the foreman's way of telling him that, with Wing set to marry, his own role as ghost husband was as good as over. Call it truth or make-believe, fact or fantasy, it was time for them all to turn the page and forget about Han.

Lu Beiping smiled bitterly. Now a new character had written herself into the drama that he and Autumn had so carefully scripted—the thought made him just a tad uneasy.

Dusk was gathering when he saw the workers off, and the sky was threatening rain. Instead of herding the cattle back into the freshly cleaned corral as he usually did, Lu Beiping gave a loud call in the direction of the hollow—*Leeleelooloowaaaaaah!*—then bounded down the slope to the creek, dug Han's blouse out of the crack in the rocks, stuffed it in his satchel, and drove the herd, which had gathered round him of its own accord, down the mountain in the direction of camp.

The grove to which Wing had been assigned lay near the second bend of the creek; it was here that Lu Beiping had confronted him on the eve of the typhoon. Perhaps by the foreman's conscious design, Wing was responsible for an area bordering on the clearing where Han was buried, not far from the sector Choi tapped. Over the past few days Lu Beiping and Autumn had surveyed all the possible routes through this grove, gotten their equipment ready, staked out a spot, then hacked a path through the swift-growing jungle grass so that anyone passing through the area would walk instinctually toward the location they'd chosen. Everything was ready, and whether their scheme succeeded or not was now out of their hands.

Taking a shortcut through a patch of vine-tangled forestland, Lu Beiping and the cattle emerged on the far side of the creek, where he hid behind a clump of bushes at the edge of the water so that he could secretly observe any movements on the trail below.

No! This was a disaster. Fong, the wild card, who'd been humping her manure baskets a short distance behind Wing while keeping up a steady stream of flirtatious chatter, now came running up, clearly planning to cut in front of him. This was the classic image of Seeking Peer Support—"revolutionary peer mentorship" was as crucial to romance as it was to Production, and a photograph of this young "integrated" couple chasing each other through the rubber grove with baskets of fertilizer swinging from their yokes would have made a perfect front-page image for the *Agrecorps Daily Dispatch*. Lu Beiping tensed. Better for Wing to be in front—much as Lu Beiping detested Fong, he wouldn't want her to get the treatment they'd intended for her husband-to-be. Not only would it be too cruel, it would mess up his and Autumn's entire plan.

How pathetic! Wing was no match for the Woman of Steel he had chosen to marry. Laughing, she overtook him easily, then went racing off down the trail ahead of him. Good god—if this were a model-opera movie, there'd be a swell of dramatic music right now. But just as Fong started down the path that Autumn and Lu Beiping had cut through the grass, she took a running jump and launched herself into the air, heedless of the twin Heavy Burdens that swung from her shoulders, sticking her chin out and kicking her legs apart in an imitation of the triumphant flying split so often employed by the Fearless Heroines of the silver screen. Beautiful!

Lu Beiping breathed a sigh of relief. Saved by the Revolutionary Leap. Right at the Point of No Return—another well-oiled model-opera movie phrase—Fong had jumped clear over the sprig of maid-engolds that Lu Beiping and Autumn had stuck in the earth to mark the spot. Trying his best to keep up with Fong, Wing came huffing and puffing down the trail after her, and before Lu Beiping could blink there was a loud *whunk* and Wing and his manure baskets spilled into the tall grass. At first Lu Beiping heard only a soft gasp of surprise as Wing struggled to right himself, then abruptly the young man began wailing at the top of his lungs like a pig being slaughtered.

—*Auuugh! Heeeeeelp!* Wing's strangled cries echoed through the forest. Initially Fong didn't slow her pace, just glanced over her shoulder to laugh at her fiancé's pratfall, but when his shouts didn't cease and it became clear that something was wrong, she dropped her baskets and came running back, adding her shrieks of dismay to Wing's screams:

—Oh my god! What happened? You're bleeding! Oh my god, Wing!

—I stepped in a hog trap, Fong! Augh! One of those stupid Tamchow hill men . . .

—A what?

—*Auuuuuuugh!*

—*Help! Help!* Fong's urgent soprano rang out over Wing's anguished moans. *Is anybody here? Come quick! We've got an emergency!*

A flock of roosting birds exploded out of the treetops, flapping in every direction and heightening the chaos.

Lu Beiping, lying among the bushes on the far side of the creek, sniggered to himself. Here he was, in the traditional movie villain pose: the Class Enemy crouching in the underbrush, ready to launch his Nefarious Counterrevolutionary Plot. This was a role he'd never before had the chance to play. Trying his best to stay coolheaded, he tied Alexei, the new lead bull, to a nearby vine and, while the knocking of the clapper summoned the rest of the herd out of the surrounding forest, strode down the slope and waded across the creek toward the scene of the crime.

The dusk was deepening, and the forest lay in deep shadow. A handful of workers who'd been busy spreading manure in neighboring sectors had heard Wing's and Fong's cries of distress and rushed over to help. Lu Beiping saw the blue-white flame of a tapper's head-mounted carbide lamp wavering toward him out of the gloom, then recognized the face beneath it—Choi.

While a small crowd gathered round the wailing Wing, Fong made out Lu Beiping's approaching figure and called out urgently:

—Come here, Lu! Thank god it's you. You're a more experienced forester than any of us—do you know how to open a hog trap?

Shouldering his way through the onlookers Lu Beiping saw, in the blue lamplight, the crude spring-loaded trap clamped on Wing's right foot. Wing's brand-new canvas army sneaker had split in two, and blood oozed from the crack.

Wing wriggled backwards instinctively upon seeing Lu Beiping, but he nonetheless beseeched him in a choked voice:

—Hey, Lu! . . . Urgh, ack! Can you help me?

—Hmm, Lu Beiping said as he bent to examine the trap: I'm sorry to say it, but I don't know how to open one of these. All I know is that you'd better not move. The more you struggle, the tighter it'll grip.

—Oh my god! Fong cried, sounding like she was on the verge of tears. What are we going to do, then? He won't be crippled for life, will he? Will he?

—Let's all quit jawing and do something! Choi cut in. Everybody hoist him up and carry him to the infirmary!

—No! Wing groaned from below. Don't do it! Don't move me!

—Here's an idea, Lu Beiping said. I just saw one of the migrants from Whitesands cutting timber over there in the forest. I'll bet he knows how to open a hog trap. Wait here. I'll be right back.

Without further ado Lu Beiping slipped into the bushes. Fong leaned down to say something to Wing but he pushed her away with a groan of irritation, probably still resenting her for baiting him into a chase game. There was nothing left for Fong to do but stand at the edge of the crowd, wiping tears from her face. Choi and the other hands hung uselessly around Wing, exclaiming sympathetically and trying to make helpful suggestions, while nearby in the trees the creek kept up its constant, burbling commentary.

Before long Lu Beiping came running back. He was carrying a satchel now, and his face shone with sweat.

—The woodcutter's on his way, Lu Beiping said, panting for breath. His name's Autumn. Lu Beiping bent over, his hands on his thighs, and stood gazing downward for a moment, as if either examining Wing's wound or arriving at a decision; then he looked up and said in a stern voice: Wing, before he arrives, I want to ask you a few questions.

Reflexively Wing tried to clamber to his feet, then he flopped down immediately with a gasp of pain.

—What . . . what are you trying you do?

Glancing over his shoulder, Lu Beiping scanned the crowd for Choi and saw her staring wide-eyed at his satchel, backing away through the press of bodies.

—Choi, wait!

He rushed over and grabbed her by the shoulder. Choi twisted away vehemently. Two older male workers stared at them in surprise.

—Whatever's wrong? Something the matter with you two?

—Lu! Fong cried, suddenly realizing what was going on: You—you—stop it! You've got something up your sleeve!

Just then Autumn's sinewy silhouette materialized out of the shadows.

—Stay here, Fong! Lu Beiping shouted at her as he succeeded in getting a grip on Choi's arm. Everybody else can go back. We'll take care of bringing Wing back to camp.

Autumn, bare-chested and clad in a checkered waistcloth, strode over to them and said without looking at Lu Beiping:

—Who stepped in the trap?

Seeing Wing, he stooped to assess the damage. As he inspected the trap he said in a mild voice:

—I see, this is a number-three trap. Won't kill you, but it hurts a sight, eh?

—Hold on, Autumn, Lu Beiping said, stepping between him and Wing. I have a couple questions for Wing first.

—Bastard! You're trying to blackmail me! Wing moaned. You won't get anything out of me, not even if you beat me to death! Fong, he's just jealous of me because you—

By now Fong had calmed down and stood gazing with a mixture of fear and mounting suspicion back and forth between Choi, Lu Beiping, and her panic-stricken, trash-talking fiancé. In the light of the blue flame that hissed atop Choi's headlamp, Fong watched Lu Beiping open his satchel and draw out a tattered blouse cut in an outmoded style.

Wing burst into sobs.

The grove hands, reluctant to withdraw from the scene, stood a short distance away with worry etched all over their faces, debating in hushed voices while pricking up their ears to catch snatches of conversation that drifted their way.

. . . set that forest fire? Did you jump in the creek? Tell me!

I, I, I . . . yes . . .

What were you burning? Why were you slinking around . . .

. . . grave money for Han . . . my dad told me to burn her things . . .

Their voices, wafting on the orchard cross-breezes, faded in and out of hearing.

. . . what terrible thing did you and your father do to Han? Tell us!

. . . I, I . . . doing homework with her . . . slept together . . . I saw my dad . . . f-f-fire . . .

Darkness seeped through the grove, and the creek's sibilant whisper seemed to emanate from the shadows. The workers, straining to hear their voices, made out only bits and pieces and had no notion what it all might mean. Then they saw Fong bury her face in her hands and run away sobbing into the trees.

That night the fat rainclouds that had been massing over Mudkettle Mountain all afternoon broke open at last, unleashing a torrential downpour.

What a glorious sound! A bedraggled Autumn burst through the door of the hut, accompanied by the rapturous roar of rain. Lu Beiping shook a finger at him and bellowed:

—Enemy of the People! How dare you assault a soldier of the Revolution using a hog trap? You miserable, unrepentant reactionary! The two of them fell to laughing, then Lu Beiping said: You're a cruel man, Autumn. How'd you think to use a hog trap? Is there some sort of precedent for that?

—Precedent? Autumn said. Not everything I do has got a rosewood story behind it, Bei. These hills are a cruel place to live in. If you're not two steps ahead of all the savage things that might harm you out here, not to mention the savage people, you'll live a short life.

Autumn had made an exception to his usual habit and donned a sleeveless cotton undershirt to ward off the chill of the late March night. Lu Beiping, seeing that his friend was completely soaked, tossed Autumn a set of dry underclothes and then got to work starting a fire in the hearth stove. The stove had lain cold for several weeks now, and when the damp kindling caught it filled the room with a thick haze of smoke that sent them both into coughing fits. As Autumn changed into Lu Beiping's spare clothing, Lu Beiping caught a glimpse of his naked back and was reminded of the time Jade had done the same thing, on a cold, rainy evening much like this one. They'd gotten to talking, and soon it felt like they had so much to talk about that they might gab all night. Smudge had been with them then—and now, Smudge was giving Lu Beiping the cold shoulder. As Lu Beiping stirred the fire his thoughts began to wander, and he sighed.

—Poor Han, he said. It was right around the time we city kids arrived on the plantation that she died. It was this time of year, cold and raining on and on, it must've been freezing when she waded into the creek with no clothes on . . .

Back in the rubber grove they'd teased the whole story, piece by piece, out a whimpering, groveling Wing. Han, who'd always done well in school, had been tasked with supervising her struggling younger brother while he did his homework. Wing had just learned about the birds and bees, and insisted that he'd only do his homework if she slept with him. Later their father found out and laid the blame on Han. The "teasey blue" blouse was, just as Choi said, a gift he'd bought her, using his first farm wages. But then, on more than one occasion, Wing had been walking through the grove that Han tapped and saw his father and sister . . . Not long afterward, the grove caught fire and burned down, then Han "got the fever" and died.

—Why are you still brooding about that evil business? Autumn asked, chuckling. Careful, the bale might seep into your blood, then we'll have to whip it out of you again!

—But Autumn, Lu Beiping said, beginning to feel dejected: I'm afraid we're already in over our heads. It's not going to be pretty when the foreman hears what we've done. And then how will Kingfisher react?

—Fight when you can win, run when you can't—that's the Enlightened Revolutionary Ideology that Kingfisher's always abided by. But the way I see it, you've won this round. You're holding the trump card. I'm curious to see what your father-in-law's next move will be, now that this unspeakable thing's come to light.

—Screw him, Lu Beiping said. Let him do his damnedest. Worse comes to worst, I'll run away with you, and we can start our own driftfolk band.

—Bei . . . Autumn said, his eyes growing bright as Lu Beiping made this declaration: Hearing you say that, I know it wasn't for nothing that I weathered this storm tonight.

Autumn turned, fished around in the pile of wet clothing, and produced a plastic bag containing the familiar black book. But when he reached into the bag he pulled out, instead, a small bottle of clear liquor.

—Never fear, he said, flashing the bottle at Lu Beiping: This isn't the yam beer you've got such a terror of. The other day I made a special trip downmountain to a Loi encampment, where I traded a bundle of white rattan for this bottle of hillflower rice wine. Here, take a sniff. Isn't it lovely?

Autumn opened the bottle. A rich, mellow fragrance threaded its way through the rain-fresh evening air.

Autumn was in high spirits tonight. He seemed to have gone straight into his expressive, quick-speaking mode without passing through the intermediate tongue-tied state. Wrinkling his nose at the smell, he laughed:

—Bei, you said I'm a man of letters. Tonight let's celebrate like a real pair of literati. I've brought my book—let's lay aside our worldly cares and enjoy an evening of wine and poetry. You can play Xin Qiji, I'll be Nara Singde.

—How about I just play deaf and dumb? Lu Beiping said teasingly, aping Autumn's mouth-agape, tongue-tied pose. Let all sound by silence be surpassed! Isn't that from some poem or other? Lu Beiping caught a whiff of the liquor's heady aroma, and as he listened to the cold autumn rain pattering outside he realized how much he'd missed his conversations with Autumn. Bursting with warmth and contentment, he hummed cheerfully to himself as he puttered around the room, feeling like he could dance.

Autumn, looking on with a smile on his face, picked up a shallow bowl and an enamelware mug that sat on a table next to the stove and poured out the wine between them. Offering the bowl to Lu Beiping, he said:

—The poets of old told of a thing called the ferrufloral oath. It was a pledge of eternal friendship, the brotherhood of steel and flowers. Here, let's toast our friendship with this hillflower wine, swear our brotherhood by hill and flower—as Autumn said these words, the bowl in his hand began to shake ever so slightly—for who knows when the river will meet the mountain again. Even if we don't cross paths again after this, having known you, Bei, I feel like these years I've spent wandering through the mountains weren't wasted.

Lu Beiping gazed at Autumn and sipped his liquor. Obviously Autumn had prepared these words in advance. Tonight more than ever, his friend's lofty locution and swarthy profile reminded Lu Beiping of some storybook brigand. There was a persistent, old-fashioned air about Autumn that made him seem quite out of place in the modern world; at first Lu Beiping had found this manner a little off-putting, but now it only increased his fondness for him. Outside the rain sheeted down endlessly, thunderously. Once again Lu Beiping sensed that he'd bumped up against Autumn's bold, brash side. Autumn always came on strong like this, baring his true feelings in a sudden and vehement way that caught Lu Beiping off-guard, making it impossible to face the topic he brought up in any manner other than head-on.

For a moment, it was as if both of them really had been struck dumb. They sat looking at each other, wine vessels in hand, a giddy rush of emotion putting them both at a loss for words. In a corner of the hut a roof-leak dripped on the lid of a pot, a brisk, chiming tattoo that mingled with the loud rush of the rain.

The moment seemed to last an eternity, the time it took for an unspoken thought to travel by pack horse across many rugged, mountainous miles.

Toward the end of this moment the drumming of heavy footsteps wove its way into the roar of the rain. It grew gradually nearer and louder, then halted just outside the door of the hut. Autumn and Lu Beiping pricked up their ears and glanced at each other in surprise, but heard no further sound. Hesitant, Autumn went over and opened the door. Immediately the fetid reek of yam beer gusted in, followed by a dripping-wet figure in a broad palm-leaf hat. Was it Kingfisher? Lu Beiping stared at the man, then shuddered and took a step back when he realized who it really was. Their unexpected guest on this rainy night was the man whose name had been on their lips just a moment ago—Lu Beiping's "ghost father-in-law," the foreman.

He was drunk. Had he been celebrating Wing's marriage, or drowning his sorrows in liquor? Lu Beiping wondered. His face was flushed and blotchy, his body covered in mud, and in one hand he held a hurricane lantern at a cockeyed angle. As soon as he stumbled through the door his towering frame went limp, and he flopped down on the dirt floor and lay there motionless till the light in the hearth stove prodded him back to his senses. Looking up and seeing Lu Beiping, he dragged himself to his feet, crying:

—Dear friend! . . . Friend Lu! . . . You're a good boy! D'you know the reason I came up here tonight? So I could beg you . . . to save my life!

Tears flooded down his face. His legs went slack again, and he slumped to his knees. Prostrating himself before Lu Beiping, he knocked his forehead on the ground till the dirt floor was a muddy slick.

Lu Beiping, trying to stay calm and keep his own astonishment from getting the better of him, said coldly:

—Get up, Foreman Kau. You're drunk.

—I won't get up unless you say you will! the foreman sobbed, still kowtowing to Lu Beiping. Then he embraced Lu Beiping's legs and cried imploringly: Please, friend Lu, won't you give me back my poor Han's shirt! I'm sick to death for worry thinking about my girl, my poor, poor girl, my poor . . . ack . . .

A gob of spit, phlegm, and bile plopped onto the floor. Lu Beiping extracted himself from the foreman's grip and said in a stern voice:

—But, Foreman, I can't give you back that shirt because I don't know the whole story yet—he traded a knowing grimace with Autumn, who was still standing behind the door—So tell me, what horrible thing, exactly, did you do to Han?

With a shudder the foreman appeared to come sober for a moment. Gripping one of the roof-posts he struggled to his feet, and as he gazed up at the smoke-blackened thatch a shadow of his former aura of chilly command came over his face. With tears still coursing down his blunt, craggy features, he said with a desolate air:

—Living one life is hard enough, Lu. You've no notion how hard it is, being a leader. Two hundred men, women, and children looking to you for their supper, the old, the sick, the dying . . . I did it for them! I did it to keep them from suffering! That year the fever was worse than ever before, the whole unit was sick with it, there weren't enough healthy arms to bury the dead. You city kids came right at the tail end, I feared you pups would catch it, so I went over the mountains to see the spirit man in Lam-ko. The spirit man said, You're a leader of men, if you want to save your village, you need to sacrifice your own flesh and blood—only that can quell the fever vapors. Oh, Heaven help me! . . . Leaning on the pillar, the foreman burst into sobs: Wing's my only son, he was the only one could carry on the family line. I'd no choice but to give up my poor, poor Han for their sake . . . I couldn't bear to kill her myself, I had to ask her to take her own life, I . . . Oh! Heaven save me!

(Decades later, Lu Beiping said to Tsung: If it hadn't been for all I'd seen and heard that year, I might well have bought this compelling tale, and been stirred to compassion for the foreman's sake. Like Abraham in Lu Beiping's book of Bible stories, the foreman—so he said—had offered up his own offspring to the gods of Mudkettle Mountain, in order to redeem his people.)

—I really want to believe everything you're telling me, sir, said Lu Beiping with a grave chuckle. So, then, can you explain why Han drowned herself in the creek without her clothes on? Can you tell me who lit that grove fire, and why? Were you trying to burn Han's blouse?

At each question the foreman winced and jerked slightly as if a bullet had just whizzed past his head. Then he gave a teary laugh and mumbled in protest:

—Did I do her wrong? She said she wanted to! She said her little brother was just a pup . . . heh, oh, my poor, poor Han . . .

He hugged the post with one arm, wiping tears from his face. Then he turned, finally noticed Autumn standing just inside the door, and straightened with a gasp of surprise.

—Gah! Who are you? Are you from the Working Group?—obviously the foreman didn't recognize Autumn. He turned back to Lu Beiping and renewed his passionate, drunken plea: Friend Lu, oh please, take pity on me, leave me a way out . . . Please!

As if afraid to linger there any longer, the foreman stooped, picked up his hat and lantern, and lurched out into the rain, still crowing in a sloppy voice:

—Have a heart, friend Lu! Please! I did it to keep . . . to keep them from suffering!

Lu Beiping leaned against the doorframe and gazed out into the mist and rain, watching the foreman's lantern and palm-leaf hat wobble away into the darkness.

He remembered Kingfisher's recent visit, which had ended with a scene almost exactly like this one: a single, glowing bead of light afloat on the vast ocean of the night. Both conversations, in their own ways, had hinged on the same point—the spirits of Mudkettle Mountain. But where Kingfisher's primitive superstitions seemed to grow out of an intuitive grasp of man's place in the world, Lu Beiping could tell that the foreman's high-toned rhetoric hid an ugly twist of distorted reasoning.

He turned to Autumn, who still stood silently by the door, and made a face.

It was an eventful night. (It felt like the longest night of my life, Lu Beiping said, years later, to Tsung.)

After they'd spent a good long while laughing at each other's imitations of the drunken foreman, Autumn fell silent, head cocked again as if listening for some other noise outside the hut, then said:

—What about this blouse I've been hearing about all day? I'd like to take a peek at this piece of cloth that your dastardly in-laws are so scared about.

Of course—the blouse. Since the day Choi stuffed the "bale-crossed" garment into his satchel, Lu Beiping had known that it was in some way vitally connected with Han's death, and clearly it had the power to haunt the minds of the foreman and his son—even more than the hog trap, it had proved a potent tool for extracting the truth from Wing. But all these weeks, perhaps fearing that its evil influence might somehow rub off on him, Lu Beiping hadn't dared pull out the blouse and inspect it closely.

—Sure! I feel like a braver man with you around, Lu Beiping said, then dashed out through the rain and tugged the satchel out of the crack in the rocks where he'd hidden it. When he came running back, raindrops bouncing off of his hair, he startled Autumn with a cry of alarm: Someone's here! Who was that, peeking in the window?

Autumn stuck his head out the door. There was nobody outside, but the bushes under the low windowsill had been trampled upon, and a puddle of water gleamed in the mud.

—Do you think the foreman would send someone to spy on us? Lu Beiping said, his heart immediately growing heavy.

—I'll bet not . . . Autumn thought for a moment, then tossed his head: Devil take it! Whoever they are, I dare them to come mix with us tonight!

Autumn slowly unfolded the cloth, and Han's blouse revealed its terrible face to the lamplight. It was faded and wrinkled, like an old woman's features, and paper-thin from frequent wear and washing. Not quite a blouse, more like a loose jacket, it was tight up top and baggy down below, and most of the cheap blue dye had run, leaving the fabric pale and blotchy looking. At first glance it just looked like an old rag headed for the trash heap. Then Autumn lifted the lower hem, brought it closer to lamp, and turned away with an expression of disgust.

—Look, he said gravely: What's this filth?

Examining the near-transparent fabric in the lamplight, Lu Beiping made out several discolored patches on the lower front panels of the blouse. Over these faint, overlapping stains were two darker marks, one large and obvious, the other small and faint. And crusted on the stiff, individual threads it was possible to discern the original brown color of the marks—dried blood. These were the bloodstains of a young woman who'd been abused and humiliated, still visible after all these years.

—Blood? But why would there be blood? said Lu Beiping with a quaver of uncertainty in his voice, knitting his brow: Didn't they say she was naked when she drowned in the pool?

—You still don't get it, Autumn said savagely, flinging the blouse to the floor. Those beasts! The stains wouldn't be from just one man. I'll bet you anything both Wing and the foreman had their way with her on the day she died. It's not blood-blood, Bei, it's woman's blood, it was her time of month and still those curs were glad to do their business. She couldn't bear the shame of it, so she up and . . .

Understanding dawned over Lu Beiping.

—So maybe the reason she was naked when she drowned herself in the creek—Lu Beiping said quickly, his heart thumping—was that she *wanted* to leave behind this dirty blouse as evidence, so that people who came afterward would find out the truth?

—I don't know, Autumn said. There's some secret behind this yet. Then he heaved a deep sigh: The least we know is that this girl had a touch of pluck to her.

All at once, the string of mysteries that hung around Mudkettle Mountain unraveled itself before Lu Beiping's eyes. The fire that destroyed Sector 11 after Han's death, the sudden, uncanny, unatoned-for blaze that began near the pool after Lu Beiping had wandered into the "baleglen," were both fueled, Lu Beiping now saw, by the guilty consciences of this beastly father-son pair. They thought that fire had the power to efface all such filthy traces from this world; who could have foreseen that Lu Beiping, chosen by the whim of Fate and by a fortuitously placed scrap of paper to banish Han's memory from their household forever, would be the very one to uncover her father's crimes and bear witness to her humiliation? He was, in more ways than he'd realized before, Han's chosen one, her soulmate.

(The beginning was pure chance, but the end was inevitable, Lu Beiping sighed, once again, to Tsung: You can make light of a lot of things in this world, but Chance, no—you can't make light of Chance.)

Lu Beiping felt a rush of heat, and blood pounded in his ears. The strange sights and sounds he'd encountered in the forests of Mudkettle Mountain flashed one after another through his mind: the mysterious, ever-shifting "baleglen"; the ghostly infant's wail; the wooden cowbell, lying mute and bloody among the leaves after Alyosha's disappearance . . . Now Chance had slipped him this blouse, which even a roaring grove fire hadn't succeeded in destroying—what other explanation could there be, except that the spirits had had a hand in this? *Did I do her wrong? She said she wanted to!* . . . *Have a heart, friend Lu! I did it to keep them from suffering* . . . In this pitiful, tattered garment he saw clearly the empty reality of human power, and hidden behind it, the face of a brave, unyielding young woman, ready to be reborn out of the flames.

He picked up the blouse and spread it open again. First that scrap of red paper, now this ragged blue blouse; he felt like he was holding some unearthly object that had floated up out of the land of shadow and linked this daylit reality to the world beyond. But at the same time he couldn't help seeing the blouse as a bloody banner, fluttering proudly over Mudkettle Mountain, proclaiming the foreman's shamelessness and arrogance. At this thought his fancies evaporated instantly.

For a moment Lu Beiping thought he caught a whiff of a fetid odor, like the wind off of a swamp just across the border of the next world. He shuddered and dropped the blouse as if it had just burned his fingers.

—Enough! Autumn cried, throwing open the door and letting in a gust of night air and the loud whoosh of the rain. Let's clear the air of these stinking vapors. Put that thing away, it and your foreman's beer-breath have called up all the shadows of Hell and just about spoiled the fine, poetical atmosphere we've managed to work up tonight.

—Yeah, let's not talk about this depressing stuff anymore, Lu Beiping agreed, cramming the blouse back into the satchel. He added more fuel to the lamp, turned up the wick, exhaled a sharp puff of air, and cried Good god! as if expelling a year's worth of vexation all at once; then looked up, an easy smile on his face. He picked up Autumn's journal, which lay on top of the bed, and began riffling through it, grunting approvingly. Alright, comrade! he said. I want a full report on your recent poetic pursuits!

Down in the gully the rain drummed on the creek, its deep roar swelling and subsiding by intervals.

—Want to hear more about my rosewood tree? Autumn said, excitement re-entering his voice: I almost forgot to tell you, I've been all over the valley with Kingfisher now, and we're sure that that tree I told you about is the only red flowering pear tree in these parts, the only true amaranthine rosewood tree on all of Mudkettle Mountain! There are a handful of yellow pearwood trees, and those are rare and precious enough, but they're nothing compared to this one—a true treasure, it is!

—Autumn, Lu Beiping said, laughing: I think you're suffering from a case of rosewood-itis!

—I suffer from a lot of things, why else would I have joined the driftfolk? Autumn said with a self-deprecatory, slightly desolate-sounding laugh. But then he went on with unabated fervor: And now, I've almost got him! I tell you, Bei, felling one of those things is tough work, it's not like a chinaberry tree which you can lick through in an afternoon even if it's four hands wide. It's hard as iron. I've been at it for a fortnight. Back when you were ignoring me—

—Hey! *You* were ignoring *me!*

—I'd go up there every day and talk with my rosewood tree. I'd heat it with fire, then cool it with water, then go at it with my knife and handsaw, then do the whole thing over again . . . It's like carving a jade statue, working that wood! It takes a subtle hand.

—Seriously? It's that hard to cut? said Lu Beiping, rather awed by Autumn's description of the wood's miraculous properties. Autumn, when will I have the honor of meeting this prince of the forest you've befriended? You've got to take me up there one of these days.

—A prince of the forest! Autumn said, his face all aglow. That's a good phrase for it, alright! Takes a thousand years and all the finest essences of the earth to make a gem like that. Ha! They said they were extinct, yet I've gazed upon one myself—Autumn was pacing the room now, his eyes shining, gesticulating feverishly—But, Bei, it's a queer thing. I sawed clear through the trunk, and I've cut away all the vines and creepers I can see, but still that tree just hangs there. It won't fall. It's uncanny!

Autumn was flying high. The wind had picked up outside and was rasping through the treetops, as if someone were really at work out there with a big two-handled wood-saw. Lu Beiping, feeling a bit wicked, decided to throw some cold water on Autumn's exultation, and said:

—But, Autumn, if you're right that this is the only amaranthine rosewood tree left, won't chopping it down make it extinct for good? Do you really want to be the man who killed the last amaranthine rosewood tree?

—You're right, Autumn said, sighing. That question's troubled my mind for a long time. If you Agrecorps people weren't laying waste to the forest right and left with all your campaigns and operations and such, burning down hundred-year-old forests in a month's time, I'd leave that tree living, let it spread its seeds all over Mudkettle Mountain. But now even the best wood's doomed to be kindling. What I don't do with my saw, they'll do with bulldozers and dynamite. There's no saving it, I fear.

—So what are you going to do with the wood, then, when you finish cutting down the tree? Make some new furniture for your throne room?

Instantly Lu Beiping despised himself for saying this—even now, he still found himself slipping into a teasing, superior tone when he was around Autumn. Clearly Autumn caught the hint of ridicule in Lu Beiping's words. His face hardened slightly, but he went on, undeterred:

—No matter what it gets made into, it'll be an heirloom to pass down to future ages. People die, ashes fly, but amaranthine rosewood lives on. When you've cherished an artifact like that, your spirit'll linger over it long after you're gone . . .

Autumn paused, listening to the rain. Then he continued:

—That's how it is with amaranthine rosewood. It's a piece of eternity. You can see your forelife in it, and your afterlife too . . .

Lu Beiping felt a chill. No wonder Kingfisher said that the shadow air lay heavy over Autumn.

Autumn stood there in silence for a moment, gazing off into the rain. Then he said abruptly:

—Have you heard the story of the Three Life Stone?

—The Three Life Stone? Lu Beiping repeated quizzically. Clearly this was another relic from days of old that was missing from Lu Beiping's knowledge base.

Autumn smiled, and said in a mild tone:

—It's a story my dad told me. It's about two monks in ancient times who were bosom friends, who agreed to meet again in the next life before a stone called the Three Life Stone, a magic stone with a living soul. Amaranthine rosewood is the Three Life Stone of woods. Some friends swear to meet again before the Three Life Stone, but I don't know if there's any soul in this world worthy of meeting again under the amaranthine rosewood tree.

The rain kept blustering away. Lu Beiping was silent.

—Autumn . . . he said finally, Are you talking about me?

—Nope, Autumn replied. I don't think so . . .

Then he turned and walked into a dark, rain-loud corner of the hut, where he reached down, picked something up off the floor, and dusted it off. When he turned back again he was holding Lu Beiping's long-forgotten harmonica to his lips. He walked over, sat down on the bed, and began to play.

Lu Beiping stared in surprise.

—Hey, I had no idea you could play harmonica too!

He was playing "Erquan by Moonlight."

—You sure hide your light under a bushel, Autumn.

Lu Beiping sat and listened to Autumn play. Chords, melody, and ornaments were all well-articulated and confident. Against the background of the rain the tune sounded lost and wistful, like a lone traveler winding along a mountain path.

This is a man of many unusual talents, Lu Beiping thought to himself. As the last chord faded away, Autumn emerged beaming from within the music and said:

—When I was a little boy I always dreamed of having a shiny Dunhuang harmonica in my pocket. My family didn't have the money to buy me one, though, and when I'd finally saved up enough, the Movement started.

Lu Beiping, feeling a rush of emotion at these words, said:

—Autumn, you might think this is silly, but . . . I want you to keep that harmonica. Hold on to it as a memory of our, acquaintance, as you say. But—why the heck didn't you play for me before?

Autumn looked down, fondling the instrument. He didn't respond.

—The poets . . . Autumn began slowly, What they wrote was meant to be sung, not spoken. Poems and songs, both are likewise . . . effusions of the soul, addressed to like minds. Thence the old phrase, "the music of the strings is the speech of the heart"—Autumn intoned, lapsing unconsciously into an archaic idiom—My dad loved to tell me tales of those gentlemen of old who'd play music for their friends, smash their zithers for their friends . . . Autumn held the harmonica under the lamp and inspected it closely: So, you're really giving this to me? Well, I'm honored.

He slipped the harmonica into his shorts pocket, then went to the door and peered out into the rain. Then he walked back into the room and said, not looking directly at Lu Beiping:

—It's late. But I don't want to go back.

—Then don't, Lu Beiping said, and was surprised to hear the words come out of his own mouth.

Autumn halted. He looked up and smiled at Lu Beiping.

—Only if you say so.

His eyes alighting on the bowl and cup of hillflower rice wine that sat half-empty on the hearth stove, Autumn picked them up, handed Lu Beiping one, tapped his drink against Lu Beiping's in a toast, and downed it.

Lu Beiping threw his head back and quaffed the rest of the liquor. The wine's aroma lingered in the air, subtle and dizzying.

(I'll remember that smell forever, Lu Beiping sighed to Tsung. It's engraved in my mind, my soul, my blood. Forever afterward, all liquor, from the lowliest yam beer to fine Moutai worthy of a state banquet, has seemed coarse and cloying in comparison.)

They sat in silence. The rain had stopped. Lu Beiping snuffed the lamp and said, jokingly:

—No talking from now on. Let all sound by silence be surpassed.

If the meeting of mountain and river is the natural result of rainfall and the turning of the seasons, then surely the meeting of mountain and mountain is a rare wonder, which only the cracking of the earth's crust and the collision of slow-moving tectonic plates can bring about.

After the lamp went out neither of them were quite sure what to do. First they took off their clothes and lay side by side in bed, silent, both of them freighted with worry, frozen by their own reflexive reserve. They closed their eyes, listening to the sound of each other's breath, feeling awkward and self-conscious. When their faces touched for the first time they pulled apart immediately. But both of them noticed the shiver that this touch triggered in the other's skin.

—Too many rules, Autumn said, chuckling. I don't like not talking.

He looked over at Lu Beiping's dark, silent, motionless figure. Lu Beiping's eyes were still shut. Reaching over and patting his friend's cheek, Autumn said:

—You really want to keep playing dumb?

Still Lu Beiping said nothing. Lightly, Autumn stroked the curve of Lu Beiping's jawbone, murmuring:

—You're tired? You'd rather sleep?

Words can be a bridge, but they can also be a barrier, a protective screen.

Once more Autumn's fingertips began to travel up and down Lu Beiping's body.

Everything was dark. Autumn's touch seemed to reach Lu Beiping from out of a distant place, another dimension: out of the clouds, out of the past, out of the rustling of yellowed pages, out of black and white photos of times gone by. Lu Beiping tried to focus on the actual, physical sensation of Autumn's touch, to distill a real, solid person out of this eccentric character who'd walked straight out of the days of lords and lyres. But the sensation melted away under conscious thought, like snowflakes cupped in his hand. It was true, there was a chilly quality about Autumn; even now Lu Beiping noticed that Autumn's skin seemed just slightly colder than his own. Autumn's touch was the cold touch of another era, awakening Lu Beiping's mind to vistas he'd never considered, penetrating some deep corner of his being and, at times, striking up a great music there. Sometimes he even fancied that Autumn was an apparition, a wavering portent on the border of light and shadow sent to remind him of something, to keep him from forgetting about something, an illusion so tenuous that any sudden motion would dispel it.

Autumn's hands stopped.

—I like how you smell, he said softly in Lu Beiping's ear.

Lu Beiping couldn't see anything in the darkness. What he smelled like to Autumn he couldn't guess, but he could clearly make out Autumn's scent: a quiet, dark smell, edged with the gunmetal odor of sunlight, carrying a hint of the fragrance of wild grass. He even caught, amid the rain-washed odors of sweat and pipe tobacco, a faint, sweet suggestion of sugarcane.

There was a loud roll of thunder outside, and a silent, answering roll of thunder within.

This was the first, and only, time they truly opened up to each other, gave themselves freely to one another.

(Years later, Lu Beiping would say to Tsung: Hearing this, you might get certain ideas about me. But the thing is, it's not true. For all I know it was just one of those fleeting adolescent phases people talk about. I wouldn't say that it was the most amazing night of my life, but it wasn't too terrible, all the same. Maybe the best way to explain it is this: It was one of those secret moments in one's life when one's personality spills out beyond its normal boundaries. It's not something I'd trumpet to the skies, but I don't see any reason to shrink before it either. Or maybe it's just that my temperament wasn't as rigid and earnest as Autumn's; I didn't take things so seriously, wasn't so readily driven to extremes, to the point where this tendency could even become a destructive force. But I can't deny that in the years since, I've often thought back fondly on that night. I've never done anything like it again; I've never gone looking for it. But it's a memory I cherish, which no other friendship or romantic encounter can ever replace. To put it grandly, that was the evening when my soul came of age—when I came to understand, intimately, the many forms human affection can take, the many directions in which it can run.)

Halfway through the night the rain started up again. The sound of the wind in the treetops made Lu Beiping remember his first night on the mountain, when he lay awake till dawn listening to the wind's eerie howling, scared stiff by the multitude of noises that made up the jungle silence. After a few sleepless nights, then a few nights of dreamless sleep, he'd whimsically named this place "Dreamless Vale," imagining it to be the sphere of heaven that the Taoists sought when they sat in meditation, refining their inner gold. But tonight he dreamed. He dreamed shallowly, though his sleep was deep. In his dream, there was water. Under the water was the moon. Inside the moon there were people, and among them, you and me. In his dream he heard distant thunder, but when he woke up he found it was only his and his companion's snores. Sometimes it was loud enough to cover the keen of the wind, and when another, very soft sound crept into their dreams, neither of them noticed.

Autumn woke first, when the wind rose back to a fever pitch just before sunrise—he was in the habit of waking while it was still dark out, and at first, when he opened his eyes, he had no idea where he was. Then, turning on his side, he heard heavy breathing, and realized with a start that there was a third person in the room.

A dark figure sat in the middle of the hut, facing away from them. With a jolt of fright Autumn woke up completely, then, managing to rein in his fear, he gave Lu Beiping a sharp shove.

Lu Beiping rolled over and opened his eyes. At exactly the same moment, both he and Autumn sat up in shocked disbelief.

The ample silhouette in the middle of the room belonged to Jade.

—Don't light the lamp! came her sharp, husky voice. Her silhouette remained motionless. I don't want to see you two.

Panic and awkwardness filled the intervening silence. Jade said, her alto voice trembling:

—If Smudge hadn't brought me down here, I'd have had no mind to come at all. It's not my business!

Smudge's shadow wasn't among those that crowded the edges of the room. There was just Jade, alone, her voice echoing in the rafters.

Then she whirled around to face the dark forms of the two men—Autumn had just groped up out of bed, and Lu Beiping still sat in the corner, frozen from shock—and said with an overtone of icy laughter:

—To think *this* is the secret you two big boys were keeping from me! I, I . . . Jade stammered for a moment, as if trying to lay hands on the appropriate curse: Shame my eyes! I must've been a real rat in my last life to have earned such a humiliation as this!

Lu Beiping saw Autumn's silhouette bound forward.

—Sister, listen . . .

—No! Jade bellowed. Get back! I'm not your sister!

—Sister, Autumn insisted, Please, listen to me for just a moment—

—No, I won't listen to you! I don't want to hear it!

—I told you, Autumn went on stubbornly, I told you I wanted to make good with Four Eyes too.

—Make good? Jade spat. Good? That's what you call it? Between two *men*? Oh, it's a cruel Heaven that made me walk in on a thing like this!

—J-jade . . . Lu Beiping began at last, haltingly.

This tardy interjection called forth the full fury of the storm:

—Four Eyes! she yelled. Don't be a two-faced bastard. It's a world of trouble I've borne for this pup, and now I've had enough—enough! You say don't you want this child, you say you don't want to be this pup's pa, and now . . . you do this! Damn it, it burns me to cinders!

Then Lu Beiping, against all wisdom, opened his mouth again and started to protest:

—Jade, I didn't . . .

—You didn't? Didn't what? You *faggot* . . . Bursting into tears, Jade beat her chest while thrusting a trembling finger at Lu Beiping: Four Eyes! Me and this baby both want to be with you, and Autumn wants to be with you too. Which is it gonna be? Him? Or us? Tell me!

At that moment the darkness in the room seemed to freeze into a solid mass.

The roof leak kept belling out its limpid ostinato on the lid of the pot in the corner of the room.

Lu Beiping gasped:

—Jade, I can't . . . I can't . . . Listen, it's unfair of you two to force me like this!

In the shadows, Lu Beiping saw Autumn blanch. Then his features contracted into an expression that was sober, frosty, and remote. He turned, looked straight at Lu Beiping, and said very slowly:

—Bei, I know it's a hard thing for you to say. I can't force you. There's a lot in this world we're powerless to change. It's been good to know you, friend, and for that I'm content. So long.

Then he opened the door, admitting the roar of the rain. For a moment Autumn's bare back and baggy peasant shorts hung silhouetted in the white glare of the morning sun; then, after a moment's hesitation, he strode out into the teeming rain and was lost to Jade's and Lu Beiping's vision.

Lu Beiping turned his head away so that Jade wouldn't see the tears streaming down his face.

Chapter 14
Snakeclouds

Even after their soul-rattling clamor had faded from hearing, the drums and gongs echoed on in Lu Beiping's mind.

A thick rampart of snakeclouds loomed on the horizon. Teeming and coiling, twisting and unwinding, the bruised red tendrils with their inky black fringes spilled eastward in a great, writhing mass, like a nest of phantom vipers that had been recently disturbed. As the wind tugged at them, the clouds unravelled in places to admit shafts of sunlight or jagged windows of sky, a bright scrawl of glyphs on a blood-red background like a message from the gods unfurling over Mudkettle Mountain.

Lu Beiping made haste toward the hollow. When he walked up out of the tree-tunnel and saw Smudge hanging from the lychee tree, his blood ran cold: Autumn hadn't come back.

There'd been no sign of Autumn for the past two days. Last night Kingfisher had exploded at Smudge: This is your fault again, you imp! If Autumn doesn't come back tomorrow, I'll string you up!

The drums and gongs had been beaten by a delegation of re-eds and workers who'd marched up from camp to pay him a surprise visit, waving flags, shouting slogans, and creating a scene of jubilant pomp of the kind that usually accompanied the announcement of one of the Chairman's New Directives. Heading up the troop was Chu, drum in hand, who flourished a sheet of paper and read aloud: "On behalf of the Production Department of the Third Battalion of the Agricultural Reclamation Corps, it is our honor to present Lu Beiping, in light of his admirable efforts toward local integration and his outstanding contribution to revolutionary production . . ." What followed was an invitation for Lu Beiping to take part in an Experience Exchange Lecture Circuit for the Advancement of Mao Zedong Thought, organized by the propaganda desk at battalion HQ. After the initial hubbub subsided, Chu leaned over to Lu Beiping and whispered: Buddy, you've got it made. With the "integration" feather in your cap, once you come back from the lecture circuit you'll be a prime pick for the next personnel call . . .

Lu Beiping watched with a wooden expression as the rowdy brigade trooped off into the trees. Clearly the foreman had kept this measure up his sleeve all along: If he couldn't shut Lu Beiping up, he'd invite him away, sealing his lips with garlands and glory and the promise of going home—a watertight solution if there ever was one.

Under normal circumstances this news would've made even the most hardened, cynical re-ed jump for joy. But Lu Beiping just felt blank. And even Kingfisher, who was always acutely sensitive to goings-on down in the valley, didn't ask him what the commotion had been about.

The uncleared dinner table stood just outside the door of the lodge, and the whole family had gathered together under the lychee tree as if anticipating Lu Beiping's arrival. The yard and the tabletop glowed crimson in the snakecloud-tinted light of the evening sun. Smudge, bound at the wrists, dangled two feet off the ground, his face a mask of furious resentment; it looked like he'd been hanging there for quite some time. Kingfisher, who hadn't gotten around to beating him yet, squatted nearby, nursing his water pipe next to Stump. Jade sat stiff and erect on a wooden stool, like a hen on her nest, with Tick and Roach under her arms. Seeing Lu Beiping, the children bent their heads away, whimpering and wiping tears from their cheeks.

Lu Beiping leaned over to Kingfisher, but before the question was out of his mouth Kingfisher said loudly:

—Nope, I've been all over the mountain. Can't find hide nor hair of him.

With a lazy glance over his shoulder, Stump chimed in:

—Aye, he's gone. What's a man to do? He's found him another roost, nine parts certain. Then he gave Lu Beiping a sidelong look and said meaningfully: Hell! I've been saying all along, this hasn't a damned thing to do with Smudge.

Lu Beiping went pale. He hadn't slept a wink in two days. Stump had never spoken roughly to him before, and now there was nothing for him to do but bow and accept it. Squatting next to Kingfisher, Lu Beiping said softly:

—Kingfisher, Stump's right. This isn't Smudge's fault.

—Then you want me to take him down and string *you* up? Kingfisher said with a swift, barbed glance at Lu Beiping. Don't put on faces for me, Four Eyes. Hmph. And I said you had grit. I don't know what the hell got into my mind.

At those words Lu Beiping felt as if the ground had cracked open beneath his feet, and before he knew it he was weeping. Nothing could have stung him worse than what Kingfisher had just said; with one blow, he'd shattered the brittle shell that had been the last thing protecting Lu Beiping's heart. He sat there in a stupid daze while Kingfisher's reproach boomed in his ear:

—Gah! It makes me sick to my stomach to see a grown man cry! Listen, you all. I'm on Autumn's side in this. I feel for him. I know there's a world of worry hidden inside him which he couldn't bring himself to share with us, but he could share with Four Eyes—Kingfisher emitted a cloud of smoke, studied the fumes as they dispersed, then continued: I could tell early on that Autumn took a shine to you, friend. If he'd wanted to make good with you and you didn't, fine. There'd have been no wrong in that. But when you offer yourself to someone, you ought to stand by your word.

Lu Beiping sat gazing at the ground, silent, secretly amazed that even through his thick cocoon of mysticism Kingfisher had seen straight to the heart of his and Autumn's friendship. On a topic that seemed, more than any other, to lend itself to talk of sins and laws and the balance of light and dark, Kingfisher had a different system of logic, a different perspective.

—Jade, Stump, I know what you're thinking, Kingfisher said; then, raising the stick of mosquito incense that he used to light his pipe, he traced a character in the air:

—You're thinking, even the figure for "good" is made up of mother and son, woman and man, shadow and light. Every good thing under the sun's born out of that goodness. Good harvest, good health, good food, good luck, it all comes from the same place—Kingfisher paused for a moment to launch a gob of black spittle onto the ground two yards away—So, let me ask you this. Since that first goodness has given you every good thing you've ever known, can you make room in your hearts for every good thing born of it? Look at Smudge, Jade. He's a bale-crossed devil child, a son of darkness—do you love him? Of course you do, he's your pup, there's space in your heart for him a hundred times over! I'm not blaming you, see. Goodness, love, is something you've got to fight for. Me, Stump, and Four Eyes have all fought over you, Jade. But if we can chase after love and fight to make it our own, we can't keep Autumn from doing the same. Is it right for him to want Four Eyes instead of you, Jade?—Kingfisher rubbed his bald pate, then concluded: Last night, I couldn't keep my head to the pillow for thinking about these things. And this is what I think. If Autumn wants to make good with Four Eyes, it's not my place to get in his way.

Stump spluttered as if he'd just choked on a mouthful of smoke.

—Oy, yoy, yoy . . . Kingfish, this is loony talk! You're the one forever affrighted of light and dark getting tipped out of true. If this isn't . . .

—Stump, Kingfisher said, expelling another cloud of smoke: Where do you think you are? The Forbidden City? Are you hoping to win a prize from the Emperor for doing such a good job minding his commandments?

Jade and Stump chuckled. Kingfisher slapped a mosquito that had landed on his stomach and went on:

—Like I've always said, in this world we live in now, bearing and sowing and sharing affection ought never to be a sin. Killing, lying, and wasting are the only sins. Folks like us, who lay our souls open to the sun every day just praying we'll live to watch it rise the next morning, have got no place fussing about virtues and commandments. When goodness is to be had, have it; that's all we can do.

Nobody spoke; silence was king beneath the lychee tree. After a short while Kingfisher looked up again and said:

—What were we talking about? Right, Smudge—Kingfisher regarded the boy dangling from the branch, who stared back at him obstinately—I can't blame a woman for being jealous or a common man for being common-minded. But I do blame you, Smudge! Scurrying around spying on people, playing the secret agent! And you, Four Eyes, chickening out at the very last minute, right when things came to a head. Both of those were small-minded, small-hearted things to do. If it hadn't been for those two things—Kingfisher thumped his pipe on the ground—Autumn would be with us right now.

At that Smudge burst into tears of indignation:

—I didn't mean to! he sobbed. I didn't mean to make Uncle Autumn run off! Honest! I nay ever meant—

—Don't give me your cheap tears! Kingfisher barked: A bale-star's what you are, boy—a kin-killer! When I heard it was you that started all this I just about hit the rafters. Bounty and bliss! First you cross your own pa, and now . . . I can't hit you. I won't. I don't want the breath of shadow on me. But you're not coming down off that tree till someone smacks some remorse into you! Stump—

—I won't beat him, Stump said doggedly. I told you, 'tisn't the boy's fault. I'll not play the ugly one tonight.

—Kingfisher, Lu Beiping interjected, let's untie Smudge and keep looking for Autumn. That's more important . . . Then a new thought struck Lu Beiping, and he added: Kingfisher, when you went searching for Autumn before, did you look near his rosewood tree?

Kingfisher shook his head.

—I've been three times up and down that valley, but I've had no luck finding that little pass he took me over. It's vanished like a specter.

—Four Eyes is right, Jade chimed in: Where else would Autumn go except to his rosewood tree? He told me he'd nearly got it chopped down.

A look of alarm flashed across Stump's face, and he whispered apprehensively:

—Oy, yoy, yoy! When a felled tree still stands, your life's in heaven's hands.

Lu Beiping's heart sank. It was true; Autumn had said that he'd cut all the way through the trunk but the tree still hadn't fallen. Springing to his feet, he announced:

—I'm going back to my hut. Autumn forgot to take his notebook with him. I remember he drew a map in there that showed the exact location of his rosewood tree.

Smudge burst out sobbing again.

—Let me go! he cried. I wanna hunt for Uncle Autumn too! Please, let me go!

Kingfisher dragged on his pipe, stone-faced. No one moved. Nobody dared take Smudge down, but nobody wanted to beat the boy.

The light was draining out of the sky, the snakeclouds turning from red to black. At last Jade heaved herself to her feet and walked ponderously, tears gleaming on her cheeks, over to Smudge.

—Smudge, she said, I want you to go too, I want you to help find your uncle Autumn so they'll forgive you. They don't want to hit you, they don't want to touch . . . I guess I'm going to have to do it! They won't take you down till I do!

As if momentarily possessed by a demon, Jade began raining furious slaps on Smudge's cheeks and shoulders. Then almost immediately, her arms fell slack, and she broke down into howls of grief.

Flintlock rifle. Snakesbane bracelet. Brimstone rag. In addition to these Kingfisher had assembled a torch out of green branches, which he carried unlit over one shoulder as he stumped up the trail in front of Lu Beiping. Lu Beiping knew that those branches had also been cut from the snakesbane plant, whose sap was said to be effective against snake venom and whose smoke, if burnt, was believed to repel snakes. This time Kingfisher had broken out the heavy artillery. As they ascended the stone ledges along the babbling rivulet, then skirted the Sea's Eye and passed through the glade where the stone memorial tablet lay, Autumn's breath, the sound of Autumn's voice, seemed to linger in the air. Lu Beiping followed wordlessly behind Kingfisher, leading Smudge by the hand. After ducking under several curtains of vines and hopping over a few fallen branches, they were soon swallowed up by the cavernous darkness of the jungle that filled the central bowl of the mountain.

He'd left all his feelings of bitterness and regret behind him in the hollow—let them slip with finality to the ground. As they were about to walk out the door Jade had complained that she didn't feel well, and Stump wanted Lu Beiping to stay behind and take care of her. What's *he* know? He's a city boy, Kingfisher scoffed. Laughing, Jade pushed Lu Beiping out the door, saying: Go do your business. I'm no fool, I can tell which is the more important matter right now. Lu Beiping could make neither head nor tail of this, and as he followed, perplexed, behind Kingfisher as they hiked up the trail into the jungle, he felt as if he'd been tossed into yet another unfathomable mystery, as if a vast, rumbling wave of the unknowable had bowled him over, wiping his mind clean, erasing everything.

Nothing could be more unknowable than this wilderness, Lu Beiping thought. It feels like it really ought to be capable of erasing everything.

Catalpa, ironwood, red lauan, pepper tree, parrot camphor, cane-leaf pine, dragonbone gentian . . . The path Kingfisher chose wasn't the same one by which Autumn had led him into the high valley; that time, they'd bushwhacked through stands of wild cane choked with vines, but now, everywhere Lu Beiping looked there were glades of towering, ancient trees rising from a rugged, ravine-cut landscape; the forest was still overhung with vines, but it was more spacious and airy. If they weren't on such urgent business, this expedition would have felt like a stroll through a museum of rare tropical woods, where no doubt Autumn, had he been with them, could have regaled them for hours with exuberant lectures on history and botany. When he found the notebook, Lu Beiping had remembered what Autumn said to him the other night: *Back when you were ignoring me, I'd go up there every day and talk to my rosewood tree.* The others, hearing this, had nodded in agreement, saying: That's Autumn for you, he's got a strange cast of mind. Everyone became freshly optimistic about the possibility of tracking down Autumn, and Kingfisher, glancing at the map, had known exactly where to look for the tree. Now it was almost dark, but the forest still glowed with a faint, sourceless light that filtered down through the canopy, reflected off the trees' broad crowns and thick trunks. Kingfisher, cigarette dangling from his lips, padded along at an unusually brisk pace, weaving and bounding among the trees like a leopard who'd long since eaten his way through the entire jungle. Before long all three of them were covered in sweat. Kingfisher seemed to be in a good mood. They paused for a moment while he lit another cigarette, which he offered first to Lu Beiping and then to Smudge; then he turned and hollered up into the pitch-dark valley, and as the long chain of echoes died away against a backdrop of eerie jungle noises Kingfisher chuckled to himself, and Lu Beiping and Smudge chuckled too.

The breeze picked up, and fat water droplets began splashing down. Before they could find cover they were completely soaked, and Kingfisher's cigarette had gone out. They laughed again. Peering up through the dense treetops they saw that the sky was still a clear, deep blue, a sign that this was not real rain but rainforest-made rain, a product of the jungle's own interior microclimate. Before long the rain stopped, and billows of mist started rising from among the trees' gnarled roots. Quick, it's the vapors! Kingfisher cried. Let's get going! The three of them hurried on.

The trail became steeper—if you could call it a trail, since it seemed to exist pretty much only in Kingfisher's mind. Threading his way through the forest, he guided them on a route almost free of obstacles, rendering the machete that hung at Lu Beiping's hip a useless encumbrance. Lu Beiping gazed up into the canopy's teeming shadows and wondered just how big this rainforest was. Kingfisher, Stump, and Autumn felled trees up here every day, yet all their work had amounted to no more than clipping a single hair from the mountain's skin. They'd taken only what they needed, Kingfisher had said; after they "weighed anchor" this place would revert entirely to wilderness. In those days "wilderness" was a dirty word—"Liberate the Land!" and "Vanquish the Wilderness!" were two slogans popular among workers on reclamation campaigns, and Fong, seeing him lope back into camp with skin tanned to the color of charcoal, liked to tease him by saying things like: Looks like you're regressing into a state of nature! At that point Lu Beiping had no way of knowing just how fragile this wilderness was, how close to the brink of extinction his society had already pushed it, in its ignorance of other definitions of civilization besides its own. Already the Agrecorps campaigns had whittled away significantly at Mudkettle Mountain's rainforests, and by the time Lu Beiping finished his cushy stint on the Experience Exchange Lecture Circuit, this tract of rare, primeval wilderness would have disappeared almost completely from the earth.

Now it was totally dark. First Lu Beiping turned on the long-handled flashlight that he carried on a strap hanging around his neck, then Kingfisher and Smudge turned on their own small flashlights as well. Probed by their three frail flashlight beams, the forest seemed even huger. The trunks, branches, vines, and aerial roots that surrounded them retreated into the darkness, and the darkness itself became liquid, thick and palpable, engulfing and dissolving everything, rendering the forest abstract. Their location, the lay of the land, the direction in which they were heading all became highly theoretical matters. Kingfisher stopped, examined the map by the light of his flashlight, then took Lu Beiping's flashlight and cast its more powerful beam over the big, dark shapes of the surrounding trees, saying:

—There's a creek just down there. We cross it, skirt the bluff on the far side, and that'll bring us to the foot of the little pass where Autumn discovered his rosewood tree. If he hasn't run off for good, he ought to be nearby.

Sure enough, Lu Beiping could hear the faint gurgling of water. In the darkness his hearing had become acute, and he was now aware of the eerie symphony of noises that filled the jungle: the shrill cries of birds, the deep croaks of toads, the occasional loud howl of some nameless beast; even, to his highly suggestible ears, what sounded like the hoarse rasp of a saw in the branches overhead. As soon as he focused his attention on the sound it disappeared, leaving only a buzzing in his ears. Against this multitude of noises Kingfisher's voice rang out again and again: *Autumn! . . . Are you here? . . . Where are you, Autumn? . . . Answer me! . . .*

Nothing but echoes.

Grief and remorse tackled Lu Beiping like a panther dropping out of the branches.

—Uncle *Auuuuu*-tuuuumn! Smudge called out. Where *aaaaaaare* you? His bright childish voice was painful to hear. Lu Beiping didn't dare join in; he knew that the moment he opened his mouth he would probably burst into tears.

Kingfisher led the way, hollering as he walked. At first his cries sounded lazy and offhand, and he didn't even pause to listen for a response. Calling for Autumn awakened hope, but it also to drew despair dangerously near. Lu Beiping followed in silence with leaden steps, every shout seeming to attach another lead ingot to his feet. After they hopped over the creek Kingfisher stopped shouting, came to a halt, and his square face appeared in the glow of his flashlight.

—Do you hear something? Kingfisher asked.

Worry and alarm were written all over his brow. A shudder of fear ran through Lu Beiping as he remembered the weird, stentorian rumble he and Autumn had heard when they'd ventured up here to round up the cattle, like a roll of subterranean thunder emanating from a neighboring valley.

But he heard no sound, except for the usual din of the forest.

Kingfisher's next question was even more unsettling:

—I smelled something, Four Eyes. Can you smell it?

Lu Beiping and Smudge both breathed in deeply through their noses. Lu Beiping smelled only the usual jungle odor, that mixture of fruit, rotting leaves, and humid air that so closely resembled the smell of semen. It was strongest in the morning, much fainter now in the evening. Smudge said he could smell roasted yams, and Lu Beiping knew that that was the smell wild ginseng plants gave off at night. Smudge complained that he was hungry. Kingfisher said nothing, just spat out his cigarette and used it to light the torch made of snakes-bane branches that he'd been carrying. As the torch ignited with a whoosh, the smoke and flames transfigured his face into a forbidding, fiery mask. Sure enough, the torch's fumes smelled like sulfur, but even more pungent. In the branches overhead Lu Beiping heard a flurry of wing beats as a flock of birds took to the air, fleeing the smoke. Only many days later would Kingfisher tell Lu Beiping what it was he'd smelled that night: an animal scent, either the smell of a snake or of a man. But just then he didn't want to scare either Lu Beiping or Smudge, so he said nothing, just lit the torch.

The torchlight drove the shadows away temporarily, then the darkness seemed to well back in like a rushing tide. The darkness was more like a living thing now, dancing and retreating as the flames ebbed and leapt. We're here, Kingfisher murmured. This ought to be the spot. He cast the torchlight in a circle around them, and Lu Beiping saw that they were standing on a gentle slope where a few trees rose like towering islands out of a sea of dense underbrush. At the edge of the ring of light he could make out the foot of a bluff, which gave this glade a sheltered, cozy feel, as if it might lie just a hundred yards from his hut and not in a distant corner of a godforsaken wilderness. Lu Beiping even thought he caught a hint of Autumn's scent, that smell that he remembered so clearly from the night they spent together.

Encouraged by this sensation, he called out softly: *Autumn! Are you here?* He didn't feel at all sad, just as if he were waking up a sleeping friend, and he kept on yelling: *Autumn! Are you asleep? Autumn! Wake up, answer us!* As he shouted, a quiet feeling of excitement stole over him.

There was no answer—not even an echo.

Just at that moment Smudge's bony fingers dug painfully into Lu Beiping's arm. The instinctive fear conveyed by the boy's touch sent an ominous premonition shooting through him. Now, suddenly, he heard it: a snatch of that hoarse, sobbing wail, the voice of the Child Crying from Beyond the Grave. Immediately he pricked up his ears, straining to hear more; but the terrible, spectral cry was gone, vanished like an apparition. He didn't know whether Kingfisher and Smudge had heard it too, but it was impossible to ignore the tendrils of panic creeping up slowly from deep within his gut.

—Look! What's that?

In the torchlight, through the smoke, Lu Beiping made out a wisp of something caught on the branch of a short understory tree, fluttering soundlessly, almost invisibly, in the breeze. Lu Beiping strode over and trained the white glare of his flashlight beam on the object. In the combined light of flashlight and torch, he saw that it was a torn piece of thread, the ripped cotton fibers undulating ever so slightly in the slow flow of air. At first glance Lu Beiping knew without a doubt that it was a thread torn from Autumn's shorts. He even thought he caught a whiff of Autumn's body odor: that faint, peculiar smell of sugarcane. But he said nothing of this to Kingfisher. No, he said, I have no idea what that is. He'd already drawn so close to hope that now, for fear of extinguishing it, he couldn't bring himself to embrace any hopeless version of reality, even one supported by reliable evidence.

Kingfisher began calling for Autumn again, a new urgency in his voice.

—Autumn! Autumn! Where aaaaaaare you?

Still no answer. After what seemed like a very long time the echoes straggled back out of the darkness, faint and distant.

Suddenly, Smudge sang out nearby:

—Come look! A tree! A big, chopped-down tree!

All the hairs stood up on Lu Beiping's neck. As the ball of torch-light glided through the darkness toward Smudge's voice, he took a deep breath and followed.

The glow of the torch and the restless flashlight beams revealed the body of a huge fallen tree. Only the very bottom of the trunk was visible; the tree's upper half melted away into the darkness. The trunk, severed at its base, showed a cross-section about as big around as a man could circle with his arms. The rippled growth rings had a jade-like patina, and the wood shavings that littered the ground nearby looked brittle and lustrous, like flakes of shell, and glittered faint gold. In the fitful firelight it was difficult to make out the wood's color—it was probably black, maybe dark purple—but the sap that had beaded along the rim of the trunk was black and crusted like dried blood. The area around the tree had been cleared, and all the epiphyte roots and bands of lichen that clung to the bottom portion of the trunk had been carefully cut away. A familiar long-handled machete and a big-toothed handsaw lay nearby, the bluing of their blades gleaming in the torchlight. On the other side of the tree sat a crude metal watering can with a long, tapered spout, for what use Lu Beiping couldn't guess.

Every detail spoke of the diligent attentions of the woodcutter. There were smoke stains and water stains on the wood, footprints and splashes of sweat in the soil; the only thing missing was the man himself.

He was gone. After they'd combed every corner of the site with torch and flashlight, they still had found no trace of the living being they'd hoped to find—no sign of Autumn.

—Kingfisher, Lu Beiping said in a strained voice: You're sure this is the tree? You're sure this is the right place?

Kingfisher stood, still holding the smoldering remains of the torch aloft, gazing in silence at the fallen tree.

—*Uncle AUUUUU-tumn! Uncle AUUUUU-tumn!* Smudge yelled, refusing to give up, casting his flashlight beam every which way.

—Don't shout! Kingfisher barked. Then he sat down on the stump, lit his cigarette from the dying torch, and began to smoke.

—Here, let me check again! Lu Beiping said, and though he knew he was deceiving himself he took out the black notebook and began flipping through it by the light of his flashlight, searching for the map that showed the location of the rosewood tree. Wafting off of the pages he smelled a hint of the clean, lucid fragrance of hillflower rice wine.

Before he found the map the notebook fell open to the second half of the poem called "Stanzas Written to the Tune of 'A Golden Thread.'" This was the poem he'd stumbled upon the day after the typhoon, leafing through Autumn's journal in the glade by the stone tablet—the poem Autumn's father had copied down for him the night he smuggled him out of the village, which the Qing courtier Gu Zhenguan had written three centuries earlier for his friend who'd been sent into exile, Wu Zhaoji.

Once again Lu Beiping read the lines penned in that harsh and forceful script:

(II)

> *I too have suffered the caprices of Fortune's hand.*
> *Yet, throughout my trials, I have remained*
> > *To your memory, true;*
> > *And it sears me through*
> *To have failed you, whose benevolence knew no end.*
> > *Once, all Jiangnan did celebrate*
> *Our names, and our glory to Heaven commend;*
> > *But could the heartsick pining of the Sage undo*
> > *Li Bai's wrongful sentence, or lessen his hardship's weight?*
> *Of all my misfortunes, this most I rue:*
> *That I have lost both my wife, and my closest friend.*

Could there be any fate
More desolate?
These, my utmost sorrows, I lay bare to you.

I was fifteen, you twenty-two; for a few brief years
You were my brother and my teacher by equal shares.
Now the blissful dawn
Of our youths is gone;
Reeds are withered by frost, men by earthly cares.
So let us less often at verses play
But save our strength, and redouble our prayers—
Stay well, friend! For I hope someday to fan
The ink-spidered sheaves you've laid away
All these troubled years, and then pass them on,
Bequeathing your name to the indifferent heirs
Of a brighter day.
Still so much to say,
But I must end here. Yours truly, Guan.

Before Lu Beiping reached the end of the poem his glasses were blurred with tears. He closed the book, threw back his head, and yelled hoarsely into the black vault of the night:

—*AUUUUUUUUU-tumn! Where ARE you? AUUUUUUUUU-tuuuuuuuumn!*

Smudged began sobbing wildly. He pounced on Lu Beiping and clamped him in a fierce embrace, burbling through tears:

—Whatever happened to Uncle Autumn? I didn't mean it, honest! I was sad, that's all . . . sad you and Autumn made good together and forgot all about me . . . sad you didn't love me as much as him . . . I'm sorry, Four Eyes, I'm so sorry!

Smudge's grip tightened on Lu Beiping's shoulders as he sobbed louder and louder, overcome by a frenzy of grief.

Goodness, love—always those two words. Lu Beiping hugged Smudge tight, patting his bare back and marveling that even a child's need for love could be the fiercest of imperatives, to be ignored or trivialized at one's peril. A human life is a speck of dust on the earth's surface; and affection, love, is such a trifling thing, yet the most necessary of all things for a living being—the most mundane, yet the most sacred, good, upon which the hopes of every human life rest.

Kingfisher's solemn features materialized out of the darkness in front of Lu Beiping. He murmured:

—Where's Autumn? Where could he be? A wild goose doesn't fly off without a farewell honk or two . . . Then he trailed off mid-phrase, shuddered, and stood with his mouth hanging open as if struck by a sudden realization.

At the same time a flash of understanding went off in Lu Beiping's brain. He thought of the big bull Alyosha, who'd vanished whole and wailing into the wilderness, remembered the bloodstained cowbell and the pool of fresh blood spreading beneath the carpet of leaves. He strode over to the tree and renewed his search, looking for some sign of Autumn, something, anything, like the Dunhuang harmonica he'd given him as a present, which Autumn had had in his pocket the morning he left.

The fallen amaranthine rosewood tree lay still and silent among the shadows.

There was no blood, not even a fleck, much less a last token like a cowbell or a harmonica. Or—Lu Beiping turned suddenly, and searched the tree branches for that single cotton thread torn from Autumn's shorts, off of which Lu Beiping had fancied he'd caught a whiff of Autumn's scent. But the thread was gone, carried off by the wind.

The smoldering torch butt in Kingfisher's hand gave a final flicker and went out.

Darkness flooded in on all sides, swamping the silence. No—it was silence that enveloped the darkness, swallowing it down into its cold, still depths. The silence thickened into a viscous fluid, oozing and hardening around the peaks and valleys of Mudkettle Mountain. As if this place had never woken from immemorial slumber, as if all memory and imagination lay frozen here, as if this silence were the original silence out of which the world was born.

Just at that moment, from far down the valley, came a faint noise echoing over the treetops: a thin, delicate sound like a piece of eggshell china shattering. The three of them stood still, listening. Kingfisher was the first to identify it—it was the cry of a premature, newborn child.

Translator's Acknowledgments

This translation took shape over many years, and any artistic project that takes so long cannot be a solitary affair by virtue of the number of lives it has paralleled. As the book goes to press I am indebted to all those people who left their mark on it in ways both tangible and intangible, whether they knew it or not: people who helped, inspired, offered encouragement, gave honest criticism, hashed out ideas with me, or simply were patient as the years elapsed and the English version of the mysterious Chinese novel *The Invisible Valley* grew slowly in my head and on my hard drive.

Thank you first to Perry Link and the UC Riverside Department of Comparative Literature, who contributed in the most direct and material way to the English translation's completion. Their support, in the form of a visiting scholarship in autumn 2010, allowed me to finish the novel's first draft in a crucial three months in the crisp desert sunlight of southern California. Professor Link's graduate students Tian Xi, Wang Hongjian, and Anne Chang were some of the first native Chinese speakers to read and comment on the translation. Thank you also to Tony Fok, who facilitated a trip to Hainan Island in 2009 that allowed me to see the novel's setting with my own eyes, giving me both an emotional and physical tie to the real experiences of the sent-down youth.

Thank you to all the friends and teachers who read chapters, gave guidance, and offered moral support. If you feel your name belongs on this list, it does. In particular I'd like to thank: Professors Ed Kamens, Jing Tsu, and Kang-I

About the Author

Like many Chinese writers of his generation, Su Wei spent his teenage years being "re-educated" through farm labor in the countryside, working for ten years on a rubber plantation in the mountains of tropical Hainan Island. He is known for his nonfiction essays as well as for his highly imaginative novels, which are seen as unique in their treatment of the Cultural Revolution. He left China in 1989, and since 1997 he has taught Chinese language and literature at Yale University. *The Invisible Valley* is his first book to be translated into English.

Austin Woerner is a Chinese-English literary translator. In addition to *The Invisible Valley*, he has translated two books of poetry, *Doubled Shadows: Selected Poetry of Ouyang Jianghe* and *Phoenix*. Formerly the English translation editor for the innovative Chinese literary journal *Chutzpah!*, he also co-edited the short fiction anthology *Chutzpah! New Voices from China*. He holds a BA in East Asian Studies from Yale and an MFA in creative writing from the New School.

Sun Chang at Yale, who helped steer me as I began the project; Jenny Blair, Olivia Gunton, and Dan Nagler, enthusiastic readers of the novel's first drafts; my writing teachers John Crowley, Sigrid Nunez, and Patrick McGrath; fellow students Winston Len and Francis Gonzalez at the New School; Noa Wheeler, whose ear I bent numerous times for advice about navigating the world of book publishing; Li Ling and Wang Xiulu, with whom lasting friendships blossomed over discussions of *The Invisible Valley*, and whose faith in me has buoyed my spirits along the way; all my translator friends from Paper Republic; and recently, my students in China, whose enthusiasm continues to buttress my belief that language study and literary translation are meaningful ways to spend one's years.

Now for the big one: Thank you to Su Wei himself, who on a whim and a hunch handed over his novel to an ambitious 21-year-old, offered unstinting support and no pressure, and spent countless hours with me poring over the book and plying me with stories and memories. More so than most translations this one was in fact co-created with the author, and this book is the child of our friendship. Thank you also to his wife Liu Mengjun and his daughter Emily, to the *san'er* and *si'er* (their numbers change constantly), and to Ah Kuan and Su Wei's family in Guangzhou, who welcomed me on the other side of the world. If *The Invisible Valley* was a bag of magic beans, then you are the beanstalk up which I'm climbing.

Lastly, thank you to Nikki Greenwood, first to explore Mudkettle Mountain with me, who helped me dream up names for ghosts and spirits and who never cut me any slack; and to my parents, who always supported my resolve to complete this unconventional project, who, even when they must have had their doubts, waited and had faith in me.